THE DEEP, DEEP SNOW

ALSO BY BRIAN FREEMAN

THE FROST EASTON SERIES
The Crooked Street
The Voice Inside
The Night Bird

THE JONATHAN STRIDE SERIES
Alter Ego*
Marathon
Goodbye to the Dead
The Cold Nowhere
Turn to Stone (e-novella)
Spitting Devil (e-short story)
The Burying Place
In the Dark
Stalked
Stripped
Immoral

THE CAB BOLTON SERIES
Season of Fear
The Bone House
*Cab Bolton also appears in *Alter Ego*

THE DEEP, DEEP SNOW

BRIAN FREEMAN

BLACK
STONE
PUBLISHING

Printed in the United States of America

First edition: 2020
ISBN 978-1-09-407132-9
Fiction / Mystery & Detective / Police Procedural

3 5 7 9 10 8 6 4 2

CIP data for this book is available
from the Library of Congress

Blackstone Publishing
31 Mistletoe Rd.
Ashland, OR 97520

www.BlackstonePublishing.com

For Marcia

The first thing you should know about me is that I believe in signs. Omens. Premonitions. I grew up believing that things happen for a reason.

That's the only way to explain why I'm alive.

You see, I've spent a lot of time thinking about who I am, because I don't know where I came from. I'm a mystery to myself.

I was born in late October or early November, but I don't know the exact day. When I was five years old, I picked October 31 for my party. Halloween. I thought that would make for a cool birthday.

Whatever the real day was, I was left on Tom Ginn's doorstep when I was about a week old. His house used to be a church, with a white steeple and a wall of stained glass windows. At night, in the darkness, my birth mother probably thought it was still a church, and I guess that's where you take a baby you're planning to abandon.

She left me in an old Easter basket, strangely enough, nestled among green paper curly cues like a white chocolate bunny. I was dressed in a cotton onesie with faded pink stripes and a bonnet with flaps tied in a bow under my chin. The temperature outside was thirty-nine degrees. Obviously I don't remember that night, but sometimes I think about what it must have been like to be alone, freezing, crying, with no idea what I had done to be cast away. She left no note to tell me why.

Tom Ginn wasn't home at the time. He was forty miles away, night-fishing under a cloudless, moonless sky in his favorite spot on Shelby Lake. You don't realize how many stars hang in the heavens until you experience one of those nights. Tom had a tent set up on the shore and a portable propane grill for cooking whatever he caught on the lake. It was a Saturday, his first night off in four weeks, and he was planning to camp on the beach until morning.

If he'd done that, I would have died.

Either the cold would have killed me, or an animal would have dragged me off. The woods near us are filled with wolves, raccoons, bears, and wolverines. We even have a mythical monster called the Ursulina that many townspeople swear is no myth. Any one of those predators would have torn a little baby limb from limb and consumed me. Thinking about it still makes me shiver.

Tom had no idea about any of this. He was enjoying the night on the placid water. The air was fresh and sweet, tinged with the scent of pine. His boat was at the mouth of a cove between the trees where it was utterly still. There was just him, the lake, the wilderness, and the stars. It's a big, big place that makes you feel small. He was sipping hot black coffee from a thermos and jigging for walleye. He'd been out there for an hour without any luck, but he was in no hurry.

That was when God sent him the sign.

Like an angel, a snowy owl swooped down from the treetops and landed on the other end of the boat. Tom was so shocked that he couldn't even take a breath. His mouth hung open with the jug of coffee at his lips. The owl perched there and watched him with its stoic, unblinking eyes. Its head was a perfect white, its body checkered over with white and gray. Breaking the silence of the night, the owl squawked out a loud, raspy call. When Tom didn't answer, the owl called to him again and again, each time with an urgent impatience.

To Tom, the owl's voice sounded like the same word over and over.
Home.

Later, he would say that he knew this was no ordinary moment in his life. He would tell everyone that it wasn't just the owl calling to him. It was me.

"*Okay,*" *he announced finally.* "*Okay, I'm going.*"

The owl unfurled its wide wings, soared into the sky, and vanished. Right then and there, Tom brought the boat in and packed up his camp. He drove the forty-mile trip along the two-lane highways faster than he'd ever driven in his life. He had no idea what was waiting for him, but when he got home, there I was. Screaming to the world. Blue with cold.

He never located whoever had left me there. My mother was long gone. When he didn't find her, Tom Ginn, the thirty-year-old, never-married, youngest-ever sheriff of Mittel County, adopted me himself. He named me not with his own name but after the place he'd been when God brought us together.

Shelby Lake. That's me.

Tom became my father, and he raised me. You won't be surprised to learn that he has always been my superhero, my whole world, my idol, my life. I worshipped that man from the time I could walk. You also won't be surprised to learn that I've spent many of my free hours at the local raptor center, volunteering with the injured owls who are brought there for rehabilitation.

Growing up in Mittel County, I knew that I would be a police officer like my father. I was already helping the secretary, Monica Constant, answer the phones in the sheriff's office by the time I was thirteen years old. It wasn't the life my father wanted for me. He thought I should go to college, leave this remote wilderness behind, and chase other dreams far from home. But my choice was to stay here and follow in his footsteps. That's what I did.

I'll be honest with you. I've always felt a little guilty that I was alive at all. I mean, God went to an awful lot of trouble keeping me here, right? When I was a girl and my father told me about finding me on his doorstep, I asked him: Why me? I'm nothing special. Why was I saved?

He told me that was something I would have to figure out for myself, even if it took me a long time to do. And he was right. All these years later, I finally have an answer that I can live with.

But that's the end of the story. I need to take you back to where it started.

The mystery began ten years ago, on July 17, a perfect summer afternoon. I was twenty-five years old back then. That was the day another snowy owl appeared in my life like the return of a messenger.

To me, the arrival of an owl could mean only one thing.

I was being called to rescue a child.

PART ONE
THE UNWANTED VISITOR

CHAPTER ONE

On the day that Jeremiah Sloan disappeared, I was teasing Monica Constant about her dead dog.

That sounds cruel, but you have to understand that Monica's Alaskan malamute had died nine years earlier after a long and very pampered life. She cremated Moody, which isn't unusual, but she kept his ashes in a flowered urn that she took with her to work in a special purse every single day. Vacations, too. If you asked her why, she would explain that if she left Moody at home and her house burned down, then she would have no way of differentiating between the ashes of her house and the ashes of her dog.

Monica wasn't about to take any chances.

And yes, I would tease her about this whenever I could.

On that particular July afternoon, my partner, Adam Twilley, was leaning against the open door that led to the parking lot, with a cigar between his lips. My father couldn't see him, which was the only reason Adam felt bold enough to smoke in the office. The warm wind blew in and sprayed a plume of ash from the end of his cigar onto the yellowed linoleum floor.

"Monica?" I called, pointing to the little gray sprinkle of ash. "I think Moody needs to go out."

To her credit, Monica always giggled at my lame jokes.

"Shelby, what am I going to do with you?" she said with a little shake of her head, using the same grandmotherly tone she'd used with me since I was a girl.

Monica and I went way back. It's a little weird when you work with people who used to change your diapers. She joined the sheriff's department as a secretary right out of high school and had never worked anywhere else over the past three decades. That's the thing about a small-town place like Mittel County. Loyalty runs deep in these parts. When you find your place in the world, you stay there.

She went back to reading us the latest police reports out loud. Adam and I were both in our chocolate-brown uniforms. Normally, we would be out on the roads together, but it had been a slow Friday so far. I was only half paying attention to what Monica was saying, because my father was in his office behind closed doors, and the muffled conversation inside was getting loud.

"Oh, this is sad," Monica announced in her high-pitched twitter of a voice as she squinted at the computer screen. "Poor old Paul Nadler wandered away again in Stanton. They want us to be on the lookout for him."

Adam snorted from behind his cigar. "On the lookout? Stanton is an hour away. Nadler is what, ninety-four? Do they think he's running a marathon or something?"

"Come on, Adam," I chided him. "The man has Alzheimer's."

"Yeah, I know, but this is like the sixth time he's walked out of that care center without anybody noticing. Somebody either needs to bell that cat or figure out how to lock the damn door."

Adam was right about that. Stanton was in the next county over, so it really wasn't our problem, but I felt sorry for Mr. Nadler and angry that the senior facility couldn't keep him safe.

They typically found him within a couple of hours, but a lot can happen to an old man in that amount of time. Once he walked into a stranger's house two blocks away and fell asleep in a closet. Another time he actually climbed the hundred-foot Stanton fire tower. Sooner or later, he was going to get hurt.

"Let's move on, Monica. What else is on the list?"

I was a little too brusque with her, but Monica gave me a sympathetic smile from the other side of the room. She could read my mind. I wasn't upset about Mr. Nadler's memory problems. I was worried that someday I would find myself in the same situation with my father.

"We've got a report of a stolen pickup truck in Martin's Point," she went on. "A white Ford F-150. That is such a nice vehicle. I've always wanted one of those."

I grinned at the idea of tiny Monica Constant driving one of the world's largest trucks. She rattled off the license plate, and Adam and I scribbled it down in our notebooks. This was the fourth stolen vehicle report this month. It was summer. Cars around Mittel County had a way of going on joyrides when kids were off school. Martin's Point was a lakeside town fifty miles south of us, which meant it attracted tourist families with bored teenagers who quickly discovered that the locals don't always lock their vehicles.

"Anything else?" I asked.

"Oh, yes. Mrs. Norris says she saw a man skulking outside her bedroom window last night. According to her, he was, quote, 'ogling her lasciviously while in a state of undress.'"

"A state of undress?" I asked. "Was he undressed or was she?"

"I think she was."

"So we're looking for a blind man," Adam joked from the doorway. "That should make it easy."

I couldn't help laughing. Adam was right about that, too.

Nobody with good eyes would be ogling Mrs. Norris. "Did she give a description of the man?"

"No, she didn't see him. Her bedroom window was open, and she says he was making some kind of snuffling sound, like heavy breathing. She thinks he came from the motel across the highway."

"All right, we'll wander over there later. I'm sure Rose won't be surprised at another complaint from Mrs. N about one of her guests. Is that all?"

It didn't matter if that was all.

Before Monica could say anything more, the door to my father's office flew open with a bang, interrupting us. I saw a slim, tall, annoyingly attractive woman in the doorway, and she saw me sitting at my desk.

"Violet," I said coolly.

"Shelby," she said with equal frost in her voice.

Violet Roka and I had been frenemies since high school. My one claim to fame in Mittel County—well, other than being the baby in the Easter basket—was being part of the girls volleyball team that won the state championship in my senior year. Believe me, that's a big deal in a small town. There's still a billboard about us on the highway. Violet's family moved to the area when she was a junior, and she promptly went out for the team and squeezed out my best friend, which didn't help us get along. She and I became the two biggest rivals with the two most stubborn personalities, but Coach Trina had managed to get it through our heads that we could accomplish more together than apart. The truce lasted until we brought the trophy home. Since then, we hadn't exactly been close.

At twenty-six years old, she was a newly minted lawyer who'd already gotten herself appointed to the county board after one of the members resigned in the middle of his term. One thing Violet never lacked was ambition. She'd been using her newfound clout to hassle my father about everything he was doing wrong as the county sheriff. I didn't like it one bit, but Dad let it roll off his back the way he did everything in life.

Violet didn't linger in the office. She shrugged a purse over her shoulder, clicked across the floor in her sky-high heels, and pushed through Adam's cloud of cigar smoke into the parking lot. Adam gave her one of his crooked James Dean smiles, but Violet didn't swoon.

When she was gone, my father strolled into the common area to join us. Adam quickly flipped his cigar to the asphalt outside and hummed an innocent tune.

"What did Violet want?" I asked.

"Oh, she always has something to complain about," my father replied with a wrinkle of his bushy mustache. "Apparently, now I'm not doing enough to combat climate change."

"What exactly can you do about that?"

"As you'd expect, Violet had a list prepared."

"Was there anything else? It sounded like the two of you were arguing."

"It was nothing, Shelby. Don't worry about it."

My father was the most honest man I knew, but that also meant he was a bad liar. I didn't know what he and Violet had been arguing about, but it was more than climate change. Whatever it was, he chose not to share it with me.

Dad wandered over and perched on the side of Monica's desk, where he perused the summary of police calls. "Mr. Nadler again? I can't believe they keep losing that man." Then without looking up, he continued: "Oh, and Adam? Was that a cigar I saw in your hand?"

"Definitely not, Tom," Adam replied, although he wasn't fooling anyone, because the smell had already permeated the basement.

My father sighed and shot me a sideways glance. "How about

we solve a little crossword puzzle for Adam, Shelby? Let's try this one. 'An unwanted visitor in a tableware emporium.' Four letters."

Dad loved crossword puzzles. He and I had spent twenty years doing them together over breakfast in the local café. His clue took me just a moment to figure out, and then I said, "Bull."

Because a bull in a china shop would definitely be an unwanted visitor.

"You got that, Adam?" my father told him with a wink. "Bull."

Adam stared at his feet and coughed. "Sorry, Tom."

"No more cigars in here, got it? Let's try not to burn down another building."

"Yes, sir."

Monica and I both covered our smiles.

That was my father. He never needed to yell or shout or throw his weight around to get what he wanted. He had a way of charming you even as he made you feel like dirt for disappointing him. His voice was soft, like piano music, which sounded strange coming from such a big man. He stood six-foot-two, with a shaggy head of snow-white hair and a mustache that kept growing out of control like a weed. Even during the winter, his skin had a deep, leathery tan. His build was bulky and broad-shouldered in a way that sent a quiet message of strength.

Anyway, now you've got the picture.

That was July 17. A slow day. The four of us were in the Mittel County Sheriff's Office, located in the basement underneath the town's Carnegie Library. It was an old space, cold in the winters, humid in the summers. We could hear the thunder of children's running footsteps overhead. The linoleum peeled at the corners. The ceiling tiles were water-stained.

For me, that particular moment will always be stuck in time. Me at my desk. Dad and Monica with the police reports in hand. Adam in the open doorway. That's how it was when the world changed.

"Wow, will you look at that?" Adam suddenly said.

He squinted into the sunshine in the library parking lot and shook his head with a kind of awe. I asked him what was up, but Adam looked transfixed by whatever he saw and didn't say a word. We all converged on the doorway, and I got there first. The sight took my breath away.

Outside, not even twenty feet away, Adam's motorcycle was parked in the lot. Perched atop the bike's side mirror was a snowy owl. Motionless. Serious. Regal.

Staring at it, I felt the strangest, coldest sensation down my entire body.

"It's just an owl," I found myself murmuring out loud, because we lived near the national forest among predators and prey. There wasn't anything especially unusual about a snowy owl taking a rest before flying back to the trees.

Except at that very moment, the phone rang on Monica's desk. We all jumped at the noise, and the owl took flight with a cry. Right then and there, I knew.

Something had happened.

Monica skittered across the floor with her short little steps and grabbed the phone. She wasn't much bigger than a bird herself. She listened to the voice on the line and was barely able to get in a word, because I could hear a panicked woman shouting at her through the receiver.

When Monica hung up, I looked at her, waiting. So did Dad and Adam.

"That was Ellen Sloan," she told us. "Jeremiah is missing. She thinks someone took him."

CHAPTER TWO

Dad led our parade of vehicles down miles of dirt road into the heart of the national forest. Adam and I followed, with me at the wheel. Dennis and Ellen Sloan brought up the rear, and they had Adrian, Jeremiah's sixteen-year-old brother, in the car with them.

This was a lonely place for a ten-year-old boy to vanish.

The town where we live is named Avery Weir, but long ago, people simply started calling it Everywhere. This being Mittel County, we say we live in the Middle of Everywhere, but the truth is that we're closer to the middle of nowhere. The deer outnumber the people around here by a significant multiple. We're still ahead of the wolves, but they're gaining on us. We're surrounded by hundreds of square miles of woods, creeks, and lakes. The nearest interstate highway is two hours south. Towns are spread out by dozens of miles, and they have great names. Witch Tree. Eagle Ridge. Martin's Point. Blue Diamond Lake.

We were thirty miles north of Everywhere when I saw the cloud of dust settling as Dad's squad car slowed and stopped. I saw a child's bicycle tipped forlornly on the shoulder of the road in a nest of thistles. The blue frame was caked with dirt. In the forest on either side of us, dense stands of paper birches and white pines fought for the sunlight. The July air was sticky and warm. Insects whined from inside the tangled brush, and songbirds danced back and forth across the road in flashes of color.

My father got out of the cruiser and assessed the bike with his hands on his hips and his mouth crushed into a dour frown. His brown, flat-brimmed sheriff's hat was securely placed on his head. The midafternoon summer sun was high and bright, but the denseness of the woods meant you couldn't see far through the shadows. It had been dry that week, so the ruts in the dirt road showed no tire tracks or footprints. The bicycle was the only evidence that a boy had been here.

Adam and I joined Dad on the road. So did the Sloans and their oldest son.

I knew the Sloans well in those days. Everyone did. Despite how spread out we are, there are zero degrees of separation in an area like ours. We know each other's stories and secrets, probably more than we should. When you all grow up together, it's also hard to get past who you were in high school. No matter what you go on to do in life, you're still the baseball star, the homecoming queen, the party girl, the volleyball champ. The Sloans had that problem. People talked about Dennis and Ellen like they were still Jack and Diane from John Mellencamp's little ditty, but that wasn't fair. Dennis had a master's degree in forestry management. Ellen had bought the failing market on Everywhere's main street and turned it into a moneymaker.

Ellen was thirty-six that year, two years younger than her husband. She was smart, cool, blond, blue-eyed, tough enough to make a shoplifter confess with nothing but one of those icy stares of hers. She was the strong one in that household. That was what made it so hard to see her struggling to keep it together. I saw the tremble in her fingers. I heard her breathing, which was quick and loud through her nose. She kept touching her hair and pushing it back in place, as if that were the only thing she could control at that moment.

Her life was her two boys, and one of them was gone.

My father put a hand on the shoulder of Jeremiah's older brother and gave the teenager a reassuring smile. Adrian was a meaty kid on the high school football team, but at that moment, he looked as if the slightest breeze would knock him down.

"So is this where you found your brother's bike?"

"Yeah."

"Did you move it at all?"

"No, I didn't touch it."

"Did you search the woods around here?"

"Yeah, sure I did. Jer wasn't anywhere."

Dennis Sloan muttered an expletive under his breath and marched to the side of the road, his boots crunching on rock. He didn't have the patience to stand around answering questions. He cupped his hands around his mouth and bellowed into the woods with big pipes that would fill a room. "Jeremiah! Jeremiah!"

His booming voice scared a few birds, but that was all. There was no answer. That didn't stop him from hollering again. He was a handsome park ranger with the strong physique of a lumber-jack, and strong men always labored under the illusion that they could solve any problem if they swung a little harder, talked a little louder, or ran a little faster. Life didn't work that way.

My father let Dennis shout himself hoarse. Then he went on in the same level voice he always used. Panic was boiling over on that road, but my father was an oasis of calm, like the eye of a storm.

"Adrian, why don't you tell us what happened?"

The teenager kicked at the dirt with his sneaker. "Jer and I went to work with Dad at the ranger station. We hung out there most of the morning, and then I figured I'd ride my bike for a

while. I was going to go by myself, but Jer threw a fit about coming with me. So I let him go along just to shut him up."

"Why didn't you want him to come with you?"

"I like to ride fast. He slows me down."

"What did the two of you do?"

"Nothing. We rode, that's all. I thought we could make it to
Talking Lake, but we didn't get that far before we got hungry.
There's a campground about a mile north of here, so we stopped
to have lunch. Mom made sandwiches for our backpacks. Jer
wolfed his down, and then he started bugging me."

"How so?"

"Oh, he was batting a shuttlecock around with his badminton
racket. He'd whack it and chase it, and he nearly hit me with it
a couple of times. It pissed me off. He was collecting rocks, too,
and he had to show me every one he found. He wouldn't leave
me alone."

"So how did the two of you get separated?"

"Jer wanted to go back, but I wasn't ready to leave. I mean, he
made such a stink about coming with me, and then he wanted to
head out before we did anything. I said fine, go, I don't care. And
he got on his bike and went back the way we came."

"You let him go," Ellen murmured to her son.

Her tone was gentle, but the lack of anger in his mother's
voice actually made the accusation cut deeper. I could see the kid
folding up like a flower.

"You *let your brother go*. Alone. Out here."

Adrian bit his lower lip and looked miserable. "All I did was
give him a head start, Mom. I was going to catch up to him."

"Are you sure he headed south?" my father asked, before
Adrian disintegrated completely. "Is it possible he went the other
way toward the lake?"

"No, I saw him go. He was heading toward the ranger station."

"Was there anyone else in the campground while you were there?"

The boy squatted to pry a few prickly burs from the cuff of his jeans and flick them into the brush. "No."

"What did you do next?"

"I hung out for a while."

"Doing what?"

"Shooting at the crows. Just to scare them. I didn't hit them or anything."

"You carry a gun?"

"Sometimes." Adrian flipped back his windbreaker to reveal the butt of a revolver jutting out of the pocket of his jeans.

"Boys need to know about guns, Tom," Dennis interrupted, as if my father had been casting aspersions on his parenting. "The safest thing is to teach them when they're young. You know that."

"I do know that, Dennis. I'm just trying to figure out what happened. Did you ever let Jeremiah handle your gun, Adrian?"

"A couple of times, but only if Dad was around."

My father was silent for a while. That was one of the things he'd taught me about police work. Silence is your friend. People can't stand silence, and they feel like they have to fill it up with something. Usually, they end up telling you things they never meant to say.

But Adrian kept his mouth shut.

"Okay, Jeremiah took his bike and left," my father went on eventually. "You were alone in the campground. Did you see or hear any cars on the road?"

"No."

"What about voices?"

"No. I said I was alone."

"How long did you stay there after Jeremiah left?"

"I don't know. A while."

"Five minutes? Fifteen? An hour?"

"I told you, I don't know. I wasn't looking at what time it was."

"But eventually, you got on your bike and headed back the same way?"

"Yeah."

"Okay, tell me the rest."

The teenager heaved a sigh. "I found Jer's bike. He was gone. I don't know anything else."

"Did you move the bike at all? Is this exactly where you found it?"

My head snapped up, as if someone had jabbed me with a live wire. I'd been on edge for months, watching for little things like that. I wondered if anyone else had noticed that Dad was repeating himself.

Adrian did. He looked puzzled and annoyed. "You already asked me about that."

Dad's composure broke for a moment, but he recovered with an easy smile. "Just making sure."

"Well, I didn't move it," Adrian said again.

"What did you do next?"

"I looked for Jer, what else? I looked everywhere. I shouted and shouted. I rode back to the campground to see if I'd missed him somehow. Then I started back toward the ranger station. I figured maybe he was walking, like the bike crapped out or something, and I'd pass him on the way. But I didn't. I rode all the way back and told my dad."

"You have a phone, right? Why not call?"

"Signal sucks out here. Anyway, I was too freaked. I just wanted to get back and tell my dad."

"Did Jeremiah have a phone with him?"

"Yeah, but it was dead."

"He's always forgetting to charge it," Dennis interjected. "I called it over and over. It keeps going to voicemail."

"Well, we'll check with the phone company and see if they can tell us anything," Dad said. "Adrian, what was Jeremiah wearing?"

"His Sunday suit."

My father's brow furrowed in surprise. "Really? Why?"

Ellen was crouched by her son's bicycle on the shoulder of the road. Her fingers reached out and touched the front tire and spun it slowly. She spoke without looking up. "We lost my father a couple of weeks ago. Jeremiah was very close to his grandfather, and he took it hard. He wore the suit to the service at the cemetery, and he's been putting it on ever since. I tried to make him stop, but after a while, I just let him do it."

"He wore Nikes, too," Adrian added. "Purple ones."

"Okay. Adrian, is there anything else you can tell us?"

"No, nothing. Really. I don't know what happened to him." He shot a pained look at his mother. "I'm so sorry, Mom."

Ellen didn't look back at her older son. She stood up again, brushed the dust from her clothes, and fixed her stare on my father. Her voice was barely a whisper, but she hammered out every word. "Someone *abducted* my boy, Tom. You need to do something right now. I want roadblocks. Helicopters. Alerts in every police department throughout the state. I want my son's picture on TV. I want him on highway signs. I want the whole world looking for Jeremiah."

She was barely holding back the hysteria that I knew was inside her. It was like lake water thumping against the surface ice, trying to get out.

"Ellen, none of us will sleep until we find your boy," Dad assured her. He drew himself up to his full height, and when he was like that, you just had to believe everything he said. "I know you're scared, but there hasn't been a stranger abduction in this county ever. Ever. It's easy to think the worst, but let's focus on the likelier explanations first. We need to search the woods around here. If Jeremiah left the road for any reason, he can't have gone far. We'll put out the word and have fifty townspeople here in a few minutes and we'll blanket the whole area. We've got hours of daylight left to find him. It's also possible—likely even—that Jeremiah simply hitched a ride back to town with somebody he knew. He could be at a friend's house right now. Kids don't think about the panic they cause when they forget to tell their parents where they've gone. Shelby and Adam will check the whole town while we're out here searching the woods. Okay? Trust me. We'll find him."

I knew my father believed that.

If I'd been in his shoes at that moment, I probably would have said the same thing. You try not to make promises you can't keep, but Dad still believed that most stories had happy endings. Someone in town would find Jeremiah. Some hero would take him home, and Ellen would cry, and Dennis would hug his boy, and the rest of us would exhale with quiet relief.

That was how we all thought it would go. The boy would be back in his mother's arms by nightfall.

But we were all wrong.

CHAPTER THREE

Ten years old. That was Jeremiah's age.

I still remember what it was like to be a kid in the summertime in Mittel County. When I was that age, I used to do exactly what Jeremiah did—take my bike down the dirt roads with my hair blowing in the wind, ride to one of the dozens of lakes around here, and swim in the cool water with fish brushing up against my bare legs. Those days felt like they lasted forever. The sun came up early and went down late. When I finally got back home, I'd be wet, dirty, tired, and ready to do it all over again.

Rose Carter was my best friend back then. Rose was the girl who got booted off the Everywhere Strikers when Violet went out for the high school volleyball team. It wasn't my fault, but Rose and I were never as close after that. I think she held it against me that I stayed on the team.

But when we were ten? We did everything together.

I would make up puzzles and mysteries for us. She and I would hike into the woods to hunt for signs of the mythical Ursulina. We'd find what looked like footprints in the mud, and we'd measure them and take pictures and bring them all back to my father to show him what we'd found. He would swear that our evidence was very, very persuasive, and we believed him when he said he would consult with people in the government about what we'd discovered.

Rose and I explored the whole county in those days. We went everywhere, just the two of us, and the Ursulina was the only monster that ever crossed our minds. We didn't worry about being alone miles from home.

We never imagined a bicycle lying on the side of the road.

Ten years old.

Dad used to keep a picture of me on the mantle from when I was that age. Hands on my hips, hair in my face, annoyed and impatient that I had to take a break for even a moment from the whirlwind of being a child. I suppose every parent has a picture like that.

If I look in a mirror even now, I can still see hints of the girl in that old photograph. I haven't lost that faraway look in my brown eyes or the stubborn crinkle in my forehead. I was a medium girl then, and I still am, not short, not tall, not heavy, not thin. My hair looks dark enough to be black, but you'd have to see me in the sunlight to know it's more like chocolate. It's straight as an arrow even on the most humid July day. I keep it parted in the middle and just long enough to frame my face. I have a few freckles, too, sprinkled like pepper across the bridge of my nose.

When I look at that picture now, I think: that girl wasn't afraid of anything. It's hard to find things you like about yourself, but I'll go with that one. I don't scare easily.

Ten years old.

It can be a dangerous age, too. You're not just a little kid anymore. You're starting to become a person, but you haven't lost the wonder of being a child. You have no sense of your own limitations. That's a good thing and a bad thing.

I thought about Jeremiah at that age, trying to figure out the world.

I knew him better than most kids in the area, because his best friend and next-door neighbor was Anna Helvik. Anna was the daughter of my friend and former volleyball coach, Trina, and I was over at Trina's house all the time. Anna and Jeremiah were often with us. He was a shy kid, not saying much when you talked to him. Anna was the brave one, like me, the girl who would go anywhere and do everything. Jeremiah looked happy to trail behind her and play Spock to her Kirk. He was sweet, always with a big smile, the polite kid who called me "Miss Lake." I liked him.

Where was he?

I kept going over Adrian's story in my head. I thought about Jeremiah heading out of the campground on his bike. I tried to picture this short, skinny boy flying down the road through the national forest. His little legs pumped up and down on the pedals, and his backside probably lifted off the bicycle seat. His badminton racket jutted out of his backpack. His hair whipped like strands of fine straw, long enough to fall over his eyes, with a cowlick sprouting from the back.

But you know what really struck me?

That Sunday suit he was wearing.

They'd put Jeremiah's grandfather in the ground two weeks earlier, and this little boy still couldn't take off his Sunday clothes.

I didn't know if it would help us find him, but it told me one thing. Jeremiah was lonely. That's what worried me, because if I could see it, then so could others.

The ones who saw a boy like that as prey.

CHAPTER FOUR

"So what do you think?" Adam asked me as we drove back toward Everywhere. "Where's the kid?"

I didn't answer immediately. I was watching a caravan of cars pass us in the opposite direction, filled with searchers ready to fan out shoulder to shoulder to hunt for Jeremiah in the woods. They were our friends and neighbors. Around here, when someone's in trouble, the word goes out, and people drop everything to help.

"I hope he's in town with a friend," I said finally, "and we just haven't found him yet."

Adam took off his sunglasses and waited until I turned my head and stared back at him. "Shelby, you know he's not in town."

"He might be."

"Without his bike? How did he get there? Somebody had to drive him, and by now, the whole town knows he's missing. If anybody knew where he was, they'd have called. The fact is, he's either still in the forest, or else—"

I waited. "Or else?"

Adam shrugged and replaced his shades on his face. "Hey, you're thinking what I'm thinking. You just don't want to say it."

He was right. I didn't want to say it, so I said nothing.

We drove on in silence. It was ten more miles before we reached the southern border of the national forest. Dennis Sloan worked at the ranger station and welcome center at the park entrance. There was a stop sign ahead of us marking the main highway cutting through Mittel County. Going left would take us east toward Stanton an hour away. Going right led toward block-long towns like Witch Tree and Sugarfall that were situated deep in the kind of woods where Goldilocks got lost.

The checkerboard streets of Everywhere were directly ahead of us. Century-old brick buildings lined the main street, which was dominated by the county courthouse and its acre of green lawn and historical statues. Next to the courthouse was the boxy library that housed the sheriff's office downstairs. The rest of the street was made up of shops that had been around for years. The small market owned by Ellen Sloan. The bakery with green-frosted sugar cookies that have always been a weakness of mine. The hardware store. The Post Office. The Nowhere Café, where Dad and I ate nearly every day of our lives.

You can imagine the jokes. Where do you eat in Everywhere? Nowhere.

Some of the shops had closed over time, leaving empty buildings with rusted signs and broken windows covered over with plywood. It's like a funeral for a friend when a main-street shop closes, because you know it's never coming back. This isn't a place where new customers come to live and shop. Every census report whittles down Mittel County by another few hundred people. Either they die or they leave for better jobs and bigger towns. People aren't having enough babies to compensate.

Adam and I parked outside the Nowhere and then went door to door at all of the shops in less than an hour. No one had seen Jeremiah that day. Searching the outskirts of town was going to take longer, because most neighbors lived half a mile or more from each other, in houses carved out of a few acres of forest, with long dirt driveways winding through the trees. I drove toward Jeremiah's house, but Adam stopped me when we were barely out of the town center. He grabbed my arm and pointed at the parking lot for our one-story K–12 school, home to the Everywhere Strikers. I'd gone there. Adam had gone there. We'd all gone there. It was summer, when kids wanted to forget about school, but there was a beat-up red SUV parked in the far corner of the lot.

"I recognize that Bronco," Adam said. "The Gruders are back."

I groaned. Will and Vince Gruder were our local bad boys. The ones who kept the county flush with drugs. "Think they know something?"

"I think we should ask."

I pulled into the lot and parked our cruiser next to the Ford Bronco. Adam and I both got out. The SUV's rear windows had been covered with duct tape, so we couldn't see into the back. Hundreds of bugs were splattered across the windshield, and the front seats were a mess of fast-food wrappers and Walmart bags. A plastic jalapeño, wearing a sombrero, dangled from the rear-view mirror, with "Welcome to El Paso" printed across the green skin of the pepper.

I knew what the jalapeño meant. Will and Vince traveled to Mexico every summer, and they cooked what they brought back into meth in a lab hidden somewhere in the woods. We'd chased them for years, but they were sly like foxes about covering up their business and had never spent so much as a day inside the Mittel County jail.

There was no sign of the Gruders outside the school, but I heard the springy thump of a basketball behind the building. Adam heard it, too, and he headed off across the green grass without a word to me. I jogged to keep up with him.

I was used to Adam taking the lead. Technically, he and I were both deputies, but he was three years older. You can guess where that left me in the pecking order, at least in Adam's mind. It didn't help that I was the daughter of the sheriff. It also didn't help that Adam had asked me out in high school when he was a senior and I was a freshman, and I'd shot him down. Adam didn't hear the word "no" very often. He was used to girls falling for the jeans, the shades, the smirk, and the tight little curls in his short brown hair. He wasn't tall, but he had the cool factor going for him back then. Cool kids weren't my type. Not that I knew what my type was.

Adam was a good cop but a little reckless, because he always felt like he had something to prove. He'd grown up in the shadow of his mother, who was a local hero in Mittel County. She'd competed in the Winter Olympics in Lake Placid and taken home a silver medal in cross-country skiing. She was pretty and TV-friendly, and she'd parlayed her success into a lot of money in sponsorships. Sooner or later, Adam was going to inherit some big bucks. Maybe that's why he never looked happy living an ordinary life. I think he always felt that his mother wanted him to do something more with her DNA than hand out traffic tickets on the county roads.

The two of us went around to the rear of the school building, where the athletic fields were arranged in a giant rectangle. The basketball courts were closest to us, and we saw the Gruders playing a fierce game of one-on-one with a white-and-purple basketball. As I watched, one of the brothers sunk a hook shot through the rusted hoop, but I didn't know which brother it was. They were identical twins, twenty-two years old.

"That's Vince," Adam said, reading my mind.

"How do you know?"

"Because Vince can shoot, and Will sucks."

We strolled over to the court. The Gruders saw us coming,

and they dribbled the ball to the fence to meet us. Both wore jeans and high-tops, and both were bare-chested, with sweat dripping in streaks down their suntanned skin. They had the same long, greasy blond hair and the same green eyes and even the same nose rings in their right nostrils. They were tall and skinny, and I could smell pot on their breath.

"Deputy Twilley," Vince announced, as if we were all old friends, "and Deputy Lake. Look at that, our two favorite law enforcement professionals are here to welcome us home. You want to shoot some hoops with us?"

"When did you get back into town, Vince?" Adam asked, ignoring the small talk.

"A couple of days ago. We rolled into Witch Tree late on Wednesday."

"Where did you go on your trip?"

"Oh, here and there. We hit us some beaches, drank us some beer. What's summer without a road trip, right? Still, there's no place like home. Nothing beats the scenery around here." As he said this, Vince gave me an up-and-down look that belonged in a brown paper wrapper.

"We're looking for Jeremiah Sloan," Adam said impatiently. "Have you seen him?"

Vince bounced the basketball in his hand. "Who?"

"He's Adrian Sloan's little brother," I told him. I noticed that Will Gruder kept scratching his leg with his foot, and I shot a quick glance at the ragged cuffs of his jeans, which were loaded with sharp little prickly burs. When I saw that, I quickly added, "I mean, you guys know Adrian, don't you?"

The two brothers exchanged looks, and the look from Vince said *Shut up*.

"Sure, we know Adrian," Vince said. "Football player, right? What's up with his brother?"

"Jeremiah is missing," Adam replied. "We found his bike on the dirt road that leads to Talking Lake. There's no sign of the boy. His parents are pretty worried."

Will shot a concerned glance at his brother. "He's missing? Really? I mean, we just—"

"Hey, that's too bad about the kid," Vince interrupted before Will could say anything more. "Wish we could help you out, but we haven't seen him. If we spot him hanging around, we'll give you a call."

"When did the two of you last see Adrian?" I asked.

Vince didn't blink. He just stared right through me. "Adrian? Heck if I know."

"Are you sure you didn't see him today?"

"Today? No, we haven't seen Adrian since we got back. Not sure why we would. You guys need anything else? Or can I get back to kicking Will's ass on the court?"

"Go ahead."

Vince grabbed his brother's shoulder and dragged him back to the basketball court. I waited to see what Will would do, and sure enough, he glanced back at me with a shifty, nervous expression that told me the two of them were lying. I turned my back on the brothers and walked away toward the front of the school. This time, Adam had to jog to catch up with me.

"What the hell was that about?" he asked. "Why were you asking about Adrian?"

"Burs."

"Huh?"

"Will had prickly burs stuck to his jeans and shoelaces. A lot of them."

"So?"

"Adrian Sloan did, too. He was picking them off while Dad was talking to him."

Adam looked back at the brothers, who were hanging around on the court and watching us go. "You think the Gruder boys were with Adrian? Because of a few prickly burs? That's pretty thin, Shelby."

"Yeah, I know. Maybe I'm wrong about this, and it's nothing. But if I'm right, then Will and Vince saw Adrian in the national forest today. And that means Adrian's lying to us."

CHAPTER FIVE

When you're in the midst of an investigation that involves a child, you always feel as if your heart is in your mouth and you have to remind yourself to breathe. So it was a relief when Monica called us to say she had a report of an unidentified, unaccompanied minor in our old town cemetery. I told her we'd check it out immediately. My first thought was that Jeremiah had gone to visit his grandfather's grave, and I allowed myself to hope that our fears had been misplaced and we'd have the boy back with his parents soon.

The dead of the Mittel County Cemetery have always been like friends to me, because the graveyard backs up to our house. When I was a girl, I used to wander the cemetery trails at night with a flashlight, hunting for ghosts. Rose thought it was creepy and wouldn't go along, but the place never bothered me. Remember, I'm the girl who doesn't scare easily. I still walk in the cemetery whenever I can. Sometimes I'll take my guitar and sing songs for the dead, because they're good listeners and don't heckle me when I'm off-key.

Adam and I parked in the driveway of my father's house, and we hiked through the backyard toward the cemetery. The burial plots are clustered in small groves, with spruces watching over the dead like silent giants. Moss and mold adorn the older stones, some of which date back two hundred years. Even on the hottest, brightest summer day, it's cool and dark there, and you can't see far because of the tree trunks packed closely together.

I called, "Jeremiah! Jeremiah, are you here?"

Adam shouted, too. "Jeremiah! Hey, Jeremiah, can you hear us?"

We didn't get any reply except the trill of cardinals.

"Let's split up," I suggested.

Adam took a path to my right, and the woods quickly swallowed him up. I went in the opposite direction. Every now and then, I called Jeremiah's name again. Distantly, I could hear Adam doing the same, but after a while, his voice faded away. The cemetery meanders over acres of hilly land, and as I explored the individual groves, I saw winged angels, crypts guarded by carved lions, fallen crosses, and massive trees toppled by storms, with mushrooms growing out of the stumps. The whole area had a peaty smell.

I'd walked these trails countless times and knew many of the names on the graves by heart, but this time, I felt an odd sense of unease being here. That's because I knew I wasn't alone. Someone was in the trees, spying on me. Every now and then, I heard a twig snap, betraying a footstep. It could have been an animal digging in the leafy brush, but I didn't think so. I kept looking over my shoulder, but the trails were empty, and I didn't see anyone near the graves.

"Hello?" I called. "Who's there?"

There was no answer, so I tried again. "Jeremiah? Is that you? Come on out, I know you're there."

I kept walking, but when I glanced back, I spotted a tiny flash of yellow disappearing behind the trunk of a black oak. It was someone wearing a hoodie. Small, definitely a child. I couldn't see a face, but whoever it was knew they'd been spotted. I heard my stalker sprinting away, and I took off in pursuit, but I was chasing someone with the grace and speed of a deer. Little stabs of yellow whipped in and out of view through the trees and left me behind.

"Hey! Hey, stop!"

I broke into a field of headstones scattered along a shallow hillside. Shadows stretched across the lawn, and the forest itself was gray. My spy in the hoodie had vanished. If it was Jeremiah, he wasn't wearing his Sunday suit anymore.

"Shelby?"

Deputies aren't supposed to scream, but I screamed in surprise. Someone was right behind me. I whirled around, and the man who was there backed away, raising his hands as if to assure me that he came in peace.

I knew him.

Oh, yes, I knew him. He was just about the last person I wanted to see.

"Keith."

He stood there, looking as awkward as me. His lips moved, but he didn't say anything, as if his mouth didn't know what to do. Talk. Smile. Frown. Kiss me.

"Long time," Keith said finally. You'd be amazed how much meaning you can pack into two little words. We could both tell you the exact date when we'd last spoken. November 14. Last fall.

"What are you doing here?" I asked him.

He nodded his head toward a flat stone on the ground, newer and brighter than the weathered graves around it. "Colleen."

"Oh. Sure."

"I suppose that surprises you."

"Why should it? She was your wife."

Keith tossed his head, flipping back his messy brown hair.

It was a nervous gesture he used a lot. He was lanky and tall, wearing khakis, old brown shoes, and a rust-colored pullover. He limped when he moved, because he had an artificial limb below his right knee. He wasn't classically handsome, but handsome faces have never been that interesting to me. His face had character, like a book that offers you something new every time you read it. His eyebrows were thick and dark, his nose long and slightly crooked, his chin narrow and protruding. He and I had the same kind of eyes, colored like raw brown sugar and a little sad. Whenever I looked in his eyes, I knew there was a lot going on inside.

Keith Whalen. He was eight years older than me. When I was a senior in high school, he taught my English class. I know, what a cliché, the girl with a crush on her English teacher. He read Thoreau, and I swooned. Yeah, that was me, but it's not that simple. We'd all heard stories about his injury in the war, his mood swings, his opioid habit, his troubled marriage. I didn't see any of that in the classroom. I just saw a broken man sitting on the desk, taking us all to Walden Pond with that "Tupelo Honey" voice of his. To me, if he had personal struggles, that only made him more attractive, and I was the teenage girl who could fix it all.

Don't worry, it was nothing more than a Harlequin Romance fantasy in my head. Nothing happened when I was a student. But dead fires have a way of coming back to life.

"So how are you?"

Keith shook his head the way he had when one of my answers disappointed him in class. "Do you really care how I am, Shelby? If you're just making small talk, we don't need to do that."

"I care."

"Okay. Sorry, I suppose that sounded harsh. It's just that the last time we talked, I thought that you—"

"Don't misunderstand me," I interrupted with coolness in my

voice. "I'm still a police officer. Nothing's changed. But you asked me if I care, and I do."

He got a little tic in his cheek. I knew I'd hurt him. I was trying to hurt him.

"You're honest. I guess I prefer that. Well, since you asked, the fact is, I'm not doing well at all."

"That's too bad, Keith."

"You may not think I loved Colleen, but I did. I miss her. And yes, I know she was a better wife to me than I deserved." Keith eyed the grave, as if Colleen were still listening to him. "You know, I've picked up the phone a hundred times to call you, Shelby."

"It's better that you didn't."

"Yeah, that's what I figured. I never told anyone. Your secret is safe. I mean, I assume you wanted it to be a secret."

"I don't want to have this conversation, Keith."

"Okay. That's fine." But I could sense his disappointment. "What about you? What are you doing here?"

"Jeremiah Sloan is missing. Didn't you hear about it?"

"No. Town news doesn't come my way like it used to."

"Well, we had a report of a kid here in the cemetery. We were hoping it was Jeremiah. Have you seen him?"

Keith hesitated. "No, I haven't. At least I don't think so."

"You don't sound sure."

"Well, someone was around here. I don't know who, but somebody was watching me from the trees when I was talking to Colleen."

"Yellow hoodie?"

"That's right. I didn't see a face." Keith flipped his hair again. I made him uncomfortable. "What happened to Jeremiah?"

I explained, and his face grew cloudy.

"You think he was abducted? Around here?"

"I'm trying not to think about it. I'm just trying to find him."

"Well, I know Jeremiah likes to go off by himself and explore. I've seen him on my property a few times this year. Mostly in the woods, but he would come up to the house and barn, too."

"Oh? Why?"

"I don't know. He didn't say anything when I tried to talk to him. Ellen and Dennis only live a mile away. I just figured he was out hunting for the Ursulina."

I stared back at him with a frown on my face. I didn't like the joke. Not from him. Not after what had happened.

"I suppose I should check in with Dennis and see how he's doing," Keith went on, "but he and I don't really talk much now."

"Why is that?"

"Colleen worked for Ellen at the mini-mart, remember? Ellen's not exactly a fan of mine anymore."

"It doesn't matter. Right now, they need all the support they can get. If you want to call Dennis, you should."

"I will."

"I need to go, Keith."

"Sure. Good luck. I hope you find Jeremiah soon. I mean, I'm sure he's okay and all, but it's rough when a kid is missing."

I didn't say anything more. There was a lot I could have said, but I didn't. When I looked at Keith, I remembered coming out to the cemetery last winter with my guitar and singing that Sheryl Crow song, "My Favorite Mistake." I turned away and hoped we were done, but I knew he couldn't let it go. I hadn't gone ten feet when he called after me.

"Hey, how come you never asked me the question, Shelby? Tom asked me. Adam asked me. You never did."

I stopped and let him stare at my back.

"Is it because you were afraid of what I'd say?"

My shoulders heaved with a sigh. I turned around and faced

him again. "I didn't ask because I knew what you'd tell me, and I figured I'd know if you were lying. I didn't want to have to live with that."

Keith closed the distance between us with a little sway in his hips from his artificial leg. He didn't look surprised by my doubts. "Well, I'm sorry to put such a burden on you, Shelby, but I want you to hear it from my mouth. I'm telling the truth. I didn't kill my wife."

CHAPTER SIX

I had to put the confrontation with Keith out of my mind, because I found the grave of Jeremiah's grandfather in the same grove where Colleen Whalen was buried. There were footsteps in the newly turned dirt, but they looked crusty and dry, dating back to the interment two weeks earlier. No one had been here recently. I was disappointed because I realized that Jeremiah probably hadn't been the child lurking in the cemetery grounds.

My little fairy in the forest hadn't gone away, however. I was still being watched. When I started up the sloping trail that led back toward our house, I saw a dot of yellow come and go behind a fat old beech tree that the locals called Bartholomew. I walked quickly to get ahead of whoever it was. Where the trail crested the hill, I was invisible, so I darted off the path and took cover. Soon, quick footsteps rustled through the brush in pursuit.

"Gotcha!" I exclaimed as I jumped back on the trail.

A ten-year-old girl froze in front of me. She was dressed in a yellow hoodie, jean shorts, and sneakers. She was tall for her age and skinny as a pencil. When she pushed the hood from her face, her sunny blond hair came free, and she stared up at me with huge blue eyes.

"Hi, Shelby."

"Anna Helvik! What are you doing here? It's not safe to be skulking around the woods. You shouldn't be in the cemetery by yourself."

Wow, did I sound like a mother, or what?

I suppose I was as close to a surrogate mother to Anna as she was likely to have. I'd been there for her first steps. I'd babysat for her whenever her parents were away. When her mother, Trina, had gone to Chicago for cancer treatment five years earlier, I'd been the one to move into their house for a month to take care of Anna. It was the least I could do for Trina, because she'd always been much more than a coach to me.

I saw Trina every day throughout high school. Like most teenagers, I'd gone through my share of angst and despair back then. I was finally old enough to understand what it meant to be abandoned as a baby, and I took out my anger about it on everyone around me. I was angry on the volleyball court. I was angry with my father. I was angry at my boyfriend for wanting sex and even angrier when I gave it to him. For two years, I was a really unhappy kid, and the only person who kept me from going off the rails was Trina. She never gave up on me.

She was still my closest friend, despite the fifteen-year age difference. I told her everything. She was literally the only other person in the world who knew the truth about me and Keith Whalen. Even my father didn't know, because he probably would have had to fire me if he did.

Trina was tall, blond, and gorgeous, and Anna was already growing up the same way. Trina's husband, Karl, was a handsome man, but the girl standing in front of me was a miniature replica of her mother. She was also stubborn and fearless, and I like to think she got some of that from hanging out with me.

"Talk to me, Anna. Does your mom know where you are?"

"I have my phone. She can call me if she wants to know where I am."

"What about your dad?"

"He's on the road."

That was no surprise. Karl Helvik had a technology job and traveled a lot. Trina was still a coach and math teacher at the high school. The two of them didn't always have as much time for Anna as they wanted, so I filled in whenever I could.

"How did you get here?"

"Bike."

"Well, what are you doing here anyway? Why were you hiding?"

"I was just hanging out. First I was spying on Mr. Whalen. Then you came and I figured I'd spy on you, too."

"People don't like it when you spy on them."

"It's just a game. It's no big deal."

There was a sullenness about her that was unusual for Anna. She'd always been a smart, sweet, mischievous kid, but she'd been standoffish with me for months. I was trying not to take it personally. Trina called it an early case of teenageritis, and maybe she was right. Anna had always been a few years ahead of other kids in most things.

"Well, let's call your mother and get you home."

"She's not there."

"Where is she?"

"She's over at Jeremiah's house."

I closed my eyes in sadness, because suddenly it made sense to me. Of course, Anna had heard what happened. Of course, she was upset and scared. Jeremiah was her best friend.

"You know he's missing?"

"Yeah. Mom said."

"Well, we have people all over town looking for him, Anna. We'll find him."

"Uh-huh."

Anna was only ten, but she seemed to know I was spouting empty promises. My father had done the same thing with the Sloans. I guess we can't help ourselves from telling people what they want to hear.

The two of us walked together in silence, and I put my arm around her shoulder. She was so scrawny at that age, nothing but bones. I saw an ornate stone bench near the fringe of a cemetery grove, and I guided her there and we both sat down with the peaceful headstones arrayed in front of us. The trees hummed with birds and bugs. Sunshine streamed across the grass, but the bench where we sat was in the shadows, and I could feel the cold, damp stone through my pants. I hunted in my pocket, where I kept a few sour balls for when I wanted a quick candy fix. I handed one to Anna, and she unwrapped it and put it in her mouth. I kept my arm around her, and I was pleased that she didn't pull away. At least for a little while, things felt normal between us.

"Is that why you're here? Were you looking for Jeremiah?"

Anna shivered a little. The sour ball made a little bump in her cheek. "Yeah, he and I would hang out here sometimes."

"Did you find him?"

"No."

"Can you think of other places that he might have gone? Do you and he have any secret hideouts?"

"No."

"Are you sure? I remember Rose and I used to bike over to the drive-in before they tore it down, and we'd hang out behind the big screen. You guys don't have a favorite spot like that?"

The girl balanced her chin on her fist. "Nope."

"How are things at home? Does Jeremiah have any problems with his brother? Or his parents?"

"I don't think so."

"What about problems with other people? Does he have any trouble with bullies? Are there kids who give him a hard time?"

"No. Everybody knows Adrian is on the football team, so they don't mess with Jeremiah."

I tried to sound casual with my next question. "What about adults?"

Anna's brow crinkled. "What do you mean?"

"Well, has anyone been bothering him? Or making him uncomfortable? I know you and he are really close, Anna. Jeremiah probably tells you things he wouldn't tell anybody else. Even his parents. Know what I mean? And if there's something like that, I need to know about it, even if he told you to keep it a secret."

Anna sat silently for a long time, and I could see on her pretty face that she was struggling with what to say. Finally, she spoke softly while staring at her feet. "We're not."

"Not what?"

"We're not close. We're not friends anymore."

"You and Jeremiah? Since when?"

"I don't know. A while."

"Do your parents know?"

"I didn't tell them about it."

"Why not?"

"Mom's got her own problems. She and Dad have been crying a lot. They don't think I know, but I know. I figured they didn't need me bothering them with my stuff."

When I heard this, I had two more things worrying me.

Something was wrong in Trina's life, and she hadn't told me about it. And Anna had ended her friendship with Jeremiah without telling her mother. The apple didn't fall far from the tree in that family. I loved Trina, but people sometimes saw her as cold, because she shared so little of herself.

"So what happened between you and Jeremiah? Why aren't you friends anymore?"

"Nothing happened."

"Come on, Anna. You two have been best buddies since kindergarten. Something must have happened."

"I just don't want to be friends with him. Does he have to be my friend?"

"No. He doesn't. But he's missing, and here you are looking for him. That makes me think you still like him."

"Well, I don't." I watched tears begin to slip down her cheeks. Her lips pushed together, and her eyes were red. "I just want to go home now. Can you take me home, Shelby?"

"Sure. Of course. I'll take you home." I got up from the bench, but then I knelt in the grass in front of her and brushed the tears away from her cheeks. "Hey, Anna, you know you can tell me anything, right?"

"Yeah. I know."

"Well, this is really important. Do you have any idea at all what might have happened to Jeremiah?"

I saw a look of terror spread across this little girl's face. Honestly, I'd never seen anyone look so scared. She cried harder and threw her arms around my neck and hugged me as if I were the only one who could save her from whatever evil thing was out there.

Then she whispered in my ear, barely getting the words out.

"I think the Ursulina got him."

CHAPTER SEVEN

The Ursulina.

It's a story as old as the town. I'm sure you know about Bigfoot and the Yeti and Sasquatch, those shaggy eight-foot monsters that walk upright through the forest. Our creature is like that, but with a twist. The legend of the Ursulina says that it can also take human form. A pioneer family in the old, old days found that out when they rescued a starving fur trader and let him spend the night in their cabin. They awoke to the horror of a giant brown beast with nine-inch claws and curved fangs who proceeded to feast on every one of them.

So you can understand why we're still a little nervous about strangers around here.

Dad told me about the Ursulina when I was only five years old. I loved stories like that, the scarier the better. Tourists love it, too. In the fall, we hold an annual festival called Ursulina Days. The town sells Ursulina T-shirts and mugs and magnets. People dress up in Ursulina costumes, and true believers come from around the world to search our woods for the monster. We even offer a cash prize of one hundred thousand dollars to the first person who brings in an Ursulina, alive or dead. So far, no one has collected the money.

Nine months before Jeremiah disappeared, Ursulina Days fell over my twenty-fifth birthday weekend on Halloween. Monica recruited me to be part of the events. In addition to her job as the sheriff's department secretary, Monica was volunteer board chair for the Friends of the Library. She was planning a Halloween event for kids on that Saturday, and Monica always gets what she wants. She may be quirky and grandmotherly, but if you get in her way, she'll give you a little giggle and then mow you down.

I've mentioned that I sing, right? I play guitar, and I write songs, too. I don't claim to be very good, but I've done it since I was a little girl. Every now and then I'll let my arm get twisted to perform at story time for the local kids. So Monica asked me to write an Ursulina song for the Halloween event. She already had an artist doing scary decorations and a writer who'd written a children's story about the Ursulina that he was going to read aloud to the kids. She wanted me to do the music, and of course, I couldn't say no to her. I didn't find out until after I'd agreed that the writer who would be working with me was Keith Whalen.

It didn't bother me at the time. Yes, I'd had a major crush on Keith when he was a teacher and I was a student, but that was years ago. Of course, I'd be lying if I said I didn't still find him attractive.

Keith owned a rambler on fifty-or-so acres of hunting land at the end of a dead-end road off the main highway. Most of the land was undeveloped, but there were a few trails that had been there for decades and a creepy little jewel of a lake hidden away in a wooded valley. Trees grew right out of the water, and their branches drooped like Spanish moss. With not much sunlight breaking through the treetops, it looked like a pond out of a Grimm fairy tale where scary things might lurk below the surface. We called it Black Lake. The Striker girls used to swim there now and then during the summers, because it wasn't far from Trina's house.

I went to Keith's place around Labor Day to talk about the Halloween show. His wife, Colleen, was there when I arrived. I knew her pretty well, because she worked at Ellen's mini-mart. She was always meek and quiet, with a cute face and mousy brown hair cut into bangs, the kind of woman who looked as if she would melt in a spring shower. I could tell immediately that things weren't good between her and Keith. It was nothing they said, but I recognized the faces of two people who were going through the motions of marriage and life. I'm sorry to say that my instinct was to blame her for making him unhappy. I still saw Keith as this complicated, interesting, romantic figure from my school days. He was my Heathcliff, and being with him gave me the same goosebumps I'd felt as a teenager.

He took me to a writer's cottage on their property that he'd converted from the family barn. It was on the other side of a hill a quarter mile from the main house and painted apple red. You could see Keith's personality in the place, with its hardwood floors, 1920s-era posters of Paris and London, jazz playing from hidden speakers, and a loft where (I could tell) he often slept, rather than in bed with his wife. He had bookshelves filled with dozens of classic novels, everything from *Cannery Row* to *The Moonstone*. He kept a little shrine, too, of his military days, just mementos hung on a bulletin board near his desk. Photographs of friends he'd lost. His dog tags. A silver-and-blue St. Benedict medal on a chain. His Purple Heart. I wanted to ask him about those days, but I could tell that some subjects were off-limits.

While I sat in an old leather recliner in the barn, he acted out his story of the Ursulina. It was full of horrible deaths and blood dripping from people's faces, and I knew it would scare the snot out of the kids, which is the whole point of Halloween. I told him he should get it published, and he flipped his brown hair and looked at me as if I were crazy. But I knew he was secretly pleased.

After we met, I wrote a song I could play between sections of the story, with a chorus that would have kids singing with me after they heard it for the first time. It went like this:

> *Ursulina! Ursulina!*
> *Look at those teeth and claws!*
> *Ursulina! Ursulina!*
> *Look at those big brown paws!*
> *Ursulina! Ursulina!*
> *Is he a scary beast? Ayup!*
> *Ursulina! Ursulina!*
> *He's gonna eat you up!*

Okay, I was never going to give Sara Bareilles any competition when it came to songwriting, but I figured the kids would love it. I wrote it in a week, and then Keith and I met in the writer's cottage again so I could play it for him. He loved the song, too. We rehearsed the whole performance many times, him doing the story, me doing the song, over the course of the next several weeks. We rehearsed way more than we needed to for a half-hour children's program. And we talked. We had long talks about things that mattered. He talked about teaching, and reading, and living without a leg, and being married to a high school sweetheart who sent one man off to war and got a very different man back.

I talked, too. I talked about my father, about Trina, about Anna. I talked about my belief in signs and omens and about the challenges of growing up as a mystery girl with no past. I talked about my crush on him in high school. We laughed about that, but I was no fool. Telling him the truth about my feelings carried us across a dangerous line.

The Halloween show was a big hit. Monica was thrilled. We had nearly two hundred kids and parents gathered in the town park outside the courthouse, and they oohed and aahed and screamed at all the right scary parts. Afterward, everybody was singing my Ursulina song. It was as close as I was ever likely to get to being a celebrity, and I was flying high. So was Keith. We hung around together as afternoon became evening and the festival wound down. We were tired but exhilarated. Everyone was coming up to us and telling us what a great show it was. We drank it all in.

As night fell, we went back to his place to continue the celebration. Colleen had already gone home and was asleep in the house. Keith said she slept a lot, because that's what depressed people do. He and I went to the old barn, and we put on music, and we uncorked a bottle of Macallan that he saved for special occasions. The more we drank, the more he opened up. He grabbed novels from his bookshelves and read some of his favorite passages to me. He caressed his St. Benedict medal and talked in a hushed voice about losing his leg. He told me about his troubles with his wife.

You know where this is going.

I knew where it was going, too, but that didn't stop me. I'm sorry. You may not be able to forgive me for what I did, and that's okay, because all these years later, I haven't forgiven myself. I was drunk, it was my birthday, and I let myself indulge a high school fantasy with a married man. God, I was stupid.

A mistake like that was bound to have consequences.

But never in my life did I imagine the consequences would include Colleen Whalen dead outside their house with a bullet in her brain.

CHAPTER EIGHT

After we left the cemetery, Adam and I dropped Anna back at her house, and then we headed to the Nowhere Café. We found my father drinking weak coffee and reassuring the worried neighbors crowded around him that we were doing everything we could to find Jeremiah.

The Nowhere is where people in Everywhere gather. It's more than a local diner dishing up pancakes and venison stew. It's our meeting hall, our water cooler, our ground zero for news and gossip. Black-and-white photos of earlier generations of Everywhere residents watch us from the walls, and someday, photos of us will take their places. We meet in the red-cushioned booths and along the lunch counter to talk about weather, sports, politics, religion, cooking, vacations, holidays, and the latest rumors about who was zooming who.

Half the town was there that evening. I knew all of the faces, but I could see something in them that I hadn't seen very often before. Fear. They were afraid, because Jeremiah was still missing. The innocent explanations for what might have happened to him were fading away, and if it could happen to the Sloan boy, then it could happen to any of their children, too.

I hung in the back of the diner near the glass door. Adam went off to flirt with the counter waitress, Belinda Brees, as he usually did. Belinda was another Striker girl from my high school volleyball team. Her nickname in school was Easy Breezy, and I don't suppose I need to explain why.

While Adam put the moves on Breezy, I watched my father take questions from the crowd. I didn't like what I saw.

His brown sheriff's uniform was crisply starched and neat as a pin. He'd changed clothes after searching through the dirt and brambles of the national forest. His mustache was trimmed, and he'd tamed his thicket of snow-white hair with a brush. One thing Dad never did was to allow the people of the county to see him at anything less than his best. He stood ramrod straight, emphasizing his height, and as the townspeople grilled him, he remained almost supernaturally calm.

And yet he wasn't. I knew him. I could see the way his fingers were clutched around his thermos so tightly that his knuckles turned pink with exertion. He didn't look at people as he talked to them. His soft blue eyes were unfocused, a sign that his mind was spinning to the point of overheating. The muscles in his tanned face were tight. Like everyone else, my father was beginning to realize that he'd misjudged this situation. This was not just about a boy who wandered away. In the time we'd spent digging through the woods and searching the town, precious hours had been lost.

Nobody paid attention to me. This was the kind of situation that reminded me that I was still just a young deputy. And a woman, too. The people who wanted answers talked to Dad or Adam, as if my opinion didn't count for anything. Even my father was guilty of that sometimes. I'd called to let him know that I thought Jeremiah's brother might be hiding things from us, but Dad wasn't ready to bother the family with more questions, not simply based on my hunch. I felt as if he were patting his little girl on the head.

"Coffee, Shel?"

Belinda Brees appeared at my side with a Nowhere Café mug and a white plastic pitcher of coffee. The coffee was terrible, but I drank it anyway, the way I always did. Dad and I came to the Nowhere for breakfast six days a week at six in the morning, and we had dinner there on most days, too. Without the Nowhere and the occasional kindness of strangers, I'm pretty sure my father and I would have starved, because neither one of us could fry an egg without setting off the smoke alarms.

I sipped the coffee, which was scalding hot. The voices around us were loud, and Breezy and I spoke to each other under our breath.

"Terrible thing, huh," she murmured.

That was the word we all used. Terrible. It was a numb word, the kind of thing you say when reality is too hard to stare in the face.

"Yeah."

"Hard to believe someone took him. Not around here. But it's looking like that, isn't it? Wow."

I didn't say anything or make any guesses. I just listened to Tom handing out hope to the people in the diner. I wanted to be an optimist like him, but we were running out of optimists in Everywhere.

"Hey, have you talked to Trina lately?" I asked Breezy.

"Yeah, she was in for the fish fry on Friday with Karl and Anna."

"Did she look okay to you?"

"As far as I could tell. Why?"

"Oh, it's something Anna said. It made me wonder if anything was wrong."

"Well, you'd know better than me."

That was true. The others on the team hadn't stayed close to Trina after high school the way I had. We'd all drifted apart. Three of the girls left town to go to college and never came back. Rose still resented being booted from the squad in favor of Violet Roka, and Violet had never been close to any of us. And then there was me and Breezy.

She was the wildest of the Striker girls. We were good friends, but we were as different as a head-banger and a country star. She was much taller than me, which helped in our school days because she could unleash a vicious spike from the attack zone. (My own specialty was a booming overhand serve.) She was skinny and always wore long-sleeved shirts, even on the hottest summer days. Breezy had dabbled with drugs since I'd known her, and I suspected she had track marks on her arms that she didn't want anyone to see. Her hair was long, straight, and black, with shiny purple streaks, and when she was working she usually had it pulled back into a ponytail. She had a plain face, and her teenage acne had trailed her into adulthood.

She was the only one of our group who'd gotten married after high school, but she'd divorced a couple of years later when her husband skipped town for the North Dakota fracking fields after cleaning out their bank accounts. I knew he was bad news, because he'd been my boyfriend before he was hers. And yes, I warned her, but girls don't always listen to other girls about that sort of thing. Since the divorce, she'd lived alone in a mobile home in Witch Tree, but the word among the local men was that Easy Breezy didn't often sleep alone.

"The Gruders live over in your area, don't they?" I asked her. "Near Witch Tree?"

Breezy rolled her eyes at the mention of their name. "Oh, yeah. They sure do."

"They're back in town. Did you know that?"

"I didn't. It must be a recent thing, because they've been gone for a few weeks. They can get pretty loud over there, and the noise blows my way."

"Do you see them a lot when they're in town?"

Breezy gave me a strange look. "What's that supposed to mean, Shel?"

"It's just a question."

"Well, they're at the Witch's Brew a lot, and so am I. No law against that, right?"

I knew this was one of those times when people saw the uniform and not me. Even close friends never forget that you're a cop. Breezy had a history with drugs, and there I was asking about two of the region's suspected drug dealers. That was bound to make her nervous.

I leaned close to her ear and whispered. "Off the record, Breezy. I just want to know who the Gruders hang out with."

"Why?"

"Because Jeremiah disappeared right after they came back to town. Maybe that's a coincidence, maybe not."

She rejected the idea with a firm shake of her head. "You're way off base, Shel. Vince and Will wouldn't touch a kid. They may be dirt bags, but I don't see them doing that."

"They sell drugs. It's a violent business."

"Yeah, but you mess with a kid, and the whole town gets involved. You think they want that kind of attention? No way."

"Have you ever seen them with Adrian Sloan?"

"Jeremiah's brother? No. He's too young to be in the bar. What is he, sixteen?"

"Yeah, but the Gruders sell their crap at the high school, right? Could Adrian be involved?"

Breezy glanced at the Nowhere's long lunch counter, as if she needed an escape from our conversation. "I don't know, Shel. You're talking to the wrong person."

"Would you tell me if you did?"

"Probably not. But in this case, I really don't know. I haven't heard Adrian's name from Will or Vince, but that doesn't mean anything. Okay? Now I have to go."

Breezy refilled my mug of coffee and waded back into the crowd. Her tease-me smile returned to her face. She put a hand on the shoulder of every man she passed and gave it a squeeze. They looked back at her like she was strawberry shortcake swimming in whipped cream.

I was alone again. Adam wolfed down a burger at the counter. I hadn't eaten anything myself, but I wasn't hungry. I pushed through the diner door and brought my coffee out to the main street and climbed into the cruiser. I opened the window. The evening had cooled down fast, and the smoke of someone's firepit was in the air. It was dusk and would be dark soon, and wherever Jeremiah was, I didn't like to think of him spending the night away from his family.

Not long after, the door of the café opened, letting out a burble of noise. My father had broken free from the inquisition. He stood in the doorway, straight as an arrow, not letting on that anything was bothering him. He saw me in the cruiser and crooked a finger at me, and I scrambled out of the car to join him. The two of us headed across the street to the library. Dad used his key to let us inside, and we took the stairway down to the basement.

The lights were on. Monica Constant was still on the phones, calling seemingly everyone in town one by one. Her eyes looked up at us hopefully, but it only took a glance for her to realize there was no news. Dad beckoned me into his office, and I followed him. He sat behind his desk, laying both hands flat on the impeccably neat surface. Always keep a clean desk, he'd say. Your desk should be as perfectly organized as your mind. I think that staying organized was his way of keeping the wolf in his brain at bay. And we both knew the wolf was in there, stalking him. Dementia had claimed both of his parents.

I stayed standing. We were silent for at least two minutes, and finally I had to say something.

"Dad, there was a ninety-nine percent chance that Jeremiah would be home safely by now. You made the right call."

My father nodded. I wasn't telling him something he didn't already know. "Unfortunately, Shelby, it's looking more and more like we're dealing with the one percent this time."

"So what do we do next?"

He inhaled long and slow. "I'm heading back to the forest. We're still searching the area where the bicycle was found. These people will search all night if they have to. I'm proud of them. A terrible thing like this brings out the best in everyone."

I thought that was a generous sentiment, but also a little naive. People who are scared and upset usually take it out on someone, and that someone was likely to be my father. If we didn't find Jeremiah, he'd be the one they blamed.

"What do you want me and Adam to do?" I asked.

Dad reached into his in-box and drew out a single sheet of paper. He put on reading glasses and examined it as he tapped a finger on his desk. "Mrs. Norris called earlier to complain that she had a Peeping Tom outside her window last night. She thought it was someone staying at Rose's motel. Normally I'd be laughing about another complaint from Mrs. N, but I'm not laughing anymore. The motel is just down the highway from where the Sloans live. You better go check it out, Shelby."

CHAPTER NINE

I stood on the county highway at the base of the steep drive-way leading to the Rest in Peace Motel. From where I was, I could see the timber frame of Ellen and Dennis Sloan's house not far down the road. The sky was almost dark, and lights burned in every window. Cars and trucks were parked up and down the shoulder, and I knew friends were providing support to the family. I was happy that the Sloans weren't dealing with this alone.

Adam returned to our cruiser from a modest yellow cottage on the opposite side of the highway, where Mrs. Norris had lived since FDR was elected. We'd flipped a coin to decide who got to talk to her this time.

"Mrs. N can't give us many details about her mystery stalker," he reported. "She calls him Snuffle Man. Said his heavy breathing sounded like some kind of obscene phone call."

"And this was last night?"

"Early this morning. Around five o'clock or so, before daylight. She was sleeping, but Snuffle Man woke her up he was so loud. He was right outside the open window."

"And is she sure it was a person? Sounds like it could be a deer snorting to me."

"Yeah, Mrs. N says she screamed and grabbed her shotgun and went running to the window. You don't mess with a double-barreled ninety-five-year-old who sleeps in the raw. She made sure to tell me that, by the way, like I'll ever get that image out of my head. Anyway, she spooked whoever it was, and he took off. She thinks he headed across the highway to the motel."

"But she couldn't give a description of him?"

"No. Too dark to see."

I peered up the asphalt driveway at the Rest in Peace Motel, or the Peaceful Rest, if you want to be fussy about its real name. Rose had inherited the place two years earlier when her parents died in a car accident. This was where she'd grown up, but I knew Rose had never wanted to be in the motel business like her parents. She liked to be on the go, and running the Rest in Peace kept her inside the office nearly every single day, which she hated. She was fixing it up and already had plans to sell it as soon as she could find a willing buyer.

Rose wasn't married, and she was an only child. It's funny, when we were kids, I was a little jealous of her because she knew who her parents were. And then, just like that, her mom and dad were gone. You'd think that kind of tragedy might have brought two old friends closer together again, but it really didn't. I offered to stay with her for a while after the accident, but she was pretty firm in saying no. I knew that Rose and I were never going to hunt for the Ursulina together the way we did as kids, but I still missed the closeness we had in those days.

The motel was an L-shaped one-story building with twelve rooms. The doors were all freshly painted red, and blooming flower boxes decorated the windows. A dense stand of pines towered behind the motel walls. It was the high season, and every door had a car parked in front of it. The highway advertisement

featured two painted signs dangling from hooks below the motel's
name. One said No Pets and the other said No Vacancy.

"Full house," Adam commented.

"Yeah, let's go see if Rose remembers any snuffly breathers."

We climbed the driveway to the bungalow in the woods that
doubled as the motel office and Rose's residence. We opened the
swinging screen door and went inside. The television behind the
motel counter was blaring a home fix-up show, but no one was
in the office. I saw real estate books on the desk—Rose was going
after her realtor's license—and another laminated sign reminding
guests about the no-pet policy. Around here, pets were prone to
wandering into the woods and getting eaten.

I rang the counter bell.

"Hey, Rose, you around? It's Shelby."

The back door of the small house was cracked open, letting in
a few flies that buzzed around us. I heard a muffled reply, and not
long after, Rose appeared in the doorway, carrying half a dozen
clay flower pots planted with daisies and African violets. She wore
a camouflage tank top and jean shorts underneath. Rose had always carried a couple more pounds than she liked, and her exposed stomach had the tiniest roll. Her skin was moist with sweat
and dirty with paint and potting soil. Her reddish-brown hair was
tucked under a beret.

"Hey, Shelby," she said. "Hey, Adam. Have you been here long?"

"Just got here."

"Oh, good. Sorry I'm such a mess. I was out in the garden,
and I've been touching up paint on the doors half the day." She
dropped into the office chair and swatted away a fly with one of
her motel brochures. "What's up? You guys find Jeremiah yet?"

I shook my head. "No."

"Damn, that's so awful. He's such a great kid. I can't believe
this. I just saw him yesterday."

"Where was this?"

"Right here at the motel. Jeremiah and Adrian both help me out sometimes during the summer."

"Doing what?"

"Oh, Adrian moves furniture and other heavy stuff. Jeremiah helps me unload boxes. Soap, shampoo bottles, new towels, that kind of thing. Ellen likes to make sure the kids have plenty of summer chores, and there's never a shortage of things to do around here. Plus, Jeremiah's a little chatterbox, and I like that. He hangs out around the office with me."

Adam and I exchanged a glance.

"Does he meet a lot of your guests?" I asked.

"Some, sure."

"And you said he was over here yesterday?"

"For a couple of hours in the morning."

"Did he seem okay?"

"Oh, yeah, he was fine."

"Did anything unusual happen?"

"Unusual? No, just the same old, same old. Guests check in, guests check out, guests always need something. It's go-go-go all day long."

"Do you remember Jeremiah talking with any of your guests yesterday?"

"I suppose he did, but I don't remember anyone specifically. People assume he's my kid, so they talk to him."

"What was he doing while he was here?"

"Not much. I was too busy to put him to work, so he was batting around a shuttlecock outside for a while, until he lost it in the trees. Then he was working on a jigsaw puzzle in the corner."

"Did he mention having problems with anybody?"

"Problems? You mean, like with one of my guests? No, he didn't say anything like that."

"Mrs. N says she had a Peeping Tom outside her window last night. She thinks it was someone from the motel. Did she talk to you about that?"

Rose rolled her eyes. "Oh, yeah, of course, she did. Every week it's something different with her. Complaining is what keeps Mrs. N alive."

"Do you have any idea who this man was?"

"Not a clue."

"She said he breathed really loud. Does that remind you of anybody staying here? Like a guest with allergies or something like that?"

"A loud breather? Seriously? You think I pay attention to that? The only problem I have is with people who are too loud at other things. Moms don't like it when the walls start shaking right next to their kids' heads."

"What about men staying here on their own?" Adam asked. "Do you have anybody in a room by themselves? No wife or girl-friend tagging along?"

"I don't get it, why are you guys so on about this? Jeremiah's missing, and you're worried about somebody peeping Mrs. N?" Rose cocked her head, trying to figure us out. Then a flush of horror spread across her face. "Oh, man, you don't think—? One of *my* people?"

"My father asked us to cover all the bases," I explained. "The thing is, if Jeremiah was hanging out here yesterday, maybe he met somebody …"

Rose swore. She took off her beret, wiped her forehead, and put it back on. "This sucks. I can't believe it."

"Single men, Rose," Adam repeated. "Anybody around here fit the bill?"

"Yeah, one guy."

"Who is he?"

"I don't know. Nondescript. Thirties, I think, tall and skinny,

buzz cut. He said his name was Bob. Bob Evans, like the restaurant. He paid cash for three nights upfront, and he said he didn't
want maid service."

"That didn't raise red flags with you?" I asked.

"This is the Rest in Peace, Shelby. Around here, anything less
than an active smell of decaying flesh doesn't worry me much."

Adam peered through the office window at the motel parking
lot. "Is his car here? What does he drive?"

"A big gray Cadillac, I think." Rose stood up and eyed the
lineup of vehicles. "Yeah, the car's here. He's in room 106."

Adam didn't wait for me or discuss what we should do next.
He banged through the screen door and took long, determined
cop steps down the row of motel rooms. If there was a chance to
be a hero, Adam was always right there. By the time I caught up
with him, he was thumping his fist on the door of room 106. I
went over to the gray Cadillac and squinted through the windows
to see if I could spot anything inside.

I did.

The floors were thick with dirt and pine needles. Bob Evans
had been in the woods. I also saw a large water canteen and a plastic bag tipped over on the back seat, spilling out a head of romaine
lettuce and a small container of dried fruit chips. I recognized the
logo on the bag. It came from Ellen Sloan's mini-mart.

I spun back to the motel room door. No one had answered.

"He's in there," Adam told me. "He's trying to ignore us, but
I hear somebody moving around."

"This could be our guy, Adam. Be careful. The boy could
be inside."

"Mr. *Evans*," Adam shouted, banging louder on the door.
"*Police.*"

The motel room door opened two inches. A chain lock dangled across the space. I saw one nervous brown eye and a round

face that dripped sweat. I also noticed a noxious smell busting out of the shut-up space.

"What do you want?"

"I want you to open the door, Mr. Evans," Adam told him.

"Why? What for? I haven't done anything."

"Then you won't mind if we take a look inside."

"Well, I do mind. I paid for the room, it's mine, you have no right to come in here."

He was right. We didn't. But in the midst of the standoff between them, I heard the thump of something inside the motel room, like the sound that someone would make who was trapped behind a locked door.

"Adam, he's got somebody in there!"

Adam heard the noise, too. As Mr. Evans shouted in protest, Adam slammed a shoulder against the motel room door and ripped the chain lock away from the frame. He piled through the doorway and tackled Mr. Evans to the ground. I leaped over the two of them like a steeplechase runner and landed in the middle of the worn, stained gray carpet. The only other door in the room was the bathroom door, which was closed. I heard the same heavy thud from the other side that I'd heard before.

"Jeremiah! Jeremiah, is that you? It's Shelby Lake, everything's okay."

I ran to the bathroom door and yanked it open. The instant I did, something erupted from inside, collided with my legs, and knocked me flat on my back. A snuffling, grunting noise filled my ears, and something huge and black began licking my face with a slobbering tongue. I shoved the thing away in horror and scrambled to my feet.

Adam had a knee shoved into the back of Bob Evans and already had cuffs around the man's wrists.

"Let him go!" I screamed.

Adam hadn't caught up to what was going on. "What? Why?" "Let him go! It's a pig! It's a pig!"

I said it several times, and I may have added an adjective in front of "pig" that began with the letter *f*.

The victim who'd been trapped inside the motel bathroom was a miniature pig, all black, probably at least a hundred pounds, looking like a beer-bellied drinker at the local bar. The animal snorted its way over to Bob Evans, who was still trapped under Adam, and shoved its flat nose into the man's face.

"Snuffle Man!" Adam exploded. "This is what Mrs. N heard? The guy was chasing after his *pig*?"

"Looks that way."

Adam flipped the man over and grabbed his collar. "I don't believe this. Why were you hiding it, buddy? You could have gotten yourself killed."

"The motel doesn't allow pets," Bob Evans gasped from the floor. "The penalty's like a hundred bucks if you bring one in the room."

Adam shook his head in disgust and freed the man. The two of us were breathing heavily as the shot of adrenaline drained from our systems. When I glanced at Adam's belt, I saw that he'd gone so far as to unsnap the holster clip on his gun. We were all lucky. This could have gone south very fast.

A pig. A pet pig.

Not a child.

I got out my phone to call my father and give him an update. The Rest in Peace was a dead end. We were no closer to finding Jeremiah.

CHAPTER TEN

After we left the motel, Adam and I drove the short distance down the highway to the Sloan house. Trina Helvik answered the door, and I could see a crowd of people behind her. It looked to me as if half the town was waiting for news with Ellen and Dennis. Adam and I needed to search Jeremiah's bedroom for clues, but I asked him to start without me. I wanted to talk to Trina first.

She grabbed a sweater and followed me down the steps. We made our way along the fringe of an elaborate garden, where the flowers had shut themselves up against the cool night. The house lights threw our shadows across the grass.

"How is Ellen doing?" I asked Trina.

"Oh, she's in rough shape as you'd expect. Ellen isn't the kind of person who can just sit there and do nothing. She likes to be in control of the world, and this is something she can't control."

Trina always had good insights into what made people tick. That was what made her a successful coach. Control was how Ellen Sloan lived her life, with everything in its proper place. The garden at her house was like that, manicured in neat, colorful rows and free of weeds, with decorative fencing to keep out the rabbits. Her mini-mart was the same way, with every box of cereal or can of soup in perfect alignment with the one next to it.

"Have you discovered anything at all about where Jeremiah might be?" Trina asked.

"No. Nothing yet."

"That's so sad. That poor boy. I hope he's okay."

"I know. Me, too."

Trina's face was stoic like a good Scandinavian, but she was also a parent with a daughter the same age as Jeremiah. I knew what Trina was thinking, that it could just as easily have been *her* child who disappeared.

"Did you get my message? I found Anna hanging out in the cemetery this afternoon."

"I did. Thank you for bringing her home, Shelby. Sometimes that girl is so headstrong." She added with a smile, "She reminds me of a certain high school volleyball player I used to coach."

"A little bit," I agreed.

"Did Anna say what she was doing there?"

"She was looking for Jeremiah. She's very upset about him."

"Aren't we all."

The two of us kept walking through the Sloans' large, sloping backyard. The forest loomed at the end of the grass. If you hiked into those woods, eventually you would find yourself on Keith Whalen's land a mile away. The trails led past Black Lake, where the Striker girls used to swim on Saturday afternoons. Trina would join us there sometimes, bonding with her players. It was during those lazy days, laughing together and telling stories, that I began to see her as a friend even more than a coach.

Trina was six inches taller than me, statuesque and athletic, like a blond model out of a Dale of Norway ad. She had a natural beauty that could make you self-conscious about your own flaws. Pale blue eyes, sharp little nose, a face so symmetrical that each side looked like a mirror of the other. At forty years old, she'd given almost nothing back to time, except for the faint lines that bent around her lips when she smiled.

However, to me, she'd been at her most beautiful five years earlier, when she was completely bald and hugging her daughter as Anna cried into her shoulder in a hospital bed. I was crying too. So was her husband, Karl. The one who should have been crying was Trina, but instead, she held all of us together with an inner strength that I envied. She had every reason in the world to be bitter, but I never saw one ounce of anger or self-pity from her throughout the entire experience.

"Anna told me that she and Jeremiah aren't friends anymore," I said. "Did you know about that?"

"Yes, it was pretty obvious. They haven't spent time together in months."

"Did you ask her why?"

"I did, a couple of times, but she wouldn't open up to me about it. I didn't want to push her. I figured she would talk about it when she was ready."

"Well, if you can get her to tell you anything more, that would be helpful."

Trina cocked her head in surprise. "Why?"

"Just in case it's related to something going on in Jeremiah's life that led to his disappearance. At this point we have to consider everything."

"I suppose so. That's an unpleasant thought."

We stood in silence for a while. Where the trees began, I saw a young doe feeding on the leaves, its body barely kept upright by spindly legs. Looking at my best friend, I debated whether to ask her what was wrong. If she was keeping a secret from me, she had her reasons, and like Anna, she would talk about it when she was ready. Except Trina rarely opened up to me. She was happy to let me lean on her, but she resisted being vulnerable herself. For a while, I'd assumed it was because she still saw me as a teenage girl and that she was more open with her other friends. Then I realized that I was wrong. Trina had acquaintances, coworkers, and neighbors, but in many ways, I was her only real friend.

"Anna thinks something is going on with you," I murmured.

Trina was staring at the doe. "She said that?"

"Yes. She said the two of you have been crying."

"Karl. Not me. I don't cry."

It always puzzled me that she was so proud of that. "So what's going on?"

"Now isn't the time, Shelby. You have other things to think about."

That was classic Trina. She was always pretending that she was protecting me when she was really protecting herself. It was a defense mechanism, a way to keep emotions at arm's length. I could have let the subject drop, but I'd learned long ago that I needed to keep knocking on the door until she answered.

"Is it you and Karl? Are the two of you having problems?"

"Oh, no. Karl is wonderful."

"Then what?"

Trina swayed slightly on her feet. She would do that beside the volleyball court, too, when she'd seen us making a mistake and was gathering her words for how to tell us. She never spoke off the cuff. She thought about everything so that she wouldn't have to regret it later. I was still struggling to learn that lesson myself.

"It's back," she said.

That was all she told me, but she didn't need to say anything more. There were not two words that could have frozen my soul more than those. It gets cold around here in the winters, but never as cold as that moment on July 17.

"Trina, I—"

That was all I managed before my throat closed up. I had so many things to say, but I didn't say any of them. I took two steps to close the distance between us and wrapped my arms around her. I held on for a long time. She reacted stiffly, as if embarrassed by our closeness. Physical displays of affection made Trina uncomfortable, but I didn't care.

When I found my voice, I said, "What do you need? How can I help?"

"There's nothing you can do right now, Shelby. But thank you."

"I'm here. Day or night."

"I know that."

"Any time you want to talk, we can talk. Or not talk. If you want to sit there and say nothing, that's fine, too."

Trina put a hand on my shoulder, as if she wanted to comfort *me*. Then she pointed at the back porch of the Sloan house. "You're sweet, but we'll have to do this later."

"What? Why?"

"Ellen's here."

I turned around and was jolted back to my other reality.

Ellen stood on the house's redwood deck with a cigarette in her hand. I hadn't even realized that she smoked. In the porch light, her face was all bone and shadow, like a skeleton's. She stared at the sky, as if she needed God to give her answers. Eighteen months ago, she'd lost her mother, and then two weeks ago, her father. And now her youngest son was missing. It would test anyone's faith.

She saw the two of us on her lawn. She saw *me* on her lawn. I knew this wouldn't be good, and it wasn't. She crushed her cigarette into a flower pot. She stormed down the steps and stalked toward me. With every step, she fell to pieces. By the time she was in my face, tears flooded down her cheeks, and her skin was beet red with fury, and her whole body quivered. She screamed at me in the darkness from six inches away.

"How dare you even show your face here? Where's my son? Where's my son? Your father promised me he would find him. Why isn't Jeremiah back here with his family? I told you! I told you, and none of you listened! I told you I wanted roadblocks and helicopters, and all Tom Ginn could do was stand there and tell me everything was going to be all right. It's not all right! Jeremiah is gone! He could be anywhere!"

Ellen's arm reared back like the cocking of a gun. She was going to slap me, and I tensed, waiting for it. Then she stopped herself at the last moment. Her open hand sank back to her waist, and her eyes squeezed shut. Her knees buckled beneath her. She slid down to the wet grass and buried her face in her palms.

Trina knelt and put an arm around her shoulders. Ellen leaned against her. They were two mothers, both staring into their own versions of hell.

"Ellen, I swear to you, we are doing everything we can to find Jeremiah."

Ellen's cries died out slowly, and her eyes opened. With Trina's help, she stood up, and I could see that her pant legs were soaked with dew from the grass. Her fever had broken; she'd cried herself out. She wiped her nose and cheeks with her hands, and she took a loud breath. She was calm again, in control, in charge. I had to admire her for that.

"I talked to Violet," she told me. "I conveyed my concerns to her."

"What concerns?"

"Simply put, Tom's not competent to handle this investigation. I know he's your father, Shelby, but we're talking about my son's life. I'm not going to sugarcoat this. I want him off the case. I want this handled by professionals. I should have insisted on that from the beginning. As it is, we've lost the most important time we had to find Jeremiah."

I tried to take my emotions out of it and not be defensive. I was a deputy, not a daughter. "Ellen, bringing in strangers isn't the way to go. Nobody knows Mittel County and the people around here better than my father."

"Maybe so, but he doesn't have the experience or resources for a case like this. This is bigger than Mittel County. Plus, let's not kid ourselves, Shelby."

"Kid ourselves about what?"

Ellen stopped, as if she'd gone too far. "Nothing."

"No, go ahead, what are you saying?"

She looked right at me. So did Trina. The fact is, I knew what Ellen was going to say before she said it.

"Tom's no longer up to the job. Mentally, I mean. I know you may not be ready to face it, but that's the truth. He's going the way of his parents."

"You don't know that."

"Take off the blinders, Shelby. I'm sorry, it's sad, but that's what it is. You think I didn't hear him ask Adrian the same question twice?"

"One question. Come on."

"It's not just that. It's been getting worse for months. Everybody in town has seen it."

I looked at Trina. "Everybody?"

Trina turned her eyes down to her feet and said nothing.

"Violet already talked to the county board," Ellen went on like a steamroller. "They've been in touch with the governor. He contacted the FBI and made a formal request for their child abduction team to take over the investigation. They'll be here in a few hours. It's done, Shelby. Tom is out."

*

Hours later, at two in the morning, I broke from the tangles of the national forest land onto the dirt road. I'd gone back there to join the search, but my flashlight battery was dead. I was exhausted, and the sweat on my body had turned cold. My skin was bleeding where the branches had scratched me. I bent and put my hands on my knees as I got my strength back. Gnats swarmed around my warm breath. The noise of the crickets in the brush was deafening. When I stood up again, I stared out into the nighttime woods. Dozens of other dancing lights dotted the forest like fireflies. Every few seconds, someone called Jeremiah's name in the distance. Shoulder to shoulder, the people of Mittel County hunted for the boy through the dark hours.

My father stood alone by his cruiser. His car was parked near Jeremiah's bicycle, which lay where it had been abandoned and was now cordoned off by police tape. Dad still had his thermos of coffee in his hand, which he'd refilled at least three times over the course of the night. He'd had that dented thermos as long as I could remember. It was the same one he'd been using on his boat the night he was visited by the owl. The night he'd found me.

I walked over to him. He didn't even notice me at first, because he was so caught up in his thoughts, as if thinking hard would bring Jeremiah back. He held himself with the stiff, proud bearing of a tin soldier. As a kid, I remember thinking that bullets would just bounce off him.

"Jeremiah's not out there, Dad."

He drank his coffee. He was still focused on the forest. "I know."

"If he'd wandered off by himself, we would have found him by now. He couldn't have gone that far."

"You're right."

"We should call off the search until daylight. Someone's going to get hurt out there."

My father noticed the blood on my face. "What about you? Are you okay?"

"I'm fine. But we're not going to find him like this."

"No. We're not."

The lights of the searchers reflected in his eyes and made his face look pale. A mosquito landed on his forehead and began feasting on his blood, but Dad didn't even bother brushing it away.

"What do you want me to do?" I asked.

"Go home, Shelby. Get a couple hours of sleep."

"You should too."

"No, I'll bring the people in. Then I'll go back to the office."

"I'll go with you."

He shook his head. "Tomorrow's going to be a busy day. You need to be ready for it."

I was too tired to argue with him. "Okay. Good night, Dad."

I began walking past the lineup of vehicles parked together like train cars on both sides of the dirt road. My own cruiser was near the far end.

"Shelby," he called after me.

I stopped and turned around. "Yes?"

"I'll find that boy."

I tried to summon a smile, because as of the next morning, I knew he wasn't going to be the one in charge of finding him. "I know you will, Dad."

Then he went on as if a brand-new thought had sprung into his head. "Listen, it may be nothing, but Mrs. Norris was complaining about a Peeping Tom outside her bedroom window last night. She thought it was someone staying at the motel. You should probably check it out."

I stared at him. He was dead serious.

"Sure," I replied, my voice cracking. "Sure I will."

I made it all the way down the road to my cruiser before I began to cry.

CHAPTER ELEVEN

I squinted through the windshield into the darkness as I drove home.

Around here, you have to be alert for night creatures. I had to brake hard near the ranger station to avoid a raccoon that rose up and gave my headlights a cold, disinterested stare with its masked eyes. The animal hunched its craggy shoulders at me and then slouched into the woods. He was lucky. Over the years, like most of the people here, I'd left behind my share of roadkill. Your first deer is a rite of passage for the young drivers of Mittel County.

The glow of stained glass windows welcomed me home. From the outside, our house still looked like a church. The steeple still pointed at the sky, although Dad had long ago replaced the cross with a weather vane. He kept the wooden siding painted church white, and he always left the downstairs lights on overnight to illuminate the windows for passersby. The multicolored panels told the story of Jonah and the whale. When I was four years old, I used to hide under my blankets with a flashlight and pretend that I was inside the belly of the beast. It felt surprisingly safe there.

I climbed the stairs to the second floor. My room was at the back, with a sharply slanted ceiling and hardwood floor. A row of windows overlooked the cemetery. My walls were filled with pictures of me and my father. My first day on the job, with him next to me, beaming with pride. Me in a dress for an eighth grade school dance. Dad's twentieth anniversary party as sheriff. Things like that. I had volleyball trophies on my dresser and yellowed copies of the newspaper from our state championship and one of the balls we'd used in the winning game. Ten stuffed owls of different sizes were lined up on my window ledges. In one corner of the room, beside the bed, was a rocking chair, along with my guitar.

I took a shower and washed off the day. I opened one of the windows, which made me shiver because I was still damp. I spent a long time staring at the woods. I was naked, but I didn't worry much about modesty, because no one was around to see me, and the animals didn't care what I looked like. Eventually, I crawled under the blankets, and I wasn't even aware of falling asleep. I blinked, and the darkness was gone, and early morning light streamed into the bedroom.

It was five thirty.

Someone was ringing the bell at our front door.

I put on a robe and ran downstairs. When I threw open the door, I found Keith Whalen standing there. He was still dressed as he had been in the cemetery the previous day. His beard line was heavy on his face. He didn't look as if he'd slept.

"Keith."

"Sorry to bother you so early."

"What are you doing here?"

"Well, actually, I never went home last night. Somehow I couldn't bring myself to leave the cemetery, so I slept in my car. I was heading out this morning, but I saw your cruiser and figured you were here."

"Not for long. I have to get ready to go."

I hoped he would get the message. I didn't want him here. But he

lingered on the doorstep anyway. He flipped his hair back, his usual
nervous gesture. "Hey, would you mind if I used your bathroom?"

"Okay. Go ahead."

I opened the door wider and let him inside. It was pretty
impressive coming into our house, because Dad had left the great
space of the church wide open when he converted the place. Voices
echo, and you still feel as if you should talk in a hushed tone.
Keith had never been here before, and he drank in the arched
windows and the high ceiling with its crossbeams.

"Wow. Beautiful."

"Yeah, it's pretty nice."

"You fit here, Shelby."

I had nothing to say to that. "The bathroom's over there."

"Thanks."

He went to do what he had to do, and I waited next to the
front door. That was rude, but I wasn't offering an invitation to
stay. He came back a couple of minutes later, admiring some of
the church paintings that Dad had saved. When he looked at me,
I saw him take note of the outline of my body, and I was uncomfortably aware of the fact that I wasn't wearing anything under the
robe. He looked away quickly, but I knew we were both having
the same memories, no matter how much I tried to crowd them
out of my mind.

"Thanks," he said again.

"Sure."

"Did you find whoever was lurking in the cemetery yesterday?"

I knew he was stalling, because he didn't want to go.

"It was Anna."

"Anna Helvik? Trina's daughter?"

"Yes."

"You and Trina are pretty close, aren't you?"

"Yes, we are."

He didn't say anything more, but he still didn't leave. I was impatient, partly because I needed to get back into town, partly because spending time with Keith was like watching a movie highlights reel showing off all of my questionable decisions in life. I didn't know what he was expecting. I was hoping it wasn't sex, because I wasn't entirely sure I would say no. Whatever else had happened between us, I still felt the same old attraction to him.

"What do you want, Keith?" I asked finally. "What are you doing here?"

He didn't answer immediately. Then he shrugged and said, "I hate being home these days. I feel like Colleen is haunting me."

"I'm sorry to hear that. But as they say in the bars, you don't have to go home, but you can't stay here."

"I know. This is awkward for you. It is for me, too. When I saw you yesterday, I was reminded of all the rough edges we left behind. I suppose there's nothing we can do about that."

"No. There isn't."

"Okay. I'll go."

As Keith went by me onto the threshold, he was close enough to brush past my body, which gave me a little shock of electricity. Then he turned around before I closed the door.

"One more thing, Shelby."

"What is it?"

"I also wanted to tell you—just so we're very clear about it—I had nothing to do with Jeremiah's disappearance."

His words came out of nowhere, and I couldn't hide my surprise.

"Why would I think you did? Is there something you haven't told me?"

"No."

"Do you know anything about what happened to him?"

"Nothing at all."

"Then why say something like that?"

"Because sooner or later, I'll be a suspect. And I want you to know right now that I'm innocent."

"What makes you think you'll be a suspect?"

Keith shook his head sadly. He flipped his hair back again. "Because of Colleen. Because the whole town thinks I murdered her. I guarantee you, people are already making up stories about me and Jeremiah. They need someone they can blame for this, right or wrong, and I'm the easy choice. Everybody is looking for an Ursulina, Shelby. They won't stop until they find one."

*

After Keith left, I wondered if he was right. Were people really talking about him as a suspect?

And if so, what were they saying about me?

I didn't think anyone knew about my affair with Keith, but I might have been naive about that. Everyone saw us hanging out together after the Halloween fair. It doesn't take much more than that to get whispers flying through the town. Rumors are like motor oil here, lubing up every conversation, and sex is a favorite topic. I wouldn't have been surprised to find out that tongues had been wagging about me and Keith.

My relationship with him was a one-time thing. Literally one time. But the damage was already done.

Little wonder I had decided at that point in my life that I was better off without dating, romance, hookups, or sex. Between my job and my friends, I didn't have time for men. Some of the local guys would have liked to change my mind, but the rule of numbers in a small town meant that pickings were slim.

Sure, I'd dated. Most people around here figured my high school boyfriend and I would get married, but that was never going to happen. He was cute, and you have to learn about sex somewhere, but I knew it was a short-term thing. After that, I went out a few times and endured a few fix-ups. None of them turned into anything serious.

And then there was Keith.

By the morning after Halloween, I was already regretting what had happened with him. Actually, I was regretting it as I drove back home overnight at three in the morning. Keith called the next day, but I ducked his call. He called four more times over the next week, and I let all of them go to voicemail. I was determined never to talk to him again and never see him again.

That lasted until the evening of November 14, when Adam and I responded to the 911 call at his house.

We found Colleen Whalen dead in the tall grass. Shot in the head. Keith said he'd come home from a hiking trip and found her. He blamed a burglar for the crime. He said much of his wife's jewelry was missing, including her wedding ring and an expensive watch she'd given him for their anniversary.

And a gun.

A gun he owned had disappeared, too.

There was no way to prove he was lying and no way to prove he was telling the truth. Did my father believe him? No. Did Adam? No. But not believing someone didn't mean you could put them in jail.

Did the people of Everywhere believe him? No. The rumors and gossip in town all declared Keith guilty.

What about me? Did I believe him?

I'd thought about that question for months, but I still had no answer.

All I knew is that while I was standing over Colleen's body, Adam asked Keith how things were in their marriage, and Keith replied, "Fine."

That was a lie. I knew it was a lie. But I didn't say a word.

CHAPTER TWELVE

I met my father at the Nowhere Café an hour later. He hadn't slept at all, but sometime during the night he'd ironed his uniform, and his hat wasn't even a single degree off-kilter. He was eating a plate of scrambled eggs and bacon at the counter, and he had the newspaper folded in front of him to the daily crossword puzzle. Breezy was late getting to work, and the coffee pot in the diner was already getting dangerously low.

Everything looked normal around here, but in fact, nothing was normal at all. This was Saturday. Day two. Jeremiah had been gone for an entire night.

"Morning, Dad," I said as I took the seat next to him at the counter.

"Hello, Shelby. Did you sleep?"

"A little. I wish you had, too."

"Something tells me I'll have plenty of free time when the FBI arrives."

"So they're really coming?"

"The governor called me personally to ask for my cooperation.

Also, the statewide media has picked up the story. It's all over TV. I imagine we're going to be inundated very soon."

I looked around at our sleepy café. It wouldn't be sleepy here much longer. We were about to be swarmed by strangers asking questions, giving us suspicious looks, digging into our private lives, and studying our behavior as if we were exotic animals at the zoo. Cops. Reporters. Volunteers. Gawkers. You could almost feel the town holding its breath, waiting for the invasion like the return of the mayflies. Most of us who live here don't really trust outsiders, for the simple reason that outsiders who come here don't really trust us.

"Maybe it's a good thing," I said, trying to put the best spin on what was ahead. "We need more manpower. We need technology. This is bigger than us, Dad. It's all about Jeremiah."

"Of course it is."

"Plus, it's not like they don't need us. We know the area. We know the people. They don't."

"You're right."

But being right didn't change the fact that this was our town, our people, our boy, and our mystery, and the whole investigation was about to be taken out of our hands. We didn't have to like it.

I heard the jingle of the diner's front door. Breezy flew in, ninety minutes late, looking stressed and breathless. In unison, everyone in the booths silently pointed their fingers at the empty coffee pot behind the counter. She stopped at the door long enough to hang up her windbreaker and tie up her ponytail, triggering disgruntled rumbling from those of us who needed more caffeine.

"Yeah, yeah, keep your pants on," she announced loudly. "Dudley wouldn't start again."

Dudley was her 1998 Ford Escort, which she'd nursed through twenty years of Mittel County winters. The patient had been on life support for a while. When it ran, its engine sounded like a bicycle with a baseball card taped in the spokes. Breezy had been working extra shifts morning and night to save money, but as fast as she earned it, she spent it on other things.

She went behind the counter, and the aroma of the brewer soon took the edge off everyone's nerves. While we waited, Breezy leaned her elbows on the counter in front of me and Dad.

"Any news?"

I shook my head.

"Hell's bells," Breezy said. "I hear the FBI's coming. Is that right?"

"They are," my father replied.

"Soon?"

"Any minute."

Breezy looked around the café with a hungry expression that was different from what the rest of us felt. I could read her mind. For her, the arrival of strangers meant tables crowded with out-of-towners who left large tips. That may sound heartless, but I couldn't really blame her. Newcomers meant money in the cash registers of the local economy. It didn't matter why they were here.

"How's Dudley?" I asked.

Breezy swore. "The starter just grinds. We may be near the end of the road."

"How'd you get here?"

"I called Monica, and she gave me a lift on her way in. Hell if I know how I'm getting home tonight."

I knew Breezy, and I wasn't worried. With men pouring into town, she'd have plenty of offers for a ride.

"Hey, you're right, by the way," she told me.

"About what?"

"The Gruders are back. I couldn't sleep. They were playing their radio in the woods half the night. You know what that means."

Yes, I knew what that meant. More meth around the county.

More emergency calls to the hospital in Stanton. More lives ruined. On any other morning, that would have been our first priority.

Breezy went off to pour coffee for the rest of the diner. Dad studied the clues of the crossword, but I noticed that he hadn't filled in a single word. His pencil sat unused on the counter, and the point of the pencil was perfectly sharp. Dad liked to say that chaos began with the littlest of things, like a dull pencil. He picked up the paper and squinted at the puzzle.

This wasn't just entertainment for him. He did crossword puzzles because he'd read that doing them was like calisthenics for the brain. He knew he was struggling. I knew it, too. Apparently, everyone in town knew.

"Sixteen across," I said, peering at the paper. "That's an easy one. Ten letters. 'The beacon in the storm.'"

Dad blinked as he reflected on the clue, but the answer didn't come. He stroked his snow-white mustache and grimaced. I think that moment was the first time I ever saw him as old.

"I guess I'm more tired than I thought, Shelby."

"Lighthouse," I prompted him.

He stared at the empty little squares on the page. "Yes, of course. What was I thinking?"

He picked up the pencil, wrote "L" in the first box, and then put it down again without finishing. He turned over the newspaper and instead focused on the mug of coffee that Breezy had placed in front of him.

"I really didn't think it was possible," he said to me in a quiet voice. "I didn't want to believe it. A child abduction. Here."

"We're not cut off from the world, Dad."

"No, I suppose not." My father took a sip of coffee and glanced over his shoulder at the others in the diner. "Everyone's saying it must have been a stranger who took him. They don't want to consider the other possibility."

"What do you mean?"

"It might not be a stranger at all. It might be one of us."

I didn't say anything, but I realized that Keith Whalen had been right. Soon we would all be turning on each other. We'd be looking for someone to blame. We'd be hunting for an Ursulina hiding among us.

The bell on the diner front door jingled again.

Monica Constant pushed into the café like a little tornado. She had an enormous satchel purse draped over one shoulder that looked as if it weighed as much as she did. Her brown eyes were huge behind round glasses. She wore a flouncy pink dress that was decades out of style. She patted her kinky strawberry hair to make sure it was just so, and then she took a seat on the counter chair next to me, where her feet dangled well above the floor. The first thing she did was remove a velvet case from inside the purse and put the urn for Moody, her dead dog, on the paper place mat. The urn was six inches high, made of turquoise ceramic, and hand painted with lilies of the valley.

"Hello, you two," Monica squeaked.

Dad turned his head and gave her his usual charming smile and then picked up his newspaper again.

I said, "Good morning, Monica."

She tapped a fingernail on the place mat and gave me a pointed look.

"And good morning to you, too, Moody," I added.

"Thank you, dear," she said with a playful dance of her eyebrows. Then she dug a sheaf of papers out of the deep bowels of her purse. "I checked at the office before coming over here. I have the summary of overnight calls."

"Did the Stanton police track down old Mr. Nadler?" I asked, hoping for a little good news.

"Well, if they did, they didn't send out a follow-up report.

Not that this would be the first time things fell through the cracks over there. I'll call later and find out."

"Thanks."

Breezy showed up in front of us again with a cup of hot Twinings tea and a blackberry scone. "Here you go, Monica, my treat. Thanks for the lift this morning. You saved me."

"Oh, please, Witch Tree is right on my way, dear. I was happy to do it."

Monica lived an hour's drive from Everywhere in a small town called Sugarfall on the western edge of the county. On some winter mornings, her commute took two hours or more. Even so, she was typically at the office ahead of all of us, and I couldn't remember a day she'd missed for weather or sickness. She was a rock.

I watched her dip the tea bag in her cup and nibble at the scone by picking off pieces with her red-nailed fingers. To me, she'd always been ageless, the kind of woman who looked the same year after year. She was precise and organized, with a great memory for details, which made her a perfect partner for Dad at work. I was pretty sure she'd thought about being a partner for Dad in other ways, too, but he'd always been too busy as a sheriff and father to think about getting married.

Dad gave up on the crossword puzzle. He slapped down the paper with obvious frustration and stood up from the counter. "I'm heading to the office."

"Okay, I'll be there in a minute," I told him.

He left, tipping his hat to the others in the diner. They smiled back at him uncomfortably. Monica's eyes followed him discreetly as he headed out the door and across the street toward the Carnegie Library.

"He's not very good today, is he?"

"Not very good," I agreed.

"Stress makes it worse. He'll bounce back."

"I hope so."

"He's going to need you, dear. Are you ready for that?"

"Of course, I am."

She patted my back. "Well, count on me to help you, Shelby. Believe me, this situation will grow you up fast."

She meant nothing by her comment, but I felt a little annoyed. It made me realize that the people around here still saw me as young. Twenty-five years old, but not grown-up, not ready for life. Monica, Dad, Adam, Trina, Ellen. To them, I was just a kid, and maybe they were right. I was still the girl who didn't know who she was or why she was alive.

I still didn't know why God had bothered to save me, and I didn't feel any closer to figuring it out.

But I had no time to think about myself. Somewhere outside, distantly, I heard the guttural throb of an engine getting closer. Monica and I both looked at each other in confusion. The others in the café heard it, too, and people gravitated from their booths to the diner window and then outside to the street, where a crowd was gathering.

I hurried outside with Monica next to me.

The throb got louder, almost deafening, making all of us cover our ears. I looked up in the sky and saw a black helicopter slowly descending toward the open grass yard in front of the courthouse. Down it came, like some giant insect, and when it was nearly on the ground, I could see white letters painted on the side.

FBI.

Monica leaned toward me as the helicopter engine cut out and the rotor blades slowed. "An unwanted visitor in a tableware emporium," she murmured in my ear.

I shook my head, not sure what she meant.

"Remember Tom's crossword clue yesterday? We were talking about a bull in a china shop. Well, dear, now we've got one."

CHAPTER THIRTEEN

Special Agent Bentley Reed of the FBI didn't look impressed with the basement office of the Mittel County Sheriff's Department. He was a city man, and this was the country. He was as tall as my father, with mocha-colored black skin, thinning hair that gave him a very high forehead, and a trimmed goatee flecked with gray. He was dressed in a pinstriped blue suit with leather shoes shined to such a bright finish that I was scared to look at them directly for fear of blindness. He was smart. I could see that in his eyes, which moved fast and didn't miss a thing. I guessed that he was in his forties, and he had the bearing of an ex-military man. He didn't walk, he strutted. He didn't talk, he commanded.

Violet introduced him to us, and we all got the message loud and clear. Bentley Reed was in charge.

Our entire county team was gathered in the basement, about a dozen of us. Dad had called in all the shifts for the early morning meeting. I stood next to Adam, who was quietly seething at the prospect of taking a back seat to the Feds. Adam never took orders well, even from my father.

Agent Reed took off his suit coat and folded it carefully over the back of a chair. He stood in the center of the room with eight other federal agents behind him, eyeing the surroundings with the same disdain their boss did. I could feel their impatience, the pros staring at the small-town cops who'd wasted so much time before calling them in.

Reed had a throaty voice like a drumbeat that filled the room.

"Sheriff Ginn, I want to thank you for making your whole team available to us and for your partnership in this investigation. My colleagues and I are members of the FBI's Child Abduction Rapid Deployment team, and we have one goal. That's to find Jeremiah Sloan and bring him home safely to his family. Unfortunately, he's already been missing approximately nineteen hours. That's not good. In a potential abduction situation, every second counts, so we're already playing catch-up, and we need to move swiftly."

I glanced at Dad, whose face was as blank as marble before it was carved. He knew he was being chastised.

"Jeremiah could still be lost in the woods," he pointed out.

Reed nodded. "Yes, we're aware of that possibility. We have heat-sensing technology in the helicopter, and we'll be launching a grid search over the forest in less than an hour. Of course, again, time has hurt us here. If Jeremiah spent a night outside, the boy's body temperature has likely dropped. That will make him harder to detect. As far as a ground search goes, one of my team is a veteran of wilderness search-and-rescue operations, and he'll be leading the search process and coordinating volunteers from the general public. As news gets out about this case, we're going to have a lot of people showing up to help, which is both good and bad. I know you've had locals out searching already, but we'll be going over the entire area again from the beginning."

Translation: Who knows what you people missed?

"Next, let's talk about the sex offender registry," Agent Reed went on. "Where do we stand on interviews with people on the list?"

"We haven't talked to anyone yet," Dad began, but Reed cut him off.

"So we're nowhere on that. Got it. Okay, we've identified nearly a hundred level-two and level-three sex offenders in Mittel and Stanton counties. I want in-person interviews and alibis from every single one of them. Talk to their neighbors, too, and show them Jeremiah's photo. I also want the state patrol showing that photo at every gas station at every exit on the interstate. Ditto for every gas station within a two-hundred-mile radius of the national forest. If Jeremiah was taken out of the area, this guy had to fill up somewhere. And let's get copies of the guest registers from every motel and resort in both counties, so we can run them against criminal records."

Behind Agent Reed, his team keyed notes furiously into their phones. Several of them were already coordinating their next moves with each other in whispered tones. These people had worked together before, and I couldn't help but be impressed. Reed may have been arrogant and condescending when you met him, but he was a pro. As painful as it was to admit, Violet had been smart to bring him in.

"We need a command post," Reed went on. "Large, somewhere we can process physical evidence as we gather it and set up our computers. Ms. Roka, what do you suggest? What's available in town?"

"There's a gym at the school," Violet proposed. "Will that work? It's wide open, and no one's using it during the summer. We've got power in the space, and we can bring in dozens of tables as needed."

"Perfect," Reed went on. He jabbed a finger at a special agent on his right who didn't look much older than me. "Next, media. Tiffany Ball is our media relations specialist. We're already getting plenty of queries, but we want to control the message, so Tiffany will be working with all of you and the boy's parents to craft a press release, profile, and media kit regarding the disappearance.

Same for social media. I expect to hold a press conference early
this afternoon, once our infrastructure is in place. Questions on
any of that?"

My father and the rest of us stood in shell-shocked silence.
Life moved at a slow pace in Mittel County. Not so at the FBI.

"Excuse me, Special Agent Reed?"

It was Adam. He stepped ahead of the other members of our
team and squared his shoulders.

"Yes?" Reed said. "You have a question?"

"Yes, sir, I'm Adam Twilley. I'm Sheriff Ginn's senior deputy."

There was no such thing as a senior deputy, but that didn't
stop Adam from staking his claim to the job. Agent Reed looked
Adam up and down from his boots to his curly brown hair and
analyzed him like a computer. I could tell what the print-out in
his head said, and I'm pretty sure Adam could, too.

Lightweight.

It wasn't fair, but Adam didn't always give the best first im-
pression. He looked like what he was, a kid with a motorcycle.

"Okay, Senior Deputy Twilley, what's your question?"

"I want to know what our role is going to be."

Reed's face bent into the tiniest smile. "Well, right now, I sure
as hell could use a cup of coffee if you wouldn't mind."

The agents broke into laughter that went on longer than was
comfortable for any of us. Adam's face turned several shades of
crimson.

"I'm kidding, Deputy," Reed went on. "All of you have an ex-
tremely important role to play. You know this area backwards and
forwards. You know the people. You know the roads, businesses,
all the things that we don't. So we're counting on you to give us
your expertise on everything local. Make sense? Sheriff, you on
board with that?"

My father nodded his agreement. "We'll give you anything you need. We know every inch of this county, that's for sure. I'm sure you can count on our colleagues in Stanton to help on their end."

"Excellent."

"I have a suggestion," Adam broke in, pushing his luck with Agent Reed. "You should probably designate a liaison between you and your team and the police here and in Stanton. Someone who can coordinate the flow of information between us. Make sure nothing gets missed."

"A liaison. Are you volunteering, Senior Deputy Twilley?"

"If you want me to, sure. I'd be happy to do that."

Reed stroked his chin with his thumb and gave Adam another careful look. "Well, the idea of a local liaison working directly with me is a good one. I like your suggestion, Twilley. However, the last thing I want to do is come in here and deprive Sheriff Ginn of his senior deputy. That doesn't seem right."

Adam's face fell as he realized he was being passed over for the assignment that he'd suggested. Instead, Reed's gaze floated around the room from person to person among the sheriff's team.

It landed on me.

"You," he said, jabbing a finger in my direction. "What's your name?"

"Deputy Shelby Lake."

"Not a senior deputy?" Reed said with a flash of his white teeth.

I couldn't help smiling, too. "No, sir, just a deputy."

"How long have you been with the department?"

"Seven years."

Reed turned to my father. "Sheriff, do you have any problem with assigning Deputy Lake to me during this investigation?"

I watched Violet open her mouth to object, but then she closed it again without saying anything.

"None at all," Dad replied. He gave me the fastest little wink.

"All right. Deputy Lake, if you're okay with that, consider yourself conscripted."

"Of course. Thank you, sir."

"That'll be all for now, everyone," Reed continued. "You'll have assignments in fifteen minutes, and senior staff will meet again before the press conference in three hours. Remember, everybody, we've got a ten-year-old boy out there. Let's go find him."

That was all.

I was afraid that Adam was going to have a stroke. He shot me a look that was black with jealousy and rage. Adam and I liked each other, and none of this was my fault, but I knew this was going to be a problem between us. As the meeting broke up, he stormed out of the basement without a word to anyone else. Agent Reed watched him go. He knew what he'd done, and he didn't care.

Of course, I wasn't dumb. I knew why Reed had picked me. He assumed I was young, I was pliable, and I would do what I was told.

"Deputy Lake?" Agent Reed towered in front of me. "The first thing I want to do is talk to the Sloans. I'd like you with me."

"Absolutely."

"Just so we're clear, the parents are suspects until we prove otherwise. That's not for public consumption, but when things like this happen, it's usually somebody close to the child. Our first job is to rule the parents out, so we can move on to others. Got it?"

"Got it."

"Ditto the brother. What's his name? Adrian? I want to reinterview him about exactly what happened out there."

I wasn't sure I should say anything, but I barreled ahead anyway. "In fact, sir, I'm a little concerned that Adrian hasn't told us everything he knows."

Reed studied me with a glint in his eyes. "Oh? How so?"

I explained about the Gruders and about the burs on their pants. I was ready for Reed to dismiss my suspicions the way my father and Adam had, but instead, he called one of his agents over immediately and asked for background research on Will and Vince. Then he turned back to me and gave me a thumbs-up.

"That's an excellent observation, Deputy," he told me. "Has anyone talked to Adrian about this yet?"

I glanced at Dad, who was close enough to overhear, and I felt like a traitor. "No."

"Well, let's talk to him right now and get to the bottom of this. If he's hiding something, we need to know what it is. The fact is, I never met a sixteen-year-old boy yet who didn't lie the first time you asked him a question."

CHAPTER FOURTEEN

"Any affairs?" Agent Reed asked me.

I eyed him across the front seat of my cruiser as we drove down the highway toward the Sloan house. My guilt about Keith Whalen was the first thing that popped into my head, and I hoped it didn't show on my face. "I'm sorry, what?"

"Dennis and Ellen Sloan. Is there any talk around town about either of them cheating?"

"Why does that matter?"

"When people try to cover up affairs, bad things tend to happen. We always have to be conscious of possible motives."

"Well, there's been gossip about Dennis for a long time. I don't know whether any of it's true. He also drinks more than he should. He's had a couple of DUIs over the years."

"And Ellen?"

"Not that I've heard about. She's a straight arrow."

"What about money problems?"

"I don't think so. Ellen's store does well, and Dennis must make a pretty good living with the forestry department. I imagine they'll be inheriting money and land from her father now, too. He passed away a couple of weeks ago."

"What about abuse? Violence? Any calls for domestic disturbance at their place?"

"No, nothing like that. We get our share of domestic issues, but I've never heard about a problem with the Sloans." I added after a moment, "It must be ugly for you and your team, always looking for the worst in people."

Reed watched the trees going by on the highway. His long legs were squeezed under the dashboard. "I find kids. We've got a ninety percent success rate doing that. Nothing else matters."

"I wasn't saying—"

"I know what you were saying, Deputy. And yes, you're right. It's ugly sometimes. The reason I ask these questions is that people who have secrets typically don't like to share them. They lie to their spouses, they lie to their friends, they lie to their doctors, they lie to cops. Even when their kid's life is at stake, they lie. Honestly, I don't care where Dennis Sloan sticks his dick. I care whether he's being blackmailed about it, or whether some girl he dumped has a grudge against him, or whether his kid saw Daddy doing something he shouldn't and told somebody else about it. All those things make kids disappear."

Like I said, Reed was smart. And tough. But he wasn't going to let anyone's feelings get in the way of what he had to do. When I listened to him talk, I could hear an unwanted visitor stampeding through the china shop, with dishes crashing to the floor in his wake.

We arrived at the Sloan house. Before we got out of the cruiser, Reed opened the glove compartment and grabbed a listing of the vehicle's mechanical specs in a plastic slip cover. He shoved the plastic case inside his suit coat pocket.

"What are you doing?" I asked. "What's that for?"

"Visual aid," he replied without further explanation.

Ellen and Dennis met us at the door. Their faces were drawn, and their eyes were red with tears and exhaustion. There were others inside the house with them, just as there had been the previous day. Relatives. Friends. Kids from Adrian's school. Trina must have finally gone home, because I didn't see her. Everyone looked fragile, as if tensing for the moment when the phone would ring and they would find out whether the news was good or bad. The teenagers clustered around Adrian. The men clustered around Dennis. The women fussed and looked busy and left Ellen alone. She was independent and needed her space.

Agent Reed introduced himself with firm handshakes for both parents. He was an entirely different man in front of the Sloans. His hostile impatience vanished. He radiated compassion. And yet I watched his eyes and knew he was registering everything in the room and taking the measure of all the people who were gathered there.

"Is there a place we can talk?" he asked. "Somewhere private?"

Dennis nodded and led us downstairs. The walk-out basement was a man cave, built with log beams and stuffed with toys. Large-screen television. Pool table. An old-style slot machine from a Vegas casino. It was just the five of us. Ellen, Dennis, Adrian, Agent Reed, and me. The adults sat on a leather sofa near the television, and Adrian staked out a high-top chair at the wet bar. I kept an eye on him. The boy squirmed like a caterpillar on a hot sidewalk.

Reed took them through a long checklist of everything that was being done. The sheer length of the list made it sound like the whole world was looking for Jeremiah. I could see visible relief on Ellen's face, and she shot me a quick *I-told-you-so* look. That was fine. Anything that gave her a moment's comfort was fine with me.

Then Reed shifted gears.

"One thing I need from you right away, Mr. and Mrs. Sloan, is a list of all the adults in Jeremiah's life."

Ellen took a moment to focus. "What?"

"Teachers, doctors, friends, coworkers, neighbors, any adults that Jeremiah would see on a regular basis."

"Why do you need that?"

"We want to talk to all of them."

"Oh. Well, of course, we can do that. Dennis and I will sit down and come up with names."

"Thank you."

The real meaning of Reed's question only dawned on Ellen slowly, and I watched a horrified realization grow on her face. What he was saying was: Someone close to you could have done this. You can't trust anyone. Your friends are all suspects.

"Mr. Sloan, how did you find out that Jeremiah was missing?" Reed asked.

"I was at the ranger's office when Adrian came running in."

"Who else was there?"

"Two other rangers were with me. There were a few tourists, too. A married couple from Iowa, I think. And two twentysome-things with backpacks."

"Were these other rangers in the office with you all day?"

"Yeah, they were."

"And do you have a registry of people who were camping on the national forest grounds on Friday?"

"Sure. We have that."

"I'll need a copy."

"Yeah, of course. You bet."

"Mrs. Sloan, what about you? How did you find out about Jeremiah?"

Ellen had been watching the back-and-forth with her husband carefully. "Dennis called me. I was at the mini-mart. And yes, Agent Reed, I can give you the names of any number of customers who can verify that I was there all day."

Reed offered her a sympathetic smile. He knew she'd figured it out. First, make sure the parents weren't involved. "I appreciate that. Please understand that this kind of information is necessary as part of our routine background in a case like this."

Then he swung around to face the teenager in the high-top chair. "It's Adrian, right? Come on over here and join us."

His tone made it clear that this wasn't just a suggestion. Adrian slid off the chair and took a seat on the sofa far from his mother and father. He stared at his feet and ran both hands through his hair, leaving it messy. He had the same thick black hair as his father.

"You a football player?" Reed asked with a friendly smile. "You've got the build for it."

"Yeah, I am."

"So was I. High school, and college, too. What do you play? Tackle?"

"Yeah."

"I figured. Okay, Adrian, I know you're worried about your brother. We all are. I know you want to help us find him. So I need you to answer some questions. It's very important that you be honest with me."

The boy shrugged. "Sure."

"First of all, do you know two brothers named Will and Vince Gruder?"

Adrian looked up sharply and realized that Reed's pleasant smile had vanished. The whites in the boy's eyes grew three times larger. His reaction told me I'd been right about Adrian not being alone in the national forest. I knew it told Agent Reed the same thing.

"The Gruders?" Dennis interrupted with a puzzled expression. "What do they have to do with this?"

"Adrian?" Reed asked quietly.

"Yeah, sure, I know them. Everybody does."

"Are they friends of yours?"

"No. I just know them. That's all."

"I hear they sell drugs."

"Maybe. I guess. I don't know."

"When did you last see them?"

The boy shifted nervously on the sofa. "I don't remember."

"Were they in the campground with you yesterday?"

Adrian didn't answer, and Reed leaned forward. His stare made the boy wilt.

"I'm asking you a question, son. Were you with Will and Vince Gruder yesterday before your brother disappeared?"

The Sloans looked back and forth between Adrian and Agent Reed, and they began to realize that their son had been lying to all of us.

"*Adrian*," Dennis interjected like the snap of a whip. "Answer the man's question. Were you with those two assholes?"

"No! No way. I was alone. I told the sheriff that."

Reed slid the plastic case with my cruiser's mechanical specs partly out of his coat pocket. "Adrian, do you know what this is? It's a search warrant that gives me the right to search your bedroom. See, I think you did some business with the Gruders yesterday, and I think we're going to find evidence of whatever you bought in your room. Now we can all wait until I finish my search, or you can save us the time and tell us what I'm going to find in there."

The silence ticked away for a few seconds, but to Adrian, it must have felt like hours.

Finally, he murmured, as if speaking in a whisper would hide the truth from his parents. "Meth."

"*Meth?*" Ellen screamed and shot to her feet. "Are you crazy? Are you out of your mind? What are you doing with something like that? Why would you have anything like that in your room? Adrian, say something!"

Agent Reed stood up, too, and he put up his hands for calm.

"Mrs. Sloan, I know this is upsetting, but right now, let's keep the focus on Jeremiah. For the moment, this isn't about drugs, it's about finding your son. Adrian, I'm going to ask you again. Did you meet Will and Vince Gruder yesterday while you were out with your brother?"

The teenager began to cry. Tears streamed down his cheeks, and his chest heaved. He could barely choke out the word. "Yeah."

We didn't have time to ask more questions.

Dennis flew off the sofa. He was over his son in a split-second. "You lying sack of ... You made this happen! You did this to your brother!"

Agent Reed and I both leaped across the space, but we were too late. Before we could get there in time to stop it, Dennis Sloan sent a fist flying with an awful crack of bone into Adrian's mouth.

CHAPTER FIFTEEN

When we arrived at the school that was being transformed into the FBI command post, I found Violet standing among the red lockers that we used to haunt as teenagers. There was a display case on the wall highlighting photos and mementos from our championship volleyball season. I stood next to her, shoulder to shoulder, and we didn't speak right away. In one of the photos behind the glass, I could see the two of us, both diving for the same ball and nearly cracking heads. Trina had had to work long and hard to keep us from getting in each other's faces.

"You were good," I told her, like a peace offering.

"So were you. Wow, you had a serve."

"But you were better on the court."

Violet nodded, as if that wasn't even a matter for debate. "It seems like a long time ago."

"Yes, it sure does."

The same seven years had passed for both of us, but I couldn't help thinking that Violet had grown up faster. She was only a few months older than me, but she was already a lawyer and serving on the county board. People listened to her and respected her. Soon enough, she'd be running the whole area.

"We were stars back then," Violet went on. "That was cool."

"Well, you're still a star."

She glanced at me to see if I was kidding, which I wasn't. "Didn't you like it?"

"The attention? No, not really. To me, it was about winning the game. I didn't care about anything else."

"Interesting." Violet turned away from the display case and was done with nostalgia. "How are things going with Special Agent Reed?"

"He's good. You were right to bring him in."

"I know."

"I'm sure you think he should have taken Adam with him, not me."

"Adam has more experience, but Agent Reed knows what he wants."

I wasn't sure if she intended a double entendre with that comment.

"I heard there was some excitement," she went on.

"Yes, there was. Dennis hit Adrian."

"Dennis," Violet said, with a sneer in her voice that made it clear she was no fan. "I wish I could say I was surprised. How is Adrian?"

"Swollen jaw, a couple of loose teeth."

"Did you arrest Dennis?"

"Adrian begged us not to. So did Ellen. Given everything that's going on, we didn't think it would help the situation to have Dennis cooling his heels behind bars. He feels bad about what he did. But Adrian lied about what happened in the forest, so I understand why Dennis is upset. If we'd known about the Gruders upfront, that might have changed the whole search."

"What does Ellen say? Was this the first time?"

"You mean, that Dennis struck Adrian?"

"That he struck either of the boys."

"So she says."

"Well, if Ellen says that, you can take it to the bank. And I'm sure she would have told me if there had been problems before."

I knew that Violet and Ellen had a close history together. When Violet's family had first moved to the area, she was an outsider who didn't fit in. She was a smart, pretty girl from the city joining a school with kids who'd been together in the same cliques their whole lives. It was a tough transition, and I didn't make it easier for her. She was just as good as me on the volleyball team, which I resented because I was used to being the best. So it's not like I gave her a warm welcome. No one in town did.

Except Ellen Sloan. Ellen hired Violet as a part-time worker at the mini-mart. They worked together nearly every day during the school years and throughout the summer months while Violet was in high school and college. It was Ellen who really saw something special in her and encouraged her not just to go to law school, but to come back to this area after she did. I thought Violet would be gone from Mittel County just as fast as she could, but she proved me wrong.

"What about Adrian?" Violet asked. "Is he in trouble?"

"He says what he bought was for his own use. An experiment. There wasn't enough to sell, and he's underage, first time offense. Plus, we want him to talk so we can finally get the Gruders for distribution. He'll need a lawyer, but chances are, he can get off without jail time, and eventually he can get his record expunged."

"I'm going over there later. Ellen asked me to spend the evening with her. I'll make sure they get a good lawyer who can work everything out."

"I'm glad."

"Where are the Gruders? Have you found them?"

"Yes, they were over in Stanton. The police picked them up and are bringing them back here."

"I hope they know something useful about Jeremiah."

"I hope so too."

"Well, I'll let you get back to Agent Reed." Violet walked away, but then she hesitated and retraced her steps. She was taller and thinner than me, and she was dressed in style. "It's not personal, you know."

"What's that?"

"My disagreement with Sheriff Ginn."

"He's my father. That makes it personal to me."

"I understand, but you have to face reality. Tom has done great work for this county for decades, but he's not fit for the demands of the job anymore."

"I disagree. And that's up to the voters, not you."

"It's up to the county board if we think there's a problem."

"He's fine," I said sharply.

Violet put a hand on my shoulder, which I shrugged off impatiently. "No, Shelby," she told me with more caring and concern than I would have expected. "He's not fine. He's getting worse. Sooner or later, you'll see that for yourself."

CHAPTER SIXTEEN

Will and Vince Gruder sat like greasy bookends on either end of the bleachers in the gym. Their hands were cuffed behind their backs. As usual, I didn't know which was which. Both of them wore tie-dye tank tops from an El Paso bar with a logo of a drunk parrot on the front. I was sure they knew why they'd been brought in, but they made a point of looking unimpressed with the FBI men in their suits.

"So which one are you?" Agent Reed asked the first of the brothers.

"Vince."

"Okay, Vince. Let's not waste time. You're in trouble. So's your brother. Judges are tired of meth wreaking havoc in their towns. Making and selling it will get you ten years, maybe more."

"I don't know what you're talking about," Vince replied.

"Adrian Sloan says you do. He says you sold him drugs."

"Adrian Sloan can say whatever he wants, but he's lying. The Stanton police didn't find anything on us. Go ahead and search our place in Witch Tree, man. It's clean. You can play tough guy all you want, but you've got nothing."

I was standing next to Reed, and I reacted hotly and jumped into the middle of the interrogation. "We know you've got a lab in the woods, Vince. You were blasting music out there half the night."

"Wasn't us. We were sleeping like babies."

Reed bent forward and leaned his foot on the bleacher. "Look, Vince, you're not stupid. You know what this is all about. We're more interested in finding Jeremiah Sloan than we are in you. If you tell us what happened with Jeremiah and Adrian yesterday afternoon, we'll talk to a judge about going easy on the drug charges. This is a one-time-only daily deal. Grab it before it's gone."

"Oh yeah? Well, I'm not buying what you're selling."

Reed straightened up and casually jerked a thumb at one of his colleagues. "Okay, forget it. Get this one out of here. I'll talk to his brother. Nobody says the deal has to be for both of them. One's all I need."

"My brother's got nothing to say!" Vince retorted loudly. As he was yanked to his feet, he repeated in a voice that Will could hear on the other end of the bleachers. "You got that? Will's not saying *nothing* to any of you!"

Reed waited until Vince was dragged out of the gym. Then he shoved his hands in his suit pockets and wandered down to the far side of the bleachers, where Will Gruder danced uncomfortably on his butt cheeks as he waited for us. Reed took his time before talking. He sat down next to Will, too close for comfort, and casually stretched out his arms on the bench behind him. Will tried to mimic his brother's tough-guy pose, but it didn't work.

"You must be Will," Reed said after a while.

"Yeah, so what?"

"Your brother tells me he's not interested in a deal. Are you smarter than he is?"

"We don't need a deal. We haven't done anything."

"Sure. I believe you. Trouble is, I'm not the one you need to convince. Who's a judge going to like better, Will? A dropout like you who's been in trouble since he was fourteen or some nice small-town football player like Adrian Sloan? A kid whose little brother is missing. That wins a lot of sympathy points with people. In fact, what's a jury going to think when they hear that you and Vince were out there in the national forest with Adrian when Jeremiah disappeared? They're going to assume you two had something to do with that."

"We didn't!" Will burst out. He nodded his head at me. "She saw us! Her and that other cop, Twilley. We were here at the school playing basketball yesterday. Then we went to the bar in Witch Tree, and we were there until after midnight. No way we had anything to do with that kid going missing."

"But you were out there, right? The two of you met Adrian in the campground, and you sold him meth. He already told us you did." Reed squeezed in until he was practically breathing in Will's ear. "Come on, kid. We're talking about a missing ten-year-old boy. Help us out. If you give us a clue and we find him, hell, you'll be a hero. A judge is going to like that."

Will glanced at the far end of the bleachers to make sure that Vince wasn't in the gym anymore. His nose was running, and with his hands cuffed, he couldn't do anything about it, so he bent over to wipe his face on his knee. "I'm not talking about drugs. You can't ask me about that. Got it? I'm not saying anything about what went down with Adrian."

Reed cocked his head at me. He shot me a look that said: *This is your town. What do you want to do?*

"All right, no drugs," I interjected. "But we better like what you have to say, Will."

"We didn't have anything to do with that kid going missing. No way. We didn't even know about it until you and Twilley told us."

"But you were there."

Will's knee bounced nervously. "Yeah. Yeah, okay, we were there."

"What happened?"

"Nothing! Nothing happened, that's what I'm saying! Vince and me, we set up a meeting with Adrian in the campground. We were supposed to meet him like one o'clock or so."

"To do what?"

"To do whatever. I told you, no questions about that. Got it?"

"Okay, no questions. Go on. When did you and Vince get there?"

"Like one fifteen or so. Adrian was there, but so was his little brother. Vince wasn't happy about that. And the kid was being annoying, getting in our faces and asking all sorts of questions. What were we doing, what were we talking about. Vince figured the kid was going to blab to his parents about seeing us. So he told Adrian, either the kid goes or the meeting's off."

"What happened?"

"Adrian told his brother to beat it. Said he should take his bike and start heading back to the ranger's office. He said he'd catch up with him in a little bit."

"What time was that?"

"I don't know. One thirty maybe."

"Did Jeremiah go?"

"He argued for a while, but Adrian gave him ten bucks. That did it. The boy got on his bike and took off."

"Which way?"

"South."

"You're sure? Away from the lake?"

"Yeah. Back toward the ranger station."

"What did you and Vince do?"

"We wrapped up our business with Adrian. Then the three of us smoked for a while and hung out. Around two o'clock or so, Vince figured we better blow, so we got in the Bronco and left. Adrian said he was going to have another cigarette, so he stayed behind."

I was practically holding my breath. "Did you see Jeremiah?"

"We saw his bike."

"Where?"

"Tipped over on the side of the road like a mile south of the campground."

"Did you see the boy?"

"No."

"Did you stop?"

"No. We figured the kid was in the woods taking a leak or something. No big deal. We didn't think anything was wrong."

"So Jeremiah left at one thirty, and you left half an hour later. Is that right?"

"About that, yeah."

"When you were in the campground, did any vehicles pass by on the road? Or did you see any people?"

"Nah, it was quiet."

I shook my head in frustration. I couldn't believe we could get this far and come away with nothing. We knew approximately when the boy had disappeared, but beyond that, we were no closer to finding him.

Agent Reed was unhappy, too. "Okay, Deputy, let's get this piece of crap out of here."

"You're letting me go?" Will asked.

"Hell, no, nobody's letting you go. You're dealing meth. The county cops are going to lock you up, and then twelve nice people of Mittel County are going to send you away for a long time. You and your brother."

I took Will by the shoulder and began to push him toward the other end of the gym, but he broke away from me and spun around, nearly falling down. "Wait, wait, wait, I've got more. We can talk. We can do a deal. Vince and me, we saw something."

Agent Reed stood up from the bleachers. His dark eyes shot through Will like lasers. "What did you see?"

"First a deal. No charges. You forget about what Adrian Sloan told you."

"We're not making any promises until we hear what you have to say."

Will looked back and forth between my face and Agent Reed's. His nose was running again, and he was in full panic mode, watching the next ten years of his life tick by behind the bars of a cell.

"A truck," he sputtered.

Reed's eyes narrowed. "What?"

"As we were driving north toward the campground, we passed a truck. It was maybe two, three miles before we got there. Thing was on the side of the road. Parked, engine running. Local plates, but I don't remember the license. There was somebody inside, but we couldn't see who it was."

"One person or more than one?" I asked.

"I only saw one."

"Man or woman?"

"I'm telling you, I don't know."

"What kind of truck?"

"White," Will replied. "A big pickup, an F-150. Look, I don't know who was in it, but they were just hanging out there on the road. When we headed back south later, the truck was gone. So was the kid."

CHAPTER SEVENTEEN

A white F-150.

You couldn't pick a more popular truck around these parts, but on the day Jeremiah disappeared, a white F-150 had been reported stolen in the lakeside town of Martin's Point, which was fifty miles south of us. That didn't sound like a coincidence. When I checked with Monica, she told me that the truck hadn't been found yet, which was unusual for stolen vehicles around here. Most joyriders abandoned them within a couple of hours.

Agent Reed and I made the drive to Martin's Point. Fifty miles probably sounds like a long way, but to us, it's a trip to the dentist. Shopping for a new coat. Lunch with a friend. When you live out here, you get used to driving an hour to do just about anything.

"There's a whole lot of nothing in this place," Reed commented after we'd driven ten miles on the highway without seeing another soul. "Living here would drive me crazy."

"Time moves a little slower in the country," I agreed.

"It does that when you're dead, too."

"Let me guess. You're a city man, Agent Reed."

"I am."

"Where did you grow up?"

"Minneapolis."

"Well, you weren't all that far from the north woods living there, right? A couple of hours?"

"Yeah, but I didn't get much farther than Uptown when I was a kid. I like having people around. Trees, not so much. I know small-town people probably hate cities, but give me a downtown neighborhood any day. This might as well be the dark side of the moon."

I'd heard that sentiment from visitors many times before. "I don't have anything against cities. I love going to the city. Most of us around here do. But then we're happy to head home and leave you with the traffic and the noise and the pollution."

"Well, you're right about the traffic," Reed said. Then he changed to an entirely new subject and took me by surprise. "Tell me about the murder here last fall."

I knew what he was talking about, but I froze and said stupidly, "Murder?"

"Was there more than one?" he asked slyly.

"No."

"Okay then. Violet tells me that a woman was shot and killed here last November. Her husband was a suspect, but the sheriff didn't have enough evidence to make a case against him."

"That's right. The victim's name was Colleen Whalen. Her husband is Keith."

"So give me the details."

"Do you think the murder has something to do with Jeremiah's disappearance?"

"Probably not, but murder isn't a common occurrence around here. Neither is child abduction. When two unusual events happen in the same area, my first instinct is to wonder whether they might be connected. Plus, Violet says that the victim's house isn't far from the Sloan house. They were neighbors, right?"

"Yes."

"Okay, you tell me. Could there be a connection?"

"I don't see how. Colleen's murder was months ago. November fourteenth."

"Tell me what happened."

"All right."

I blinked as I drove, thinking about that day. I was shocked at how quickly Keith had been proven right. The FBI had only been in town for a few hours, and already he was on their radar screen. I was also focused on the sky ahead of us. Over the trees, I could see dark clouds pushing our way, blotting out the sun. A summer storm was getting closer.

"Deputy?" Reed asked.

"Sorry. Looks like severe weather coming in. I was thinking about Jeremiah. A kid in a storm, you know? I don't like it."

"Neither do I."

"Anyway, November fourteenth was a Saturday," I went on, rattling off the details we'd unearthed in the investigation. "Colleen Whalen spent most of the day shopping in Stanton. She had dinner by herself at an Applebee's restaurant and paid the check at seven forty-five p.m. There was nothing on her credit card after that and no calls on her cell phone. If she went straight home, it would have taken her about an hour to make the drive. That puts her back in town around nine p.m."

"And her husband?"

"Keith Whalen says he was out hiking all day at Shelby Lake."

Reed looked at me curiously.

"Yes, that's how I got my name. Long story. Keith said he had a sandwich in his car in a parking area near the lake. He fell asleep. When he woke up, it was late in the evening. He headed home but says he didn't get back until almost midnight. He found his wife dead in the grass outside their house, with the front door open. She'd been shot in the head. He called 911, and I responded to the call along with Deputy Twilley. There was no gun found at the crime scene. When we searched the house, we saw that a jewelry box in the master bedroom had been rifled. Keith said that an expensive watch had been taken from his nightstand, too. And Colleen's wedding ring wasn't on her finger."

"So the idea is that his wife came home and interrupted a burglar, who killed her and escaped."

"Yes."

"Is that a common thing around here, armed robbery?"

"No."

"Were there any witnesses who could confirm that Whalen was at Shelby Lake like he said? Or what time he got home?"

"No."

"Did Whalen own a gun?"

"Yes, he told us that he owned a Taurus Centerfire revolver but that it was missing. The caliber of the bullet we recovered from Colleen Whalen was consistent with a gun like that, but of course, without the gun itself, we couldn't test it."

"And what did Mr. Whalen say about the state of his marriage?" Reed asked.

I gripped the wheel tightly. "He said it was fine."

"Did his neighbors agree? I hear it's tough to keep a secret in a small town."

"Keith has a troubled past," I said carefully. "He lost a leg in Afghanistan. He suffers from depression and probably PTSD. It's safe to say his marriage showed the strains of that. Colleen worked with Ellen Sloan at the mini-mart, and Ellen told us that Colleen wasn't happy."

"So the murder victim knew Jeremiah's mother?"

"Yes, but I wouldn't read too much into that. Everyone knows everyone else around here."

Reed pursed his lips. "Keith Whalen was never charged in the murder?"

"No. Honestly, the sheriff didn't believe Keith's story, but there was no way to prove that a burglar *didn't* do it. He talked it over with the county attorney, and they concluded there was too much reasonable doubt to get it past a jury."

"Probably true," Reed agreed. Then he added, "Do you know what kind of vehicle Keith Whalen drives?"

"A Toyota Highlander, I think."

"So not a white Ford F-150?"

I turned my head and stared at him. "No."

"Good to know."

After that, we were silent until we reached Martin's Point.

*

Martin's Point is built on the shore of the region's largest lake, much bigger than any of the other lakes in Mittel County. It was a quiet little town for a long time, but the city people had discovered it about twenty-five years earlier. They built summer homes all around the lakeshore, and upscale resorts and B&Bs had sprung up to accommodate vacationers. Antique shops and gourmet restaurants followed. The success of Martin's Point took its toll on the other towns in the county. Some of the rustic cabin resorts that had prospered for decades went under as tourists found more upscale amenities by the lake. You can still find the ruins of several old resorts deep in the woods, slowly being overrun by Mother Nature.

My most vivid memory of Martin's Point was taking Anna Helvik there on a Sunday afternoon five years earlier. That was when Karl and Trina were away in Chicago for her cancer surgery. Anna was five years old then but already smart for her age. She knew something was wrong with her mother. I took this beautiful blond child to the lake, where we cruised on my father's boat under the bright sunshine. We fished, and Anna caught a crappie. She struggled to hold the slippery, squirming fish in her small hands and giggled the whole time, until it stopped struggling as it died. I watched Anna shake the fish, as if to wake it up. When it didn't, she bawled, and it took me most of an hour to get her to stop. When she was finally calm again, she wiped her face and asked me, "Is that what's going to happen to my mom?"

That was when I started crying, too.

That night, when we were back at her house, I stood outside her bedroom and listened to her pray before she went to sleep. Over and over, she said, "God, I'm sorry for killing the fishy, I'm sorry for killing the fishy, I'm sorry for killing the fishy."

I remember thinking: I would take a bullet for that little girl.

Anyway, Agent Reed and I arrived in Martin's Point, and I parked the cruiser near an ice cream parlor on the far end of the main street. The shop owner was also the owner of the F-150 that had been stolen the previous day. Unfortunately, we were one block from the town's sandy beach, where dozens of tourists tanned on any given summer day. The bus stop from the town of Stanton was immediately across the street. The large town parking lot was behind us, and anyone walking from their car toward the water would have passed where the truck had been stolen. So this location had hundreds of suspects and not a security camera anywhere in sight.

The store owner's name was Bonnie Butterfield, which I thought was a great name for someone with an ice cream shop. She gave us free ice cream when we introduced ourselves. I'm not too proud to turn down things like that. I picked a flavor called Ursulina Poop, which was chocolate-hazelnut ice cream swirled with fudge and studded with nuts and malted milk balls. It was terrific. Agent Reed got vanilla, and I rolled my eyes at him.

Bonnie took us outside and showed us where her truck had been parked half a block from the store itself. It was out of view from inside the parlor. She'd discovered it was missing when her husband arrived at one o'clock and mentioned that the truck wasn't in its usual spot. She'd seen it there about eleven o'clock when she went outside to meet the mailman, so the theft had occurred sometime in the two hours or so in between.

She also told us with some embarrassment that she'd left her truck unlocked with the keys in the cup holder. She'd been doing that for years without any problems. I wasn't surprised, because half the families in this area couldn't even find their house keys if you asked, but this time, it was Agent Reed who did the eye rolling.

After our conversation with Bonnie, we stopped in at every store along the main street to see if anyone had witnessed the theft, but no one had seen a thing. We located the mailman, too, who was no help. There wasn't anything else for us to do. Half an hour later, we were in my cruiser on the way back to Everywhere.

"What did you take away from all that?" Reed asked me, as if I were a trainee at Quantico.

I thought about it as I drove. Then I said, "The time."

"That's right. What about it?"

"The truck was stolen sometime between eleven and one. The Gruders passed the truck on the national forest road around one fifteen or so. And we're at least a ninety-minute drive from where we found Jeremiah's bicycle. So if this was our guy, he didn't waste any time. He must have driven straight there."

"Exactly," Reed said. "Whoever took the truck knew where he was going. He had plans."

CHAPTER EIGHTEEN

That night in Everywhere, the rain came.

After I took Agent Reed back to the command post, he set me free until morning. I drove to the Nowhere Café and parked on the main street, where rivers ran through the gutters and the downpour drenched me immediately. It was ten o'clock. All the shops were closed, and the only light I could see was from the window of the diner. Even so, the street was still crowded with cars bearing out-of-state plates. The café was open late to accommodate a full house of strangers. Print and TV reporters. Volunteers and curiosity-seekers, all sharing posts on Instagram and Facebook. Our little town was suddenly the epicenter of the daily news.

Inside, I squeezed to the end of the lunch counter and found an open stool next to Adam. He'd switched out of his uniform into casual clothes. He wore a tight-fitting white T-shirt, ratty blue jeans, and a baseball cap backward on his head. His brown curls poked out from under the rim. He had a bottle of Bud in front of him and two other empty bottles on the counter. He glanced at me with a resentful stare as I sat down.

"Busy day, Shelby?"

"Yeah. Pretty much."

"Well, it must be nice to be in the middle of all the action."

"Come on, Adam. I didn't ask for this."

"Yeah, but you got it, didn't you? Maybe if I had perky little tits, Agent Reed would have picked me."

He was trying to get a rise out of me, but I kept my mouth shut rather than fire back at him. I knew he was drunk and didn't know what he was saying.

"So did you find Jeremiah?" Adam asked.

"You know we didn't."

"Did you find *anything?*"

"We're still looking for the missing truck."

"You mean all those Feds crawling over town and they still don't have a damn clue what happened? What a shock. It's almost like they don't know this area from the holes in their asses."

"Adam," I murmured sharply. "Keep your voice down. You want these reporters to know you're a cop and you're drunk? If Agent Reed hears about it, you're going to be in big trouble."

"Oh, what's he going to do? Give me a crap assignment? You know what I spent my day doing, Shelby, while you were hanging out with the feebs? I was visiting camp sites on my motorcycle. Talking to Bubba and Dixie in their RV about whether they'd seen anything strange. Sticking my head inside every outhouse to make sure nobody was hiding there. Reed was very insistent about that. Check every toilet, he said. Supposedly they found a kid gagged and bound inside a porta-potty on one case, but if you ask me, he was making that up. You got a body, you bury it."

"*Adam,*" I hissed at him again. "Don't talk like that."

He went back to his beer. "Whatever."

Breezy arrived to rescue me with a glazed donut, which she knew was my favorite. She'd already put in a fifteen-hour day but

looked none the worse for wear. She was whistling, and I suspected that the pockets of her apron were stuffed with tips. She'd
borrowed new clothes, too. Somewhere during the day, she'd
traded her red mock turtleneck for a button-down white blouse
sheer enough to give the world a look at the skimpy purple bra she
was wearing underneath. Enough buttons were undone that the
girls practically spilled out when she leaned over.

"Is he still being Mr. Grumples?" Breezy asked, eyeing Adam
next to me.

"Oh, yeah."

"Poor baby," she said, sticking out her tongue at him. "The
FBI won't let you play with them?"

"Shut up, Breezy," Adam retorted.

She reached out and patted his hand, and she tugged on her
blouse to make sure he had a good view. "Sorry, sweets. I don't
mean to poke the bear. Drink up, the next one's on the house.
When I'm in a good mood, I figure the world should be, too."

I checked my watch. "It's late, Breezy. You guys ever going
to close?"

"Maybe at eleven. Look at this place. I've made more money
today than I'd make in two weeks normally. I mean, I feel a little
bad about it, but still. No offense to our local boys, but I wouldn't
get a twenty-five percent tip around here if I served them stark
naked. Today? That's my average."

"Lots of reporters on expense accounts, huh?"

"No kidding. I hope this keeps up for a few days. I'll have
enough to retire Dudley and get a new car." Then she closed her
eyes in disgust with herself. "Oh my God, did I just say that?"

"Yeah. You did."

"Sorry. I got carried away."

"Hey, I get it. Just keep it to yourself."

Breezy pasted the flirty smile back on her face and went off to serve the strangers in the diner. I looked toward the front window, where rain continued to pour down from the night sky like a deluge. A drumroll of thunder made the building shake.

"Jeremiah's out there in this," I said quietly, underneath the noise of the café.

Adam heard me. "Yeah, I know. It sucks."

"Do you think he's alive?" I leaned close enough that Adam's beer breath was in my face.

"If he is, it might be better if he weren't," Adam replied. Being drunk has a way of making you speak the truth even when you're better off with a lie.

I swore, because I didn't want Adam to be right, but he probably was. I'd held onto the hope all day that this was a mistake. An accident. But suddenly, there was a truck. The truck changed everything. Someone had gotten into a stolen truck, and two hours later, Jeremiah vanished without a trace, leaving his bicycle on the road. I couldn't find an innocent explanation for that.

"Have you seen my father?" I asked.

"Yeah. He went home."

"What about Monica?"

"She left an hour ago."

"Okay. Thanks."

"Hey, Shelby?"

"What?"

"Sorry for being a dick."

I winked at him. "What else is new?"

I finished my donut and waited for the sugar to kick in, but it never did. I watched the rain, which was hypnotic. Every now and then, lightning flashed over the Carnegie Library across the street like a broken branch. I thought the storm might pass if I waited long enough, but the downpour kept on. Eventually, I climbed off the stool and left money on the counter. I gave Breezy a 30 percent tip, which didn't amount to more than a dollar. I figured she'd laugh about it anyway.

"I'm heading home," I told Adam.

"Yeah, see you in the morning."

I listened to the thunder. "You still got your bike outside?"

"Yeah."

"Well, drive carefully."

"Always."

*

The rain did finally quit. The roads were a mess, slick with mud and leaves and fallen branches, but at least I could see where I was going as I drove home. When I got there, the lights were on, giving the house a saintly glow through the stained glass windows. Dad's truck was in the driveway, but when I called for him inside, I got no answer. I checked his bedroom, which was empty. The bed didn't have a wrinkle and was made with hospital corners, as always.

When I looked through the windows at the backyard, I saw him. He'd built a screened-in gazebo out there years ago as a playhouse for me. The light inside made it look like an oasis in the darkness. I went out the back door and trudged through the muddy grass, leaving footprints. A firefly winked at me near the trees. Inside the gazebo, I found Dad in one of the wicker chairs. He was still in his uniform, sitting straight up with perfect posture. The daily crossword puzzle was folded up in his lap, with only a handful of words filled in. He had his phone on the table in front of him, as if waiting for it to ring.

Something told me it hadn't rung all day.

"Hi, Dad."

He gave me the kind of smile that lets you know in a glance that you're loved. "Hello, Shelby."

"Mind if I join you?"

"Please."

I sat down next to him. We didn't talk for a while; we just listened to the buzz of insects hiding in the grass. Eventually, he asked about my day, and I gave him an update. We were silent again after that, until he looked over at me and said, "I owe you an apology, Shelby."

"For what?"

"I should have listened to you about Adrian and the Gruders."

"It was a hunch. I got lucky."

"No, you were observant, and I didn't take you seriously."

"Don't worry about it, Dad," I said, but I liked hearing it.

Somewhere during the day, he'd slipped off to see the town barber and get his hair cut. When I looked at him in profile, I could still see his face looking like it did in photographs from twenty-five years earlier, when his hair and mustache were dark brown. He'd been leaner then, but just as serious. I remembered the proud expression on his face in the first picture Monica had taken when he held me as a baby. It was a long time before I understood what it meant to him to find me on his doorstep in that year of all years. He'd lost his father to Alzheimer's four months earlier. His mother to the same damn disease five months before that. Enter Shelby Lake into his life. He used to say that I'd saved him as much as he saved me.

"I have to ask you something, Shelby."

"Sure, Dad. What?"

"I don't want you to panic when you hear it."

"What is it?"

His hand trembled a little with nervousness. "What's the name of the boy who disappeared?"

I stared at him. "Dad, I—I don't—"

"Just his name, Shelby. Please."

"It's Jeremiah, Dad. Jeremiah Sloan."

He nodded as if it were one of the answers in his crossword puzzle that had eluded him. "Of course, it is. Thank you. I was able to remember everything else about the past two days, but not that. Weird, isn't it? It was just gone. Like a chip of paint falling off the wall. This has been a bad day. I know it'll go up and down, but this was a bad day."

Dad was being clinical about it to protect me. I knew he would never show me the depth of his frustration, but it was there. I looked away so he wouldn't spot the sadness on my face, but I could never fool him.

"You don't have to pretend, Shelby. We'll just take it as it comes."

"I know."

"It can move fast, or it can move slow. And there are new drugs now. Hopefully, we'll hardly notice it for a while."

"I know," I said again, choking on the words.

Funny how I could feel myself getting older at that moment. The teenage girl, the volleyball player, was slipping away from me into the distant past and leaving me alone. It was as if Jeremiah had taken what was left of that side of me with him when he disappeared.

"Trina's sick again," I added, not knowing why I felt the need to tell him that when he had his own troubles. "She told me about it last night."

"I'm so sorry."

"I don't want her to be alone going through this again. I'm just worried she won't open up and let me in. Or anyone else. Not Karl. Not Anna."

"Some people can't do that."

"I know. That's not who she is."

"All you can do is be there for her. She has to decide for herself what she needs."

"I know," I said again.

Sitting there, I felt a wave of anger at the world. It's that helpless frustration we feel when fate deals a blow to someone we love, and there's no one we can blame and no one we can scream at.

"Do you want to bring out your guitar?" Dad asked, trying to pull me out of the hole I was in.

"No, thanks. I'll take a rain check. I want to be by myself for a while."

"I understand, Shelby. Go on. Get some sleep."

I stood up and bent down to kiss him on the top of the head. While I was there, I put my arms around him and didn't let go. He held on to me, too. We didn't need to say anything. There was nothing we could do about the future.

I turned and left the gazebo and hurried upstairs to my bedroom. When I stood by one of the windows looking down on the backyard, I saw the light of the gazebo go out, and I could just barely make out my father as he returned to the house. With him gone, there was nothing but wilderness outside. I opened the window and breathed in the humid air through the screen. The night was quiet and still after the wild storm, with barely a leaf moving in the trees.

Then, out of nowhere, a barn owl swooped down in front of me, its huge auburn wings spread wide. I jumped back with a shout. For an instant, I saw its monk-like face staring at me as it crashed against the second-floor screen, and then after the impact, it spiraled away down to the ground. When I peered out again, I could see the bird on the grass below me, hopping as it tried and failed to fly on a broken wing. I sprinted for the stairs to rescue it.

You know me. I believe in signs.

That one felt like a bad omen of what was to come.

CHAPTER NINETEEN

I do regular transports of injured birds for the Stanton Raptor Center, so I keep heavy cardboard boxes and falconry gloves in a shed near the house. With Dad's help, I was able to get a blanket over the owl and secure him inside a box, which I put on the floor of the front seat of my cruiser. I called my friend Jeannie Samper, who runs the center, and she said she'd be there to meet me. Jeannie was used to calls at all hours during the summer season, and I'd never once seen her fail to get up in the middle of the night to receive an owl, hawk, or eagle in need of help.

Stanton is an hour's drive east from Everywhere. The highway was dark and empty and still slippery from the heavy rain. There was a lot I could have been thinking about as I drove, but I put it all out of my mind and simply stared down the tunnel of my headlights and kept a watch for deer and moose. I could hear the occasional rustle of the owl shifting inside the box.

I made it to the raptor center just before midnight. The facility was really just Jeannie's house and a few acres of land, located well outside the busier Walmart section of town. She and her husband and four kids were squeezed onto the upstairs floor, while the downstairs, garage, basement, and outbuildings had been converted into areas to treat and house several dozen birds of prey at any given time. Jeannie was a ruthless fund-raiser, and the equipment and care she provided rivaled anything you'd find at a veterinary hospital.

The garage was open as I drove up the muddy, twisting driveway through the woods. However, the person who met my car wasn't Jeannie. A man I'd never seen before came up to my driver's window with a smile, and I rolled it down.

"You must be Shelby. Jeannie said you were on your way. I'm Dr. Lucas. I understand you have a little patient for me."

"Yes, it's a barn owl that flew into my window. I'm worried he may have a broken wing."

"Well, let's get him inside and take a look."

Dr. Lucas didn't look more than thirty years old. He wore a white lab coat over a red-checked flannel shirt and stonewashed jeans. He had long sandy hair that hung loose to his shoulders. I'd never been much of a fan of long hair on men, but on him, it worked. He had a thin frame and narrow face, and his eyes were warm and very blue. When he smiled, the skin around his eyes crinkled and made you want to trace the lines with your finger, as if you were exploring a map of an exotic new place.

When I got out of the car, I saw that he was taller than me but not a giant, only about five-foot-ten. He shook my hand. His grip was firm, and his hands were soft. I took him around to the passenger side, and he reached inside to take the box with the same gentleness you would use with a newborn's cradle. As the box moved, the owl inside got scared and began moving about, and Dr. Lucas murmured, "It's okay, buddy, we're here to help. Don't worry."

I liked this man.

"I'm sorry to get you out of bed in the middle of the night," I told him.

"Oh, I wasn't sleeping. Wide awake and staring at the ceiling. I was actually pleased to get Jeannie's call."

"And you're a vet?" I asked, which sounded like a stupid question as soon as it came out of my mouth.

"Two years now," he replied with a grin, as he carried the box inside the garage. I followed him past the lineup of glass windows at the back into the treatment room. "Don't worry, I passed all my tests. I can take a dog's temperature like nobody's business."

I laughed. In fact, I may have blushed a little.

"Sorry, what I mean is, I usually see Dr. Tim over here." Dr. Tim was the sweetest, most capable vet on the planet and about two hundred years old. He'd volunteered his time at the raptor center ever since Jeannie started it.

"Yes, I recently joined Tim's practice in Stanton," Lucas told me. "He's planning to retire in a couple of years. When he does, I'll take over the business."

"Dr. Tim retire? That's hard to imagine. I was pretty sure they'd have to take him out of the clinic feetfirst."

"Well, that may still be true. It took me a few months to convince him to let me come on board, and so far, all he's done is cut back his hours a bit. But that's okay. When you do something you love, why would you want to quit? Anyway, I'm in no hurry. As far as I'm concerned, he can stay on as long as he likes. I'm just happy to learn the ropes."

There was something refreshing about meeting someone else like me who wasn't in a huge hurry. Sometimes I feel like the world is filled with nothing but Violet Roka's, who rush to finish one day in order to get to the next.

"Do you live in Stanton?" I asked.

"I do. I moved here about a year ago. I was actually born around here, but my family moved away when I was ten. I grew up in Kansas City, and then I went to vet school at Kansas State."

"But you moved back here? I don't hear that a lot."

"Oh, it's a complicated family drama. My grandfather needed help, and I was the only one willing to uproot myself to go back home. I guess the fact that I still thought of Stanton as home even years after we moved away made me realize it was something I needed to do."

"I know exactly what you mean."

I was enjoying my conversation with Dr. Lucas, but I heard a tapping behind me on the row of windows that separated the treatment room from the garage. When I looked over my shoulder, I saw Jeannie Samper waving at me.

"Don't worry, I've got this," Dr. Lucas told me. "You don't have to stay in here. Go talk to Jeannie."

"Are you sure? I'm happy to help. I've done it before. I'm practically a vet tech."

"It's fine. If I need another pair of hands, I'll shout."

I felt the tiniest twinge of disappointment at being dismissed, but I left him alone with the owl. Outside the treatment room, Jeannie greeted me with a hug. I apologized for coming so late, but she waved it off as if it were nothing. The two of us watched Dr. Lucas through the glass as he tended to the owl. You can always tell someone who loves animals. His movements were quick, firm, and tender as he prepared to sedate the bird in order to X-ray its wing.

"So Dr. Tim has a partner now," I said. "Amazing."

"Yeah, I never thought I'd see the day," Jeannie agreed. "I like Lucas. He's very capable. And very charming."

"He sure seems to be."

Jeannie winked at me. "Unmarried, too."

I shrugged off her comment. Jeannie's mission in life was to fix me up. "Yeah, well, who has the time?"

"Uh-huh. You never have time if you don't make time, Shelby Lake. Come on, let me fix you a cup of tea, and we can chat."

I had an hour's drive home ahead of me, and I was anxious to get back on the road, but I never turned down tea with Jeannie. She grew her own, and her kids sold it at farmers markets during the summer. Once you'd had her tea, you really couldn't drink store-bought anymore.

Jeannie led me up an old narrow staircase with boards that creaked and shifted under my feet. In the second-floor family room, I plopped down on her threadbare sofa as she went into the kitchen to boil water. She had a homemade, lemon-scented candle burning; that was the only light. The doors to the other upstairs rooms were closed. Everyone else was sleeping.

She returned shortly with tea for me in a china mug that looked as if it had been around for decades. The flower design on it was faded. She had her own tea in a ceramic mug with a logo for the Stanton Raptor Center. Nothing matched around here, and that was fine.

"Here you go, sweetie."

Jeannie sank into a glider opposite me and pushed herself relentlessly back and forth with one leg on the floor. She was forty years old, with prematurely silver hair that was tied in a bun behind her head. Having four kids, she always said, was what had turned her gray. She was tall and very heavy, but her weight didn't slow her down. I'd never seen her when she wasn't busy doing three things at once. As she drank her tea, she turned on the television and muted it, fanned herself with a magazine, and fiddled with the baby monitor that let us listen to the noise of her six-month-old, Hildy, in the nursery.

Life for Jeannie was a constant juggling act, but she never showed any stress about it. Despite the pressures of running the raptor center, she and her husband managed to find time to homeschool all of their kids. Their oldest, Matthew, was sixteen, as deeply religious as his parents, and had already been accepted to college at Northwestern in the fall. The two middle kids were just as bright.

"What an awful thing about Jeremiah Sloan," Jeannie said. "Are you any closer to finding him?"

"Not so far."

"If this happened to one of my kids, I think I'd be driving up and down every street in the county shouting their name. Dennis must be a wreck."

"He is. They all are."

"People are saying that someone grabbed him. Is that true? It's hard to believe around here."

"We're not sure what happened yet," I said cautiously.

"Well, I have two boys. Don't rule out the possibility that Jeremiah wandered off on his own and got into trouble. That's what boys do."

"We're not ruling anything out yet."

Jeannie opened her mouth as if to say something more, but then she closed it again. She sipped her tea, and her round face in the flickering glow of the candle looked troubled. She played with a loose strand of her gray hair and pushed back and forth in the glider.

"Jeannie? Is there something else?"

"Oh, I'm sure it's nothing. I shouldn't say anything. I don't like to be a gossip."

"Jeremiah's missing. This is no time to hold something back."

Jeannie put down her mug on the coffee table between us. No one could hear us, but she leaned forward in the glider and whispered anyway. "Well, you know I see Dennis a lot. Either he's over here, or I'm in the ranger station."

"Of course."

Dennis's job in the national forest meant that he was often discovering birds that needed treatment at Jeannie's center. When healthy birds were ready to be rereleased into the wild, Jeannie worked with Dennis to do so deep in the forest land. That shared bond had made them good friends over the years.

"There was this odd little thing last fall," she went on. "It makes me kind of uncomfortable to talk about it. I mean, I know the kind of man Dennis is, and I've made peace with that, but I don't like being recruited as a coconspirator."

My eyes narrowed with concern. "Go on."

"I was with him at the ranger station, and he asked if my son Matthew would be willing to babysit for Jeremiah that Saturday night. All night. He was wondering if Matthew could sleep over at his house."

"Why didn't he have Adrian do it?"

"That's the thing. Ellen and Adrian were both out of town. She was off at some retail conference in New Orleans, and Adrian went with her."

"Ah." I got the picture.

"Yes, you see why it bothered me, right? Dennis was going to be gone all night, and he wanted a babysitter from Stanton, not Everywhere. He didn't want the news getting around. I was pretty sure he was having an affair and looking for a way to hide it."

"Well, I doubt it's the first time, if you believe the rumors."

"Oh, I'm sure that's true. Like I say, I know Dennis, warts and all. I wasn't crazy about it, but I agreed to let Matthew do it. He's been trying to save money to buy a telescope, and Dennis was offering a hundred dollars to have him stay over. I knew Matthew could use the cash."

"So what happened?"

"Well, it seemed to go fine. Matthew and Jeremiah hung out watching TV and playing video games during the evening, and then he got Jeremiah ready for bed around nine thirty. No problem. Except I got a call from Matthew at one in the morning. He was in a panic."

"Why?"

"He went to check on Jeremiah before he went to bed himself. The boy wasn't in his room."

"He was gone?"

"Yes. Matthew was about to call 911, but I told him first to search the house and then walk around the yard to see if he could find the boy anywhere. That's what he did. Matthew found Jeremiah hanging out on the back porch below his bedroom window. He said he'd climbed down to watch the stars."

"So what's the problem?"

"Well, Matthew was pretty sure that Jeremiah was lying. The boy wasn't in his pajamas anymore. He'd changed clothes. And his shoes were all muddy, like he'd been off in the woods somewhere. Matthew asked him about it, but the boy swore he hadn't been anywhere. He said he went out in the middle of the lawn, and that was that."

"But?" I asked, because I could tell the story wasn't over.

"But Matthew said something else, too. He told me the boy looked really, really scared. I mean, the poor kid was trembling. It was like Jeremiah had seen a monster."

CHAPTER TWENTY

I slept through my alarm on Sunday morning. Instead of waking up at five thirty, I woke up at seven. My father was already gone. His cruiser wasn't in the driveway. I got ready quickly and then made my usual stop at the Nowhere Café for breakfast. Like last night, the tables were filled with out-of-towners.

I called out my order to Breezy and took a seat at the counter next to Adam. He was on the same stool he'd been at the previous night, looking as if he'd never left, except for the fact that he was back in his deputy's uniform. His eyes were bloodshot and rimmed with dark circles, his hair was dirty, and he had a pot of coffee and four aspirin on the counter in front of him, the universal clues of someone nursing a hangover.

"You get the license plate?" I asked.

"What?"

"Of the truck that ran you over."

"Ha. Funny."

I laughed, but Adam didn't. He popped all of the aspirin onto his tongue and washed it down with coffee.

"Has my father been in here?"

"Yeah, he already went over to the office."

"I bet he complimented you on your appearance."

"The subject came up," Adam replied.

I laughed again, because I could imagine how that conversation had gone. "Well, don't let Agent Reed see you looking like this. He won't be impressed either. He'll send you off to investigate more toilets."

Adam's face had the mournful look of a bloodhound. "Too late."

"Why? Reed's already been in here?"

"No, I did something stupid last night."

I didn't like the sound of that. "Oh, Adam, what did you do?"

"I was pissed off about getting shut out of the investigation. And I was hammered. So I called him."

"You didn't."

"Yeah, I did."

"Did you talk to him?"

"I left a message. It was an epic rant. I'm pretty sure my career is over. What the hell, it's probably better that way. I suck. Everything I touch, I screw up."

I put a hand on his back, because Adam looked as if he might cry. I'd never seen him so upset. "Hey, come on. It happens. Cut yourself some slack, okay? It's been a tough couple of days for all of us, and none of us have gotten much sleep. Besides, you don't report to the FBI. You report to my father."

Adam shrugged off my reassurance. He was feeling sorry for himself, and I couldn't really blame him. "If the FBI wants me gone, I'm gone. Reed talks to Violet, Violet talks to Tom, Tom kicks me to the curb. You know that's how it goes."

"I'll talk to Agent Reed," I promised him.

"It won't do any good."

"You don't know that. And no matter what the FBI or Violet says, Dad's not going to fire you for one mistake. He may read you the riot act, but that's all. He knows you're good at the job."

Breezy showed up in front of me, bringing coffee and a short stack of blueberry pancakes. She looked as bright as the morning sunshine, her long hair was washed, her makeup was neatly done, and she had a spring in her step. I wasn't sure if it was the prospect of another day of big tips or whether she'd gotten lucky last night. Or both.

"Adam telling you his tale of woe?" she asked.

"Yup."

"He kept saying he was going to call that FBI guy, and I said, don't do it! I tried to cheer him up, but he wanted to mope instead." Breezy leaned over the counter until she was practically in Adam's face. "And you know, Adam Twilley, most men like the way I cheer them up."

"Knock it off, Breezy," Adam fumed. "I'm not in the mood."

I changed the subject before Adam blew up again. "So how's Dudley? Back in the land of the living?"

"Yeah, for the moment. Kenny at the Witch Tree garage went over to my place yesterday and tinkered with the engine. I was able to get it started this morning. Of course, then I practically ran out of gas on my way in. I thought I had a spare tank in the shed, but no such luck. I was afraid Dudley was going to sputter out before I made it here."

Breezy tended to ramble when she talked, so I tuned her out as I ate my pancakes. I had this strange habit of eating pancakes like the phases of the moon, and my breakfast was waxing gibbous when I heard Adam mutter a curse under his breath. His face looked gray as death. I followed his eyes and saw Agent Reed in the doorway of the diner. The FBI man wore a dark suit and had reflective sunglasses over his eyes. He beckoned me with his finger.

"Stay put," I murmured to Adam. "Don't say anything."

I figured we didn't need a confrontation between Adam and

Agent Reed in front of a dozen reporters. As it was, questions about the investigation flew as soon as they spotted Reed, but he stood near the door without responding, as if he were stone deaf. I left my pancakes behind, threw some money on the counter, and hurried over to join him. He held the door open for me, and we stood on the sidewalk together outside.

"Good morning, Deputy Lake."

"Hi. Listen, I hear that Adam left an unfortunate message for you last night, and I just want you to know—"

He cut me off. "If Deputy Twilley has anything to say, he can say it to me himself. Don't fight his battles for him."

"Sure. Of course."

"We don't have any time for distractions. There's been a break in the case."

I felt my heart rise into my mouth, giving me a bitter taste. I was afraid of what he would say next. "Did you find Jeremiah?"

Agent Reed shook his head. "No, but we found the missing F-150."

*

The white truck was in a parking lot near the beach at Shelby Lake.

Obviously, this was an area I knew well. I'd spent many hours here throughout my life, looking out at the cove where my father had moored his boat between the trees and thinking about the strange circumstances that had brought him home to rescue me. This was my sacred place, the small lake that had been touched by God.

To everyone else in Mittel County, of course, it was just a quiet destination for avid fishermen like Dad or Adam and teenagers looking for a make-out spot where the cops wouldn't find you. Its location wasn't really all that far from Martin's Point, where the truck had been stolen, but it felt remote compared to that busy tourist town. If you'd swiped a truck and wanted to party in a place where no one would find you, this was a good spot.

The same was true if you'd kidnapped a child.

In the early morning hours, the F-150 was the only vehicle in the parking lot. It was wet with leaves and pine needles that had been swept from the trees. The area was paved, so there were no tire tracks. An FBI forensics team surrounded the truck, examining it inside and out. Another team patrolled the beach, hunting for evidence of anyone who had been here, and still another team hunted through the park's garbage cans.

At least twenty cops and volunteers were spread out through the surrounding forest, on a search for Jeremiah.

"Who found the truck?" I asked Agent Reed.

"A fisherman got here at dawn. He remembered the media reports about the F-150 and called it in."

"Is there any way to tell how long it's been here?"

Reed surveyed the parking lot with a frown. "No, our search grid hadn't covered this area yet, so we don't know when the truck was abandoned. Hopefully, someone will come forward and let us know whether they saw it in the parking lot in the last couple of days."

One of the FBI forensic analysts, who was robed completely in white, called Agent Reed over for a conversation.

I stared at the F-150 and tried to connect the dots in my head.

On Friday morning, this truck had been parked half a block from Bonnie Butterfield's ice cream parlor in Martin's Point. It had been stolen sometime after eleven o'clock, and barely two hours later, the Gruders had spotted someone in a white F-150 near the spot where Jeremiah disappeared. Maybe it was this truck. Maybe not. Now it was Sunday morning, and the truck from Martin's Point had been found abandoned in an area that was nowhere near the national forest.

Reed returned and peeled off his sunglasses. "There's nothing in the truck."

"No evidence that Jeremiah was inside?"

"No evidence that anyone was inside. The truck has been wiped down. No fingerprints anywhere, not even inside the flat bed. In your experience, are teenage joyriders that good at covering their tracks?"

"No."

"Yeah, that's what's I think, too. Kids didn't do this. It was a thorough job. Someone didn't want us finding anything."

"You think this is the truck, don't you?"

"Without more evidence, we can't be one hundred percent sure. But if you want to know what my gut tells me, then yes, this is the truck, and yes, it's connected to Jeremiah's disappearance."

"What does that mean?"

Reed studied the searchers in the forest, pushing shoulder to shoulder through the underbrush. "If Jeremiah was inside that truck, then either someone brought him here to the lake after kidnapping him, or someone abandoned the truck here to throw us off the scent and make us search in the wrong place. Either way, I don't like the fact that he's done with it."

I understood the implications.

If the kidnapper was done with the truck, then it was possible he was done with Jeremiah, too. Neither of us wanted to say it out loud, but I began to fear that we would never find the boy alive.

Sunday was already off to a bad start, and as Agent Reed and I stood near the waters of Shelby Lake, it only got worse. I heard the ping of a text arriving on my phone. It was Monica Constant sending me a message. I checked it and then gave Reed the news.

"The police in Stanton have found a body."

CHAPTER TWENTY-ONE

No, it wasn't Jeremiah.

The body was Paul Nadler, the ninety-four-year-old Alzheimer's patient who had wandered away from his nursing home on Friday morning. We'd feared for months that something bad would happen to Mr. Nadler when he made one of his escapes, and something finally did.

A river runs through the heart of Stanton. It's not a big river like the Mississippi; it's more of a creek that ebbs and flows with the rainfall. On Friday, when Mr. Nadler disappeared, it would have been a trickle under the Oak Street bridge, but on Saturday night, the heavy storm would have swelled it into a torrent racing through the land south of town.

The Oak Street bridge was only four blocks from Mr. Nadler's nursing home. Anyone sitting under the bridge deck would have been invisible from the street, so it wasn't a surprise that no one had found him. The Stanton police suspected that he'd died down there, and the next day, when the rains came, his body had been picked up by the swollen currents and tumbled downstream. An organic farmer driving into town for the Sunday open-air market had spotted Mr. Nadler's body two miles south of town on the grassy riverbank beside the highway.

Nadler was dressed the way he'd been when he wandered away on Friday, in a blue button-down dress shirt, a plaid blazer with patches on the elbows, pleated tan slacks, and natty wing tips he'd probably owned for thirty years. His leather wallet was found still buttoned into his back pocket, and it contained twenty-six soggy dollars, a frequent-buyer punch card from a long-closed Stanton restaurant, and a laminated photograph of his late wife. His face in death was utterly peaceful.

The discovery of a dead body so soon after Jeremiah's disappearance triggered Agent Reed's rule that when two unusual things happen in close proximity, it was important to look for connections. As a result, the FBI forensics team took control of the death investigation and was planning to oversee the autopsy. However, there was no sign of foul play and no violence to the body other than the postmortem injuries of the river currents. To me, it looked as if Mr. Nadler had gone to sleep under the bridge and never awakened. All in all, in the grand scheme of things, it didn't seem like a bad way to leave this world.

Even so, it made me sad. I was sad for Mr. Nadler dying alone. I wondered what he remembered of his life when he left and whether he had any thoughts about his family or friends. Most of all, I was sad because when I looked at the body on the riverbank, I didn't see Mr. Nadler's face. I saw my father's face. I saw my proud, strong father stripped of who he was, unable to pick up a fork and tell you what it was used for. I had a vision of the future, and it filled me with dread.

"Do you need me here?" I asked Agent Reed.

"No, not for a while. Do you have somewhere you need to be?"

"I thought I would walk the route from the nursing home to the river bridge and see if Mr. Nadler left anything behind."

"Okay. That's a good idea. Come back here when you're done."

But I could tell he knew that this man's death meant more to me on a personal level than I was sharing. I was sure Violet had told him about my father, and it wasn't a big leap from there.

I drove alone into the heart of Stanton, past the chain restaurants, past the Walmart. I found the three-story senior apartment building where Mr. Nadler had lived. It didn't look much different from the outside than a building where twenty- and thirty-somethings would live. Two cars from the Stanton Sheriff's office were in the parking lot, and no doubt they were breaking the bad news to the residents and staff.

I parked in front of the building and crossed the street. There was a mailbox, a bus stop, and a McDonald's on the opposite side. One of the times Mr. Nadler had disappeared, he'd been found in the children's playland inside McDonald's, jumping with the kids in the bouncy castle.

Oak Street ran next to the McDonald's through a leafy suburban neighborhood. As I walked on the sidewalk, the sun came and went through the trees. Death shouldn't have been stalking such a perfect Sunday morning. Ahead of me, I could see the river bridge. It took me only a few minutes to get there on foot. I walked halfway out onto the bridge, then looked down over the railing at the swift waters below me. In the hours since the rain, the level had already dropped, but it was still a miniature version of whitewater rapids rushing around gentle curves toward the southern end of town. When I looked behind me, I could still see Mr. Nadler's apartment building a few blocks away.

I retraced my steps to the riverbank and made my way down the grassy slope, which was wet and slick. A concrete walkway bordered the river, but the water level had risen above it. I peered under the bridge itself, trying to see between the support posts. Staying above the waterline, I side-stepped along the sharp slope of a retaining wall under the bridge deck. I was surprised to find someone sitting there, only inches away from the rushing water.

It was Dr. Lucas from the raptor center. He hadn't noticed me yet. He was staring at the current as if he were hypnotized.

"Well, hello," I said.

He looked at me when he heard my voice. I'd startled him, and he had to place me in his memory. "Oh. Hello. It's Shelby, isn't it? This is a surprise."

"Yes, I didn't expect to see you again so soon. How's my owl?"

"I expect it to make a full recovery. The injury to the wing wasn't serious."

"That's good. I'm glad to hear it."

He took note of my uniform. "I'm sorry, Jeannie didn't mention that you were with the police."

"Mittel County, not Stanton. There was a body found downriver this morning. I'm here with the FBI to make sure there's no connection to the missing boy from Everywhere."

"Yes, I know about the body," Lucas replied.

"Oh?"

"He was my grandfather. Paul Nadler. That's my name, too. Lucas Nadler."

I carefully slid down onto the concrete slope next to him. The river slapped loudly against the stone. It was darker and cooler here in the shadows of the bridge. "I'm so sorry. You mentioned your grandfather last night, but I didn't make the connection. I don't think Jeannie ever mentioned your last name."

"Yes, that's the vet world. I'm always Dr. Lucas, never Dr. Nadler. I prefer it that way, to be honest. It's more personal."

"Well, I apologize for pulling you away in the middle of a family crisis. I mean, to take care of the owl."

"No, I was glad to do it. I needed to think about my work for a while and not about Grampa Paul. I've been a wreck since

Friday, not knowing where he was. At least something like this reminds you how people pitch in to help. The police and the people
at the facility have been great. Jeannie, too. The two of us drove
all over town looking for him."

"I know this didn't end the way you were hoping. All I can say
is, I saw his body. There were no signs of distress or pain."

"Yes, I was there earlier when the Stanton police called me,
and I thought the same thing. He looked as if he'd just slipped
away. Still, I wish I'd been with him. The police think he probably
came down here to the river from the nursing home, so I figured
I'd come here, too. I figured maybe his spirit would be hanging
around for a while. I suppose that sounds foolish."

"No. It doesn't."

Lucas smiled at me. I thought the same thing I'd thought last
night. He had a nice smile that went from his mouth all the way
up into his blue eyes. His long blond hair was messy across his
shoulders.

"I came back to Stanton because Grampa Paul needed help.
I was hoping to take care of him myself, but by the time I moved
here, it was obvious he needed more care than I could give. That's
why I moved him to the facility. It's not a bad place, even though
it can be awfully depressing."

"We got the reports over in Everywhere every time Mr. Nadler
wandered away. It seemed like they couldn't keep track of him."

Lucas laughed sadly. "Well, don't blame them too much.
Grampa Paul was like Houdini. An escape artist. We tried GPS
trackers; he found a way to take them off. The elevators were
locked out, but somehow he always managed to slip away from
the dining room. The police would call when they found him,
and I'd go talk to him wherever he was and take him back there.
He hated it. He'd cry when I left. It broke my heart."

It broke my heart, too.

"If you don't mind a personal question, did he know who you were?"

Lucas's face got a faraway look. "Occasionally. Just for a moment or two. Most of the time, no. I was in there somewhere, though. He'd talk about things we did together when I was a kid, but he didn't realize that it was me sitting there with him. Still, I liked hearing the old stories. It was a comfort knowing there were bits and pieces of him that the disease hadn't taken, even if he couldn't connect them to reality anymore. He'd talk about this resort we used to visit during the summers, and for him it was like we'd just been there the previous weekend. Or he'd laugh about the ant farm he built for me and how all the ants got loose and sent my grandmother screaming out of the house. I remember when that happened. I was probably seven at the time. But he thought the two of them still lived in the old house. He'd ask me over and over where my grandmother was. To him, she was still alive. Still the most beautiful woman he'd ever met."

"That's sad, but it's sweet, too."

"Well, as I say, it was nice knowing the disease hadn't wiped out everything."

The two of us were quiet for a while. I was comfortable sitting with him. It occurred to me that he was one of the few people I'd met who had been through what was ahead for me. I didn't like talking about it, but Lucas made me feel safe.

"My father," I murmured.

He looked at me. "What about him?"

"It's starting."

Lucas understood immediately. "I'm so sorry, Shelby."

"Yeah. Thanks."

"How old is he?"

"Only fifty-five. It's early onset. His parents went the same way."

"There are things that can be done now to slow it down."

"I know. We'll explore everything."

"Well, if I can help at all—"

"I appreciate it." I checked my watch and saw that a lot of time had passed while I was sitting there. "I really need to go."

"Of course."

I pushed myself to my feet and brushed dirt off the slacks of my uniform. "What's next for you? You came home because of your grandfather. Will you leave now that he's gone?"

"No, I don't think so. I like it here. I always have."

"Well, good. And thank you again for taking care of the owl last night."

"It was my pleasure."

"Goodbye, Dr. Lucas."

"Please, let's drop the 'doctor,' okay?"

I smiled. "Okay. Lucas."

"I really am sorry to hear about your father, Shelby. Believe me, I understand what you're going through. If you'd like to talk more, I'm always happy to do that. Maybe we could meet for dinner sometime."

It was a kind, generous offer that also sounded suspiciously like a date.

"Maybe we could," I replied. "I'd like that."

CHAPTER TWENTY-TWO

Agent Reed and I had an hour alone as we drove back to Everywhere from Stanton, and I used the time to try to save Adam's job. Yes, I knew he wouldn't lift a finger to help me if the tables were turned, but I didn't want to see him get fired for one stupid mistake. So I talked up Adam as much as I could, and Reed heard me out. Then, without a word, he took his phone from his pocket and played me the voicemail message. It was even worse than Adam had described it. He was obviously so drunk he could hardly talk, and I could hear the beat of the rain and rock music in the background as he tried to form his words. Most of what came out were four-letter obscenities. At some point, the reality of what he was doing must have dawned on him because he cut it off in midsentence. But the damage was already done.

"Well, that was bad," I admitted, because there wasn't anything else I could say.

Agent Reed didn't react, other than a grim little smile. He simply put his phone back in his pocket. I was silent for the rest of the drive.

When we reached Everywhere, we went directly to the Sloan

house. There was still a crowd of neighbors inside, helping the family. Trina was back, and she answered the door. She led us into the living room where Ellen and Dennis were waiting. Reed wanted to give them an update about the F-150 before news broke in the media. I knew the discovery didn't bode well for finding Jeremiah, so when Reed asked to be alone with the Sloans, I was happy to bow out of the conversation. The three of them went downstairs. Trina and I left the other neighbors in the living room and went upstairs to see Anna, who was hanging out in Jeremiah's bedroom.

The door to the boy's room was at the end of the hallway. I headed that way, but Trina stopped me with a hand on my shoulder. We hadn't turned on the light, so her face was in shadow. I didn't see any emotion there, which wasn't unusual. Even so, I knew she had something to say to me.

"Shelby, we haven't told Anna about the cancer. Not yet."

"I understand."

"I just didn't want you to say anything to her."

"Of course. I won't say a word. But she's a smart kid, Trina. She already knows something's wrong."

"I know. I'd planned to tell her this weekend, but then, with Jeremiah—"

"Yeah. There's never a good time."

"No, there's not." Trina took both of my hands. "Listen, I have to ask you something. A favor."

"Anything."

"Hear me out before you say that. Look, I'm going to do whatever I need to do to beat this again. You know me, I'll fight with every breath I have. But I'm a practical woman. I'm a coach, and being a coach means being prepared for every eventuality, including losing the game."

"Trina—"

"No, wait. Listen to me. You know I don't get sad about things.

Life is what it is. I had to deal with all of this the last time it happened. I'm not afraid for myself, but I am afraid for Anna. You know how hard it is not having a mom. I worry about her going down the wrong path because I'm not there. So if the worst does happen, I'd like you to be there for her. I need to know she has someone. Not just her father; she needs another woman in her life."

"You know I will. You don't even have to ask."

She squeezed my hands tightly. "Think hard about this, Shelby. I'm not saying be her friend. You're already her friend. This is a very different kind of responsibility. And I know you're likely to have your hands full with Tom."

"Don't worry about that. Don't worry about anything except your fight. Focus on what you need to focus on. I'll always be there for Anna. There's never a question about that."

If I didn't know Trina as well as I did, I would have sworn that I saw tears in her eyes. She didn't say anything more. With a cracked smile of gratitude, she waved me toward Jeremiah's small bedroom. I walked down there, but Trina stayed in the hallway behind me. I understood that she couldn't go inside. I tapped the door gently with my knuckles to alert Anna that I was coming in.

It was a boy's room, painted midnight blue with posters of dinosaurs taped on the walls. The floor was messy with metal race cars and rainbow-colored Legos scattered around like land mines for bare feet. Jeremiah had dirty underwear and socks piled in the corner, and they had the slightly rancid smell of a boy who didn't shower as often as he should. I saw an open can of yellow Wilson shuttlecocks tipped over on his dresser. It was easy to imagine Jeremiah in the campground, whacking one of those shuttlecocks with his badminton racket and chasing after it.

His bed was unmade. He had *Jurassic Park* sheets twisted into knots. Anna sat on the bed with her legs crossed. She had a pile of rocks in a plastic ice cream bucket in front of her that she was

building into a column on top of a hardcover copy of a Rick Rior-
dan book. The rocks were a shiny mixture of flat beach stones, all
smooth as if they'd been polished and rounded by water.

I pulled a plastic chair over toward the bed and sat down in
it. Anna didn't look at me. She kept stacking rocks with a quiet
intensity, choosing them carefully so they went one on top of the
other. The tower in front of her was almost a foot tall. She had a
look about her that said nothing in the world was more important
than what she was doing at that moment.

"Hey, Anna," I said softly.

"Hey, Shelby."

"What are you doing?"

"This is a Karen."

"A what?"

"A Karen. Last fall we went on a field trip. The teacher showed
us how the Indians made Karens in honor of their ancestors by
stacking stones together. Jeremiah and I thought it was cool."

I smiled. "Oh, a *cairn*. Okay. So why are you making a cairn?"

The girl picked up each stone as if it were sacred. "They're for
dead people."

"Are you talking about Jeremiah?"

"Yes."

"Anna, we don't know that Jeremiah is dead. You shouldn't
think that. We all hope he's fine and will be back home really soon."

Anna placed another rock, and she was careful and precise
about it. When she was done, she shook her head. "No, he's dead."

"Why do you think that?"

"He told me."

I glanced at the open door to the bedroom. I wanted to make
sure no one else in the house had come upstairs to hear any of
this. "Jeremiah told you he was dead? How did he do that?"

"He came to visit me when I was sleeping last night. He was

all wet, like he'd been in the rain. He told me that he was dead but that it was okay and I shouldn't feel bad. But I do. So I told him I would make a Karen for him."

"Anna, that was just a dream."

"No, Shelby. I saw him. He's dead."

She lifted one more stone out of the ice cream bucket and put it on top of the others, but her hand began to shake. This time, the tower of stones fell down over the book and onto the sheets. Anna frowned, and her lower lip trembled, but she didn't cry. She picked up all of the rocks and put them back in the bucket, and then she chose two stones and started over.

"In your dream, did Jeremiah tell you what happened to him?"

"No. He didn't talk about that."

"Do you have any idea where he was?"

"In the woods."

"Did you recognize the woods? Was it the national forest?"

Anna shook her head. "I don't know. It was just somewhere in the woods."

"Did you see anyone else? Was anyone with him?"

"No. He was alone, because he was dead. But there was a cross."

"What?"

"A cross. He was standing next to a birch tree, and somebody had carved a big cross in the trunk of the tree, like with a knife or something."

You may think I was crazy to ask her about these things, but there were worse places to look for answers than inside a child's dream. Sometimes that's how they share secrets when the real world is too scary for them. And I've always believed that dreams can carry clues, too. No matter what had happened between them, Anna and Jeremiah had been best friends. If he was going to find a way to send a message through anyone, it was her.

"Thank you for telling me about this, Anna, but how about we keep your dream between us. Okay? Can you do that? I think it would upset people to hear you talking about Jeremiah being dead."

"I understand."

"But it's good that you told me. That's the right thing to do. Remember what I said in the cemetery on Friday? You can tell me anything. It doesn't matter what it is. I'll always protect you no matter what."

Anna put down the stone she was holding. She stared into the bucket of rocks, and then she finally looked up. Our eyes met. "No, Shelby. You can't protect me. He's going to get me."

"What are you talking about? Who's going to get you?"

"The Ursulina."

I reached out and stroked her hair. "Oh, honey. Oh, is that what you think? Anna, the Ursulina isn't real. It's just a story. You shouldn't believe it, and you shouldn't be scared of it."

"No, you're wrong. It's real. It came after Jeremiah, and it got him. And now it's going to come after me next."

"Why do you think that?"

The girl rubbed one of the stones from the cairn between her fingers, but she didn't answer me.

"Anna?"

"I can't say anything about that. It's a secret."

"A secret? What kind of secret? Anna, I really need you to tell me."

"No, I can't. We swore we wouldn't say anything."

My heart started beating a little faster. "Was this a secret between you and Jeremiah?"

"Yes."

"Does this secret have anything to do with why you and Jeremiah aren't friends anymore?"

She bowed her head and nodded.

"Anna, what happened? Please tell me."

But the girl shook her head vigorously and pressed her lips shut.

"Well, can you tell me *when* this happened?"

"It was months ago. I don't know when. The leaves were all over the ground."

The leaves were falling.

Autumn.

I remembered Jeannie Samper telling me that her son Matthew babysat Jeremiah one night the previous fall. And that Matthew had found Jeremiah sitting out on the deck below his bedroom, terrified by something he'd seen.

"Anna, I heard that Jeremiah sneaked out of his room one night last fall. Do you know anything about that?"

Her eyes got wide with surprise, and I knew I was right. We were talking about the same night.

"Where did he go?"

"The woods," she said after a long pause. "He went into the woods behind his house."

"Did you go with him?"

"No! No! I didn't do anything, I swear, I didn't do anything!"

"It's okay. You're not in any trouble. What was Jeremiah doing? Why did he sneak out?"

Her eyes went to the window and then the open closet door, as if to reassure herself there were no monsters to be found.

"To hunt for the Ursulina," she told me, as if it were the most natural thing in the world. "Remember last Halloween? You sang about it. And the man with no leg told that story."

I closed my eyes and felt terrible, because I couldn't help thinking that this was partly my fault. "Yes, I remember."

"Jeremiah said if we found the Ursulina, we'd be famous. But I told him it was too dangerous. He said he didn't care, he was going to find it all by himself."

"And that's what he did?"

"Yes."

"And he didn't tell anyone about it?"

"Just me."

"Okay. Anna, what happened that night? Why was Jeremiah so scared when he got home?"

Anna grabbed a pillow and clutched it to her chest like a stuffed animal. "He was out there, and he saw—he saw—"

I spoke softly. "What did he see, Anna?"

"He saw it. He saw the Ursulina."

A little sigh came out with my breath. "Anna, whatever Jeremiah saw, it wasn't the Ursulina. Believe me. The Ursulina is a myth. It's not real. The stories we told on Halloween, those were just funny things we made up."

"No, Shelby. Jeremiah saw the Ursulina."

"How do you know?"

Anna didn't answer. Now she was crying.

"Anna? It's okay. Tell me. Why are you so sure Jeremiah saw the Ursulina?"

The girl reached out and grabbed my hand. She whispered to me. "Because he saw it kill somebody."

CHAPTER TWENTY-THREE

I went downstairs and found Ellen and Dennis Sloan, who were still with Agent Reed. Jeremiah's parents were shooting silent, hostile stares across the room at each other, as if they were prize fighters on opposite sides of the ring. Since Friday, the stress of losing their son had already begun to split them apart.

I knew I was about to make it worse.

"I'm sorry to interrupt, but Anna Helvik told me something about Jeremiah that may be important."

Ellen studied me with cool surprise. "Anna did?"

"Yes."

"Anna and Jeremiah haven't talked in months."

"I know."

Ellen looked at Agent Reed, as if inquiring whether he was going to allow me to get in the middle of this. As far as Ellen was concerned, I was just a young deputy who'd gotten a job because my father was the sheriff. But Agent Reed gave me the slightest nod, which was the signal to continue.

"Did the two of you know that Jeremiah sneaked out of his bedroom one night last fall?" I asked.

Ellen shook her head to dismiss the idea immediately. "Jeremiah? That's ridiculous. He wouldn't do that."

But Dennis's reaction on the other side of the room was different. He swallowed hard and looked away from his wife. Ellen noticed the uncomfortable expression on his face.

"Dennis?" she said sharply.

"I did know that," he admitted.

"You did? Why didn't you tell me about it?"

"I talked to Jer. He said he wouldn't do it again. I figured we didn't need to make a big thing of it."

"Well, why did he sneak out? What was he doing?"

"It was stupid. It's the kind of thing boys do. He told me he was hunting for the Ursulina. He and Anna were obsessed with it back then, remember?"

"You should have told me," Ellen snapped. "I can't believe you kept this from me."

"I didn't want to worry you."

But I knew that wasn't the real reason, and the real reason had to come out, regardless of the consequences for Dennis and Ellen.

"Mr. Sloan, how did you find out about this?" I asked.

Dennis's flushed face got redder. I could see him thinking: *Does she know?*

"I caught Jer climbing back inside," he replied. He quickly added with exasperation in his voice, "I don't understand why you're asking about this. It was last year. As far as I know, Jeremiah didn't do it again. Believe me, I checked his room every night to be sure. How is any of this going to help you find my son?"

I realized that Agent Reed was right. People lie. They lie about everything. They lie to protect themselves. They lie even when their child's life hangs in the balance.

"Mr. Sloan, I talked to Jeannie Samper. She told me what happened."

Ellen looked at me with angry frustration, but I think she already suspected that I was opening a door that would be better left closed. "Jeannie Samper? From the raptor center? What does she have to do with any of this? Agent Reed, I think we've had just about enough of this nonsense."

But Reed could see the stricken look in Dennis Sloan's eyes. "Mr. Sloan? I think it would be better for all of us if you simply answered Deputy Lake's questions."

Dennis's face was a mixture of shame and rage. "Fine. What do you want to know?"

"Did you ask Jeannie Samper if her son Matthew could babysit for you that night?"

"Yes." His voice was like the crack of a bullet.

"Matthew Samper?" Ellen interrupted. "When was this? Where was I?"

I held up my hands. "Mrs. Sloan, let's just try to get through this, okay? Mr. Sloan, you asked Matthew if he could stay here all night, isn't that right?"

Dennis spat the word at me again. "Yes."

"So you weren't actually home when Jeremiah sneaked out?"

"No."

The realization dawned on Ellen's face, which turned gray as charcoal and just as hot. It's one thing to hear rumors about infidelity. It's another to have the truth thrown at you while your child is missing. I could see the wheels turning in her mind, and then she finally spoke.

"New Orleans, right?" she asked calmly with a cold glance at her husband. "I took Adrian with me on that trip. Is that when it was?"

Dennis hung his head. "Yes."

"Who was it? Breezy? It's always her. You're always running back to her. How long has it been going on, Dennis? How many *years*?"

"Ellen, do we have to do this now?" Dennis pleaded. "What

does it matter who it was? Yes, I was out all night. Yes, I wasn't alone. It has *nothing* to do with Jeremiah."

"Mr. Sloan, I'm sorry," I interrupted, "but we really do need to verify your whereabouts that night."

"Why on earth does that matter?"

I didn't tell him anything more. I waited without explaining. I could see Agent Reed getting impatient with Dennis, too.

"Mr. Sloan, tell us where you were," he barked. "Answer the question."

"Fine. Whatever. I don't know what difference any of this makes. Yes, I was with Belinda Brees."

"In Witch Tree?" I asked.

"No. We went to a hotel in Martin's Point. We spent the night."

Ellen shot to her feet. I knew she wanted to storm away, but she didn't. She needed to hear the rest. She needed to know why this was coming up now.

"When did you get home?" I asked Dennis.

"About ten the next morning. It was Sunday."

"What did Matthew Samper tell you?"

"He said he checked Jeremiah's room about one in the morning, and Jeremiah was gone. He searched the house and found him on our back porch. My son told him he was just out looking at the stars, but Matthew said he didn't think that was true. So I talked to Jeremiah about it. Eventually, he admitted he'd gone out on this crazy expedition to find the Ursulina. I told him he could have gotten hurt and that he was never to do anything like that again. He swore to me he was done. As far as I know, that was that."

"Was Jeremiah frightened when you talked to him?"

"Of course he was. Scared to death."

"Did he say why?"

"He's a little boy. He felt guilty that I'd found him out."

"Is that all?"

"Yes, that's all."

"When was this?"

"Last fall. November."

"What date?"

"I don't remember."

"Mrs. Sloan?" I asked quietly. "Do you remember?"

I could tell that Ellen had already guessed the truth, because she put her hand over her lips with a kind of frozen horror. "My conference was the weekend of the fourteenth." Then she went on, as if we could read each other's minds. "Is that possible, Shelby? Do you really think—?"

"Yes, I do," I replied. "It was November fourteenth. That was the night Colleen Whalen was shot and killed. I think Jeremiah was there. I think he saw it happen."

CHAPTER TWENTY-FOUR

I finally did what I should have done months ago.

I confessed.

We were all gathered in the dark, dank sheriff's office. Me. Dad. Monica. Adam. Violet. Agent Reed. Before we could start talking about what to do next, I told them that I had something to say. And that was when I laid it all out. I told them exactly what had happened on Halloween night during Ursulina Days. How Keith and I went back to his place together. How we talked. How we drank. How we had sex in the old barn with his wife asleep in the main house a quarter-mile away.

The face I didn't want to see as I confessed was my father's, but I had to look at him anyway. He had this sad, sad expression that was like a knife in my heart. I knew he was disappointed in me for what I'd done. The affair with a married man. And worse, concealing it when I knew things that might have changed the direction of a murder investigation. Keith Whalen's marriage hadn't been fine, no matter what he'd told us back then. He'd cheated with me only two weeks before her death. If Colleen knew, if she'd found out, if he'd told her, then he had a motive to kill her.

The next step in the investigation was to question Keith. Not just about Colleen, but about Jeremiah, too. If I was right that Jeremiah had seen Colleen Whalen being killed—if that was what had terrified him the night of November 14—then Jeremiah was a witness to murder, and witnesses were always at risk. The question was what the boy had actually seen. Anna didn't know. Jeremiah hadn't told her *who* the Ursulina was. But Keith was the obvious suspect.

I wasn't going to play a role in the interrogation. I knew that. My father was the natural person to question Keith, but Violet suggested in her usual pointed way that Dad's relationship with *me* had poisoned his involvement in the case. He didn't argue with her. I assumed Agent Reed would take over, but Reed thought a local cop should take the lead.

So that meant Adam would question Keith.

Adam jumped at the chance. He was hungry for an opportunity to prove himself after his drunken voicemail the previous night. Strangely, when I looked at him, I realized that he didn't look like a kid anymore. He wasn't James Dean on his motorcycle. The last couple of days had sobered and matured him. I felt the same way about myself. Maybe that's what happens when you have to confront your mistakes.

We drove to Keith's land, which was located down a dead-end road from the main highway. As the crow flies, we weren't even a mile from where the Sloans lived. It was an easy hike through the forest for a ten-year-old boy. Keith wasn't in the main house, but his car was outside the garage, so I guessed where he was. I led the parade over a shallow hill to Keith's renovated barn.

It was midafternoon under bright sun, a beautiful day and humid enough to make me sweat and make my uniform stick to my skin. I stayed outside alone and listened to the raucous blackbirds while Adam and Agent Reed went inside. I didn't think they would be there long. Once Keith realized that he was a suspect,

I assumed he would ask for a lawyer and shut up. That was the smart thing to do.

But Keith was impulsive and had other ideas. I had only been waiting there for a couple of minutes when Reed returned and waved me toward the barn.

"I thought we agreed I shouldn't be part of this," I said.

"We did, but Whalen doesn't want a lawyer. He wants you. He says he'll talk to us but only if you're there."

I didn't want to do it, but I went inside.

The barn assaulted me with memories, mostly bad ones. I remembered the jazz music playing, although it was silent now and every footstep echoed from the wood floor to the high ceiling. I could hear my guitar and feel the strings under my fingertips as I sang the Ursulina song. I could smell the mustiness of the barn and the peat of the whiskey we drank. I remembered the crackle and ash of the roaring fireplace and the smoke that burned my eyes. There, in front of the fire, was the white sheepskin rug where I'd made my foolish mistake.

Keith sat in a leather recliner, watching me. His eyes said that he knew what I was remembering, and he was remembering the same things. The rest of us took up chairs around him, and Adam sat in the middle like judge and jury. Adam removed his deputy's hat with both hands and carefully placed it next to his chair. He smoothed the sleeves of his uniform and kept his black boots flat on the floor.

"Okay, Shelby's here. Are you willing to talk to us?"

"Why not?" Keith replied. "I don't have anything to hide. I didn't kill my wife. I didn't have anything to do with Jeremiah's disappearance. I'll save you the trouble and repeat what I told you eight months ago. I was at the lake all day. I came home late. It was nearly midnight. I found Colleen dead outside our house. She'd been shot. I called the police. That's all I know."

"Except you told us back then that there were no problems

between you and Colleen. And now Shelby tells us that you and she slept together only two weeks before your wife was killed. That's a pretty important detail to omit."

Keith didn't look surprised that I'd exposed our relationship. I wanted to sink down through the floor of the barn as I watched his face. I'd done the right thing, but I'd also betrayed him.

"Yes, Shelby and I slept together. That was a mistake. My mistake. It was a huge error of judgment on my part, and I take full responsibility for it. It happened one time and never again, but I shouldn't have concealed it from you."

"Was that the only time during your marriage that you were unfaithful?"

"Yes, it was."

"Did you feel guilty about it?"

"Of course, I did."

"Did you tell Colleen what you did?"

I watched Keith hesitate. "No."

"You kept the affair from your wife?"

"Yes."

"Did she suspect?"

"Not that I know of."

"Do you think other people in town suspected something between you and Shelby?"

"I don't know. I don't see how they could."

"Was there chemistry between the two of you? Were you attracted to her?"

Keith's mouth was tight. "Yes. Obviously."

"Was your wife there for the Halloween show?"

"Yes."

"Do you think she could see the attraction?"

"I have no idea."

"Were you acting strangely after the affair?"

"Maybe. I don't know."

"Don't you think your wife knew that something was wrong?"

"I don't know!" Keith retorted again.

He lost control for only a moment, but his outburst was like the ding in a windshield that begins to grow into a crack. Adam knew it, too. He was wearing Keith down with his questions.

"Let's talk about Jeremiah. You told Shelby on Friday that you saw Jeremiah Sloan on your property several times this year. He would come up to the house and the barn."

"That's true."

"Why did he do that?"

"I have no idea."

"But you knew the boy."

"Of course."

"Did you talk to him?"

"Sometimes."

"What did you talk about?"

"Nothing of consequence. He said he was out exploring. I didn't think anything of it."

"Did he mention anything about the Ursulina?"

"The Ursulina?" Keith shot me a puzzled look. "No."

"Did he say anything about being near your house on the night your wife was killed?"

Keith's eyes widened with concern. "No."

"And yet Shelby says you were afraid you would become a suspect in Jeremiah's disappearance."

"Yes, I did say that."

"Why would you be afraid of that if you did nothing wrong?"

"Well, here we are, Adam. Does that answer your question?"

"We're getting a warrant to search your property. What are we going to find when we do that?"

"Nothing."

"Are we going to find Jeremiah?"

"No, that's crazy."

"If the boy's here, it would be better to tell us now."

"I don't know what happened to Jeremiah. I had nothing to do with his disappearance. You can look all you want."

Adam stared down at a folder in his lap. "I reviewed the notes from when we talked after Colleen's murder last fall. Do you still take psychotropic medications in conjunction with PTSD from your military service?"

"Yes."

"Did you take any of those medications on the day your wife was killed?"

"I'm sure I did. I take them every day. I told you that."

"Do you still suffer from night terrors?"

"Yes."

"The leg you lost. Does it hurt? Your back, your neck?"

"Yes."

"In fact, you're in almost constant pain, aren't you?"

"Yes."

"Does that take an emotional toll on you, too?"

"Yes."

I felt as if I were watching the drip-drip-drip of a water torture. Keith was calm, but each question chipped away at his psyche, which wasn't all that strong to begin with. He needed this interview to end. I could see him glance at me in frustration as if I could rescue him from this, but I couldn't.

This would only end with him telling us what he'd done. When I looked into his eyes, I knew he was hiding things. That was the problem I'd had from the beginning. I knew him too well.

Adam shook his head in sympathy. He was Keith's friend now. He scooted his chair closer and leaned forward.

"Look, Keith, I know the burden you're carrying. You went

through hell overseas, physically and emotionally. I get it. I respect it. Like you say, you're in pain every day. All kinds of pain, the kind that the rest of us can't appreciate. Colleen couldn't appreciate it, could she? She didn't understand. She wanted to, but she didn't. And you wanted to be the husband she needed, but you couldn't do that either, could you?"

Keith didn't take his eyes off me. Adam was talking, but Keith was looking at me. Like he needed me to offer him some kind of absolution. I found it hard to stare back at him, but I did. I knew I was the one who could break him, and I had no choice.

I mouthed: *Tell them.*

Then again: *Tell them.*

And he did.

"Okay," Keith murmured, opening up the floodgate. The water came crashing through. "You're right. I couldn't be the husband that Colleen needed. I never could. She was never happy."

"Because of you."

"Yes."

"You had a bad marriage, and it was your fault."

"Yes, it was."

"You blamed yourself for putting your wife through hell, and then you went and cheated on her."

Keith blinked over and over. "Yes, I did."

"That made you feel guilty."

"Of course."

"Did you lose sleep over it? Did you lay awake thinking about it?"

"Yes."

"It was like a constant weight in your gut making you sick."

"Yes, it was."

"So what did you do?"

Keith said nothing. His breathing came faster and faster.

"Did you tell her?" Adam asked.

I saw sweat on Keith's face. He still said nothing, but his emotions began to come apart.

"I think you told her," Adam went on. "Come on, Keith. November fourteenth. You told Colleen what you did. You told her about the affair. You couldn't stand the burden anymore. You couldn't keep the secret. So you told her. Right?"

Keith inhaled and held his breath. The seconds ticked by, and he didn't breathe.

Then he finally spoke.

"Yes, I told her."

I looked away in disgust. With him. With myself. Of course he'd told her. Of course he'd lied about it to me. He'd lied about everything.

"You admit you told her about the affair," Adam went on coldly.

"Yes."

"Was it that day? November fourteenth?"

"Yes."

"The two of you argued."

"Yes."

"She was hurt. Devastated."

"Yes, she was."

"She went to Stanton. You were apart all day."

"That's right."

"And when she came home, you kept arguing, and you lost control, and you shot your wife."

"No, I didn't do that."

"You took the gun—your gun—and you killed her."

"No."

"Did you see Jeremiah? Did you know he was watching?"

"I didn't see him, because I wasn't there."

"When did you find out that he knew what you'd done?"

"I never found out anything like that. That's not the way it happened."

"Keith, you've told us the truth about everything else. Why lie to us now?"

"I didn't kill Colleen!" Keith's voice rose as he denied it again. I couldn't resist staring at him. I had to see his face. "Look, I know you don't believe me. Yes, I had a bad marriage, it was my fault, I cheated on my wife. She was going to leave me and divorce me. All of that's true. But I didn't kill her. It wasn't me. I came home from the lake and found her dead."

Adam shook his head, as if Keith were a child making up a lie. "A burglar shot her? Really? You're sticking with that?"

"It's the truth," he told us, and his eyes begged me to believe him.

But I didn't.

I didn't believe him.

All those months later, I finally accepted what had been in front of me from the beginning.

I'd slept with a man who killed his wife.

CHAPTER TWENTY-FIVE

The next day, we searched under a sky blanketed with clouds. We searched for Jeremiah.

The FBI canvassed Keith's house, barn, and land. Dozens of agents hunted for DNA, blood, hair, fiber, and fingerprints that would tell us whether Jeremiah had been there. They looked for freshly turned earth and the ash of fires that could be sifted for bones. Dogs traveled the land with their noses to the ground, sniffing for the smell of a body buried underground.

Keith limped back and forth throughout the search, wearing a path in the damp grass. Every now and then, he looked at me, and I looked back at him. Whatever feelings we'd had for each other were gone.

We'd cordoned off the road to Keith's house. Beyond the police tape, dozens of people spied on the search. There had been no official announcement, but news of what was going on spread faster than a virus here. The whole town had gotten the word that Keith Whalen was a person of interest in the murder of Colleen Whalen and in the disappearance of Jeremiah Sloan. Ellen and Dennis were among the crowd outside, holding a vigil for their son.

I was still an outcast. I wondered if I'd still have my job soon. My father could only protect me so far. At first, I stayed near the barricade on the dirt road to keep the search area secure, but it was obvious that rumors had spread about me, too, and I heard an undercurrent of nasty gossip with my name on it. Ellen Sloan's stare was icy, as if the loss of her son was my fault. I was upset to think she might not be entirely wrong. If I'd said something earlier, if I'd admitted the affair when we first began investigating Colleen's murder, then maybe things would have turned out differently.

Eventually, I asked one of the other deputies to take my place, and I simply waited on the high fringe of Keith's property to watch the evidence being gathered. The morning passed slowly, and so did half the afternoon. A spitting drizzle made the day miserable. My hair, my face, my uniform were all wet.

Still the FBI swept the land and carried out bags of material to be analyzed in their lab. I wasn't sure if I was more concerned that they would find something or that they would find nothing at all.

Late in the day, my father came and found me on the hill. We hadn't talked since my revelations the day before. I felt sick to my stomach about what he would say. He stood next to me as we observed the search going on below us, and I waited out his silence with desperate impatience.

"Am I fired?" I asked when I couldn't take the tension anymore.

Dad tugged at his mustache. "What do you think? Should I fire you?"

"I don't know."

"Do you want to be fired?"

"No."

"Well, take it easy. You're not fired. I'll have to reprimand you. A formal letter will go in your file. And I think a suspension of some kind is in order. You made a very serious mistake, Shelby.

You concealed important information about a suspect in a murder investigation."

"I know."

"I expect better from you."

"Yes, sir."

"More to the point, you should expect better from yourself."

I didn't reply. I didn't have to. He knew I felt the sting of his words. And he wasn't done with me.

"I'm not going to be sheriff forever, Shelby. We both know that. The next election is in November, and Violet has already suggested that I should step down gracefully. That's what I'm inclined to do. You know I was hoping to be here long enough that you could run to succeed me, but obviously you're not ready for that."

The truth hurt.

"Obviously."

"I love you, Shelby. I'm sorry."

"I love you, too, Dad. Don't be sorry. This was my screwup."

My father walked away down the sloping grass. I watched him go, and I knew I would always remember how he looked at that moment, still in control of his world for a little while.

After he left, I couldn't stay there. I had to go. I turned around and hiked through the long grass until I couldn't see Keith's house or barn anymore. His land went on for many more acres, but the woods took over. I saw a rough trail matted down in the underbrush, and I followed it. I knew where I was. I could keep going for less than a mile and arrive where the Sloans lived. This was the route Jeremiah would have taken, flashlight in hand, on November 14. I'd always thought of him as a shy follower, not a brave kid, but there he was, alone at night, out looking for the Ursulina. Just like I'd done at the same age.

I'd been on this trail many times myself over the years. Sometimes I'd come here alone, sometimes with Rose, sometimes with

Trina and the rest of the Striker girls. I recognized old-growth trees that had been here my whole life. I saw glacial rocks where I used to sit and listen to the birds. If you dug down under the moss, you'd find places where I'd scratched my initials.

Another quarter mile took me to the place we called Black Lake. It was the haunted lake in the valley with the trees sprouting from the water, where we would dare each other to swim after we told scary stories about what was lurking below. The wind scraped low branches across the lake's surface and caused ripples. By the shore, I saw a high boulder we used to climb to jump into the water. I could still hear the echo of our squeals and screams. I climbed the boulder again, like I used to do when I was a kid. It was high enough for you to think you were queen of the world up there. You could see the whole lake edge to edge, and it was really just a large pond, barely a hundred yards across. Part of me thought about taking off my clothes and jumping in the way I had years ago. But I didn't.

Below me, I saw a clearing where we would lay after swimming. You couldn't really call it a beach, because there was no sand, just a few feet of low weeds where we would spread out our towels.

When I looked closely, I saw something in the clearing.

What I saw made me jump down the sheer side of the boulder near the water, almost twisting my ankle in the process. I fought through an overgrown patch of snakeroot and broke into the open, and there they were.

Stones.

Towers of stones.

At least two dozen of them, made from the kind of flat gray rocks I'd seen in a plastic bucket in Jeremiah's bedroom. Some of the towers were only a few inches high; others had tumbled over and lay in piles; others had somehow survived the wind and rain to stay standing a foot or more above the weeds. I knew what these were. These were cairns.

Built for the dead.

I had no doubt that Jeremiah had built them. He'd seen a woman killed on this land, and this was his way of making peace with it. But it wasn't just the stones themselves that caught my eye. Something sparkled in the brush near one of the cairns, as if it had been placed atop the tower and fallen down. It was shiny even under the dark sky and the thick cover of trees. I knelt and stared at it. It was a ring, made of yellow gold, with a single large square-cut diamond mounted in the center.

A wedding ring.

I put on a plastic glove from my pocket and picked up the ring to examine it. There was no inscription. Nothing to identify its former owner. Even so, I knew whose finger it had been taken from. Hurriedly. In the dark. While her dead body was still warm.

When I looked at the still surface of the lake, I also knew what we would find when we searched under the water. The stories of Black Lake hiding something horrible were true.

Colleen Whalen's jewelry had never been stolen by a burglar.

It had been here the whole time.

*

You see, Keith made a mistake.

Panicked people covering up crimes often do.

He'd put all of his wife's jewelry in a plastic bag that night. His expensive dress watch, too. Maybe if he'd disposed of the pieces separately, we wouldn't have found them, but when the FBI dragged the silty, muddy lake bed, they located the plastic bag, filled with water under its loose knot. Everything Keith had removed from their bedroom was still inside.

I imagined him frantically gathering up things that night to make us believe that a thief had killed Colleen. But would a thief leave her diamond ring behind? No. So he ripped it off her finger as he was heading for the woods and must have shoved it carelessly in his pocket. Somewhere on his way to the lake in the darkness, he'd lost the ring. And sometime after that, Jeremiah had found it.

But Colleen's jewelry wasn't the only thing that Keith had hidden to get away with murder and hide his guilt.

He'd put the gun in the bag, too.

The gun that killed her.

With that discovery, we finally had everything we needed to solve Colleen's murder. Dad arrested Keith Whalen and took him away. Soon enough he would be headed to trial and then headed to prison. I was pretty sure that he would never be coming home.

CHAPTER TWENTY-SIX

Looking back, I think of the search for Jeremiah in two phases. The beginning and the end.

I say that with the perspective of time, because like I told you, all of this happened more than ten years ago. I'm no longer the young twenty-five-year old I was then. I didn't know it at the time, but with the arrest of Keith Whalen, the beginning was about to be over. There was never really a middle in this case, just years of nothingness. And the end—well, the end was still a long way into the future.

Six weeks after Jeremiah disappeared, school began again without him. Summer was over. Life was moving on for everyone in town. The FBI had left town three weeks earlier with the case still formally unsolved. There were no more volunteers filling up the motels. The media had long since let the mystery fall out of the headlines. News feeds the beast, and when there's no news to report, the beast moves on to new territory.

It's not like we were going to forget Jeremiah, but there comes a point in every investigation where there are simply no more clues, and no matter how hard you try, you can't create them. You can keep the file open. You can pull it out every few months and read it again and try to think of things you've missed. And then you realize that all you can do is put the file back and wait. Wait for something to happen. Wait for a break in the case that might never come.

I could see all that ahead of us as I sat in the Nowhere Café that September night with Dad, Monica, and Adam. We were finally getting back to our old routines. I was texting Jeannie Samper about my next volunteer shift at the raptor center. Monica was reading spicy excerpts of a romance novel to Moody in his urn. Adam was flipping through the pages of a motorcycle magazine. Dad had his newspaper open to the crossword puzzle.

"A destination for the well-meaning traveler," he announced to the three of us as he twirled a sharpened pencil in his hand. "Four letters. Anyone? Any ideas?"

I was the only one paying attention. "Do you have any of the letters, Dad?"

"I don't."

I thought hard about the clue, but that's the worst way to solve a puzzle. You can't force it, you have to let it come to you. Sooner or later, at the strangest times, the answers would pop into my head, long after they didn't matter anymore.

A destination for the well-meaning traveler. I had nothing.

Dad waited until it was obvious that I couldn't help him, and then he buried himself in the other clues of the crossword again. He looked oddly free. Ever since he'd decided not to run for re-election, a burden had been lifted from him. He no longer had anything to prove. It had been good for his mind, too, without the stress. He was a little sharper. He'd had fewer incidents. All that was good. But I was under no illusions about where this was going, and neither was he.

I saw Breezy behind the counter wielding a knife on a cherry pie. She wandered over to our booth with a slice of pie à la mode for Adam. He hadn't ordered it, but she knew what he liked. She wore a big red button on her jean shirt that read Sheriff Twilley. Adam had been passing them out for weeks.

"On the house," she told him with a wink. "Or is that too much like a bribe now that you're going to be a big shot and all?"

A satisfied grin crept across Adam's face as he cut into the pie with his spoon. "We'll just call it a campaign contribution."

Yes, Adam was going to be my new boss. I'd made my peace with that. Only days after my father announced he was stepping down, Adam had let me know that he was running to replace him. His mother was happy to see him doing something important with his life. Most of us thought he was still too young, but he had the advantage of being the only candidate interested in the position. He'd also courted Violet Roka, and Violet had persuaded the county board to endorse him. So we all knew the job was his. Being young wasn't necessarily a problem. Dad had been young when he got the job, too.

I had a hard time wrapping my head around the idea of Sheriff Twilley, but I hoped he'd grow into it. I had to admit he'd changed over the course of the summer. I hadn't seen him with a drink since he launched his campaign. He'd dialed back the sexual innuendo and flirting with every girl he met, including me. He'd even asked my opinion on a case a couple of times. All in all, this was a new Adam. I guess sometimes the position makes the man.

Was I disappointed that Adam's decision meant I wouldn't be sheriff of Mittel County myself? Not really. I'd never been ambitious in that way. Dad had been hoping to hand the keys to me, but I didn't care. Anyway, I had his health to think about. I had Trina and Anna to think about, too, because Trina wasn't doing well. My life was going to be busy enough.

So you see, we were all moving on.

I listened to the murmur of talk in the diner that night, and I realized I hadn't heard Jeremiah's name once. Not once. That was a first. The talk was about the new school year, the end of the state fair, the end of summer, the grouse hunting season, the announcement that Rose was putting the Rest in Peace up for sale, and the lineup of country concerts at the Indian casino near Stanton.

But not Jeremiah.

Most locals thought they already knew what had happened to Jeremiah. To the police and FBI, the case was still open, but not to the people here. They blamed Keith Whalen. He was guilty. If you murdered your wife, it wasn't a big leap to imagine killing a child to cover it up. You could have surveyed anyone in the diner that night, and they would have told you that Keith had discovered that Jeremiah saw him shoot Colleen. Maybe the boy had confessed it one of the times he'd wandered up to Keith's house. Or maybe Keith had seen the boy and his cairns near Black Lake and asked him why he was building those little towers of stone on his land.

However it happened, Keith found out. So he kidnapped Jeremiah and killed him and hid his body in one of those remote places in the north woods that no one would ever find. Maybe Anna's dream was right and he'd carved a cross on a birch tree near the grave, too.

Jeremiah wasn't coming back. The man who'd killed him was already in jail. The people of Everywhere were ready to put this tragedy behind them and start living their lives again.

But first, Jeremiah had to be avenged.

First, the past had to be erased.

As the four of us sat in the booth at the Nowhere, Monica's phone rang. Her emergency phone. She answered it, her face fell,

and she looked at us with an expression that said we should all
have been expecting this.

"Fire," she said.

*

The flames had already consumed most of Keith's house by the
time we got there. Even from a hundred yards away, I felt the
ferocious heat on my face. Gray smoke billowed against the black
sky, and we had to cover our mouths and noses to keep the poison
out of our lungs. Ash fell around us and floated like snow in the
air. Night turned to day. The crackle of burning wood sounded
like the growl of the Ursulina.

As I watched, the roof of the house caved inward and the
walls bent and collapsed in mountainous showers of sparks. On
the other side of the shallow hill, I saw a second plume of smoke,
where the barn burned, devouring my memories. There was nothing to be done. None of it could be saved. The firefighters used
their water on the surrounding grass and trees to keep the flames
from spreading to the forest. Fortunately, the wind barely moved
that night, and after a while, a light drizzle began to fall, sizzling
into steam as it tamped down the flames.

Six teenagers sat in handcuffs in the back of two of our cruisers. They were all boys from the high school. Adrian Sloan was
among them. We'd caught the kids as they were scrambling to escape the scene. They'd stayed too long to watch their handiwork.
I knew they'd be punished, but I didn't think a judge would be
too harsh with minors, not when one of them had lost a brother.
They'd probably get community service. After a while, their records would be cleared, and we'd all get on with the business of
forgetting that Keith Whalen had ever lived in Everywhere.

I stood there for hours that night, hypnotized by the fire.

Even after it was out, I stayed. We had to make sure it didn't catch again, and I was one of the volunteers who spent the entire night watching over the hot, soggy funeral pyre. When it was safe enough to get close, I walked the perimeter with my flashlight to see if anything had escaped. Any little piece of Keith and Colleen. I did the same at the barn. But the fire had been thorough and consumed everything except a few scorched beams and shards of melted glass.

Was this justice?

All I can tell you is what I believed that night. I believed that Keith lied to me. I believed he murdered his wife and covered it up, and I believed that twelve good men and women would pronounce him guilty. Was it an accident? Was it a crime of passion that got out of control? Was it a burst of rage that bubbled up out of the horrors of his past? Possibly. That was up to the judge and jury, and they could decide how long he would spend behind bars. Either way, he would pay for his crime.

But Jeremiah?

Call me naive if you want, but I wasn't convinced that Keith Whalen had really taken that boy. If he had, we would have found Jeremiah's body hidden under the water of Black Lake, like the evidence of Colleen's murder. But we didn't find him there.

No.

We hadn't solved the mystery yet. We didn't know the truth about Jeremiah. Back then, I wasn't sure we would ever know what really happened.

I remember wandering alone beside the remnants of the fire that night. You could say it's burned into my memory. As I picked my way beside the ruins, I said one word aloud to myself. Just one word. Otherwise, I was quiet, feeling awed by the devastation.

"Hell," I murmured, staring at the scene.

There was plenty in that twisted panorama of destruction to

remind me of hell, but actually, I was thinking about Dad's cross-word puzzle. Like I told you, the answers usually come at the strangest moments, long after you've given up.

Hell.

The destination for a well-meaning traveler was hell. That was the where the road of good intentions usually led us.

PART TWO
THE WELL-MEANING TRAVELER

CHAPTER TWENTY-SEVEN

Anna and I glided on cross-country skis through the fresh bed of snow filling the cemetery trails. She took the lead up and down the hills, and I followed. With each breath, we exhaled clouds of steam. The skeletal branches of the trees cradled the snow and shook wet, cold blasts into our faces as the wind blew. My cheeks felt numb. It was January 22, a bitter and blustery Monday morning, during one of those days-long stretches of winter gray where you wonder if the sun still exists.

Ahead of me, Anna brought herself to a stop halfway down the shallow slope. She leaned on one of her ski poles and stared into the thick of the forest. I pulled up beside her. Among the shaggy pines and flaky white trunks of the young birches stood the massive gnarled body of the famous Mittel County beech tree we called Bartholomew. The tree had survived storms and fires for more than two hundred years. Its roots dug into the ground like fingers, and its many fat arms made it look like a troll that had been turned to stone. If you grew up in Everywhere, you almost certainly paid a visit to Bartholomew on a sixth grade science outing.

Two of Bartholomew's finger-roots had grown apart over the decades to create a deep hollow like a cave. I'd written a song once about Barty's Hollow, one of the songs I played for kids on my guitar during Sunday story time at the library. The chorus went like this:

It's big enough to build a house
But don't you go inside
'Cause wolverines and sleeping bears
Use the cave to hide!

"Think there's a sleeping bear inside?" Anna asked me. She remembered the song, too.

"Could be," I replied. In fact, the hollow made a perfect den, so I wouldn't have been at all surprised to find a black bear sleeping through the winter there.

"Maybe we should check it out," she said. "There could be cubs by now."

"Or we could just let sleeping bears lie."

Anna shrugged. She unhooked a plastic bottle from her belt and squirted cold water into her mouth. We'd been outside for twenty minutes, and the bottle was already partially frozen. I watched her eyes go from Bartholomew to the other trees around him, searching one by one among the birches. She did that wherever we were in the woods. I don't think she realized that I noticed it, but I knew what she was looking for.

A cross.

After all this time, she was still hoping to find Jeremiah.

Anna peeled a red balaclava from her head, letting her blond hair cascade below her shoulders. Her creamy skin had a pink flush from the cold. At twenty years old, she was now a beautiful young woman. She'd grown up tall and lean, with curves to make the rest of us jealous. She had dark eyebrows above pale-blue eyes and a face that looked stolen from a painting. When she smiled, she was the spitting image of her mother, and I felt like Trina was still with me.

But Anna hardly ever smiled.

We weren't even a quarter mile from our destination, but Anna made no effort to push off on her skis. It was like this whenever we came here. When we could see the cemetery grove ahead of us at the base of the hill, she would stop and procrastinate, hoping I would change my mind.

"It's not much farther," I said, although we both knew that.

Anna refused even to look down the hill. She unzipped one of the pockets on her ski jacket and extracted a pack of cigarettes. She lit one and inhaled, and then she held it between two fingers and extended it in my direction, offering me a puff. I shook my head, saying nothing. She knew I didn't smoke. She knew I hated the fact that she did. We played this same game all the time.

"Barty's sick," Anna said, nodding at the tree.

"Oh?"

"Yeah. I met a guy at a bar in Stanton last week. He's a forestry major at the college. He says it's some kind of bark fungus. He showed me photos at his place. Barty might not make it more than two or three more years. Sucks, huh?"

I didn't like to think of Bartholomew toppling over and taking a couple of centuries of Mittel County history with him. Of course, I knew the point of the story wasn't to tell me about Barty's fungus. It was to let me know that she'd been in a bar the previous weekend, met a stranger, and slept with him.

"We should go," I said, not taking the bait.

Anna fluffed her blond hair with both hands. "I don't know why we have to do this all the time."

"We don't do it all the time. We do it on Mother's Day and on January 22."

"Well, Mother's Day is only four months away. Let's wait."

"Come on, Anna."

"I'm cold. It's freezing out here. It's stupid to go at this time of year. I told you I didn't want to come out here."

"This won't take long. Then we can head home."

Anna shook her head, and her jaw hardened with stubborn resistance. "I'm not doing it this time, Shelby. I'm sick of this. You can go by yourself if it means so much to you. Tell her I said hi."

I pulled off my own balaclava, and the wind slapped my face, as if it were mad at me. "Look, go home if you want, but it's been ten years, Anna. Ten years."

"Do you think I don't know that?"

"I know you do. I think that's why you don't want to go. I'm just saying, you'll regret it if you miss this one."

Anna tilted her head and blew smoke toward the trees. "Blah blah blah. God, Shelby, give it a rest, will you? I know you're into the spiritual New Age stuff, but I'm just not, okay? Coming out here doesn't change a thing. If it makes you feel better, great, go for it. But I hate it."

"Okay. If that's how you feel, then go."

Anna threw her cigarette into the snow. Awkwardly, she lifted up her skis and turned around on the trail, forcing me to glide a few steps forward to make room for her. I twisted around to watch her over my shoulder. She settled into the tracks we'd made and with a giant shove on both ski poles, she launched herself toward the crest of the hill, heading back the way we'd come. Her arms and legs pumped. Her loose hair flew behind her. A few seconds later, she slid across the top and vanished.

It was just me and Bartholomew now. I wondered if he really was sick.

I tapped my poles on the slope and let gravity whisk me downhill past the dense trees. A couple of minutes later, I reached the clearing, where I slowed to a stop. It had been a mild winter until recently, melting most of the early season snow, but January had taken us back to the deep freeze. Six inches of fresh snow had covered up some of the flat headstones that we usually saw here. It was like missing old friends. Even so, I relished the peace and silence here. The grove, like the bears, was in hibernation until spring, although a few deer tracks tiptoed through the fresh powder to let me know I wasn't alone.

Trina was buried on the far side of the clearing.

Her headstone was built of pink marble and topped with the sculpture of an angel. With her rosy face and wings, she looked like a fairy caught in the middle of a dance. I skied that way, until the angel was in front of me and Trina was below me in the frozen ground. Her carved name rose over the snow.

"So I'm back."

I never felt strange talking to her as if she could hear me. Anna didn't feel the same way. In all the years we'd been making these visits, Anna had never said a single word to her mother. She'd always stood beside me in frozen silence, her face showing the anger she felt that Trina had left her so young. But until this time, she'd always come with me. This was the first year she'd made good on her threat to turn back and leave me to visit the grave alone.

"My father says hi," I went on.

Then I figured, why lie to the dead?

"Actually, that's not true. I told him I was coming here, but he didn't remember you. Don't feel bad. Most days he still knows me and Monica, but not too many others. He doesn't even recognize Adam anymore. He's still physically healthy, which is a good thing, I guess. I don't know, maybe he's happy, too. I'm the one who can't handle it. It's getting to a point where I don't know how much longer I can do it myself, you know? I still have to work. Friends help out, but there's only so much they can do. I'm putting off the decision, because I don't want to deal with it. I can't even think about it."

I wiped a couple of tears from my face. I thought about what else to tell her. I always gave her an update about her husband.

"Karl changed jobs. He can work remotely now, so he doesn't have to travel as much. That's good. And he's seeing somebody. A woman he met at an IT class he was giving in Stanton. It's been a year now. It seems serious. I didn't tell you last time, because I wasn't sure it was going anywhere, but now, I don't know. He might be ready to move on. He didn't know what you'd think about that, but I told him you'd say it was crazy he waited so long."

The wind blew and swirled a little cloud of snow around the angel's face. I thought that was Trina agreeing with me.

"And Anna," I began.

But I didn't know what to say.

"I'm sorry she's not here. It's still hard for her. She's so lost, Trina. It breaks my heart."

I crouched down in the snow, so I was eye to eye with the angel.

"She hates the woman Karl is seeing, but it's not about her. I've met this woman. She's nice. Anna just can't accept it. She had a huge fight with Karl over the summer, and she left. Took all her stuff and moved out. We didn't know where she was. We were all in a panic. Breezy finally told me she saw her in the bar in Witch Tree with Will Gruder. That girl knows how to pick them, doesn't she? I mean, Will hasn't been much trouble since his brother died, but I wasn't going to let her stay there. I told her she had two choices, move back home or move in with me. So she picked me. She's been living with me and Dad for about three months. At least she has a mission in life now. She wants to find every way humanly possible to push my buttons and make me lose it with her. So far, I haven't, but the ice is getting pretty thin."

I didn't tell her the rest.

I didn't tell her about Anna barely graduating from high school and saying no to college. I didn't tell her about the girl getting fired from four jobs in eighteen months since then. Or about the boys and the bars, one after another. Or about the shoplifting charge in Stanton that I was able to get dropped when I paid the owner back.

Then again, I suppose she knows.

"Anyway, I miss you. I can't believe it's been ten years. Every time I pass your photograph on my dresser, I stop and think it's just not possible that you're gone. I don't know. Life just feels pretty empty at the moment. The thing is, I'm letting you down. That's what really hurts. I promised you I'd be there for Anna, and I can't reach her. I don't know how to get through to her. She's such a great kid, but she's in so much pain, and she shuts me out. She's going off the rails just like you feared, and I can't do anything about it. I could use your help, Trina. That sounds silly, but wow, I could really use your help right now."

She didn't answer, of course.

I laughed a little at myself.

There was nothing more to say, so I told Trina goodbye and said I'd be back on Mother's Day. Then I worked myself around on my skis to head home.

That's when I saw the owl.

He was perched on top of a stone cross on one of the headstones jutting out of the snow. A perfect, serious, white-and-gray snowy owl. We stared at each other like old friends. I hadn't seen one in a long, long time. In fact, it took me a while to remember the last time I'd seen a snowy owl, and I realized it was atop Adam's motorcycle on the day Jeremiah disappeared.

Was it another sign?

Did Trina send it to me?

You don't have to believe that if you don't want to. All I know is, later that same day Jeremiah's ghost came back into my life. And just like it had ten years ago, everything changed.

CHAPTER TWENTY-EIGHT

Winter is traditionally the slow time at the Nowhere Café. Not too many tourists come to Mittel County in January. A few ice fishermen, a few lonely artists, a few naturalists doing research. Otherwise, we have no one to talk to except each other, and we always look up when the bell rings on the diner door to see who's coming in next.

It's slow for the Sheriff's Department, too. We get busy during ice storms when cars and trucks slide off the highway, but sub-zero cold tends to keep people inside and out of trouble. The nights bring out the domestic disturbance calls, but the days can pass without the phone ringing at all.

On that Monday afternoon, Monica and I sat in a booth with my father. He was working intently on one of his puzzles, although he no longer tried to solve the actual clues. About a year ago, he'd started filling the boxes with random words. At least he was still using real words when he did. One of the next warning signs, according to the doctors, would be when he began using nonsense letters.

"Looks like you're almost done with that one, Tom," Breezy said brightly as she topped up our coffee.

She was right. Dad had filled in most of the boxes, and he

beamed when she noticed it. "Why, thank you, young lady. If I am good at one thing in this world, it's crossword puzzles."

Breezy squeezed his shoulder affectionately. She'd been "young lady" to Dad for about nine months. That was what he called all of the women he didn't recognize now. Age didn't matter in his calculations. I was still Shelby. Monica was still Monica. Everyone else in the world was "young lady" or "sir." He didn't know who any of them were.

The doctors in Stanton had told me that my father was in what they called stage five of the disease. We'd been at that plateau for about two years. If you asked him what he'd had for breakfast, he wouldn't have a clue, but he could talk about the details of police cases from decades earlier as if they'd happened the previous day. Maybe, in his mind, they had. He could still bathe and dress himself, and he made it a point to look good, the way he always had. But I wasn't comfortable with him being alone anymore, and the doctors said it was only a matter of time before he moved on to stage six, at which point I would either have to quit my job to take care of him 24/7 or find a facility we could afford. I hated the idea of either option.

Dad put down his pencil. He focused on Monica, who was crocheting a navy-blue scarf that I knew she intended as a present for him. "How's that puppy of yours?" he asked her. "Is he house broken yet? You have to stick with training once you start and be consistent, you know. Firm and consistent. Dogs appreciate that."

Sometimes we couldn't always keep up with the shifting sands of my father's mind.

"Puppy?" Monica asked, looking puzzled.

"Moody! Isn't that what you call him? Malamutes are such beautiful dogs."

Moody, of course, was sitting where he always did, in the flowered urn on the table in front of Monica.

"Oh, he's just fine, Tom, thank you for asking. Of course, puppies have limitless energy. I swear that dog will wear me out."

"I've thought about getting a dog myself," Dad went on. "Shelby loves the idea. It's good for kids to grow up with a dog. But right now, that little girl is so much work that I don't think I could handle a puppy, too."

I wondered how old I was at that moment in his mind. Two? Three?

Dad had a proud, happy look on his face, but then he glanced across the table and focused on me, and there I was, thirty-five years old. He knew me. He recognized me. But his eyes went glassy with confusion as his mind tried to reconcile the impossible contradictions. I couldn't be a toddler who wanted a dog and an adult in my deputy's uniform at the same time.

The confusion made him afraid, and I hated seeing fear on my father's face. Then, as if giving up on things that made no sense to him, he went back to finishing his puzzle.

I got out of the booth, because I couldn't stay there at that moment. Monica patted my arm in sympathy. I followed Breezy back to the lunch counter and sat down in one of the chairs. I'd left my coffee on the table, so Breezy filled another cup for me.

"Sorry, Shel. That's hard."

"Thanks."

"Where's Anna? I mean, it's the anniversary, right? I figured the two of you would be hanging out together."

"I truly have no idea where she is."

"Things aren't so good with you two?"

"Not good at all."

Breezy lowered her voice. "Listen, just so you know, I saw Anna back at the bar in Witch Tree last weekend. She was with Will Gruder again."

"Great. That's just great. Was she drinking?"

"Beer."

I shook my head. "She's underage. I could bust the place."

"I know, but don't do that. I'll talk to the owner and try to get her cut off if she comes in again."

"Is she doing drugs, too?"

"Not that I saw."

"Come on, Breezy, be straight with me."

"I am, Shel. I haven't seen her with drugs. As far as I know, she's clean."

"Thanks." I eyed Breezy, who was as thin as a sapling but had clear, bright eyes. "How about you? Are you still clean?"

She offered a cynical laugh and pulled up her sleeves to show off her bare arms.

"Cleanest I've ever been. Being on food stamps will do that to you. No drugs. No cigarettes. And hey, I've lost ten pounds. This no-money diet really does the trick."

"You need any help?"

"I need plenty of help, but you're not rolling in dough either. I'll be fine. Something will turn up."

Everyone around here knew Breezy had it rough this year. She'd never been flush, but she'd had an emergency appendectomy the previous summer, and the medical bills had cleaned her out. The diner didn't need her for extra shifts during the slow season, and there weren't a lot of ways to make money on the side in January.

Breezy leaned across the counter. She tried to put the best spin she could on my situation with Anna.

"I know you don't want to hear this, but it's actually sweet that she hangs out with Will. Most girls won't do that. I mean, the burns and all."

"It's Will Gruder, Breezy."

"I get it. He's not your favorite person. But you know, he's not dealing anymore. He paid the price in all sorts of ways. Right now he's just kind of pathetic. He blames himself for Vince's death, and he wallows in it. Mostly he drinks in the bar and reads the Bible."

"The Bible? Seriously?"

"Seriously."

"Well, if Anna wants religion, she doesn't need to get it from Will. She can come to church with me and Dad."

I knew I sounded bitter. I was feeling bitter. It was a bad day.

The bell on the diner door jangled, and all of our heads turned like trained dogs. Adam strolled inside, bringing a cold burst of winter air with him. He took off his sheriff's hat and tucked it under his arm, and he used one hand to primp the few remaining brown curls on his head. His hair had thinned over the years, but his waist had gone the other way, bulging as he added twenty more pounds. He greeted people at every table the way a politician does. He said hello to Dad, too, which I appreciated, but Dad simply called him "sir."

Adam joined me at the counter but didn't take a seat immediately. "Is Rose here?"

"Rose? No, I haven't seen her. Why?"

"She called and said she had something she needed to show me."

He slid onto the chair and eyed the morning glory muffins under a glass dome. He checked his phone, found no new messages, and put it faceup on the counter in front of him. I could smell cigar smoke clinging to his uniform the way it usually did. Now that he was the sheriff, no one was going to tell him to stop. He had money, too. His mother had died three years earlier and left him her fortune. I thought he might retire at that point, but he didn't. He was in the second year of his third term as sheriff. People kept voting for him because he was a known quantity, although he wasn't really beloved the way my father had been. And I think Adam knew it.

You can check off all your goals in life, but it doesn't necessarily make you happy. Adam had the job he'd always wanted and the money he'd always anticipated, but something was still missing. The old restless Adam was back. Physically, he'd let himself go since he lost his mother. In addition to putting on weight, he was drinking again. He was back on his motorcycle and driving recklessly when he wasn't on duty. He'd gone through a string of girlfriends. None of them had stayed.

"Did Rose tell you what this was about?" I asked.

"No. She probably wants to sell me one of those new lakeside condos in Martin's Point."

"Yeah, could be."

"Have you seen her recently?"

"A couple of weeks ago. I had her out to see how much our house is worth."

He cocked an eyebrow at me. "You're thinking of selling?"

"I might have to, depending on what happens with Dad."

"Too bad. It's a great place."

That was Adam. He had a hard time seeing past the surface of things. Yes, the house was a great place, but it was so much more than that to me. And the idea of selling it made me sick.

The café door jingled again. This time, Rose Carter stood in the doorway. My childhood best friend. She was prosperous now, like Adam. Ten years in real estate had been much kinder to her than running the Rest in Peace motel. She was thinner thanks to a Nutrisystem diet, she'd grown out her red hair, and she'd traded in her camouflage wardrobe for wool business suits. Sometimes I didn't even recognize her as the same person, but people change.

Rose stood at the entrance of the Nowhere, halfway between in and out. The door was still partially open, and people grumbled at her because of the cold air blowing inside. She had a shoebox cradled in front of her with both hands, held with the kind of tenderness you'd use for a pet who had died. Her face looked like she'd come from a funeral. The others in the diner began to notice her demeanor, and the complaints about the winter breeze died away into an uncomfortable silence.

We all knew there was something in that box.

She walked toward me and Adam with the shoebox out-stretched at the end of her arms. She put it on the counter and took two steps backward away from it, as if it had a kind of dangerous radiation that would seep into her bones. She didn't take off the lid. Adam and I traded glances, and then, with the slightest nervousness, he popped open the top of the shoebox with one hand.

I stood up and leaned over to get a better look at what was inside.

When I did, I couldn't help myself. I gasped.

There are ordinary, unimportant objects in life that wind up filled with enormous meaning because of what they represent. You can feel it. You can feel the sacredness of those things. And that was true of what was in the box. It was old, dirty, and frayed, nothing more than trash, but it was something that all of us in Everywhere had waited ten years to find.

It was a yellow Wilson shuttlecock.

CHAPTER TWENTY-NINE

Adam stared at the shoebox in complete disbelief. He reached inside as if he were going to pick up the shuttlecock, but then he pulled his hand back.

"Where did you get this?" he asked Rose.

She stood silently in the diner, and so Adam asked her again. "Rose? Where did you find this? Where did it come from?"

Others from the diner got up from their tables and began to press around us to look inside, but Adam waved them back. The only one close enough to see inside the box was Breezy, and when she did, she screamed. "Is that from *Jeremiah*?"

The buzz around us immediately intensified, and Adam slapped the cover back on the shoebox. He stood up from the chair and called to the people in the diner. "Everybody quiet, come on, pipe down. Let's get to the bottom of this. Rose? I need you to tell me where this came from."

Rose had to catch her breath, and her voice was low enough that I had to strain to hear her. "I have a listing on the old Mittel Pines Resort, and I was showing the property to a potential buyer."

"The one out near me in Witch Tree?" Breezy asked. "That old wreck?"

Rose nodded. "It's been abandoned for more than twenty years. The county took it over when the owners walked away. I got a call this morning from a Chicago developer. He was in town and asked if I could show him the place. So we went up there."

Adam was anxious for her to get to the point.

"The shuttlecock, Rose."

"Yes, sorry. Well, there are about thirty old cabins at the resort. Most have collapsed, but one of the larger cabins at the back is still mostly intact. Its chimney came down in the past couple of days. When my buyer and I were passing by, I saw something in the rubble, and I went to check it out. That's where I found this. The shuttlecock must have been stuck up in the chimney, and when it collapsed, well, there it was."

"You should have left it there," Adam said. "You should have called me."

"I guess so. Sorry, I didn't really know what to do. All I could think about was Jeremiah."

That's all I could think about, too.

I could imagine the boy whacking the shuttlecock with his racket and chasing it, because that's what boys do. And the birdies were always getting lost. Sometimes they'd get stuck in trees. Or they'd go over a fence. Or maybe, maybe, they would get stuck on the roof of an abandoned cabin. Up in the chimney where no one would see it or rescue it for years.

The diner erupted with whispers. Everyone else was thinking the same thing.

"Hang on, hang on, it might not mean anything at all," Adam insisted, throwing cold water on our dreams. "Let's not get ahead of ourselves. We need to check it out before anyone gets excited. Shelby and I will go up to the resort with Rose and see what we can find."

He was right.

There was nothing yet to tie this shuttlecock to Jeremiah. It might have been stuck up in the cabin chimney for decades, back to a time when the resort was open and families used to come up there on summer holidays to swim, camp, fish, grill steaks, and toast marshmallows over the fire. There were a thousand different children who might have lost it there.

And yet despite those doubts, we knew. We all knew.

Our missing boy had finally sent us a clue.

*

Now that Adam was the sheriff, I had a new partner to patrol the roads of Mittel County with me.

My partner was Adrian Sloan.

Adrian was twenty-six years old, still as bulky and strong as when he played football in high school. He came from two attractive parents, but he wasn't a particularly handsome kid himself. He wore his sandy hair in a flat crew cut. His nose, which he'd broken more than once on the playing field, was like a misshapen meatball. The points on his jutting ears suggested a little Vulcan blood. He didn't smile much, especially when I made jokes like that.

I was a little surprised when he wanted to become a cop, but I guess losing his brother gave him a purpose in life. Adam was reluctant to hire him, but I pushed hard that we should say yes. Adrian had put his teenage mistakes in the past, and if we rejected every cop because they'd done stupid things in high school, we wouldn't have many applicants left. He was solid and serious now. He'd married a sweet girl, and they had a one-year-old. I liked him.

Adrian drove with his hands rigidly in the ten-and-two position, and he didn't take his eyes off the bumper of Adam's car ahead of us. Even for a quiet kid, he was unusually quiet today, which wasn't surprising at all.

"I know this is really hard for you," I said.

He shrugged, although it was hard to tell, because he had no neck.

"You don't have to come along. I can call you if we find any-thing or if we have questions for you."

"I want to be here."

"I know, but if you're going to stay, you have to be a cop and put your emotions aside. Can you really do that?"

Adrian chewed on that thought for a while without answer-ing my question. The snow-covered evergreens flashed by on both sides of the highway. The cruiser was warm from the heat turned on high. "It doesn't make sense," he said finally, as if to prove he was thinking like a cop. "I don't understand how Jer could have gotten to that resort. It's thirty miles from where we lost him."

"Well, remember, this might not be related to him at all. We don't know yet."

"Yeah, but if it is? I don't get it."

"Obviously, someone took him there."

"To some old falling-down resort? Why? Why would they go there?"

"I don't know," I replied, but I could think of several reasons, and none of them was good.

Half an hour after we left the diner, we reached the town of Witch Tree, population 165. It was one of dozens of don't-blink-or-you'll-miss-it towns in Mittel County. The dense forest loomed around the main street, as if waiting impatiently to creep back in and take over the land when the humans went away. We passed the Witch's Brew, a bar and diner with a rough reputation. Then a Lutheran church that doubled as a senior center. A gas station. A car repair garage and parts store. A gun shop. And not much more than that. The few people who called Witch Tree home lived on dirt roads that crept through the woods like vole tracks on a spring lawn.

We followed Adam in the car ahead of us. Rose was in the passenger seat beside him. They turned on one of the dirt roads half a mile past the bar, and I saw a small clearing where tall trees leaned dangerously over the roof of a mobile home. This was Breezy's place. Her mailbox on the road didn't have a number; it simply said, "Breezy." Weeds poked out of the snow around the trailer, and I saw Dudley rusting under the pines near an old shed. The Ford Escort had finally died for good a few years back and never moved again.

The slick, rutted dirt road continued into the trees. Unless you lived along here, you were probably going the wrong way. We drove slowly past the driveways of a few recluses living deep in the forest. A mile later, the road ended at a T-intersection. The left half of the T was really just a long driveway. A warped wooden arrow pointed the way, and the name Gruder was painted on the arrow in black. Will Gruder lived down there. The other direction was marked with a Dead End sign, and there was still a decades-old, barely legible poster for the Mittel Pines Resort sagging next to the road. We were two miles from the abandoned cabins.

"This is pretty close to Will and Vince's place," I murmured.

Adrian frowned. "Yeah."

"Think that means anything?"

"No. No way."

But I wondered if that was just wishful thinking.

"Did you used to come up here?" I asked him.

"Me? No. Why?"

"It was a hangout when I was in school. I came out here with the Striker girls a few times. It was a popular spot for parties. Booze. Drugs. Sex. Whatever."

"Not me," Adrian said.

"Okay. Just curious."

We punched through the snow, following the icy tire tracks of a handful of cars that had come and gone here recently. The dead-end road wound through a series of sharp S-curves, following the ribbon of a frozen creek six feet down the bank below us. The trees on both sides were packed together like soldiers at attention. It was gloomy here even on a sunny day, but the winter gray made it seem like night.

Where the road ended at a turnaround, an old rusted chain was draped across a driveway that was barely wider than our cruiser. Adam parked there. The snow behind the chain was deep, but I could see boot prints, probably from Rose and her prospective buyer. It was hard to imagine anyone coming here and thinking this was the place to invest money. The Mittel Pines Resort had once been a popular summer getaway, but that was when families still enjoyed rustic vacations and there wasn't any competition from the B&Bs in Martin's Point. My father and I had spent a weekend here once when I was about twelve years old, not long before the resort closed for good. I could remember practicing my guitar by the campfire, which must have driven everyone else crazy, because the sound around here carries for miles.

We all got out of our cars. Adam climbed over the chain and led the way, and Rose, Adrian, and I followed behind him. The snow came up to my calves. The four of us walked between the trees and then across a bridge over the frozen creek, until the forest opened up and the ruins of the resort dotted a huge clearing. Most of the old cabins were rotting mounds where moss, weeds, and young trees grew among bowed walls and caved-in roofs. I saw broken doors, shattered windows, frost-covered spiderwebs, and moldy sofas abandoned in the middle of the dead, overgrown brush. Raccoons had made dens here and riddled the snow with paw prints. At least three cabins had been burned by vandals over the years and the wood bore streaks of blackened charcoal and spray-painted graffiti. It was unrecognizable from the place Dad and I had visited so long ago.

Rose pointed. "I found the shuttlecock back there."

I followed the direction of her finger to one of the larger cabins that had fended off some of the ravages of time and nature. The walls were still standing. There were holes in the roof, but it hadn't fallen. The glass of the windows was all gone, and the door hung open, and I could see where the bricks of the chimney had pitched into the weeds. Rose's footprints made a path into the middle of the bricks.

We all went over there, and Adam knelt among the rubble. He squinted and then got up and rubbed his chin and studied the clearing with a frown. This place had the terrible stillness of a battlefield after the guns had gone quiet.

Ten years.

I tried to imagine Jeremiah here. I looked around at the encroaching forest and thought of all the places you could hide a body in these woods. When the ground thawed, we'd bring the dogs, and we'd search.

The open cabin door clung stubbornly to one of its hinges. Rose stayed outside, and the three of us explored the interior. Even in the daylight, under the holes in the roof, we needed flashlights to see. The floor was a mess of glass shards and animal droppings. I saw an old mattress and bed frame that was nothing but stuffing and rusted springs. A toilet and sink had broken off from corroded pipes and toppled over. I examined every square inch of the cabin floor with my flashlight. When I pulled up the mattress, I found the corpses of two dead rats.

Nothing here suggested that Jeremiah had been inside the cabin. Not until Adrian called, "Look at this."

He was at the back wall near a brick fireplace. The floor was wet where snow had blown in through the hole caused by the collapse of the chimney. He squatted near the remnants of a walnut dresser that had collapsed, spilling out its four drawers. Nests had been built inside the drawers by animals over the years. I saw an old laminated resort brochure, with photos of what the place had looked like in its heyday. But there was something else in one of the drawers, too. Adrian highlighted them with his light.

I saw stones.

Gray and black stones. Dozens of them.

Like you'd use in a cairn.

CHAPTER THIRTY

Ellen Sloan arrived at the abandoned resort two hours later. She brought an entourage with her.

I waited to meet her outside the chain at the driveway, and cars rolled up along the dirt road one after another. Ellen and Violet came together in the first sedan. Several aides followed in two other cars. Then half a dozen print and television reporters and photographers brought up the rear in trucks that were equipped for live shots.

The media army looked ready to assault me with questions, but Violet held them back like a publicity veteran, which she was. Ellen approached me alone, wearing a white winter coat that made her look like a snow angel. She had calf-high boots and leather gloves. Her blond hair was tied in a ponytail, and she wore sunglasses. When she took them off, I saw that her eyes were rimmed in red.

"Hello, Shelby."

"Congresswoman."

That had been Ellen's title for the last three years. After Jeremiah's disappearance, she launched a nonprofit organization focused on missing children, and built a statewide reputation lobbying for improvements in child safety laws. When the eighty-year-old Congressman representing our district had finally retired, local leaders—especially Violet—had encouraged Ellen to run for the seat. She had, and she'd won. She'd spent the last three years shut-tling back and forth between Everywhere and Washington, DC. Violet was her chief of staff and legislative director.

"Your husband is already up at the resort with Sheriff Twilley," I informed her.

Ellen's face barely moved. "Ex-husband."

"Yes, of course. Sorry. Adrian's there, too."

"How is he doing?"

"Adrian's a fine officer. You should be proud."

She looked over her shoulder at the press to make sure they were a safe distance away. It had to be a strange life, always mak-ing sure that no one was listening to what you said. "Good. I'm glad to hear it. Adrian took Jeremiah's disappearance very hard, and I was worried about how he would grow up. I was horrified when he was involved in setting the fire at Keith Whalen's house, but it proved to be a turning point for him. He did the wrong thing, he got it out of his system, and he was punished for it. It helped him move on and get his life together."

"I think you're right."

"He says good things about you, too, by the way. He says he's learned a lot from you, Shelby."

"I'm glad."

"How is your father?" I didn't know if Ellen was asking out of genuine concern, or whether that was simply what politicians did with constituents.

"He's declining."

"I'm very sorry. It's a terrible disease."

"Yes, it is."

She put her hands on her hips and looked up the road toward the resort. I could see journalists taking photographs behind us. The news was already online and would be the lead story throughout the state and probably across the country by morning.

"I'm glad I was in the county when this happened. I was able to drop everything to get over here."

"Of course."

"So you really think Jeremiah was taken here?"

"It looks that way, although we can't be totally certain yet."

Ellen shook her head. "Why this place? It's so remote."

"I don't know."

"What about Keith Whalen? Does he have any ties to the resort?"

"Not that we're aware of. But we'll talk to him and see what he says."

Ellen nodded. Her lips were pursed together.

"What about you, Congresswoman?" I asked.

"Me?"

"Do you have any family connections to the resort? Would this place have had any special meaning for Jeremiah?"

Ellen shook her head. "He wasn't even born when it closed. Dennis and I took Adrian up here a couple of times when he was a boy. That's all."

Violet joined us, leaving the gaggle of media behind her. Nothing had changed between us in a decade. Violet was always moving forward, and I was standing still. I probably didn't look much different, wearing the same deputy's uniform, with nothing but a few lines around my eyes and mouth to mark the passage of time. Violet now looked more like Washington than Mittel County, with a cell phone glued to her ear, a Congressional ID on a chain around her neck, and a few streaks of premature silver running through her bobbed hair. She was a Very Important

Woman doing Very Important Things. I didn't doubt that she'd run for office herself someday.

"The press want to go up and take pictures," Violet said without even a hello.

"Adam doesn't want anyone there. We've taped off the whole resort as a potential crime scene."

"Well, I know these media people. If you don't give them something, they'll sneak in. Let one person go up there and shoot some footage and share it with the pool."

"I'll run that by Adam and let you know."

"Congresswoman, they're going to want some kind of statement from you," Violet added. "A short press conference with the sheriff would be best."

"We'll discuss that after I've talked to him," Ellen replied.

"Yes, ma'am. Oh, and I talked to the FBI. Special Agent Reed is in Nebraska working on another matter, but he agreed to be pulled away so that he could supervise this investigation again. He was pleased that there might finally be a break in Jeremiah's case. He'll be here tomorrow."

Ellen nodded. "Excellent."

I was certain that Violet hadn't talked to Adam before calling in the Feds. I was equally certain that Adam wasn't going to be happy about having this case snatched out from under his nose again. The bad blood between Adam and Agent Reed hadn't gone away.

Violet looked at me with the assurance of someone who was used to giving orders. "Agent Reed asked that the local authorities keep the scene secure and not disrupt anything on-site until he arrives with his forensics team. Please convey that message to Sheriff Twilley."

"I will."

"Thank you, Deputy," Violet said, as if we'd just met.

"Of course, Ms. Roka."

I admit there was a little sarcasm in my voice, but Violet let it roll off her back without any change in expression. She headed back to the reporters.

"I'll take you up there now if you'd like, Congresswoman."

"Yes, thank you." Then she added with a smile, "You can call me Ellen, you know. I'm not here because I'm in Congress. I'm here because I'm a mother trying to find my son."

I unhooked the chain from the driveway and let her walk through into the snow. "I appreciate that, Congresswoman."

The two of us walked side by side up the road and across the bridge toward the abandoned resort. Ellen looked at everything around us with a kind of wonder, as if she could feel Jeremiah's presence if she tried hard enough. I understood. This was as close to her son as she'd been in ten years. If we were right, he'd been *here* after he disappeared and after the fruitless search began. We'd finally found the next link in the chain that we'd missed so long ago.

When we arrived at the ruins, Adrian hurried over and wrapped up Ellen in a tight hug. He was a tough, strong cop, but at that moment, he was just a boy with his mother. I gave them space. Not far away, I saw Dennis Sloan talking to Adam, and I joined them. I passed along Violet's message about the FBI, and I saw the flash of anger in Adam's face that I expected. Just for a moment, he was a twenty-eight-year-old hothead again, leaving a drunken message on Agent Reed's phone. Then, with a resigned sigh, he became the sheriff and began barking orders to shut everything down.

Meanwhile, Dennis stared across the overgrown field at his son and his ex-wife. It had been five, maybe six years since he and Ellen finally acknowledged that the split between them was irrevocable and filed for divorce.

I could see regret in his eyes. It was obvious that he still loved her. I guess most cheating husbands don't realize that until it's too late. He was almost fifty now, with his handsome, athletic days behind him. The rumor mill said that he still hung out in the local bars and made passes at the young girls, but his come-ons were mostly pathetic now. He'd quit his job in the national forest years earlier, because he couldn't keep passing the spot where Jeremiah had vanished day after day. Now he ran a landscaping business in the warm season, and he did snow removal during the winters.

Ellen saw him, too, but there wasn't a drop of emotion in her stare. She made no move to come closer or to acknowledge him. He didn't belong to her world anymore.

Dennis zipped up the down vest he was wearing, as if he'd felt a chill. "So what do you think, Shelby? Who brought my son out here?"

"We haven't found any evidence about that yet. Hopefully, the FBI will turn up something when they search."

"Do you think it was Keith Whalen?"

He caught me off guard, and I answered before I could stop myself. "No. I don't."

Dennis didn't look surprised by my honesty. "Me neither. Keith had problems, sure. He had a lot of anger bottled up inside. I could picture him losing it and killing Colleen. But kidnapping my son and murdering him in cold blood? I never believed that Keith was capable of that."

"Neither did I."

"Well, I guess we could both be wrong. People surprise you, right?"

"Yes, they do."

He watched his ex-wife again, who ignored him as if he didn't exist at all. "Ellen always thought Jeremiah was still alive. She never gave up hope."

"But not you?"

"No, not me. I knew he was dead. That was really what split

us up. I'm sure everyone thought it was because of the affairs, but the fact is, Ellen could tell that I didn't have any hope left. She hated that. She needed to believe."

"Why were you so sure?"

"I guess I could feel it. I just knew he wasn't in the world anymore. I even had a dream where Jer came and told me he was dead. I cried, but I was sort of at peace after that. He said he was okay."

I thought about Anna's very similar dream. It was as if Jeremiah had been leaving messages with the people who loved him.

"I suppose you'll be searching the woods," Dennis added.

"Yes. When the snow melts."

"I hope you find him. For Ellen's sake. For closure. She never found any peace the way I did. She still tortures herself about it. I see her on television sometimes at Congressional hearings, and there will be this moment where she's questioning someone and she stops and gets this faraway look. And I know. She's thinking about Jer. She's wondering where he is. So it would be nice if she could stop wondering, you know?"

"Yes, I know. That's what we all want."

"He doesn't have much of a family to come back to," Dennis went on, "but I'd like to bring him home anyway. Jeremiah deserves that."

CHAPTER THIRTY-ONE

Adrian wanted to stay at the scene with his mother, so I took the cruiser myself to drive back to Everywhere. The winter night was already falling fast. I headed off along the slippery curves with my headlights sweeping past the forest above the frozen creek. When I got to the intersection that led toward Witch Tree, I started to turn left, but then I spotted the wooden arrow pointing me toward Will Gruder's house.

I reversed my turn and continued straight.

I'd been to Will's house on police calls several times, but not since the explosion at the meth lab two years earlier. Their lab had been located deep in the forest on hunting land plastered over with No Trespassing signs. It was no wonder that we'd never found it. But the explosion and fire gave it away and torched several acres of wilderness. We'd found Vince dead at the scene and Will burned over 60 percent of his body. He barely survived.

When I parked in the snowy yard, a Doberman tied up on a chain welcomed me with a murderous frenzy of barking. The house wasn't much larger than one of the old resort cabins, but it had a satellite dish pointed at the sky and security cameras mounted near the roof. Heavy-duty electrical cables ran outside, powering a refrigerator and freezer. I saw an enormous wooden cross hung on the front door.

I knocked hard, which only made the dog madder. The door opened a crack, and to my dismay, I saw Anna staring at me from inside.

"What are you doing here, Shelby?" she asked in annoyance. "Are you following me?"

"I'm looking for Will."

"Well, he's not here."

"Where is he?"

"In the hospital in Stanton. He's had joint problems since the fire, you know. Yesterday his knee locked up, and he had to have some kind of injection."

"I'm sorry to hear it."

"No, you're not."

I leaned closer and smelled alcohol on her breath. Hard stuff, not beer. "Am I interrupting a party?"

"There's no one else here."

"So are you going to invite me in?"

"Will wouldn't like it. He doesn't want strangers coming inside."

"Then how about you come outside?"

Anna sighed as if I were making a huge imposition on her life, but she grabbed a coat and joined me in the yard. The Doberman on the chain barked like a madman, but Anna snapped her fingers, and the dog shut up immediately and stiffened to attention. Anna told him to sit, and he did. His eyes followed her closely, waiting for her next command.

"He obviously knows you."

"Sure he does. Plague's a good boy."

"Plague? The dog's name is Plague?"

Anna rolled her eyes. "Vince thought it was funny."

"Well, you're good with animals."

"Better than people."

Anna hadn't zipped up her bubble coat. Underneath, she wore a short-sleeved red T-shirt that left part of her stomach exposed. Her jeans had holes in the knees. I was more concerned with what I saw tucked into her belt. An automatic pistol.

"What the hell are you doing with a gun, Anna?"

She shrugged away my concern. "Some sketchy guys come around here sometimes. People don't always know that Will is out of the business."

"You've been drinking. Alcohol and guns don't mix."

"I had one drink. It's not a big deal."

"Is the gun Will's?"

"No, it's mine."

"You own a gun? Since when?"

"Since last summer. I was having a smoke behind the Witch's Brew, and some guy tried to assault me. That's when I met Will. He taught the guy a lesson. I didn't want to get caught out again, so I got a gun."

"You were assaulted?" I asked, trying to keep my voice down. "And you didn't tell me?"

"Nothing happened. The guy barely touched me before Will took him down. I'm fine."

I took a deep breath and tried not to lose my cool. Anna was always pushing me, as if she *wanted* me to blow up at her, yell at her, ask her what the hell she was doing with her life. But I didn't. Not this time. I tried to channel Trina, who'd always seemed to levitate above the world, never getting upset, always staying in control. Honestly, I don't know how she did it.

"Anna, you keep shutting me out. I want to help you."

"I don't need your help," she snapped back at me. "What, did you have a nice talk with my mom today and she told you to crack the whip? Look, I don't care what you think you are to me, Shelby. Mom, sister, girlfriend, priest, whatever. Right now, you're my landlord and that's all."

The raw pain blew out of this girl like a tornado and nearly swept me away.

"Okay. You're right, we don't have to be close. We don't have to be anything. But as your landlord, I need you to be home tonight. Not here. Got it?"

"I have to take care of Plague."

"Find someone else to do it. Call one of Will's friends at the bar. I need your help with Dad tomorrow. I'm going out early to see Keith Whalen, and then the FBI is coming into town. You need to look after my father. That's part of our deal."

Anna didn't answer. It seemed like everything I said got under her skin.

"Did you hear me, Anna? I need you to do this for me."

"Yes, I heard you. Fine. I'll get someone else to look after the dog. What else do you want, Shelby? Why are you here? I'm cold. I want to go back inside."

"You haven't heard?"

"Heard what?"

I told her about the shuttlecock and the Mittel Pines Resort and Jeremiah. She tried to pretend that the news meant nothing to her, but this time, I was the tornado, and Anna could hardly stay standing. When I was done, she shoved her hands in her pockets and ground her boot into the snow. She covered her hurt badly.

"Do you want to talk about it?" I asked her.

"What is there to say?"

"Jeremiah was your friend."

"Yeah, well, finding an old badminton birdie doesn't bring him back, does it?"

"That's true, but we have another chance to figure out what

really happened to him. He didn't fly to that resort, Anna. It's thirty miles from where he disappeared. Somebody grabbed him off that road and took him here." I added after a pause, "And it wasn't the Ursulina."

"Yeah. I get that. I'm not a kid anymore, Shelby."

"I never said you were."

"Okay, so somebody took him. It sucks, but there are a lot of crappy people in the world."

"I know."

"What do you want with Will, anyway? He didn't have anything to do with it."

"Are you sure?"

"Yes, I'm sure."

"Have you and he talked about it?"

"No, but I know him. He's not what you think."

"You know him now. Or you think you do. Will and Vince were both hard cases, Anna. They were drug dealers. The only thing that put them out of business was the explosion. Ten years ago, they were out on that road selling meth to Adrian. They passed right by where we found Jeremiah's bike. It's not a big leap to think they grabbed him."

"Will wouldn't do that."

"The resort is only a couple of miles from this house. That's a big coincidence."

"So what? Everybody knows about the resort. I've known about it since I was a kid."

"What about Jeremiah? Did he know about it?"

Anna shrugged. "Sure."

"How?"

"I took him there."

"*You* did? Did his parents know?"

"I don't know. Probably not. It was just one time."

"When was this?"

"It was the year before he disappeared. Summer. Mom came out to Witch Tree to meet Breezy for lunch at the bar. I had to go along, because Dad was on the road. That sounded boring, so I asked if Jeremiah could come with and we brought our bikes. When we got here, he and I went off to explore the resort. I'd heard it was a spooky place. I figured it would scare him. And it did."

She smiled at the memory, but then she wiped the smile from her face and looked upset.

"Did he have his badminton racket with him? Could he have lost the shuttlecock back then?"

"No, he didn't."

"Did anything unusual happen while you were there?"

"No. I told Jeremiah it looked like the kind of place where the Ursulina would hide. I said if he was really brave, he ought to spend the night and see if it showed up."

"You said that?"

"It was a joke, Shelby. It's not like he was going to do it."

"Did he talk about the resort after that? Did he ever tell you that he went back there with anyone?"

"No."

"What about you? Did you go back there?"

"Sure. Lots of times. Will and I went out there last summer. We pitched a tent."

"Why?"

"Will said it was haunted. He said maybe we would see some ghosts. He believes in crap like that, same as you. But we didn't see anything. Now are we done, Shelby? It's freezing out here."

"Yes, we're done, but remember what I told you. Be home tonight."

"I heard you the first time."

Anna headed for Will's front door. The Doberman stirred as

she did and began to growl at me again. I turned away, but when I reached the cruiser, I stopped and called to Anna before she went inside.

"Tell me something."

"What?"

"Why Will?"

"What do you mean?"

"Anna, look at yourself. You're a beautiful girl. Why hang out with Will Gruder? Do you love him?"

"No. I don't."

"Then why?"

"Everybody hates him," Anna replied. "I like that."

CHAPTER THIRTY-TWO

I was at my wit's end about Anna, and I needed to talk to some-body. Or I needed a drink. Or both. As I neared Witch Tree, I saw the lights on inside Breezy's trailer. On impulse, I turned into the matted-down snow of her yard and parked behind her beat-up Dodge Durango, which had replaced Dudley. The yard was otherwise empty, so I hoped that meant Breezy was alone and not entertaining. She'd gotten older like the rest of us, but her reputation as Easy Breezy hadn't changed.

She answered immediately when I knocked. Her face showed surprise that it was me on the steps. "Shel."

"Hey, Breezy."

"Everything okay? You don't usually stop in here."

"I was passing by and saw the light. I thought I'd say hi. I don't want to get in your way if you're busy."

"No, it's fine, come in. The only thing you're interrupting is laundry."

She waved me inside. Pop music played on a cheap old boom box. The interior of the mobile home was compact and cluttered. I saw dishes stacked in the kitchenette sink and clean clothes folded in piles on the dinette table and reclining chair. She cleared a spot for me to sit down in the built-in booth. I spotted a couple of old photographs hung on the wall over the sink, including one of the Striker girls after our volleyball victory. We had our arms wrapped around each other's shoulders. We looked very young.

"I've got a couple beers in the fridge. You want one?"

"No thanks, but you go ahead."

"I can afford beer, Shel. Really."

"Well, okay. Sure. Why not?"

Breezy grabbed two cans of Miller Lite from her small refrigerator. She popped both cans and put one in front of me. Then she grabbed a folding chair and sat down, propping her bare feet on the table and leaning back until the chair balanced against the door of the stove. Everything inside the trailer was a tight squeeze.

She wore shorts and a pink spaghetti-strap top. A toe ring with fake jewels shined on her left foot, and a tattoo snaked up her ankle. She wore her hair long and straight the way she always had, but she'd stopped using highlights a while back and let it stay her natural brown. It was loose around her shoulders. Her pockmarked face was winter-pale. She took a swig of beer and then grabbed a remote control and turned down the volume on the boom box so that the music was soft in the background.

We drank together for a few minutes, and Breezy did most of the talking. The air in the trailer was warm, and so was the beer. I hummed along in my head to the song that was playing, "Iris," which had always been one of my favorites. When a T-shirt slipped off Breezy's pile of clean clothes, I folded it and put it back.

"Anything going on with you, Shel?" she asked after a while, because I hadn't said more than two words while we were sitting there.

"I'm just tired."

"Well, you must have had a hell of a day. This whole thing with Jeremiah is something else, huh? After all this time?"

"Yeah."

"Do you know anything more yet?"

"No, it's too early to tell."

Breezy looked at me the way a friend does who's known you for a lot of years. "You sure nothing else is wrong? You don't look so good."

I shrugged. "Anna."

"Ah."

"She was over at Will Gruder's place. We had another argument. Whatever I do, I seem to make things worse between us."

"That's not you, Shel. It's her. You can't fix what that girl's been through. Believe me, it's easy to get screwed up even when you've got two parents. I can't imagine losing your mom as a kid. But hell, why am I telling you that? You never even knew who your mom was. Or your real dad, for that matter."

"Yeah."

"I don't suppose you ever get over that."

"No. You don't. That's why I know what she's going through, feeling angry, feeling abandoned. I thought maybe it would give us some common ground, but it hasn't worked out that way. We were so close when she was a girl, but not now. I can't reach her."

"Well, kids are tough nuts to crack."

"I know."

"You're the best thing in her world. Don't give up. She'll come around."

"I wonder." My eyes drifted to the volleyball team photograph over her shoulder. I was ready to change the subject. "So I saw Violet today. She was up at the resort with Ellen Sloan."

"Yeah, I saw the media parade. I figured she was in town."

"She acted like we hardly knew each other. She kept calling me 'Deputy.'"

"Still the same stuck-up Queen Vi."

"That's her."

Breezy winked. "You know, I can tell you a juicy story if you want. If you can take off your cop's hat for a minute."

"What is it?"

"Vi and I did coke together once in high school."

My mouth fell open. "Are you kidding? Violet?"

"Yeah. In the locker room."

"That's hard to believe. She's such a straight arrow."

"Not always. It wasn't even my idea. It was her stash, not mine."

"And you never told me?"

"We kept you out of it because of your Dad. Nobody else knew. We didn't want to get kicked off the team."

"Where did she get it?"

"I don't know. If you wanted anything back then, it wasn't hard to find. Some things never change. Actually, you want to know the real dirt?"

"What?"

"I hear Ellen had a pretty serious drug problem, too. Pills."

"Who told you that?"

"Dennis."

"You still see him?"

"Oh, I throw him some pity sex now and then. He's not a bad guy. Nothing's really been the same in his world. Losing Jeremiah. Losing Ellen. Leaving his job. I feel sorry for him. Anyway, he swears Ellen was a pill-popper for years. Who knows, maybe she still is."

"Or it could be a man talking crap about his ex."

"Yeah, well, it's hard to say. Vi and Ellen are both pretty tight-assed. I suppose they've got to unwind somehow." Breezy tilted the can to her lips again and then wiped her mouth. "I miss this, you know. You and me dishing."

"Me too."

"We should do it more."

"Yes, we should."

Breezy slapped her chair down on the floor. "Hey, can I tell you something funny? Since we're sharing dirty secrets. I'm not exactly proud of it."

"What?"

"I hooked up with a guy at the Witch's Brew last week. Out-of-towner. He came over here, and we did it, and he snuck out in the middle of the night. Guy left fifty bucks on the table. Can you believe that? He thought I was a hooker."

"Oh, crap."

"Yeah, at first I felt like a slut, but then it made me laugh. It's not like I didn't keep the cash, too. I'll tell you what, it made me think. People always say you should find a way to get paid for doing what you love."

"Breezy. No."

She laughed at me. "Kidding. I'm kidding. I love shocking you, Shel."

I laughed, too. It felt good to laugh. I hadn't done enough of that lately.

We spent the next half hour making jokes the way we had back in high school. I didn't think about Anna or Dad for a while, which was a relief. I only had the one drink, but I was relaxed enough to feel a little bit drunk. We were both grinning like teenagers when we saw headlights spray across the front window of the trailer. I heard the growl of a car engine and tires pushing through the slush outside. Breezy got up and peered through the blinds.

"Well, look at me, all popular tonight."

"Who is it?"

"Adam." She swung open the door, letting in frozen air that brought goosebumps to my skin. She put up her hands in surrender. "Is this a raid, Sheriff? Two cops showing up at my door in one night?"

Adam climbed the steps, making the trailer shake. He had his hat off, and his face was red with cold. He slid off his brown leather gloves and shoved them in his pocket. "I saw Shelby's cruiser. I figured I'd better see what the two of you were up to."

"Girl time," I explained.

"I'm out of beer," Breezy told Adam, "but I've some got whiskey in a cabinet if you want some."

"No. Thanks."

The strain of the day showed in Adam's tired eyes. He rubbed his hands through his messy brown curls. His boots tracked melting snow on the floor. I squeezed over in the built-in booth to give him room to sit down, but he stood awkwardly where he was.

"Do you need anyone up at the resort tonight?" I asked.

"No, I've got it covered."

"Did you say anything to the press?"

"Yeah, Ellen and I made a statement. She said the usual things, hoping this is the break we've waited for, praying for answers, you know the drill."

"Sorry about the FBI."

"I saw it coming."

Breezy put up her feet again and rocked back and forth. "So Jeremiah was over at the Mittel Pines Resort after he disappeared. Wow. You know that means whoever took him had to drive right by my trailer. That's creepy. If I'd looked out the window, I would have seen him go by."

"*Did* you see anyone?" I asked curiously.

"Oh, no."

"No strange cars coming or going?"

"I doubt I'd remember if I did, Shel. I was barely home for days after Jeremiah disappeared. I was putting in double shifts at the diner. Those first few nights, I didn't get back here until midnight. Still, it's weird that the kid was so close to me, and I never knew it. It makes me sad. Like I should have done something to save him."

"Do you remember anything else?"

"Hey, come on, are you kidding? It was ten years ago."

"I know, but what about the Gruders? Do you remember anything about them? It's an interesting coincidence that they live so close to the resort where Jeremiah was taken."

"Well, yeah, but snatching a kid wasn't their thing. Look, Shel, I know you're not happy about Will and Anna, but I can't see those boys doing anything to Jeremiah. Adam, you talked to them, didn't you? Did you see anything weird going on?"

Adam shot me an impatient look. "Shelby and I *both* talked to them at the school that afternoon. They were playing basketball. I can't see them kidnapping Jeremiah, taking him thirty miles to an abandoned resort near their house, and then coming all the way back to Everywhere to shoot some hoops. It doesn't make sense."

He was right. It didn't make sense. And maybe Breezy was right, too. I was just looking for a reason to pry Anna away from Will Gruder.

I stood up from the booth. "Well, I better get home. Monica's hanging out with Dad, and I need to rescue her. Thanks for the girl talk, Breezy."

"Anytime."

"I should go too," Adam said. "Breezy, don't beat yourself up about Jeremiah. There's nothing you could have done."

"Yeah. Thanks."

We opened the trailer door. Old Man Winter waited for us like a ghost with frigid breath. I took one step down into the cold, but then I stopped and turned around as I thought of something else. I was reluctant to ask the question with Adam standing between us, because this was something better shared friend to friend. But I needed to find out anyway.

"Hey, Breezy? Listen, I don't mean to put you on the spot."

"What is it?"

"Well, there were a lot of strangers in town those first few days after Jeremiah disappeared. Media people. Out-of-town cops. Volunteers. They were big tippers over at the diner."

"Yeah. So?"

"So I was wondering if anyone came out to Witch Tree with you after your late shifts."

Breezy didn't react well to what I was implying. She opened her mouth as if to fire something back at me, but then she stopped. Her face pinched into a strange, unhappy expression as she looked back and forth between us. I knew I'd crossed a line by not waiting to talk to her in private. It's one thing to joke about easy sex, it's another to have your friend ask you about it in front of a man. I saw Adam flinch, as if he'd wandered into the middle of a shooting match and figured he'd better duck.

"Why do you care who came home with me? Jeremiah was already gone by then."

"I know, but if someone was out here with you, we should probably talk to them. Just in case they saw anything. Like you said, this is the only road out to the resort."

"Well, there are so many men, Shel," Breezy said sourly. "What makes you think I'd even remember?"

"I'm sorry. Look, I'm not judging you. I would never do that. This is just routine follow-up."

Adam played the good cop, which, of course, made me the bad cop. "We're not trying to pry, but Shelby's right. If you came back here with someone, you should really tell us who it was."

"Really, Adam? You think that's what I should do?"

"He could be a witness and not even know it."

Breezy shook her head. "Well, sorry, the answer is no. I was working late every night, I was tired. Nobody came out here with me. Got it? Now you can both go."

I wanted to say something else to make it right, but for now, there was nothing more to say. I'd made a mistake and offended a friend. Adam put a hand on Breezy's shoulder and thanked her and murmured an apology. Then the two of us tramped down the trailer steps into the snow, and she slammed the door behind us. We stood by our cars as the freezing cold stung our faces.

"That was awkward," I said. "Sorry."

"Yeah."

"I had to ask."

"I know. You were smart to check."

I didn't say anything more. We both got into our cars. I waited while Adam started his engine and drove into the night. I looked at the trailer and thought about going back to the door to confront Breezy again, but all that would do was make things worse.

Even so, I knew the truth. Girlfriends always do.

Breezy was lying.

CHAPTER THIRTY-THREE

I found my father staring into the flames of a roaring fire when I got home. The fireplace took up most of the north wall of the great space in our house, and he'd built it himself brick by brick. There were no lights on in the room, just the fire's orange glow. He sat in a Shaker chair, his back straight, his feet flat on the floor, his hands on his knees. I didn't let him know I was there. I watched from the wide arched doorway and wondered where he was and what he was thinking about.

Monica came up behind me. She was drying her hands on a kitchen towel. She took off her big glasses and wiped away water spots and then repositioned them carefully on her face. The glasses made her eyes look twice their size. She wore the yellow polka-dot apron that I'd given to my father when I was nine years old. It looked ridiculous on him, but on Monica it seemed to fit, even though it was so big that she looked like she was wearing a bed sheet.

"We had spaghetti," she squeaked. At almost sixty years old, she still looked and sounded the way she had my whole life. She was as sweet and perfectly preserved as strawberry jam.

"Did Dad eat?"

"Yes, he needed a little help with it. He wasn't too happy about that."

"His pride hasn't gone away, that's for sure."

"I think I'd feel worse if it had. I did laundry, by the way. I figured you wouldn't be up for it when you got home."

"I don't know what I'd do without you, Monica."

"Oh, please. There's nowhere I'd rather be."

"Is Anna back?"

"No. I haven't seen her."

I tried not to let my frustration show. I had no idea whether Anna would come home at all. She knew I needed her help, but that didn't mean anything to the girl. I thought she might stay out just to spite me.

"Are you hungry?" Monica asked. "There's still some pasta."

"I can heat it up myself. You should go home. You've got a long drive."

"Only if you're sure you don't need anything else."

"I'm sure."

Monica untangled herself from the extra-large apron and handed it to me along with the kitchen towel. She grabbed her winter coat from the hall closet, then retrieved her satchel purse and Moody's flowered urn from the table near our front door. I waved at both of them, and Monica giggled and left. I felt bad that she still had to drive an hour to get home. With me and Dad depending on her, she didn't have much of a life for herself.

I went into the kitchen and heated up a small bowl of pasta and sauce in the microwave and ate it quickly at the table. Then I joined Dad in the great space that had once been the church sanctuary. Sometimes he played music in the evenings, and sometimes he preferred silence. This was a silent night. The crackle of burning wood was enough to occupy him. Even on a January evening under a high ceiling, the fire made the room so hot that I began to sweat. My father didn't seem affected by it at all. His face had the same suntanned glow it always did.

"Hi, Dad," I said as I pulled over a chair and sat down next to him.

"Hello, Shelby. How was your day?"

"Oh, fine." Then I stopped biting my tongue and decided to be honest with him. "Actually, no, that's not true. It was a pretty tough day for all of us. Do you remember Jeremiah Sloan? The boy who disappeared?"

"It was last summer, Shelby. I'm not likely to forget it."

In fact, it had been ten long years, not six months, but I was glad that Dad knew who Jeremiah was. His mind operated like a time machine with a bug in its programming. You couldn't tell where it would carry him next. Whenever my father went traveling, he came out at a different moment of his life. Sometimes the moments were enveloped in fog, and sometimes they were crisp and clear. And you never knew how long any given moment would last.

"Well, it looks like someone took Jeremiah to that old abandoned resort out near Witch Tree. Mittel Pines. We still don't know what happened to him. The FBI is coming back into town to run the search."

"Then I should go out there."

I chose my words carefully. "Adam and I have it under control, Dad. We'll take care of it."

"Even so, they'll want to talk to me."

"Okay, don't worry. I'll arrange it."

But I wouldn't. In the morning, he'd have forgotten our conversation entirely.

"What about the F-150?" he went on with a precision that surprised me. Sometimes details flooded out with perfect recall like that. The past wasn't gone. It was still in his head somewhere, just hidden away in places he couldn't always find. If only we could help him look.

"What do you mean, Dad?"

"Well, the F-150 was abandoned near your namesake lake. That's on the other side of the county from Witch Tree. And yet you still think the truck was connected to the boy's disappearance, don't you?"

"Agent Reed thinks so."

"So why take the truck so far away?"

"I don't know."

"I've always wondered how he got away from the lake," Dad went on, as if he were still Sheriff Tom Ginn. "It's remote out there. How did he get away from that area once he left the truck behind? Did someone pick him up? Did he have another car waiting for him?"

"That's a good question," I said. And it was.

We didn't have many conversations like that anymore, and they never lasted long. I treasured them when we did. For those brief moments, I had my father back, and I remembered the man he was. I wished it could last all night, but the heat began to make me tired. As we sat next to each other, I found myself drifting off, giving in to the exhaustion of the day. I blinked my heavy eyes and tried to stay awake, but it was no use. Eventually, I surrendered to the hypnosis of the fire.

I awoke sometime later with a start. When I checked my watch, I saw that nearly two hours had passed. Dad was exactly where he'd been, still sitting straight up in his Shaker chair, his blue eyes wide awake. The fire was waning, burning down to the last embers.

A footfall landed on the hardwood floor under the archway behind me. I realized that the noise of the front door opening and closing had awakened me. When I turned around, I saw a

vanishing swish of blond hair. A girl disappeared into the shadows, and I heard the squeal of the old wooden steps as she climbed
to her bedroom.

Anna was home.

Suddenly, it felt like a good night.

*

The next morning, early, I drove to Stanton. I left Dad in Anna's
care for the day. I only had time to stop briefly at the Nowhere
Café to fill up my travel mug with coffee and take out a blueberry
muffin for the road. I wanted to talk to Breezy, but she wasn't
there for her morning shift. I still felt bad about the previous
night, and I wanted to make sure we got past it.

The winter gray hung over my drive east, like an old blanket
thrown across the sky. The roads were empty except for the occasional deer hunting for fallen twigs under the snow. I made my
way to the state prison north of Stanton, spent an hour checking
in through the bureaucracy, and then another half hour waiting in
a small conference room with concrete walls.

Eventually, they brought in Keith Whalen.

I hadn't seen him since the trial where I'd testified about our
affair. I wasn't sure how I expected him to look or what I would
feel when I saw him again. His thick brown hair had been cut
short, leaving him without a cowlick to toss back. The lines on
his face were deeper, but he still had the same sad brown eyes. He
was even leaner than he'd been in the past, to the point of being
skinny. Despite our history, not much had changed for me. I still
looked at him like he was my high school English teacher and I
was still eighteen years old.

"Shelby Lake," he said with surprise.

"Hello, Keith."

He took a moment to assess me the way I'd assessed him. "You look good, Shelby. Not very happy, but you look good."

I resented that he could still read me so well. "How are you?"

"You mean, how has prison life suited me for ten years? The days are all the same in here. After a while, you look forward to it being that way. You don't like having the routine disrupted."

"Like by me?"

"No, not you. You're a welcome distraction."

I found myself struggling for words, like this was a cocktail party and I was making small talk. "You've served half your sentence. That's good."

"I don't count the time. It's a waste."

"Do you read a lot? Do you need books? I could send you some."

"It's sweet of you to be concerned for my welfare after all this time," he replied, in a tone that made sure I knew it wasn't sweet at all. "Yes, I read. I write, too. You'll be amused to know that I turned my Ursulina story into a children's book. Isn't that what you told me to do? A publisher actually accepted it, at least until they found out about my circumstances. Then it quickly became 'thanks but no thanks.' Oh, well."

"I'm sorry."

"What do you want, Shelby?" he asked impatiently. "Why are you here? Welcome distraction or not, seeing you is hard for me on all sorts of levels. Partly because you're the reason I'm in here. Partly because I know I'm going to spend the next several months seeing your face again whenever I close my eyes. And it took me years to get you out of my head the first time."

I thought of all the things I could say to that.

Then I said, "I'm not the reason you're in here, Keith."

"No? Well, it doesn't matter. Just tell me what's going on."

"The Mittel Pines Resort," I said, studying his face for a reaction. His expression was blank.

"What about it?"

"Do you know it?"

"It's that old ruin near Witch Tree, right? So what?"

"Have you ever been there?"

"Didn't it close like five hundred years ago? No. I've never been there. What is this about?"

"We think that's where Jeremiah was taken after he was kidnapped."

Keith leaned across the table. I could smell his closeness. "Ah. I see. Is this the part where I break into a nervous sweat because you're so close to finding the body I managed to hide?"

"I don't know. Is it?"

He fired his words at me. "My story hasn't changed, Shelby. I had nothing to do with Jeremiah's disappearance. I don't know what happened to the boy. I was nowhere near the national forest that day. And since you saw me in the cemetery in Everywhere that same afternoon, I don't know how you think I managed to take the boy out to this old resort, kill him, bury him, and then get back to town in time for you to see me visiting my wife's grave."

That was what I'd expected him to say. Honestly, I'd come to this place just to hear those words from his mouth.

"You're right."

"Excuse me?"

"You're right. I don't see how you could have done it. The timing doesn't work."

"Well, doesn't that make me feel better."

"The fact is, I never really thought you were involved in his disappearance."

"That's big of you, Shelby."

"But I have to ask. Is there anything at all you can tell me about Jeremiah? Or about the Mittel Pines Resort? I'm not trying to trick you, Keith. Back then, I know you couldn't say a word, even if you knew more than you were telling us. But now, well, it doesn't really matter, does it? You're already in here. If you can help me, I wish you would."

"I don't owe you anything, Shelby."

"No, you don't."

"Regardless, I can't help you. I don't know a thing."

"Okay."

He waited, and I didn't say anything more.

"Are we done?" he asked. "Is that all?"

"That's all."

Keith stood up. He took a long look at my face, as if he were trying to memorize it. I was about to signal to the guard to take him away, but Keith stopped me by sitting down again. His jaw softened. His hard eyes were suddenly full of emotion.

"I made a mistake back then, Shelby."

"You sure did."

"No. You don't understand. My mistake was to hide the evidence."

"What do you mean?"

"Yes, I took the jewelry. And the gun, too. I threw it all in Black Lake. I admit that. It was a stupid thing to do. But the only reason I did it was to protect myself. I was desperate that night. I panicked. I knew how it would look when the police came and saw Colleen's body and my gun lying next to her. I knew that you'd tell everyone about our affair sooner or later, and then I'd have a motive to go along with a dead wife. I could see all that coming. That's why I tried to make it look like a thief did it. But I didn't kill Colleen."

I got out of the chair and waved to the guard. I wanted Keith out of there right now. I didn't want to hear this. I didn't want to listen to him lie to me again. The guard unlocked the door and came into the room and took Keith by the arm, but Keith resisted long enough to bend over the table.

"You asked if I could help you, Shelby. You asked if I knew anything about Jeremiah. Well, here's what I know. I'm innocent. I didn't murder anyone. Maybe there's no connection between Colleen's death and what happened to that boy. Or maybe you were right all along, and Jeremiah knew who really killed my wife."

CHAPTER THIRTY-FOUR

A cold case like Jeremiah's disappearance never goes completely cold. It was always in my thoughts. We kept a file cabinet in our basement office that contained everything related to the case. Search results. Photographs of evidence. Transcripts of interviews. Plus my personal notes of what had happened in those early days. Every few months, on a slow day or a Sunday afternoon, I would pull it all out and go over everything page by page to see if there was something we'd missed. After Adrian joined the force, we'd often do it together. I think it made him feel closer to his brother.

Sometimes the review left us with new questions, new people to talk to, or new places to search. None of it led to any breakthroughs, but it meant I was often on the phone with Special Agent Bentley Reed to talk about the case. He came back to town several times over the years, including on the one-year and five-year anniversaries of the disappearance, when the national media was revisiting the mystery. A strange thing happened along the way. He and I became friends. We'd have meals together. I told him about my struggles with Dad and Anna. He told me about his wife, his four kids, and his drug-addicted brother. I was pretty sure he didn't tell many other people about him.

When I got back to the sheriff's office later that morning, Reed was there to lead the investigation again, and he kissed me on the cheek. Physically, he hadn't changed much. He was an imposing man, in good shape, and I was willing to bet he could still give younger agents a run for their money at the gym. He'd shaved away his thinning hair and his goatee, probably because it had gone completely gray a while back. He wore a suit and tie, but he'd come prepared for the January weather with a hooded winter coat and North Face boots.

He was still as sharp and focused as ever. We reviewed topographical maps of the area and studied ground and aerial photographs of the ruins at the Mittel Pines Resort. The team laid out a search strategy and grid. Then, while a dozen FBI forensic specialists headed for the resort itself, Reed asked me to drive him back to the original place on the national forest road where Jeremiah had disappeared. He wanted to follow the route the kidnapper would have taken on the way to Witch Tree and see the world through his eyes.

Being Reed's chauffeur again after ten years gave me a feeling of déjà vu. As we drove, I told him about my conversations with Ellen and Dennis Sloan and about Anna taking Jeremiah to the ruins of the resort a few months before the disappearance. I also told him about my visit with Keith Whalen, even though I didn't believe that Keith was telling me the truth about Colleen's murder.

I told him my father's thoughts about the white F-150 too.

"Interesting," Reed replied as we rattled along the dirt road. "I've spent a lot of time thinking about that very same question. I don't see how the driver of the truck could have gotten away from the lake without help. Either someone met him or someone left a car for him. If that's true, there's a witness around here who knows something."

"Or we could be wrong about the truck."

"True. Do you believe that?"

I shrugged my shoulders. It would make the case easier if I believed that, but I didn't. "No, you're right. The truck was wiped down for a reason. It's connected to Jeremiah somehow."

Reed was quiet, looking out the car window at the trees. We were close to the spot. When we got there, I parked, and the two of us climbed out into the bitter cold. The forest was more open in January because the trees were bare, and you could see into the deep stretches of wilderness on both sides. Snow clogged the brush and spilled across the road in windswept ridges. Where there had once been nothing but a bicycle left behind, there was now an unofficial memorial that attracted locals, strangers, and mystery hunters at all times of the year. People came here to look for clues and pray for answers. They always left something behind. There were dozens of white crosses. Stone cairns. Stuffed animals. Flowers that had died with the coming of winter. Hand-written notes with messages of inspiration.

Come home, Jeremiah.
The lights are on for you, Jeremiah.
You're not forgotten, Jeremiah.

During the warmer months, volunteers tried to keep the site clean and well maintained, but the memorial grew forlorn over the winter as weather took its toll. Reed looked up and down the road and into the trees. We'd been here together countless times. Nothing was ever going to change, but you never knew when the ghosts would decide to talk.

Reed shoved his gloved hands into his coat pockets. "If we're right about the F-150 being connected to the crime, that means someone stole the truck in Martin's Point and grabbed Jeremiah right here about two hours later. And now it looks like whoever it was took the boy to the abandoned resort, which is another hour away."

"That's right."

"This resort sounds like a place that most locals know about but most outsiders probably *wouldn't* know about."

"Yes, unless they stayed there when it was open."

Reed nodded. "Okay, that's true. A visitor would remember it, too. On the other hand, the resort was shuttered for more than a decade before Jeremiah disappeared, right? So if our perp stayed there, it was a long time ago. The question is: Why take the boy there? Was there anything personally significant about that location for the kidnapper? It's a long way to go with a victim in the car, and there are plenty of other deserted hiding places closer to where we are. But he chose the resort."

"You think that was his destination all along," I said.

"I think so. It's not a place you come upon by accident. He knew where he was going."

My face was cold. I shivered. I couldn't take my eyes off the collection of crosses pushing out of the snow. We were alone out here, and the wind moaned and rattled the empty branches. Ten years ago, we'd been here in the summer, when the forest was over-flowing with life, full of insects and birds and plants all reaching for the warmth of the sunlight. Now that world was dead until spring.

"The kidnapping had to be a crime of opportunity," I pointed out. "No one could have known that Jeremiah would be out here. Adrian didn't even want him to come along. So the boy couldn't have been a specific target for anyone. He was just in the wrong place at the wrong time."

Reed frowned. "In other words, we're right back where we were when this all started."

"A predator."

"I'm afraid so."

I thought for the millionth time about Jeremiah riding his bike that day. I could almost hear the squeak of the wheels if I listened hard enough. I'd tried for years to think of an explanation for his disappearance that didn't go back to the horrible reality of a monster abducting him, but I always ended up in the same place.

Right here on this dirt road, in a collision of good and evil.

Right here with the Ursulina.

*

The media was waiting for us outside the resort. They surrounded Agent Reed, but he deflected their questions as we passed through the police barrier that was guarded by one of my fellow deputies. We hiked along the resort driveway and across the creek bridge, following the trail of numerous sets of footprints. In the clearing where the ruins of the old cabins were located, the FBI team was hard at work.

They'd already made one discovery. In the toilet located inside the cabin where the shuttlecock had been found, they'd identified remnants of human feces, which had to have been left long after the resort had been shut down and the water turned off. Of course, there was no way to know who had left that evidence behind. The resort had been a magnet for trespassers for twenty years, and no doubt many of them had answered the call of nature while they were here. Like everything else, the samples would go back to the FBI lab for DNA analysis in the weeks ahead.

As the search continued, the afternoon passed slowly in the cold. Darkness began to sink across the clearing. We were all hoping for fast answers, but the FBI never rushed, and that made everyone impatient. I saw Adrian patrolling the fringe of the forest, wearing a wet path into the snow. Seeing his lips move made me think he was talking to himself. Blaming himself.

I went over to make sure he was okay.

"You don't need to hang out here," I told him. "Why don't you go spend time with your parents? I'll call you if we find anything."

"No, I'm staying."

"There's a lot of ground to cover, Adrian. They'll be at this for days."

"I know, but I want to be here. I owe it to Jer."

Adrian reminded me of his father, a big, physical kid who didn't know how to deal with loss. "I've told you this before, but what happened to Jeremiah isn't your fault. You shouldn't feel guilty about it."

"Not feel guilty? Shelby, I told him to go. I was buying *drugs*, and I sent my little brother off by himself."

"Yeah, but you're not the one who took him away."

Adrian simply shook his head and didn't listen to me. I could tell that he didn't want to feel better about himself. I remembered the very first day, the very first moments after the crime, when Ellen Sloan had quietly eviscerated her older son by laying the blame at his feet. I wondered if Ellen had ever taken those words back and forgiven him, but I doubted it. Here we were ten years later, and Adrian was still echoing what his mother had said.

You let him go.

I heard a shout.

"Special Agent Reed, we need you over here," one of the members of the FBI search team called. Through the gray twilight, I saw him signaling to Reed from the opposite side of the clearing. "We've got something."

My heart sank. I had visions of what they'd found, and none of them was good. I ran through the snow, and so did Adrian. We all converged on the site from different directions. Adrian, me, Reed, Adam. The FBI analyst stood outside one of the other cabins, at least fifty yards away from where we'd found the shuttlecock. He held a large plastic bag in his gloved hand. The bag was filled with odd, multicolored objects, but I couldn't identify them at first. Then I realized that the objects were Legos. There were hundreds of them in red, yellow, green, orange, purple, and blue. Some were loose; some had been chained together; others had been built into an army of tiny robots.

"We found these scattered among the debris on the cabin floor," the analyst said. "We may be able to get fingerprints or DNA off the pieces."

I looked at Adrian. "Did Jeremiah have Legos with him that day?"

Adrian reached out to graze the plastic bag with his fingers, but the analyst pulled it out of his reach. "Yeah. He had a tub of Legos in his backpack."

"And the robots?"

"He used to build those all the time."

Agent Reed didn't look happy about the discovery. "Was Jeremiah playing with the Legos before he disappeared? When the two of you were at the ranger station that morning?"

Adrian rubbed his forehead with his thick fingers and tried to remember. "No, Mom got the box to cheer him up because he was so upset about losing our grandfather. He hadn't opened it yet."

Reed frowned, as if this wasn't the answer he wanted to hear. "Did you find anything else?" he asked the analyst on his team.

"Yes, sir. We've got a collection of rocks similar to the ones the sheriff's department found in the other cabin. We're bagging them now."

"How many?"

"There are a lot, sir. Dozens. It looks like they were gathered from the forest and creek bed around here."

I saw another scowl of confusion cross Reed's face. He buried his hands in his coat pockets and wandered away from the group. The wind blew snow across his face. I followed and quickly caught up with him. "Is something wrong?"

"This doesn't add up. How long does it take a kid to build Lego robots like that? How long does it take to gather that many rocks from the forest around here?"

"I don't know. Hours, probably." As I said that, I realized what he was driving at. "Jeremiah was out here for a while."

"Yes. If you ask me, he was here at least a day. Maybe more. But that's not what's bothering me."

"Then what is?"

"Think about it, Shelby."

I did. I tried to imagine Jeremiah here with his toys. Attaching Legos together one after another. Batting his shuttlecock around the resort. Hunting through the trees and ravines and finding rocks he could use in his cairns.

That's when it hit me.

"He was free."

"Exactly. He was free. It doesn't make sense. Abductors don't let kids go off by themselves. What was really going on in this place?"

I studied the ruins in the growing darkness.

We had to be getting closer to the truth, and yet I felt as if we were farther away than we'd ever been from finding the answers. "We just said we were dealing with a predator. A sex crime. But I don't know, is that what this feels like to you? I mean, it looks like Jeremiah was out here *playing*."

CHAPTER THIRTY-FIVE

I got home after dark with a takeout veggie burger and sweet potato fries in a cardboard box from the Nowhere Café. Thumping rap music from Anna's room drowned out every other sound in the house. I was hungry, and I had a headache, and the music made it worse. I called out to my father that I was back, but there's no way he could have heard me, so I sat in the kitchen by myself. We had an open liter of cheap white wine in the refrigerator, and I poured myself a glass.

I don't know how long I sat there. I finished my burger. I dipped my fries in ketchup one at a time as I ate them. I drank the wine, and when I was done, I drank another glass.

Anna still hadn't turned down the music. When I went upstairs, I saw that her door was closed, with a sign hung on the knob that said, Stay Out. Dad's door was closed, too. I went to my bedroom and grabbed my guitar and went back downstairs. I let myself out into the yard and hiked through the path we'd shoveled to our gazebo. I sat inside on one of the wicker chairs, and I turned on a space heater to take the edge off.

I played for a while, picking out tunes and singing. That's the

way I unwind. I did a Simon and Garfunkel song, "Keep the Customer Satisfied," and then I played "Hotel California" until I had
this vision of Don Henley with a sorry look on his face, shaking
his head at me. So I quit. I worked on the chords of a song I'd been
writing, but it wasn't coming together yet. By the time I'd played
for half an hour, the space heater wasn't enough to keep me warm.
I was freezing and my fingers were numb, so I went back inside.

The music shook the house. I couldn't take any more of it. I
went upstairs and pounded on Anna's door, and when she didn't
answer, I opened it anyway, despite the warning to keep out. The
volume inside made me cover my ears. Anna lay on her bed, wearing
a purple T-shirt and shorts and white athletic socks. I was relieved
that she was alone in the bedroom. She was reading the Bible, and
I couldn't remember when I'd ever seen her doing that. I went over
to the speakers on her dresser and yanked out the plug. The sudden
silence was blissful, but the music left a ringing in my ears.

"I think we've had enough of that for tonight."

"Tom didn't mind," she replied in an irritated voice.

"He's a kinder soul than me. Where is he?"

"In his room."

"Did the two of you eat?"

"Yeah, we had eggs. I can cook, remember? You're the one
who can't."

I couldn't argue with that. "I'm going to crash early. It was a
long day. Keep the music off, okay?"

"Whatever."

I nodded at the Bible in her hands. "Light reading?"

"Will said I should see what's in it."

"And what have you found?"

"It's pretty grim. 'Everything is purified with blood. Without
the shedding of blood, there is no forgiveness.'"

"Try some other passages," I suggested.

Anna shrugged. "So did you find him?"

"Who?"

"Jeremiah."

"We found evidence at the resort, but we don't know what happened."

"Oh."

She began reading the Bible again, ignoring me. I felt dismissed. I left and closed the door behind me. I went to my father's room and tapped my knuckles gently on his door. It was still early, but if he'd fallen asleep, I didn't want to wake him. Although I didn't know how anyone could have slept through the music Anna was playing.

There was no answer. I opened the door a crack and peered into the room. The bed was neatly made. The recliner near the window where he usually sat was empty. "Dad? Are you still up? It's Shelby."

I checked the bathroom, but that was empty, too. When I glanced at the dresser, I saw his cell phone. Wherever he was, he didn't have it with him.

I went back downstairs. There was no sign of him in the great space. I knew he wasn't in the backyard, because I'd just been there. I checked the basement, because he still liked to putter in his work room, even though I'd had to take away the power tools for fear he would injure himself. But the basement was dark. No one was there.

My heart began to accelerate. Anxiety tightened around my chest.

"Dad? Dad? Where are you?"

He didn't answer. He wasn't in the house.

I ran upstairs again and threw open Anna's door without knocking. She had headphones on, but I could still hear the blast of music between her ears. She didn't notice me until I went and grabbed the headphones off her head and threw them on the floor.

"Hey!" she shouted at me. "What the hell?"

"Where's my father?"

"I told you, he's in his room."

"No, he's not. He's not in his room. He's not downstairs. He's not anywhere."

"Well, the last time I saw him, he was in his room."

"And I just told you, *he's not there*. Now march your ass downstairs and help me find him."

Anna groaned loudly and followed me back to the ground floor. I rechecked all of the rooms, but I was wasting my time, because I knew he wasn't there. I could feel a huge, sick weight taking shape in my stomach. I went out onto the front porch and shouted into the darkness.

"Dad? Are you out there? It's Shelby. Are you there?"

The winter night was perfectly still. All of the animals and the dead in the cemetery must have heard me, but not my father.

I was shaking from head to toe as I went back inside. Anna stood in the foyer, watching me with her thumbs hooked in the belt loops of her shorts. Her blond hair was messy.

"Where is he?" I demanded.

"I don't know."

"Anna, I told you to watch him. I was counting on you."

"I did watch him. I spent the whole day with him. I made him dinner. He went to his room. I figured he was in for the night."

I clenched my fists and unclenched them. I swallowed down my rage, but it rose back up like a boat on a turbulent sea.

"Did he say anything?" I asked, struggling to keep my voice calm. "Did he talk about going somewhere?"

"No."

"Did anyone come by? Did anyone call?"

"No."

I glanced at the hallway leading past the laundry room to the garage. I had a terrible premonition of what I would find. I ran down there and pushed through the heavy door. The garage was empty, and the door to the outside was open, letting in the cold wind. The Ford Explorer we kept in there was gone. Dad's truck.

"Oh, my God."

He hadn't driven in two years. We'd taken away his license and keys. But I'd been letting Anna drive the truck since she'd been staying with us.

"Where are your keys?"

"What?"

"Your keys, your car keys, where are they?"

I was losing it. Sweat made a film on my skin, and I felt acid in my throat.

"On the kitchen counter," Anna replied. "Chill. I needed to run out and get eggs, remember? You don't keep anything in the fridge."

"*Chill?* Did you just tell me to chill? Don't you understand what's going on here? The truck is gone. My father is gone. Your keys aren't in the kitchen, because he *took* them. How many times have I told you that you can't leave your keys lying around?"

"I forgot. I was busy making dinner. What the hell do you want from me, Shelby?"

"What do I want from you?"

I could feel blood pulsing into my face. I stared at the empty garage, and I thought about Dad out on the roads, with no idea where he was or where he was going, driving off in the middle of a January night. He could be alive or dead by now. He could be hurt. He could be bleeding. He could have pulled off the road and walked into the woods alone and be freezing to death on a trail somewhere. My father. I'd failed him. I'd lost him.

What did I want from Anna?

What did I want from this girl?

I thought about what Trina would do and what Trina would

say, but Trina was gone. I wasn't her. I could never be her. I didn't have the patience of Job. I wasn't a mother. I had no idea what to do with Anna. All I knew is that I had never been so furious at anyone in my entire life. All the emotion I'd bottled up and forced down for months exploded from me like a bomb.

I screamed.

"What do I want, Anna? What do I want? I want you for one single second of your life to think about someone else. I want you to stop being a little bitch and realize that what you do affects other people in this world. I want you to be a human being and find something in that empty heart of yours. Got it? I want you to grow up, Anna! Grow the hell up! And I want you out of my house. I want you to pack your bags and go. Go now. Get away from me. Do you hear me? Do you understand me? I don't want you anywhere near me or my father or this house. Call Will Gruder and have him pick you up, and live with him for all I care, because I am done with you, Anna Helvik. Done. Finished. We are over. Get out of my sight!"

It took me all of one second to regret my outburst.

Oh, damn.

Oh, hell.

What did I just do?

I watched this beautiful twenty-year-old girl, whom I treasured, whom I loved more than life itself, disintegrate before my eyes. I wanted emotion from her, and I got it. She crumbled into pieces. She sobbed.

I tried to apologize. I said it over and over. I'm sorry, I'm sorry, I'm sorry, Anna, I'm sorry, please forgive me, I didn't mean that, I'm upset.

But you can't take the words back once you've said them. They're out there forever. I reached out to take hold of her arm, to hug her, to comfort her, but she twisted violently away from me. Her tears turned to fury. She was speechless with sorrow, humiliation, and rage. She turned and ran away from me up the stairs, and I knew, I knew, she was gone.

She was going to leave just like I'd told her to do, and she wasn't coming back.

And meanwhile, my father was missing.

*

There haven't been many times in my life when I've been a wreck, but that night, I was a wreck. I wasn't able to function. I couldn't drive. I called Adam, who told me he'd come to the house. I called Monica, who was an hour away, but as soon as I told her about Dad, she started getting dressed and getting ready to head back through the winter night to Everywhere. I probably sounded hysterical to them, and I was.

Adam arrived first. I half expected him to use his motorcycle, which he drove on off-hours throughout the winter, but he came in his sheriff's truck. He was out of uniform, and the first thing he did was ask for coffee, because I could smell that he'd been drinking. He didn't look thrilled to be here, but he hugged me and sat me down in the kitchen and tried to keep me calm.

"I've called out every deputy," he assured me, putting his cell phone faceup on the table. "They're all out on the roads, every one of them. I called the boys in Stanton, too, and asked them to give us a hand. Wherever Tom is, we'll find him."

"Did someone look in the sheriff's office? Maybe he'll go there."

"That was the first place I checked."

"I just don't know how his mind works, Adam. He could think it's years ago. He could think he's still working a case somewhere."

"Like I said, we're covering the whole county."

"It's cold. It's practically zero. If he's outside …"

"I know, Shelby. We're doing everything we can."

I stood up again, because sitting down and doing nothing was driving me crazy. "I'm so sorry about this."

"Don't be."

"He wandered off and didn't take his phone. I don't even know if he remembers how to drive. I'm going to have to do something. This is the beginning of the end. I can't let this go on."

"Worry about that tomorrow. For now, let's just focus on finding him and getting him home."

I nodded, because Adam was right. I opened the refrigerator door and closed it. Don't ask me why. I poured myself a cup of coffee and poured it out. I pulled a half-empty garbage bag from under the sink, tied it up, and replaced it with a new one. I had to keep moving and doing something, no matter how useless it was.

Finally, I ran out of power like a wind-up toy. I sat down again.

"Thank you, Adam."

"You don't have to thank me. It's my job. Besides, you and I go back a long way. So do me and Tom."

"Well, this is above and beyond, and I really appreciate it. You're a good sheriff. You know that, right?"

"I'm competent, Shelby. That's about all. Let's not pretend I'm the sheriff Tom was."

"Hey, come on. That's not fair."

Adam took a pack of nicotine gum from his shirt and unwrapped a stick. "It's okay. I'm used to living in other people's shadows. I've been doing it since I was a kid."

"What do you mean?"

He reached into his pocket and found his wallet. He opened it and took out a small photograph of his mother. It was from decades earlier, when she was a young athlete. He had a glossy magazine article folded inside his wallet, too, and he spread it out on my kitchen table. It was from a sports magazine that had done a retrospective on his mother's Olympic career after she'd died. I felt a little bit of kinship with him at that moment, despite all the differences between us. Sooner or later, we all become orphans.

"Just look at everything my mother did," Adam said.

"She was an amazing woman."

"Yes, she was."

"But?" Because I could hear the "but" coming.

"But she also went out of her way to make me feel like a failure my whole life. Nothing was ever good enough for her. I know she didn't mean to be that way. I don't blame her for it. It's just who she was."

I didn't have anything to say to that. I'd known his relationship with his mother was troubled, but I'd never heard him go that far. Adam wasn't the kind of man who typically shared personal things. He picked up the photo of his mother and stared at it, and then he put everything back in his wallet. I noticed that he folded the magazine article with care and made sure the corners of the picture stayed unbent.

"I'm just saying that you're lucky to have a father like Tom, and Tom's lucky to have you."

I nodded. He was right about that, too.

On the table in front of us, Adam's cell phone lit up with a call. I tensed, because the ringing of the phone meant there was news, and all my fears ran through my head in a single instant.

He answered the call and listened. I couldn't read his face. When he hung up, my throat was so dry I couldn't even swallow. "Well?"

"We found him," Adam said, his face breaking into a smile. "He's alive, he's fine."

"Oh, thank God!" Tears of relief began to run down my cheeks. I felt as if my whole body would melt. "Thank God, thank God! Where is he?"

"I'll drive you over there. He's at Shelby Lake."

CHAPTER THIRTY-SIX

Dad sat in his truck at one of the campgrounds near the lake. With clouds hiding the moon, I had trouble seeing the frozen cove in front of us. He was dressed for the cold in his winter coat, winter hat, and boots, and he'd even made coffee and brought his thermos with him. According to the deputy who'd found him, he was sharp and perfectly focused tonight. And yet he had no recollection of coming out here and no memory of how to get home. It was strange, the randomness of the disease. It was as if the wires in his head were loose, sometimes working, sometimes failing.

"Hi, Dad," I said, climbing into the truck next to him.

He reacted as if this situation weren't strange at all. Me showing up at the lake with him in the middle of a January evening. He looked over with a big smile, then reached out and squeezed my shoulder. "Oh, hello, Shelby. I'm so glad to see you."

"What are you doing out here?"

He blinked, as if that were an odd question. "I come here all the time."

I knew that wasn't true. He didn't drive anymore, which

meant he hadn't been here in at least two years. But it made me wonder if he'd been doing this for much of his life, and I never knew about it.

"Why?"

"Well, it's a beautiful spot. My favorite spot in the whole world. Shelby Lake. This is the place that gave me you."

"I know."

"I was thinking, all these years have gone by, and I don't believe I ever asked. Do you like the name I gave you?"

"I do. I love it." Then I realized I was quickly running out of time to ask the things I'd always wanted to ask. "But why not Ginn, Dad?"

"What do you mean?"

"Why Shelby Lake? Why not Shelby Ginn? You were the one who was going to raise me."

"Raising a child doesn't mean you own them. I thought you deserved to be your own person, separate from me. I had visions of you going off and living your life far away and seeing the whole world. I never wanted you to feel as if you were stuck here with me."

"I'm not stuck anywhere. I'm exactly where I want to be."

Dad didn't react or say anything. His eyes were lost in the darkness of the lake.

On most days, I don't think he was aware of what was happening to him. That was probably better. Time played hopscotch in his head, and he simply jumped along with it. Old friends became strangers he called "young lady" or "sir," and he had no knowledge of losing anything. But every now and then, I saw a glimmer of regret as he recognized the horror that was unfolding. He knew that his moments of clarity were growing rare, and he was too proud to say anything about it. He'd watched his parents die of the disease, and he'd always wanted to shelter me from the same thing happening to him. He wanted me to be far away when it took him over. But here I was.

"We should go, Dad. It's late."

"Let's just take five minutes at the lake, okay?"

"Sure. If you like."

We got out of the truck and hiked through the snow of the campground to a bench near the flat sheet of ice, where the lake water was trapped until spring. The wind howled at us, as if angry that anyone was here. I was cold, but my father didn't seem to notice the frigid temperature. He pointed at the narrow gap between the trees where the cove broke out onto the larger area of the lake.

"That's where I had the boat anchored. The owl just came down from the forest. And you told me where you were."

"I guess I did."

He inhaled loudly, swelling his lungs with the winter air. His white mustache looked crusty with frost. "Snow's coming soon. A lot."

"You think so?" I trusted his judgment about that. He'd lived enough seasons here to know what nature was planning.

"Definitely. A big storm. We'll be buried in it soon." He turned his head to look at me. I could barely make out his blue eyes. "Do you know what they say about the deep, deep snow?"

"What?"

"It hides every secret. It covers every sin."

"But only until spring," I pointed out. "The snow always melts."

"Yes, but sometimes that takes a very long time."

I took his hand. "Let's go home, Dad."

But he didn't move. He didn't want to go, and to be honest, neither did I. He was himself again, and neither one of us knew how long the moment would last or how many more moments like that we would have. I think he wanted to make the most of it while he could.

"It was thirty-five years ago, Shelby. On this very day."

"What was?"

"My mother died."

"I'm so sorry, Dad. I didn't know." I felt bad. I knew it had happened in January, but as far as I could recall, he'd never told me the date. I didn't even realize that he remembered it himself.

"It was the worst day of my life. Nothing else comes close. Even losing my father a few months later wasn't the same."

"I understand."

"I had a breakdown after it happened. I had to get away from here. I simply got in my car and drove. I didn't know where I was going. The snow was coming down. It was practically a blizzard and the roads weren't safe, but I didn't care. I can't say I was even aware of the time or the miles passing. Sort of like tonight."

I was still holding his hand, and I squeezed it tight.

"I drove all day," he went on.

"Where did you go?"

"Honestly? I don't know. I wasn't paying attention to signs. I stopped at a campground much like this one and just watched the snow fall. I stayed so long that I got snowed in. I couldn't go anywhere. It was pretty remote, and I hadn't taken anything with me. No coat. No food. I grew a little concerned as night fell. However, as I always say, things happen for a reason. A young policewoman came by on her way home, and she rescued me."

"That was fortunate."

"Yes, it was."

He didn't say anything for a while, as if he were caught

between present and past. The cold got inside my bones and sent a shiver up my spine. Or at least, I blamed it on the cold at that moment, rather than on anything else.

"Dad?" I said when he stayed quiet. "Are you okay?"

"Oh, yes."

"Maybe we should go."

"Yes, we should."

I led him back to the truck through the snow and helped him inside. I got behind the wheel and started the engine, but the warmth did nothing to shake away the trembling I felt. Dad was next to me, but I could feel him slipping away. He was tired, and he was about to time travel again to a new square in some other part of his life.

"This policewoman. Do you remember her name?"

"Policewoman?" he asked. He was already gone.

"Never mind, Dad."

I drove us home through the dark, empty roads. I was relieved that he was safe but anxious about when he would wander away again. Next time we might not find him. Things couldn't go on like this, and the choices I had to make for our future felt painful and close.

I thought about that and so much more on the forty-mile drive home. The same forty miles my father had driven to rescue me when I was a baby.

I thought about the white F-150 that had been abandoned near this same lake.

I thought about Breezy lying to me about being alone after Jeremiah disappeared.

I thought about Anna and the damage I'd done to our relationship.

I thought about Adam and his mother.

I thought about mothers and fathers and orphans.

Most of all, I thought about the strange coincidence that thirty-five years ago, in the middle of the deep, deep snow, Sheriff Tom Ginn met a young policewoman, and nine months later, I was born.

CHAPTER THIRTY-SEVEN

The FBI search continued the next morning at the old resort, but there wasn't anything for me to do there, so I drove to the raptor center in Stanton instead. One of our neighbors agreed to stay with Dad, but that was a temporary solution, and I knew I needed to find a permanent answer soon.

Jeannie Samper had expanded the center with two new buildings over the years. A couple of her larger donors had passed away and left the organization sizable donations in their estates. She wasn't involved in the daily operations as much as in the past. She'd had two hip replacements that limited her mobility, but her oldest son, Matthew, had come back from Northwestern to take over the management of the center. Her husband and three younger kids were involved, as well.

Fewer birds arrived for help during the winter, but I still came over whenever I could to work with the owls and eagles that had permanent homes there and to drink Jeannie's farmers market tea. And, yes, to see Dr. Lucas Nadler, too. He was now the center's primary vet. Our visits hadn't overlapped in several months, but I knew Lucas was on the schedule today.

I arrived while he was giving a presentation to a middle-school class in the newly opened visitor's center. He had Winston, a great horned owl, perched on a leather glove, and he was explaining to thirty rapt twelve-year-olds about the hunting and breeding habits of owls. When he saw me, he gave me a warm smile from the front of the room. Winston's head swiveled on his neck to observe me, too. The owl had white feathers on either side of his beak that looked like Santa Claus whiskers.

I found Jeannie in the gift shop, awaiting the swarm of kids and teachers after the presentation. She wore cheaters pushed down to the end of her nose. She didn't get up from her chair, but I bent down and gave her a hug. I was surrounded by shelves crowded with T-shirts, magnets, DVDs, hats, and stuffed eagles and owls. Visitors to the center typically didn't go home empty-handed.

"Is today your shift, hon? I didn't expect to see you here."

"No, I came by to talk to Lucas about something."

"Ah. Of course. Lucas."

"Yes, Lucas, and don't give me that look."

Jeannie took off her reading glasses and eyed the vet on the other side of the gift-shop windows. I knew what she was going to say. "I still don't understand why the two of you didn't make a go of it."

"We tried," I told her for about the millionth time.

"You tried? You had, what, one dinner?"

"One very nice dinner where we realized that we both had busy lives and no time for romance. So now I have a really good friend instead of an ex-boyfriend."

"Or you could be friends with benefits," Jeannie pointed out. "So what do you need to talk to Lucas about?"

"My father."

"Is there a problem?"

"He wandered off last night. We found him forty miles away."

"Oh, that's not good."

"No, it's not. I have some decisions to make."

"I'm sorry to hear it, hon. I guess you knew this day was coming."

"I did."

Jeannie's youngest, a ten-year-old named Hildy, wandered into the gift shop and interrupted us. She was heavily built like her mother and wore a long-sleeved T-shirt with a close-up photograph of Winston's sober owl face and the slogan, "Hoooo Are You?" Hildy gave her mother a rundown of ticket revenue with all the poise of a corporate vice president. Like the rest of Jeannie's kids, she was basically a genius.

I waited until Hildy was gone, and then I said to Jeannie, "Can I ask you a personal question?"

"Of course. What is it?"

"Do you ever lie to your kids?"

Jeannie laughed. "What, little white lies? Sure. If there's only one Snickers bar left, you better believe I'm telling them we're out."

"Not little lies. Big stuff."

Jeannie's round face turned serious, because she could see I was serious, too. "What did you have in mind?"

"I don't know. Say you'd done something wrong in your past. Would you be honest about it with your kids? Would you tell them?"

"I suppose it depends on what it is, but I'd like to think so. We all make mistakes. I don't want my kids thinking I'm perfect. Not that they'd ever believe that."

"What if it was something that affected them?"

"Like what?"

"I have no idea. Sorry. It's not important."

Jeannie wasn't convinced by my denial. "Is everything okay with you, Shelby? What's on your mind?"

"Nothing. I'm fine."

I was rescued from saying anything more by the arrival of a

crowd of chattering seventh graders in the gift shop. Jeannie was immediately busy at the register. I glanced out the windows of the learning center and saw Lucas and Winston disappearing toward the outdoor shelters for the raptors-in-residence. I waved goodbye to Jeannie and followed them.

By the time I caught up with Lucas, he had the horned owl safely back on his perch inside the screened enclosure. He returned outside and gave me a friendly embrace on the trail. The morning was cold and as gray as ever, but the snow my father had predicted hadn't arrived yet. We were surrounded by the watchful eyes of bald eagles, red-tailed hawks, barn owls, and turkey vultures.

Lucas had hardly changed at all since I first met him. His blond hair was still long and loose, and he still had the most gentle eyes that I'd ever seen. He'd taken over the vet practice in Stanton when Dr. Tim passed away four years earlier, which meant he was on-call pretty much every day of the week. Not that he ever complained. He loved what he did and had the gift of looking at ease wherever he was. That was what came of knowing who you were and being comfortable inside your own skin. The only time I'd ever seen him look out of place was when we met for dinner on our first and only date. Formal surroundings didn't suit either of us. Honestly, neither did dating.

It had been several months since I'd seen him, but we always reconnected as if no time had passed in between. I felt relaxed with Lucas in a way that I hadn't felt with anyone else since Trina died. Maybe it was because neither one of us had any expectations of the other. I didn't see him as a man, and he didn't see me as a woman. Or at least, that's what we pretended.

"How are you, Shelby? It's been ages. It's wonderful to see you."

That was all it took. That was how close to the edge I was. He didn't have to say anything more than that to get me crying. I'd been able to hold it together with Jeannie, but not with Lucas. I broke down. Everything that had happened the previous night overwhelmed me. I stood there with tears running down my face, and Lucas pulled me to his chest and held me until I'd regained some semblance of control.

When I could speak, I told him about my father's disappearance. I knew he'd been through it with his grandfather and could understand. He waited until I was done before he even said a word. He was a good listener.

Eventually, when I'd talked myself out, he said, "But Tom's safe?"

"Yes."

"Okay. Well, that's the main thing."

"I know. I just feel like I'm at a crossroads."

"It sounds like you are."

I slipped my arm through his elbow. We walked on the plowed trails through Jeannie's acreage, ignoring the chill of the winter morning. It was peaceful here under the tall trees.

"What was it like with your grandfather?" I asked him. "How did you deal with it?"

"Well, Grampa Paul was much older when I came back here, and the disease was already further along. He had some lucid stretches, but he spent a lot of time jumping through his past the way Tom's doing now. I'd been hoping to figure out a way to take care of him at home—you know, a combination of myself and in-home nurses—but I realized pretty early on that was going to be impossible. I'd have emergencies where I needed to be out the door immediately and couldn't wait for a caregiver to arrive. I'm sure you're in the same situation."

"Exactly."

"Even live-in care wasn't enough. You can't watch someone 24/7, and Paul was a wanderer. If I went to take a shower or cook a meal or read a book outside, he'd be gone. I'd literally have to lock him in his room at night, and I'd wake up and hear him rattling the doorknob to get out. It was awful. Sometimes I still hear that noise at night. It haunts me."

He looked behind us at the cages where the raptors lived. The cages kept them safe, but a cage was still a cage.

"So finally, I made the decision to put him in that facility in Stanton," Lucas went on. "Believe me, it was one of the hardest things I've ever done. The fact that I didn't have a choice didn't make it easier on either of us."

"Yeah."

"I won't tell you not to feel guilty, Shelby. If it comes down to that for you and Tom, you *will* feel guilty. All you can do is find a way to live with it. And any time you need to talk to someone who knows what you're going through, I'm right here."

"Thanks, Lucas."

"Are you at that point?"

"I don't know," I replied, and I didn't. I had no idea. "Most days, he's functional. I mean, he can do basic life stuff. He has periods where he seems entirely normal, but then he can be gone just like that. If he's going to start disappearing, I need to do something. I don't want him ending up on the side of the river like your grandfather."

Lucas gave a sad little laugh. "You know, Grampa Paul probably preferred it that way. He went peacefully, and he wasn't locked away in some room when he did. That's not so bad. But I hear you. It could have been much worse, and no one wants a loved one to pass away alone."

I checked my watch. "Well, I should go. I appreciate the talk."

"Of course."

"I made an appointment this morning to visit the facility in Stanton where your grandfather was. Just to see what it's like and get some of my questions answered. I'm not looking forward to it."

"Do you want company?"

"Really? Could you do that?"

"There's nothing on my schedule that I can't cancel."

"Well, that would be so helpful. Thank you. It won't take much time, I promise. I have to get back to Everywhere soon. I need to check on the FBI search at the resort."

Lucas gave me a puzzled look. "The FBI are back in town? Did something happen?"

"Haven't you seen the news?"

"No, I hardly ever read the paper or watch television. I usually don't know what's going on in the world. You'd be amazed how little difference it makes to your life on most days."

"Well, it's about Jeremiah Sloan," I told him.

"That boy who vanished years ago? Is there new information in the case?"

"Yes, we found evidence that he was taken to an abandoned resort outside Witch Tree after he disappeared. The FBI is searching the area to see if there's anything that would help us figure out what happened to him."

"You mean, like a body?"

"That's what we're afraid of."

"I'm so sorry." Lucas stared into the trees, and I watched his brow furrow with memories. "Witch Tree. Wow. That takes me back. I don't suppose it's the Mittel Pines Resort, is it?"

"Yes, it is. Why? Do you know it?"

"Sure. I was there for a couple of weeks every summer before we moved away. Grampa Paul used to take me there. That was one of the things I really missed about being in Kansas City. I couldn't visit the resort with him anymore."

"Hang on, your grandfather used to stay at the Mittel Pines Resort?" I repeated, just to make sure I had it right.

"It was his favorite place in the world," Lucas told me. "He loved it out there. He was so upset when it closed. I bet he stayed there practically every summer of his life. I remember sometimes when I was in the facility with him in Stanton, he'd talk about the days we spent there. He'd tell me that when summer came, we really had to go back and stay in the cabins. That was so sad. In his mind, the resort was still open, and I was still a ten-year-old boy."

CHAPTER THIRTY-EIGHT

Lucas and I stood outside the nursing home in Stanton where Paul Nadler had spent the last months of his life. I had an appointment to talk to the administrator about my father, but instead of going inside, I stood on the sidewalk and found myself unable to move. Yes, I was hesitating because I was scared to even think about my dad in a place like that. But I also couldn't get Lucas's story about his grandfather out of my mind.

"Shelby?" Lucas said, when I stayed frozen where I was. "Are you okay?"

"I'm not sure."

"Should we go in?"

"Not yet."

I looked up and down the street that ran past the three-story apartment building. I drove past this location every month when I had errands to run in Stanton, but I'd only stopped here once, after Paul Nadler's body was found by the river. From where we stood, I could see the Oak Street bridge a few blocks away. I thought about Mr. Nadler wandering out of this facility when no one was looking and taking a stroll past the neatly mowed lawns until he reached the bridge. He climbed down the slope and sat underneath the bridge deck, and at some point on that summer Friday, his heart stopped. When the rains came the following night, the river rose up and carried his body away and left him on the grassy bank outside town.

That was what had happened to him.

And yet.

I walked across the street, and Lucas followed me with a puzzled expression on his face. The parking lot of the McDonald's on the corner was crowded. I sat down on a cold bench beside the bus stop and tried to make sense of it.

"Shelby?" Lucas said, trying again. "Do you want to tell me what you're thinking?"

What I was thinking was crazy, but I said it anyway.

"I think your grandfather was the one who took Jeremiah to that resort."

Lucas shook his head. His expression made it clear that he definitely thought I was crazy. "Grampa Paul? Come on, that's impossible."

"Maybe, but hear me out. Over in the national forest, we've got a ten-year-old boy on his bicycle. He misses his grandfather so much that he won't even take off his Sunday suit. And now over here in Stanton, we've got a nice old man with dementia who loved taking his ten-year-old grandson to the Mittel Pines Resort. An old man who wandered away from his nursing home on *the same morning* that Jeremiah disappeared."

I watched Lucas struggle with what I was saying.

"Yeah, it's a weird coincidence, but that's all it is."

"Are you sure?"

"Well, it doesn't make sense, Shelby. Grampa Paul's body was found by the river here in Stanton. Not in Everywhere. Not in Witch Tree. Here in Stanton."

"You're right."

"The national forest where that boy disappeared is more than an hour away from here. And Witch Tree is, what, another hour past that? How on earth did Grampa Paul get there?"

"I don't know."

"I mean, even if he took somebody's car, it doesn't add up. You're saying he drove to Everywhere, picked up Jeremiah, went out to this resort, came back to Stanton, dropped off the car that apparently nobody realized was gone, and *then* went walking by the river, had a heart attack, and was carried away by the current? Doesn't that sound absurd?"

"Yes, it does."

"Plus, if Grampa Paul really was the one who picked him up, what happened to Jeremiah? I hope you're not suggesting that my grandfather harmed that boy. Because he didn't, Shelby. He would never, ever hurt a child. He was the nicest man I've ever known."

"I'm sure he was, Lucas."

"Then how do you explain Jeremiah never turning up?"

"I can't."

"Well, see? There's no way it happened like that. No way."

I was ready to agree with him, because everything he said was true. My theory didn't make sense. It left me with too many questions that seemingly had no answers. And yet I couldn't give it up for one simple reason.

I was right.

I knew I was right. I knew it had happened exactly that way. Paul Nadler took Jeremiah Sloan to the Mittel Pines Resort. I didn't know what happened next, but I was sure that somehow their two lives had intersected that day in the national forest.

As if to prove I wasn't really crazy, the universe took that moment to send me a sign. A real sign that helped explain everything.

We sat on the bench across from the nursing home, and a

regional bus rumbled toward us from the center of town, the way it did every hour of every day, serving Stanton and Mittel Counties. I saw it coming, and I looked at the destination on the electronic sign on the front of the bus.

It said Martin's Point.

I got up immediately and flagged the driver to stop. "Want to take a ride?" I said to Lucas.

"Why?"

"Because that's what your grandfather did."

Lucas didn't argue with me. The two of us got on the bus. Ten years ago, I was sure Paul Nadler had done the same thing. He'd walked out of the retirement home and crossed the street just as the Martin's Point bus was pulling up to the stop. He'd climbed the steps, probably said a polite hello as he paid the driver, and taken a seat. He was dressed impeccably in his blazer, checked shirt, tan slacks, and wing tips. No one looking at him would have given him a second thought or wondered if this old man wasn't where he was supposed to be.

Lucas and I had no trouble finding a seat. In summer, the bus would have been crowded, but not in January. We made a handful of stops in other towns as we made a zigzag route south, leaving Stanton County behind and crossing into the lower half of Mittel County. I saw the city limits sign as we neared Martin's Point. The road descends as you drive into town, and below us, I could see the huge swath of white marking the lake that was frozen from shore to shore. Lake homes dotted the breaks in the bare trees. We rumbled along the main street past shops and inns that were mostly shuttered for the winter. When the bus pulled to the curb, I said to Lucas, "This is our stop."

"Is it?"

"Oh, yeah."

We got out of the bus and let it pull away in front of us.

When it did, we were immediately across the street from Bonnie Butterfield's ice cream parlor. Unlike many of the other Martin's Point shops, Bonnie kept her store open year-round, because people here eat ice cream no matter how cold it gets outside.

"I know this was a long time ago," I said to Lucas, "but do you remember what kind of car your grandfather used to drive? Back when he would take you out to the resort on summer vacations?"

Lucas thought about it. "A white pickup, I think."

I pointed down the block. "Like that one?"

He followed the direction of my finger, and his eyes widened in surprise, as if I were a magician performing a trick. I realized he was beginning to think I might not be crazy after all. "Yes, just like that one."

Ten years later, Bonnie Butterfield still owned a white F-150, parked in the same place where she'd always kept it, half a block away from her shop. I wondered if she still left her keys inside. I imagined Paul Nadler getting off the bus from Stanton and seeing that truck. It was *his* truck, or at least that was what his mind told him. Mr. Nadler got in that white F-150 and headed off for the Mittel Pines Resort, where he'd spent some of his happiest days with his grandson.

But you know, every dirt road looks like every other one around here, and it's easy for an old man to get confused. I was pretty sure Mr. Nadler had made a wrong turn on his way to Witch Tree and wound up on the dead-end road that leads into the national forest.

That was where he met Jeremiah.

CHAPTER THIRTY-NINE

Dad was right about the snow coming. As I made the long drive back to Everywhere late that afternoon, it began to fall, like sand tapping across my windshield. Soon a thin white layer covered the highway, and my tires kicked up a cloud that I could see behind me in the mirror. I drove carefully to avoid slipping off the road.

Darkness was already setting in as I arrived in town. Everywhere looked like a fairy land, covered in swirling snow and lit up with the Christmas lights that we kept on through most of the winter. I parked outside the Carnegie Library. Across the street, I could see the early bird crowd at the Nowhere Café. The evening special was Swedish meatballs, and the lingonberry sauce was famous. I could see several members of the FBI team filling the booths, but not Agent Reed. He was waiting for me in the sheriff's office.

I climbed the concrete steps that fronted the century-old library building and let myself inside through the massive oak doors between two Corinthian columns. The stairs to the basement were on my left. I was about to head down to the sheriff's office when I heard a voice call to me from the darkness of the library.

"Shelby, over here."

It was Agent Reed. The library was closed, but he was wandering among the shelves and lighting up the spines of the books with his phone. I do that sometimes at night, too, if I'm working late. There's something about being alone with all those books that makes you think the characters will come to life.

Reed had a book in his hand, which he returned to the shelf. "You know, I've never asked you, Shelby. Why is the sheriff's office in the basement? It seems like a strange location even for Mittel County."

I smiled. "Oh, it was a temporary fix that became permanent. We used to have our own building, but it burned down about fifteen years ago. We moved in underneath the library while the county board debated what to do about a different space. Eventually, my father told them we'd just stay where we were. He always thought we should be out on the roads anyway, not stuck in an office."

"Smart man. What started the fire?"

"An overnight deputy was smoking."

"Ah. Not Sheriff Twilley, I hope. I can tell he likes his cigars."

"Fortunately not."

The two of us made our way to the front of the library where chambered windows overlooked the street. We sat down in overstuffed chairs that had been here my whole life. The air inside had grown cold. You could hear a pin drop in the quiet, and when we talked, our voices had a faint echo on the stone floors.

I explained to him my theory of what had happened between Paul Nadler and Jeremiah. I expected him to dismiss it out of hand as impossible. He didn't.

"I remember the old man," he replied when I was done. "I couldn't have told you his name was Paul Nadler, but I remember the body by the river. He had a peaceful look about him."

"Yes, he did."

"And you're convinced that Jeremiah went off with this man?"

"I am. I can't make all the details fit yet, but I believe that's what happened."

Reed knitted his hands on top of his bald head. "Yesterday, I said the boy seemed to be having fun out at the resort, not that he was some kind of prisoner. That's consistent with your theory."

"It is."

"Did you check with the police in Stanton about Nadler's background?"

"I did. He had no criminal record. Nadler's grandson, Lucas, says his grandfather was never abusive. There's no reason to think he planned to harm Jeremiah. Frankly, I don't think this was a kidnapping at all. I think it was completely innocent."

"Did you get a DNA sample from the grandson?"

"I did. I told him we'd need to run familial comparison on any DNA samples found at the resort."

"And what do you know about the grandson?"

"He's a local veterinarian. Solid guy."

"Are you sure?"

I felt an urge to defend Lucas. "Yes, I'm sure."

"His grandfather was missing, and the two of them had history at that resort. It's at least possible that he went out there looking for him, Shelby. I can tell you like him, but we have to cover all the bases."

"I know we do. And I already checked. Lucas was with a friend of mine, Jeannie Samper, most of that Friday and Saturday. They were searching for his grandfather. Plus, I saw him myself late Saturday night at the raptor center in Stanton. He wasn't involved."

"Well, that leaves us with several mysteries," Reed said.

"I know. If this was an innocent accident, I can't understand why we never found Jeremiah. This case should have had a happy ending."

"Unfortunately, the fact that it started out as innocent doesn't mean it ended up that way. It's possible that the wrong kind of person found them and took advantage of the situation. After all, we know that a third party got involved at some point. This wasn't just Paul Nadler and Jeremiah Sloan. Someone else wound up in the middle of it."

"Because of the F-150."

"Yes, exactly. The truck was wiped down and abandoned on the other side of the county. There's no way Paul Nadler did that. Somebody else did."

"I feel like we're back at square one."

"Oh, no, we're not. Thanks to you, we may well be a lot further along than we were before. However, our suspect pool just got bigger. Any alibis people had for Friday don't hold up anymore. We've looked at this whole case through the lens of Jeremiah's disappearance on Friday afternoon. But that may no longer be the relevant timeline. If Paul Nadler was the one who took Jeremiah to the resort, then the real question is, what happened between Friday afternoon and the discovery of Nadler's body by the river in Stanton on Sunday morning?"

I thought about the people we'd considered suspects.

Will and Vince Gruder.

Keith Whalen.

I'd seen all three of them on Friday afternoon when there wasn't enough time for them to have taken the boy to the resort and made their way back to Everywhere. But Reed was right. Things had changed. We didn't know where they'd been for the next two days.

"Here's what I don't understand," I said. "If somebody else got involved, how did they even find Jeremiah? Nobody knew he was at the resort, and I can't believe they stumbled onto him by accident. It's too much of a coincidence."

"Well, everybody in Mittel County was looking for the boy,"

Reed pointed out. "Maybe somebody saw or heard something that led them to search the resort. And there he was. We'll need to talk to everyone who lives nearby to see what they remember."

Somebody heard something.
Talk to everyone who lives nearby.

As he said that, I felt a ripple go through me.

"Somebody in Witch Tree *did* hear something."

I leaped out of my chair and headed for the stairs that led down to the sheriff's office. Reed followed on my heels. Downstairs, the lights were on, but there was only one deputy staffing the phones. I gave him a distracted greeting as I headed for the file cabinet. The Jeremiah file cabinet. I knew what I was looking for. My notes. My own personal diary of everything I'd seen and heard during the early days of the investigation.

I yanked the folder out of the drawer the way I'd done over and over at different points in the past ten years when I revisited the investigation. I flipped through the pages until I found my notes for Saturday morning.

"Breezy," I said. "She heard something."

"The waitress?"

"Yes. Belinda Brees. I went into the diner on Saturday morning the day after Jeremiah disappeared. Breezy made an offhanded comment that didn't seem important, but I wrote it down anyway, because I was still suspicious about the Gruders."

"What did she say?"

"She said I was right about Will and Vince being back in town. They'd been playing their music half the night, and it was keeping her awake. But the Mittel Pines Resort isn't much farther from Breezy's house than the Gruders'. What if the music she heard wasn't coming from Will and Vince? What if it was really coming from the F-150 at the resort?"

*

Just as it had the previous night, light blazed from the darkness at Breezy's trailer in Witch Tree. An inch of snow had already gathered over her dirt driveway, and more was falling like a slow, quiet avalanche. The virgin bed was undisturbed by tire tracks when we arrived.

I got out of the cruiser. So did Agent Reed. We made footprints In the snow and climbed the rusted metal steps of the trailer. I thumped on the door. "Breezy? It's Shelby. Breezy, are you there?"

I put an ear to the door and heard nothing but the wind around me. The trees in the dark forest surrounding the lot stared at us.

"Not home?" Reed asked.

"Her car's here."

We descended into the snow and circled the trailer. The only footsteps I saw were a few rabbit tracks crisscrossing the yard between Dudley's rusted carcass and the tree line. Breezy hadn't been outside since the snow began. I got on tiptoes to peer through the windows, but the curtains were pulled shut on all sides. I banged on the wall and called again. "Breezy? You around? Open up!"

I went to her Dodge Durango and brushed away the snow and peered inside. It was empty. I checked the wooden shed where her yard equipment was stored and shined a flashlight on the interior. There was nothing inside but old spiderwebs and pools of ice on the concrete floor.

The two of us went back to the trailer. I pulled my phone out of my pocket and dialed her number. When I listened, I could hear the muffled sound of Breezy's ringtone inside. Her phone was there.

I climbed the trailer steps again and checked the door, but it was locked.

"Does she have a boyfriend?" Reed asked.

"Lots. But I don't think this is about a boyfriend."

"Well, what do you want to do, Deputy? This is your town."

"I say we go in."

Reed nodded his agreement. He climbed the steps and threw his shoulder heavily against the trailer door. He was a big man, and the lock only held through two more mighty shoves before it gave way. The door banged open. Reed went in first, and I followed him.

Immediately, I slapped my hand over my face. The smell erupting out of the warm, shut-up space was like a hothouse of rotting lilies. I had to swallow down the urge to vomit. My eyes shot to the floor, and I wanted to scream at what I saw. Blood was spattered across the kitchenette and had settled into a sticky lake on the linoleum floor. In the middle was Breezy. She lay sprawled on her side, eyes fixed and open as she stared at me, her skin gray. Her long hair spilled across her face and was stained red by her own blood.

My friend, my fellow Striker girl, was dead.

CHAPTER FORTY

I called Adam, and it took him forty-five minutes to drive to Witch Tree through the snow. I met him outside. When he and I went back into the trailer together, I kept my arms wrapped so tightly around my chest that it felt like a boa constrictor was squeezing me to death. I held back my emotions as I stared at Breezy's body. It's not like violent death was a stranger around here. I'd seen grisly suicides by shotgun. I'd seen car accidents where people flew head-first through the windshield. But this was different. I'd known Belinda Brees since I was a girl and talked to her at the diner practically every day of my adult life. I'd sat right here with her in this trailer two nights ago. And now she lay dead at my feet.

"What the hell happened here?" Adam asked. "Was this an accident? Did she slip?"

He examined a plastic bottle of canola oil tipped sideways on the counter. The lid was loose, and oil had oozed down the front of the cabinets and made a slippery puddle on the trailer floor. Some of the oil had comingled with the blood, and I could see a sheen of oil on the bottoms of Breezy's bare feet. On the other side of the kitchenette was the sharp counter edge where her skull had struck as she fell backward. It was stained to a deep burgundy, and remnants of bone and tissue clung to the corner. Below, on the linoleum, tiny florets of brain matter were scattered around her head like spilled cereal.

Agent Reed knelt next to the body. "If she slipped, she had help. See these little sliver cuts on her shoulders? Those are from fingernails. There's bruising, too."

I bent over, reluctantly, and saw what he meant. There were four tiny crescent scratches on both of Breezy's bare shoulders beside the spaghetti straps of her top. Little discolorations marked her skin. She'd had a violent confrontation with whoever killed her, and I didn't think the timing of her murder was a coincidence.

"She must have known something about Jeremiah. That's what got her killed."

"And she kept quiet about it for ten years?" Adam retorted, shaking his head. "That doesn't sound like Breezy."

"I know, but she was hiding something when we talked to her on Monday night."

Reed's head turned sharply as I said this. "Hiding what?"

"Breezy talked about how creepy it was that whoever took Jeremiah drove right past her trailer. She said she didn't see anything, so I asked if anyone had spent the night with her in those first couple of days after Jeremiah disappeared. I wanted to know if there were other witnesses we should talk to. She said no, but I don't think she was giving us the real story. She was protecting someone."

"Any idea who?"

"No."

Reed studied the body at his feet again. "Well, it looks to me like she's already been dead for a couple of days."

"It was probably that same night we were here," I said. "She didn't show up for her shift at the diner the next morning."

He frowned. "Where's her phone?"

I looked around the cramped confines of the trailer, but I didn't see it. "It's here somewhere. I heard it ringing when I called from outside."

"Call it again," Reed told me.

I pulled out my phone and dialed Breezy's number. We heard it ringing, still muffled but louder than before. Her ringtone was Beyoncé's "Single Ladies," which fit for Breezy. The noise came from near my feet, and I realized the phone was under her body. Reed bent down with a gloved hand, nudged the body slightly at the hip, and slid out her phone with two fingers. I recognized the cheap silver pay-as-you-go phone that Breezy had used for years.

Reed tapped on the screen. He navigated to the call log and pulled up a list of dialed numbers. "What time did the two of you leave the trailer on Monday night?"

"About seven thirty."

"She didn't make any calls after you left. And there are no incoming calls either."

"If she didn't reach out to anybody, then why was she killed? No one knew we'd talked to her."

"Maybe not, but the whole town knew we'd found evidence at the resort," Adam pointed out. "This is Everywhere. News travels fast."

"So she was a time bomb."

Adam stared at me. "What do you mean?"

"I mean, as long as we hadn't connected Jeremiah to that resort, whatever Breezy knew didn't matter. As soon as we did, she became a threat. The question is why."

*

Not long after that, I said goodbye to Breezy for the last time. I still had trouble accepting the reality that I would never see her again.

Adam offered to drive Agent Reed back to Everywhere, so I was on my own. I exited the trailer into the winter night, where the snow was still falling through the swirl of lights on the police cruisers. Beyond the perimeter of the scene, I saw that a black SUV was now parked on the dirt road. Violet Roka stood outside the driver's door, looking elegant and powerful in her long wool coat. It was dark, but she wore sunglasses, as if she were in disguise. Her hands were in her pockets. I got the feeling that she'd been waiting for me.

I headed her way. The snow made my hair wet and got in my eyes, making me squint to see. My brown uniform was bulky and unflattering. As always, I felt outclassed whenever I was around Violet.

"So it's true?" she asked me.

"Yes. Breezy's dead."

Violet's face didn't react to the news. "That's what I heard. The FBI media rep called the congresswoman to give her a heads-up. I wanted to get out here ahead of the reporters, but they'll be all over this soon enough. I need to brief her before she gets any questions. What can you tell me?"

"Don't get too sentimental, Violet. Try to hold it together."

Yes, that was a cheap shot, but Violet took the hit without flinching.

"Look, I know we've never been close, Shelby. I know you think I'm an ice queen. Unfortunately, doing what I do, I can't afford the luxury of getting emotional about things. It doesn't mean that I don't feel anything. Breezy was my friend, too."

"Well, someone murdered our friend tonight."

"You're sure it was murder?"

"Agent Reed thinks so. Do you want to see her before they take her away?"

"No. I just want information."

"You should talk to Adam about that. Or the FBI. Not me."

"I want this to be unofficial for now. I'm a lawyer, Shelby. Lawyers like to know the answers before they start asking questions."

"So what do you want to know?"

"Obviously, whether Breezy's death is connected in any way to Jeremiah's disappearance."

"It's too early to say for sure."

Violet sighed. "I told you, this is off the record, Shelby. Not for the press, not for public consumption. Let's not play games."

"Okay. Is there a connection? Probably. But we don't know what it is yet."

"We're very close to the old resort. That must mean something."

"Could be."

"Is there any reason to think Breezy herself was involved in Jeremiah's disappearance?"

"Breezy? No, not at this point. Why would you think that?"

Violet took off her sunglasses. She looked uncomfortable, and I'd hardly ever seen Violet looking that way. "Let's talk in my truck."

"If you like."

We climbed inside. The interior was still warm. She had three separate cell phones mounted on her dashboard, and I had to relocate a laptop and a dozen thick manila folders to sit in the leather passenger seat. In the thirty seconds it took me to get situated, two of the phones rang and went to voicemail, and one rang again immediately after that. That was the life of a congressional aide. I was sure Violet loved it.

"What's going on?" I asked her. "What did you want to tell me?"

"This is private and sensitive information, Shelby. That's why I'm telling you, not Adam, not Agent Reed. I hope I can count on your keeping it confidential."

"Not if it affects a murder investigation, Violet."

"I don't know if it does. It's probably irrelevant. But since it involves Breezy, I thought you should be aware of it."

"Okay."

"Three years ago, Breezy tried to blackmail me. It was during the first campaign. She wanted money, or she was going to go to the press with a story about me using cocaine."

"Did you pay her?"

"No. I told her to go to hell."

"And did she talk to the press?"

"If she did, they saw it for what it was. Malicious gossip. The story never saw the light of day. I'm only telling you this because I know Breezy has been struggling with money. If she stooped to blackmail once, she might do so again."

"All right. I appreciate the information. But I do have to ask: Was the story true? Do you have a drug problem?"

"No."

"Did you have one in the past?"

"No."

"Breezy told me that you and she did coke together in high school."

"That was a very long time ago. We were teenagers. Sometimes teenagers do stupid things. How is that relevant now?"

"Breezy's dead. Someone murdered her. Everything's relevant."

"Well, I didn't kill her, if that's what you're suggesting. Believe me, if I didn't think it was worth paying blackmail over, then it wasn't worth committing murder, either."

"What about the congresswoman?"

"What about her?"

"Breezy also said that Ellen had a problem with pills. That sounds like something a politician would want to keep secret."

Violet sat in silence for a while without answering me. "Breezy said that? Breezy wasn't anywhere near Ellen in the past ten years. So let me guess where this came from. Dennis, right?"

"Are you saying he lied? It wasn't true?"

"I'm saying Dennis is still upset and angry about the divorce. He's not a credible source."

"That's not exactly a denial, Violet."

"So what? It's none of your business."

"If Ellen was abusing pills when Jeremiah disappeared, then yes, it is my business."

"She wasn't."

"Are you sure?"

"I am." She drummed her fingers on the steering wheel and stared through the windshield with a frown. "Look, all I'm going to tell you is this: Ellen struggled with the disappearance of her son. I'm sure that's no surprise. She was in therapy *after* it happened, and she was treated with medication. Hypothetically, if that resulted in any kind of problem, she dealt with it, and she's clean now."

"Okay."

"Does that answer your concerns?"

"For the moment, yes."

Violet shook her head in disgust, showing emotion for the first time. "This is low, even for Dennis. Gossiping about his wife's depression over her missing son. But I guess it shouldn't surprise me."

"You don't like him."

"No. I don't. I never have. Ellen has been my friend since I moved to Mittel County. I put up with Dennis for her sake. But she deserved better. She didn't need him. He was holding her back. She finally realized that, too."

"I guess she did."

"You know when I lost all respect for Dennis?"

"When?"

"The day after Jeremiah disappeared. I went over to their house that Saturday night to be with Ellen, and Dennis wasn't there. Can you believe that? He walked out on his wife while their son was missing. He bailed on her. I never forgave him for that."

"Why did he leave?"

"Because he was a coward. He couldn't deal with it."

"And you're sure it was that Saturday night?"

"That's right. I was there with Ellen all night, and she was alone. Dennis didn't get back until early morning."

"Where did he go?"

Violet shot a glance at Breezy's trailer. Mixed emotions spilled across her face. "I don't know for sure, but I can guess. When he came in, he reeked of booze. And he reeked of sex, too."

CHAPTER FORTY-ONE

I got out of the truck, and Violet drove away.

I surveyed the police activity that was still going on outside Breezy's trailer, and then I walked down the dirt road through the snow until the crime scene was blocked from view by the trees. It was the middle of a winter night, and I was cold, wet, and mostly blind.

The road vanished into the forest ahead of me. In the sticky heat of summer ten years ago, Paul Nadler would have driven this same road in the white F-150, with Jeremiah on the seat next to him. A sweet old man, a sweet young boy. They were in no real danger at that moment, as far as I knew. There was no reason we shouldn't have found both of them eventually. There was no reason why this story hadn't ended with Jeremiah safely back home.

All I could think was: Someone intervened. Something happened.

I was about to go back to the trailer when I heard a noise not far away. The closer I listened to it, the louder it became. I had no idea where it was coming from. It seemed to be disembodied, floating over the trees, landing on me like the sheets of snow.

Music.

Someone was playing music deep in the forest. I could even recognize what it was. "Stairway to Heaven."

Breezy had heard music ten years ago, too. She'd stood at the diner counter and talked about music playing half the night and keeping her awake. We'd both assumed it was coming from the Gruders, but listening to the music now, I realized how sound can play tricks on your ears. What Breezy heard could easily have come from somewhere else, like a pickup truck with its radio on, in the overgrown field of an abandoned resort.

I listened to the mysterious music and felt a crushing sense of guilt. Breezy had told me about the music she'd heard back then, and I'd completely missed the clue. I'd never given a thought to the idea that the music might have been connected to Jeremiah. I could have gotten in my cruiser and gone out there and saved him. The boy would still be alive. Instead, here we were.

The song in the forest called to me like a Pied Piper. I had to know where it was coming from and who was playing it. I headed back to the trailer and got in my cruiser. I took off down the dirt road, plowing and swerving through the drifts of fallen snow. When I reached the T-intersection, I stopped and got out of the car and listened. Where Will Gruder lived, down the driveway to the left, the forest was silent. The music was coming from the other direction.

From Mittel Pines.

I kept driving. My headlights lit up the old road sign that was a like a headstone for the resort. My windshield wipers dragged aside snow and ice. I could see ruts chewed through the powder, already being filled in by fresh snow.

Someone had driven here before me.

I went slowly, but I got stuck twice and had to use a shovel from the trunk to dig a path for my tires. It took me almost half an hour to drive two miles.

When I got there, I found a car parked at the dead-end turn-around for the resort. I didn't recognize it, but it was an Escalade about the size of Canada, with a bumper sticker that said Repent in red letters. I got out of my cruiser and shined a flashlight on the Escalade's interior, but it was empty. I could still hear the music, loud and close now, coming from the field where we'd searched the old cabins. There was supposed to be a deputy here guarding the scene, but I wondered if Adam had pulled him because of the blizzard.

I ducked under the police tape. One set of footprints showed me the way. I followed them through the trees until the trail opened up at the resort meadow. Snow poured from the night sky. In the field, the footprints had already been erased, but I could see the glow of a light inside one of the cabins that was still standing. Music boomed around me like a rock concert, covering my approach. I hiked toward the cabin through deep drifts.

A whiff of cigarette smoke soured the air as I got closer. The cabin windows were shattered and empty. There was no door. I inched toward the rotting wall and peered inside and saw a girl in a Lotus position on a moldy, moss-covered mattress. She had a lantern next to her. Her eyes were closed. Her boots were on the wet floor. A cigarette hung from her mouth, and as I watched, she pinched it between her fingers and exhaled smoke without opening her eyes. She wore jeans, heavy wool socks, and a blue bubble coat that had once belonged to me.

It was Anna.

When I went inside the cabin, the crunch of my shoes on broken glass alerted her. Her eyes shot open, first with fear, then with irritation as she recognized me. I shouted at her to turn off the music, but she didn't, so I grabbed her phone myself and switched off the sound that fed her speakers.

The resort went silent. My heart beat more slowly. I heard the hiss of wind and snow.

"You shouldn't be here," I told her quietly. "This is a crime scene. We're still searching for evidence."

"I didn't touch anything."

"No? What about that cigarette? The FBI will find it, bag it, and waste time running DNA on it."

"Fine. I'll pick up my butts. Okay? Will that make you happy?"

I didn't want to get in another argument with her. This girl meant more to me than anyone in the world other than my father, and I had basically thrown her out of my house and told her she was worthless. Me. The woman who was supposed to be her guardian angel.

"What are you doing out here, Anna?"

"Nothing. I'm not doing anything."

"No Bible reading tonight?"

"Why bother? God's not here. He left Jeremiah to die in this place."

"We don't know what happened to him yet."

"Yeah. Sure."

"Who owns the Escalade outside?"

"It's Will's. So what?"

"I still need to talk to him."

"I dropped him at the Witch's Brew. You can find him there. I told him I'd pick him up later. I wanted to come out here and be by myself for a while."

"Why? Why come here?"

She didn't answer. She closed her eyes and focused on her yoga position, as if ignoring me would make me go away. I thought about leaving, but I couldn't do that. Instead, I took a seat next to her on the old mattress. The smoke of her cigarette burned my throat. The cabin around us was filled with shadows and snow. I saw a dead, frozen robin in the corner.

"Anna, I want to apologize. I said harsh things that I didn't mean. I was upset about my father. It was wrong of me to take it out on you."

She was in a pose made for relaxation, but she wasn't relaxed at all. She was coiled like a spring. When her eyes opened, they were bloodshot and hurt. "Will says people apologize when they accidentally tell you what they really think."

"That's not true."

"You don't have to lie to me, Shelby. I heard what you said. I got your message loud and clear. You think I'm a worthless little bitch. At least you had the guts to finally admit it. I'm sorry my mom foisted me on you and told you to look after me. The good news is, you're done. You told me to get lost, and I did. I'm not your problem anymore, so don't worry about me."

I had no idea what to say. None. If anyone in that cabin felt like a worthless bitch, it was me.

"Anna, tell me why you came out here. Please."

"Go away, Shelby. Don't pretend you care."

"I'm not pretending. I do care. Talk to me. You can hate me if you want, but I need you to talk to me."

"Why? What difference does it make?"

"Because I love you. And you're hurting. I want to help."

"You can't help. I wish you'd just go."

"Well, sorry, I'm not going to do that. Look, Anna, we both know why you're here. Why can't you just admit that you're upset about what happened to Jeremiah? Why is that so hard for you?"

The girl scrambled off the mattress as if I'd set it on fire. She shoved her feet back into her boots and paced back and forth in the cabin. She kicked at the snow with each step.

"Can't you feel him?"

"Jeremiah?"

"Yes, of course, Jeremiah! He was here. He's all over this place."

I tried to feel what she felt, but I didn't. To me, there were no ghosts here, just the sleeping chill of winter. But I had never been connected to Jeremiah the way Anna was.

"Did you come out here to talk to him?"

"I came out here to tell him to leave me alone."

"Leave you alone? What do you mean?" And then I realized what she was saying. "You still dream about him, don't you?"

Anna pushed her blond hair out of her face. She was close to tears. "I have the same dream over and over. It's driving me crazy. I can't make it stop."

"Tell me about it."

"He keeps telling me he's okay. He says that he doesn't blame me, that it's not my fault."

"It's *not* your fault."

The girl picked up an empty, dirty beer bottle from the debris on the floor and heaved it at the wall, where it exploded into a shower of glass. "Of course, it is! Jeremiah! My mom! It's all my fault!"

I got up from the mattress and took her by the shoulders. "Anna, you didn't make those things happen. Your mom had cancer. And Jeremiah's disappearance had absolutely nothing to do with you. If he keeps coming back in your dreams, maybe it's because you're not listening to him."

I hoped that the wall between us might crumble. I hoped that she'd put her arms around me. I was praying that I'd finally be able to reach her. I was looking for anything, any kind of glimmer, even the smallest crack in the shell. But she was as lost as Jeremiah. She shrugged off my hands and backed away from me.

"You don't know anything. You don't know who I am. Will does. He knows I'm a bad person."

"Will is wrong."

"Yeah? Tell me one good thing I've done in my whole life, Shelby. Just one."

"Are you kidding? Your best friend disappeared ten years ago, and you *still miss him*. Would a bad person feel that way?"

Anna reached into her pocket and found another cigarette to light. Her fingers trembled. "Shelby, please just go now."

"I'm not going to leave you here. Let me take you home. My home. That's where you belong."

"No. I get it, you feel sorry for me, but I want to be alone right now. Okay? Let me be alone with him."

Maybe I should have forced her to go with me, but it felt like the wrong thing to do. I couldn't help her until she wanted my help.

"Okay. If that's what you want, I'll go."

"Thank you."

I headed for the cabin doorway. I was outside, under the falling snow, when Anna called to me. There was something different in her voice that reminded me of the little girl she once was. "Hey, Shelby?"

I turned around. "Yes?"

"Just so you know, you're in the dream, too."

"Your dream about Jeremiah?"

"Yeah. It used to be that I was alone, but lately you've been there, too. You're standing on this dirt road, and when I pass you, you tell me you're looking for someone, but you can't find him. And you ask me if I've seen him."

"Who am I looking for? Jeremiah?"

"No. Not him."

I was puzzled. "Then who?"

"You always say the same thing," Anna replied. "'A well-meaning traveler.' That's who you're trying to find."

CHAPTER FORTY-TWO

Even late on a snow-filled Wednesday night, the Witch's Brew was packed shoulder to shoulder with people. When I came inside out of the cold, I immediately felt warm with so many bodies pressed together around cocktail tables. The entire bar was paneled in walnut, making the place dark. Sconce lights flickered like fake candles. The heads of deer, elk, bears, and moose scowled at me from the walls. I looked around at the faces, but I didn't see Will Gruder.

People tend to notice the uniform in places like this. They figure it's never good when a cop arrives, so they gave me space. I heard fragments of conversation as I pushed through the crowd, and everybody was talking about Breezy being dead. I made my way to the bar. I was about to ask the bartender about Will when I noticed a familiar face near the back door.

It was Dennis Sloan, standing off by himself and staring into his beer as if he were alone on the planet.

"Hello, Mr. Sloan."

Dennis looked up from his drink and eyed me with an anxious stare. That's the thing about being a parent with a missing child. Whenever a police officer shows up, you think, this is it. This is the moment I find out.

"Mr. Sloan? That's pretty formal, Shelby. Is this an official visit? Do you have news?"

"No news, but actually, I do have a couple of questions for you. Could we go outside where it's a little more private?"

"Sure. If you want."

We went through the rear door into the gravel lot behind the bar. A few cars were parked back there, wearing caps of snow. The large trash bins near us smelled of old vegetables and empty wine bottles. Dennis's face was flushed red. Ten years had gone by since he lost his son, but he'd aged twenty.

"I heard about Breezy. I'm just devastated. I can't believe it. What happened?"

"We're still looking into that."

He glanced at the woods on the other side of the parking lot. Somewhere beyond those woods was Breezy's trailer. What I saw on his face looked like genuine longing and regret.

"I really liked her, you know. It was more than sex. It's not like we were in love or anything, but we were good for each other."

"When did you last see her?"

"Thanksgiving. Adrian was in DC with Ellen, so I was alone. So was Breezy. I came out here to the Witch's Brew, and we ended up having drinks and going back to her place. That's the way it was with us. We wouldn't see each other for months, and then we'd screw around and stay up all night talking. It's nice to be with someone you've got history with, even if it's just an on-again, off-again thing."

"And you haven't seen her since then?"

"No."

"What about Monday night? Where did you go after you left the resort?"

Dennis's tired eyes slowly focused. He realized what I was asking. "Are you kidding, Shelby? Tell me you don't think *I* killed her."

"We have to talk to everyone who knew her and rule them out."

"Well, I didn't go to Breezy's on Monday. I'd like to give you an alibi for where I was, but I can't. After I left the resort, I went home. Nobody went with me. I wanted to be alone. All I can tell you is, I would never hurt Breezy. No way."

"Okay."

"Is there anything else? I have to go soon. Once the snow stops, I have to start plowing driveways."

"I have a few more questions. Do you remember knowing a man named Paul Nadler? He was from Stanton."

"The name's not familiar. Who is he?"

"He *was* an old man with dementia, and he spent a lot of time throughout his life at the Mittel Pines Resort. He wandered away from his nursing home on the same day that Jeremiah disappeared. We think it's possible that he's the one who took your son there."

"And killed him? A senile old man?"

"We don't know exactly what happened, but it's more complicated than that. Given what happened to Breezy and that she lived on the only road that leads out to the resort, it's possible she knew something, even if she didn't realize it."

"If Breezy knew anything at all, she would have told me."

I held his eyes with mine. "Here's the thing, Dennis. I asked Breezy if anyone was with her on Friday or Saturday night after Jeremiah disappeared. She said no. But I don't think that's the truth. I don't think she was alone. And I think whoever was with her either knows what happened to your son, or has been hiding something important for a long time. I think that's why she's dead."

I watched him get angry, but the anger didn't last long. He shook his head with disbelief. "And you think it was *me*? That I know what happened to Jer?"

"Violet says you didn't spend that Saturday night at home. You went out, and you didn't come back until very late. I know you'd been having an affair with Breezy. It makes me wonder if you went to see her."

Dennis sighed and shook snow out of his hair. "Okay. I don't know what difference it makes, but yes, I did see her that night. Honestly, I haven't been thinking about anything else since I found out that Jer was at that damn resort. Can you imagine what it feels like to know I was so close to my boy back then? Hell, I could have shouted his name, and he probably would have heard me. I could have driven over there and saved him. But I didn't know, Shelby. I didn't know a thing about it."

"Tell me what happened that night."

He exhaled long and slow, as if talking about it was the last thing he wanted to do. "Ellen was freezing me out all day. She was in her own world. I mean, I don't blame her for that, but after a while, I just couldn't be there anymore. I couldn't take the silent treatment. So I went out. I didn't even know where I was going. I drove up and down the roads, like maybe if I drove around long enough, I'd find Jer. It was pouring rain. Hammering down. I kept thinking of him being out in the middle of that. Anyway, sooner or later, I wound up in Witch Tree. Right here at the bar. It wasn't deliberate or anything, it just happened. I stayed here until the place closed at two in the morning, but I still didn't want to go home. I couldn't face Ellen. And I was feeling wrecked about Jer. So I went over to see Breezy at the trailer."

"Did you see anyone else on the road as you were driving to her place?"

"I don't remember. It was late, and I was pretty buzzed."

"Did you hear anything when you got there?"

"Hear anything? Like what?"

"Music. Someone playing music in the forest."

"I don't think so. I'm pretty sure the rain had stopped, but I don't remember hearing anything."

"Was Breezy awake?"

"No. She was sleeping. I knocked on the door and woke her up."

"Was she alone?"

"Yeah."

"You're sure?"

"I'm sure. It's not like there's any place to hide in the trailer, Shelby. Other than the bedroom, and that's where we went. I mean, I'm not proud of it. My son was missing, and what did I do? I had sex."

"And after?"

"Breezy went back to sleep. I stared at the ceiling and thought about what a piece of crap I am. I stayed there for a while, and eventually, I got up and went home."

"What time did you leave the trailer?"

"I don't know. Sometime between two and three, I guess. I didn't check my watch."

"And you drove straight home?"

"Yeah."

"Did Breezy wake up when you left?"

"No, she was dead to the world." He frowned. "Sorry, bad choice of words. But she was tired. She was barely awake even while we were having sex. She'd pulled double shifts at the diner two days in a row. I knew she had to get up early again, so I let her sleep. I just slipped out."

"What about when you left? Did you hear music then?"

"I'm not sure, but I don't think so."

"Did you see anyone else?"

"What? I forgot about the raccoon."

"The raccoon?"

"Well, I assumed it was a raccoon. I remember going out the

door at Breezy's place. I was parked right behind Dudley in her driveway. As I opened my car door, I heard a loud bang from the shed in her yard. Like somebody bumping into a wall or something."

"Did you check it out?"

"Yeah, I went over there. The shed door was open. It was pitch-black, so I used the light on my phone to take a look around. A shelf had fallen. I figured that's what I'd heard, and I assumed an animal had done it. But I'll tell you, when I went back outside, I had the weirdest feeling. It made my skin crawl."

"What was it?"

Dennis shook his head. "I wasn't alone out there. I was sure someone was watching me. I could feel their eyes."

CHAPTER FORTY-THREE

When I asked about Will Gruder, one of the other drinkers at the bar ratted him out by pointing a finger upstairs. I knew what that meant. The owner of the Witch's Brew kept a few rooms for drunk patrons who needed to sleep it off instead of driving home. The word around town was that the rooms also got rented by the hour.

The stairs were located behind a varnished door across from the restrooms. When I climbed to the second floor, I found myself in a cold, narrow hallway, decorated with posters of black cats. There were four doors on each side, looking in on empty rooms that didn't offer much more than a twin bed and a closet-sized bathroom. The smell told me that people threw up here regularly. I passed seven open doors, but the last door on the right was closed.

The noises I heard inside told me what was going on.

I knocked hard. "Will Gruder! It's Deputy Lake. We need to talk."

The grunting from the bodies behind the door stopped abruptly, and I heard a string of profanities. Footsteps creaked on the wooden floor, and the door inched open in front of me behind a chain. I saw a redheaded girl who couldn't be more than a teenager. Behind her, the room was pitch-black.

"What do you want?" she demanded.

"Is Will Gruder in there?"

"What if he is?"

"I need to talk to him."

She looked ready to give me attitude, but I heard a male voice behind her. "Just do what she says."

The door closed again. I heard angry whispers on the other side, along with the rustle of clothes. When the door opened again, the redhead passed me with a slur about cops underneath her breath. The light was still off in the bedroom, and the shutters were closed. When I opened the door, I could barely make out the body of a man on the twin bed. The long stretch of pale skin told me he was naked.

"Get dressed, Will."

"Turn on the light so I can see."

I didn't bother with games. I knew he wanted to shock me. I turned on the light, and I kept my reaction off my face. Yes, he was naked, and his skin was mottled all over with the shiny, grotesque burns that he'd suffered in the explosion of his meth lab. Vince had died, but seeing Will made me wonder if his brother had gotten off easy. I didn't like Will, and I didn't like what he and Vince had inflicted on the people around Mittel County with the drugs they sold. But he'd definitely been punished.

He saw through the impassive look I was faking. He smirked at my discomfort. His own face was like a shiny plastic mask, with a nose that resembled the opening of a skull. His mouth was like a round cave. His eyes were unaffected, still sharp and blue, as if part of his sentence was to be able to see himself in a mirror every day of his life.

Will limped to a pile of clothes near the bed. I remembered Anna talking about his bad knee, which was wrapped in an elastic bandage. He grimaced as he stepped into a white pair of under-wear, and then he sat on the bed without putting on anything else.

"Vengeance is mine," Will murmured. "That's what you're thinking, right? I got what was coming to me?"

"I'm sorry about your situation," I told him. And I was.

He had the look of a man who was accustomed to pity from everyone he met and had no patience for it. "You can turn off the lights again if you don't want to look at me. I keep the lights off for sex. Girls won't do it if they see me. I don't blame them. I'm a monster."

I felt like I should disagree with him, but I couldn't.

"Does Anna know you're cheating on her? Does she know you bring other girls up here?"

"Anna and I don't sleep together, so I can't cheat on her."

"Oh." I couldn't hide my surprise. Or my relief. "Okay."

"Yeah, I'm sure you're happy about that. It's not like Anna hasn't offered, by the way. She's told me lots of times that she wanted to do it. I said no."

"Really."

"Yes, really. There are only three reasons a girl will sleep with somebody who looks like me. One is because I pay them. Two is because they think they're at the circus, and they want to see the freaks. Three is because they want to punish themselves. Anna's number three. That's the worst kind."

"Then why do you hang out with her?"

"I don't. She hangs out with me."

"Well, do us both a favor and knock it off. I don't want her with you. I don't want her anywhere near you. You make her feel bad about herself, and I hate that. That girl can do amazing things with her life, but she'll never get there with you dragging her down."

"You're wrong. I don't do that. She does it to herself. But hey, I get it, it's easier to blame me."

"You told her she was a bad person."

"No, I said we're all bad people. I'm a bad person. You're a bad person. We sin. That's what people do."

I had to remind myself that you can go through a lot of physical suffering and still be a jerk. Underneath it all, Will Gruder was still Will Gruder.

"Look, you got a crappy deal," I told him. "It doesn't matter that you brought it on yourself, I wouldn't wish it on anyone. If you're not dealing drugs anymore, great, good for you. If you want to spend your life reading the Bible and doling out pop psychology, that's fine, too. But leave Anna alone."

Will shrugged. "Is that all?"

"No. That's not all. I assume you heard about Jeremiah Sloan and the Mittel Pines Resort."

"Yeah. Everybody's talking about it."

"And about the death of Belinda Brees."

"Sure. That's too bad. Breezy was cool."

"How well did you know her?"

"In the old days, she was our favorite customer. Sometimes she didn't have any money, so Vince would make her sleep with us instead."

"Real nice."

Will rocked back and forth on the bed. His blue eyes were cold. "So what? Like I said, everybody sins. You weren't exactly an angel back then, were you, Deputy? Cheating. Lying. Wasn't that you?"

I ignored him, but I felt the sting. He was good at pinpointing people's weaknesses. His grotesque appearance also gave him a strangely hypnotic presence. He was like a cult leader gathering up disciples to spread his gospel, and Anna was under his spell.

"Where were you Monday night?"

"Lying in a hospital bed. My knee went out, and I had

injections. I couldn't walk. I was there Monday. I was there Tuesday. I only got out this morning. Sorry if that bums you out, Deputy, but I didn't kill anybody."

"I never said you did." But he was right. I wasn't expecting an unshakable alibi from Will in Breezy's death. To me, he was my prime suspect. "I want to talk about the weekend that Jeremiah disappeared."

"What about it?"

"The Mittel Pines Resort is close to your house."

"So?"

"So did you and Vince ever go out there?"

"Sometimes."

"Doing what?"

"Hanging out. Screwing around."

"What about that weekend? Did you go there?"

"No. We'd just got home from our supply trip to Mexico, and we were back in business. We were busy."

"The road to the resort goes right near your place. Did you see anything that weekend? People? Vehicles?"

"I don't think so."

"Did you hear anything?"

Will tilted his chin in thought. He leaned back, putting both palms flat on the mattress. "Music."

"You heard music? Where was it coming from?"

"I don't know. Could have been anywhere. We heard it both nights. Friday and Saturday. Someone was playing it pretty loud. Vince was getting pissed."

"Breezy thought the music was coming from the two of you."

"That's why Vince was pissed. He didn't want the cops getting nosy."

"Did you check it out?"

"No."

"Why not? If Vince was angry, seems to me he'd go bang some heads."

"We didn't want to attract any attention."

"What about Breezy? Did she come over to complain?"

"No. We didn't see her."

"But you had to pass her trailer when you were coming and going, right?"

"Yeah, so what?"

"Did you see anyone there?"

"Ten years ago? Who knows? Breezy always had a lot of company. All I remember is, yeah, there was music, and it was loud, and then somewhere in the middle of Saturday night, it stopped."

"It stopped? When?"

"Come on, Deputy. Late. I don't know."

"What kind of music was it?"

"A radio station, I think. Seems to me we heard commercials. I remember we could make out some Aerosmith and some Stones, too. Vince was a big Stones fan."

"Do you remember anything else?"

"It was a long time ago. So no, I don't remember a damn thing. Are we done?"

"We're done."

Will got off the bed and went back to the jumble of clothes on the floor. I could see that his knee was mostly frozen. He bent down with difficulty and grabbed a white T-shirt that he slipped over his torso, and he grimaced in pain as he did so. Then he slipped on a blue flannel shirt and left it unbuttoned.

"Remember what I said about Anna," I told him.

"Talk to her about that. Not me."

"Oh, I will."

Will gestured at his jeans on the floor. "You going to help me put my pants on, or what?"

"Are you kidding?"

"You scared off the girl, Deputy. I can't do it myself, not with my knee locked. It's not like you need to be afraid of me. I don't bite."

I rolled my eyes. "Lie on the bed. If you try anything, believe me, you'll regret it."

Will's mouth stretched into something close to a grin. He limped to the bed and lay on his back. I picked up his jeans, but as I did, something metal slid out of his pocket. I retrieved it from the floor and studied it in my palm. It was a silver chain, and on the end of it was a blue-and-silver enameled religious medal. On one side was an image of a robed, bearded figure, and on the other was a cross with capital letters circling the outside of the coin.

"This is a medal of St. Benedict, right?"

"That's right. You know it?"

"I've seen one before. What do the letters mean?"

"It's a Latin curse against Satan. It keeps him away."

"Do you need help with that?"

"We all do."

He extended his arm and cupped his fingers together. I let the coiled chain and medal fall back into his hand. He slipped the medal around his neck.

"Where did you get it?"

Will rubbed the medal between his fingers. He took a long time to answer. "I think it was a gift."

"Really? From whom?"

"I don't remember. Maybe I found it. Does it matter? It's not expensive, if you think I stole it. You can probably get one online for ten bucks. You should think about it, Deputy. Seems to me Satan must be hanging around you wherever you go."

I headed for the door. "Goodbye, Will."

"Hey, what about my pants?"

"I'll send your girlfriend up."

I went back into the cold hallway, then downstairs into the warm, crowded bar. I felt lost in a daze. I watched the seas part for me—cop in uniform again—and I headed out of the Witch's Brew into the night. The snow had finally stopped, but it left behind a silent white shroud over the world.

I got into my cruiser, but I didn't turn on the engine.

Instead, I sat there and thought about the medal of St. Benedict. Will was right that it wasn't valuable. You could walk into a flea market or a church basement and find one for a few dollars.

But I knew where I'd seen St. Benedict before. It was a long, long time ago.

Keith Whalen had kept the very same medal on a hook in his barn.

CHAPTER FORTY-FOUR

Sometimes you get to the end of a crossword puzzle, and you've filled in every answer except one. You've got most of the letters, but you can't figure out that last word, even though it's right there in front of you. Usually, that means you're thinking about it all wrong.

That's how I felt as I drove back to Everywhere. I had all the clues I needed to solve this puzzle, but I still couldn't fill in the blanks.

I drove fast and made good time. The plows had been out through the storm and had already cleared the highway and the main street through town. Even so, it was late by the time I parked in front of the Nowhere Café. I checked my watch and saw that the diner had closed five minutes earlier. The neon sign in the front window was off, but the lights were still on, and sometimes I can sweet-talk them into a last cup of coffee or piece of pie before I head home.

I got out and peered through the window. In a booth at the far back of the restaurant, I saw Monica and Dad. I felt bad that Monica had stayed late again to look after my father and that she'd have a long drive ahead of her on the snowy roads to get home. The night waitress, whose name was Patty, waved at me when I drummed my fingers on the door. She let me inside, and she still had a hot pot of coffee in her hands. I was saved.

"Take your time, Shelby," she told me. "I still have to clean up before I head out of here."

"Thanks."

"It's horrible about Breezy."

"Yeah. It is."

The diner was like a family, so I knew Patty well. I knew all of the waitresses so well that I probably had their shifts memorized better than they did. They were all friendly, all lifers in our little town. But I couldn't help thinking that none of them would ever call me "Shel" and that I would never see Breezy behind the counter again, joking and flirting with the men.

"Hello, you two," I said as I slid into the booth next to Monica. Then I noticed Moody's urn and corrected myself. "Sorry. You three."

"Much better," Monica replied with a squeaky giggle.

I leaned over and apologized in her ear for being late, but she shrugged it off the way she always did. Patty came and poured coffee for me. I closed my eyes and listened to the quiet hum of the diner. It always sounded the same and smelled the same, and at that moment, I was glad for anything in my life that didn't change. When I opened my eyes, I saw Dad sitting across from me. His white hair was combed, his white mustache trimmed. He whistled tunelessly under his breath, and I could read the signs. He was lost in time tonight, somewhere that only he could see.

For years, I had thought of my father as one of those things in my life that never changed, but that wasn't true anymore. In fact, I wasn't even sure I could believe in the stories that he'd told me long ago.

"How are you, Dad?"

He turned his warm eyes on me. "Fine, Shelby. How was your day?"

"My day?" I thought about what to say. "My day was all about Breezy, Dad. Do you remember her? Belinda Brees?"

"Do I remember her? After that diving save she made in the game last night? I love how that long hair of hers flies when she jumps. That girl is so intense on the court. Well, you all are. Trust me, you girls are on your way to the championship this year. It's going to happen."

I worked up a smile. "I hope so, Dad."

To him, Breezy and I were still two high school seniors playing volleyball. I almost envied him, because he had this strange superpower to drop himself down into another part of his life. The man with almost no memory could remember everything from some parts of the past, if only for a few seconds. I wanted that power for myself. I wanted to go back to that Sunday morning ten years ago after that rainy, rainy night. I wanted to sit right over there at the counter again and talk to Breezy.

I wanted to ask her: What happened last night?

What did you see?

What did you hear?

Who was with you?

But I couldn't.

And the fact is, I knew the answers to all of those questions, and they didn't help me. What happened? Nothing. What did she see? Nothing. What did she hear? Music, just music, blowing in with the wind.

Who was with her? Dennis Sloan.

A cheating husband with a missing son. But Dennis wasn't the man I wanted. I simply didn't believe it.

No, the man I wanted was Will Gruder. I had this insane notion that the medal of St. Benedict around Will's neck really did belong to Keith Whalen. That Will and Vince had been the ones to murder Colleen. That Keith was innocent, just like he said, and that somehow the Gruders had discovered that Jeremiah had seen it all happen. Which gave them a reason to make sure he disappeared. They'd heard the Rolling Stones booming from the pickup truck's radio that night. They'd gone out to the resort and found Jeremiah, and they'd seized the opportunity to make the one witness to their crime go away for good.

That's what I wanted the last word in the crossword puzzle to be. Four letters.

Will.

But the letters simply didn't fit the clue. Breezy didn't know anything about Will or Keith or Colleen or even Jeremiah back then. And Will didn't kill Breezy. I knew that, too. He'd been in the hospital in Stanton on Monday night. So if Will didn't kill Breezy, then I simply wasn't looking at the clue the right way.

So I did the only thing you can do when you can't solve a puzzle.

I switched puzzles.

"I enjoyed talking to you last night, Dad."

His face grew quizzical. "Last night?"

"At the lake."

"Oh. Well. I enjoyed it, too." He smiled, but I knew he didn't remember. Our time at the shore of Shelby Lake was already filed away in a part of his brain that he couldn't locate.

"You told me about the day your mother died," I prompted him. "You took a trip. You met a woman who rescued you in a campground."

He looked lost at what I was saying. He blinked rapidly, and his smile faltered. His expression told me that all I was doing was upsetting him. I wasn't sure he even remembered his mother at that moment. And certainly not a policewoman he'd encountered somewhere in a long-ago winter. They may as well have been ghosts who'd never existed.

"It's okay, Dad. It doesn't matter."

He looked grateful that I dropped it. That's what always hurt more than anything, that momentary look of panic in his eyes. I could see his mind saying: These are things I should know. Why don't I know them? Fortunately, it never lasted long, and then the curtain came down again to protect him.

Dad shouldered his way to the side of the booth and got out, looking tall and fit. The disease could be a terrible mirage. "Nature calls," he said.

I watched him make his way to the restroom, and I kept a close watch on the hallway, because the rear door of the diner was back there. I didn't want him wandering out into the snow.

Monica inched closer to me and spoke in a low voice. "What was that about Tom's mother?"

"He told me that he took a long drive after she died, and he got lost somewhere. Did he ever tell you about that?"

If anyone would know, it was Monica, but she shook her head. "I vaguely remember him taking a couple of days off, but he never spoke about what he did. Why?"

"It's nothing."

For now, this was my secret. My mystery.

I saw the restroom door open again, and my father came back to the booth. Patty came over with the final dregs of the coffee. "One last warmer-upper before you go, Tom?"

"Oh, no, thank you, Breezy. I'm likely to float away."

Patty looked uncomfortable at being called by the name of a dead woman. She looked at me with a silent question as to whether she should correct him or not. I gently shook my head.

"So you've got Dudley running again, do you?" Dad went on. "Yesterday you said he was on life support. You weren't sure you were going to get him started again. Good thing you made it to work with all of these out-of-towners around. Big tips, am I right?"

I didn't know exactly where he was at that moment, but what he was saying made me hold my breath. Maybe somewhere in Dad's head, he knew what I needed, and he was trying to find it for me. Maybe, for him, it was that Sunday morning ten years ago after Jeremiah disappeared.

Maybe he knew something that I'd forgotten long ago.

"Dudley?" Patty asked him. "Who's Dudley?"

I cringed, because I was afraid that she would jar him out of his memories when I needed him to be back in the past. But Dad simply gave one of his Santa laughs.

"Your car, Breezy, your car! Yesterday you had to rely on Monica's taxi service to make it to the diner, don't you remember? But here you are today, bright and early. So I assume Dudley is back in the land of the living."

I mouthed to her: *Yes.*

"Uh, yeah, yeah, sure he is, Tom," Patty murmured.

"Good, very good. How did you get home last night anyway? You were working pretty late. Did you find a knight in shining armor to take you out to Witch Tree?"

Patty looked completely at sea, but I felt a chill running up and down the length of my body.

"Last night?" Patty said, not understanding the game. "My husband picked me up, like he always does. We only have the one car. I'm sorry, Tom, did you want more coffee?"

"Oh, well, sure, just a little more for the road. Thank you, young lady."

I knew that Dad was gone again. Patty was "young lady," not Breezy. He was back in the shadows, among strangers he didn't know. The visits never lasted long.

But this time, he'd given me the clue I needed to solve the puzzle.

"You picked up Breezy in Witch Tree on that Saturday morning," I said to Monica. "You brought her to the diner that day, right?"

Monica knitted her eyebrows in confusion and stroked Moody's urn. "I'm sorry, dear, what?"

"Saturday. The day after Jeremiah went missing. You picked up Breezy."

"Did I? Oh yes, you're right, I did. She couldn't get Dudley started, and she called to see if I would stop at her place on my way into town. I'd forgotten all about it. But why is that important?"

I shook my head. "It's not. It doesn't matter how she got *to* the diner. What's important is how she got *from* the diner to her place in Witch Tree that night. She didn't have her car with her. She was stranded here. *So who took her home?*"

Monica looked at me for the answer. "Do you know?"

In that first moment, I didn't.

And in the next moment, in a rush, I did. Yes, I did. The snow melted around me, and I knew everything. I knew who took Breezy home. I knew who killed her. I knew how Jeremiah died, I knew how Paul Nadler's body made its way to the river in Stanton, I knew how that white F-150 had been abandoned at Shelby Lake without anyone coming to pick up the driver.

There was just one man behind all of it.

One man with a motorcycle.

"Shelby?" Monica asked me. "Who took Breezy home that night?"

"A well-meaning traveler," I replied.

*

I woke up Agent Reed at the motel.

It had been the Avery Weir Inn since Rose sold it, but we all still called it the Rest in Peace. I saw a laptop open on the bed in Reed's room, but his eyes were heavy, as if he'd fallen asleep while working.

"Shelby," he said in surprise, with a glance at his watch. "Is everything okay?"

"No. No, I don't think so. I have a question for you. Do you remember that voicemail that Adam left for you when you came to town the first time? The one that almost got him fired?"

"Of course," Reed replied with a roll of his eyes.

"This will sound strange, but do you still have it?"

He gave me a puzzled look. "Well, I'm sure we have it archived somewhere. Trust me, the FBI saves everything. It would take me a few minutes to find on our server, though. Why? What is this about?"

"I need to listen to it again."

Reed read the expression on my face. He was wide awake now. "Okay. Let me see what I can do."

He retrieved his laptop from the bed and relocated it to a circular table near the window. He sat down and began tapping the keys. I closed the motel-room door behind me, shutting out the winter air. Reed gave me a sideways glance as he typed. "So are you going to tell me what this is about?"

"Drunk driving. I'm pretty sure that's what this is about."

His fingers stopped over the keys. "What?"

"No kidnapping. No abuse. Just drunk driving."

Reed didn't push me to explain. He turned his eyes down to the keyboard and focused on his laptop again. It took him only a few minutes to find the archived recording of Adam's voicemail. The time stamp was just before one a.m. on that early Sunday morning ten years ago. He called me over to listen, and then he played it for me. I'd heard the message once before, but I barely remembered what Adam had said. I only knew it had been bad, and it was.

"*Special Agent Reed, this is Deputy Adam Twilley. Just thought I'd check in with you after a really productive day checking the toilets of campgrounds around here. Yeah, thanks a lot for the vote of confidence. I bet you thought that was funny. I bet you guys had a good laugh about that. Man, you feebs really think you're rock stars, huh? You think you're so much better than a bunch of rubes like us in the sticks. Well, you know what? You're all just a—*"

I held up my hand to make Reed stop the playback. There was no need to go on. I confess, I cleaned up what Adam had said. It was much, much worse, filled with insults and F-bombs. The fact is, I wasn't really listening to Adam's slurred, drunken voice.

I was listening to the background.

"Did you hear it?"

Reed looked at me. "Hear what?"

"The music."

He played it again, and this time he heard it, too. It was music from a car radio. Close by, so close that Adam had to be practically on top of it, Mick Jagger was croaking out "Under My Thumb."

"The music is coming from the F-150," I said. "Adam was there. He was at the resort."

CHAPTER FORTY-FIVE

At daybreak, I asked Adam to meet me.

The morning was cold and clear at the old Mittel Pines Resort. With barely a murmur of wind, every branch in the trees was still. The winter gray had vanished and left the clearing under blue skies, making the bed of snow sparkle like a field of diamonds. I hiked through calf-deep powder into the middle of the meadow and found a fallen tree trunk. I brushed off the snow and sat down. I waited.

Adam arrived ten minutes later.

I watched him come. He wore his uniform and his hat like shields that he could hide behind. He was the sheriff, but to me, he looked like a boy again, impulsive and reckless. I could see now what the years and the guilt had done to him. I tried to imagine what it was like to keep a terrible secret for so long and to see it reflected in your own eyes whenever you looked in a mirror.

As he came close to me, I watched him try to decode my own face. Did I know?

He stood over me and squinted into the sun. His shadow stretched behind him. "Shelby."

"Hello, Adam."

"What's up? Why the early meeting?"

"I have a question."

"Yeah? What is it?"

"I want to know if it was an accident."

He tried to keep his cool, but his whole body stiffened. "What are you talking about?"

"Not Jeremiah. I know he was an accident. I'm talking about Breezy. Did you mean to do it? Was it deliberate? Or did you simply get angry and push her and she fell?"

"Is this a joke?"

"Oh, no. No joke. What was the problem, did she want you to pay her to keep quiet? Violet says Breezy wasn't above a little blackmail. She needed money, and you've got a lot of it."

Adam shook his head, but he was a terrible actor. He was trembling down to his boots. "I think you've had a stroke, Shelby. We should get you some help."

I stood up from the fallen tree, and we were eye to eye.

"When I asked Breezy who went home with her on that Saturday night ten years ago, she was about to say it was *you*. Right? You took her home on your motorcycle. But she stopped and didn't say anything when she saw you flinch. Did she realize that you didn't want her to tell me? She must have wondered why. When you came back later, had she already figured it out? Did she threaten to expose you? So the two of you argued. You grabbed her by the shoulders, you shoved her, and she fell and hit her head. I really hope it was an accident. Breezy was my friend. I don't want to think you went over there to kill her."

"We're done here, Shelby. I'm leaving."

"No, you're not going anywhere, Sheriff. I need to tell you a story."

"What kind of story?"

"I'm going to tell you what happened to Jeremiah. Agent

Reed and I spent most of the night working out the details. Yes, he knows all about it, too. We must be pretty close to the truth, but you can stop me if I get anything wrong. Okay?"

Adam stared at me with hollow, empty eyes and said nothing.

"We know about Paul Nadler taking the F-150 and meeting up with Jeremiah. I bet they liked each other immediately. The old man, the young boy. Nadler probably asked him if he knew where this old resort was, and Jeremiah said, sure, I know that place. And off they went. They drove here. Right here. It must have been an adventure for Jeremiah. Hunting for rocks. Playing with his badminton racket. Putting Legos together. Playing the radio on the pickup truck. I'm sure he was thinking he'd have a great story to tell when he got home."

I glanced over my shoulder at the cabin where the two of them had stayed. It was winter now. It was summer then. But Anna was right. Suddenly, I could feel Jeremiah all over this place.

"Friday was fun, but I bet Saturday was when the fun started to wear off. Jeremiah started getting lonely. Hungry, too. I don't imagine he had much to eat in his backpack. His phone was dead. He was missing his family and wondering what to do. I don't know exactly when Paul Nadler had his heart attack, but at some point, Jeremiah must have realized that this sweet old man was gone. Just like his own grandfather. All of a sudden, the adventure began to get scary. And when it got dark on Saturday? And a thunderstorm came roaring in? That poor kid. He must have been terrified. Probably the only thing that helped was listening to the radio on the truck, but he'd had the engine running for hours. It must have been getting pretty low on gas. I feel bad, thinking about him all alone, hiding in the cabin, wondering if anyone would ever find him."

I stared into Adam's eyes.

"But someone did. You found him."

Out of the stillness, a single gust of wind whipped across the meadow and took Adam's hat off his head. It rolled away on top of the snow like an old tire. Adam made no attempt to retrieve it.

"Saturday was a rotten day for you," I went on. "I get that. You were doing grunt work for the FBI. You were tired. You were pissed off. You smelled like campground toilets. So you spent the evening drinking at the Nowhere Café and pouring out your problems to Breezy. And when the diner finally closed, you took her home. She rode on the back of your bike in the pouring rain. Not smart, Adam. You were already pretty drunk. You could have both been killed. But you made it to her trailer. What did you do when you got there? Did you drink more? Or did Breezy share any of her other stash with you? Meth? Cocaine? Heroin? Did you sleep with her, or were you too drunk and riled to make it to bed? That probably made you feel worse. Now you were really angry. So when the rain stopped, you told Breezy you were heading home. She came outside with you, and she heard the music. Rock and roll radio blaring over the trees for hours. Just like the previous night. She was sure it was the Gruders. She asked you to go over there and tell them to knock it off, and that's what you did. You drove your motorcycle down the dirt road, but pretty soon you realized it *couldn't* be the Gruders. The music was coming from the other direction. And that's when you headed to the old resort."

It was all so vivid. I knew Adam. I could see him parking at the end of that road and following the music toward the cabins like a siren. He must have suspected what he would find there. He must have realized that he was going to be a hero. What a combination of alcohol and adrenaline would have been pumping through his bloodstream.

"You came up here, and you saw it. There it was. The white F-150. Did you call out Jeremiah's name? No, probably not. You still thought he'd been kidnapped. You figured whoever did it was still around. So you searched through the cabins, and *you found him.* Safe. Alive. Alone except for that poor old man, dead on the moldy mattress. Did Jeremiah run to you? Did he hug you? Wow, what a moment that must have been, Adam. Really. I know how exhilarated you must have felt. All these people searching, all these out-of-towners, all the national media, all the Feds treating you like dirt—and you found Jeremiah. *You.* All by yourself. You were going to be on television. I mean, real television, New York talk shows. Magazine covers, too. Probably a movie. You were going to be famous."

I felt my words catching in my throat. I didn't like doing this to him. I really didn't.

"That's when you left the voicemail for Agent Reed, right? I can hear it in your voice when I listen to it. That smug triumph. You were going to show all of them, all of those arrogant Feds. Except you were drunk, and you were impatient. You should have called for backup, Adam. One phone call to my father, and then you wait there with Jeremiah until the cavalry arrives. But that wasn't good enough for you, was it? You weren't going to let anybody else take that boy home. You were going to do it yourself. You were going to drive him right up to his house and put him in his mother's arms. Nobody else. Not my father. Not me. Certainly not Agent Reed. Deputy Adam Twilley was going to save the day. But there was hardly any gas left in the pickup, was there? It was pretty much empty by then. So you said to Jeremiah: How about the two of us take a ride? You ever ridden on a motorcycle?"

I looked at the stricken pain on Adam's face.

I knew I'd gotten it exactly right.

"You could feel that boy's arms clenched around your waist as you rode. You must have been flying. You were thinking about your future and how this was going to change your life. You were thinking what it was going to be like when Ellen Sloan saw her son again. You were thinking about all those media people interviewing you and taking your picture. You were thinking about everything except what you should have been thinking about. The road. The wet pavement. The bike. You took one of the curves too fast, is that how it went down? The bike spun out? You fell. Jeremiah fell. You got up, but he didn't."

I shook my head.

"I'm trying to imagine the horror you felt, Adam, and I can't. I just can't. One split second, and all those dreams turned to nightmares. You'd found our boy, and now, instead of rescuing him, you'd killed him. You weren't going to be the hero anymore. You were going to be *hated*. Everyone in town, in the state, in the country, would know your name. Adam Twilley. The drunken deputy who let a missing boy die on his motorcycle. You were going to lose your job. You were going to jail. Your life was over. You were in a panic. What do you do? You can't let anyone know what happened. Nobody can know Jeremiah or Paul Nadler were anywhere near that resort. You had to cover it all up."

I pictured him standing over the boy's dead body on the road. Dragging him down the shoulder into the woods. Coming up with a desperate plan.

"You needed gasoline for the truck. So you rode back to Breezy's, right? You figured she'd have a tank in her shed. Except in the middle of doing that, you heard somebody outside the trailer. Dennis Sloan. He felt you watching him; he was sure someone was there. But you were lucky. He didn't find you. He left, and then you took the gas tank and went back to the resort to get the truck. You had to move fast. You needed to get everything done while it was still dark. You tried to hide any evidence that Jeremiah had been there, but you were in a hurry. There were things you missed, things you didn't know about. The rocks. The Legos. The lost shuttlecock in the chimney. You filled up the gas tank of the truck, and you put Mr. Nadler's body in the back, and you put your motorcycle in the flatbed. Then you went back to where Jeremiah was waiting for you. Was there a shovel in the pickup, or did you take one from Breezy's shed? Either way, you buried him. You dug through the wet ground and buried him. Do you still remember the place where you did it? I don't think you forget something like that. I hope you remember, because you're going to take us there, Adam."

His breaths were coming faster and faster. His eyes darted back and forth, as if he could find a way to escape if he looked hard enough.

"Then all that was left was to get rid of Paul Nadler. And the truck. So you drove all the way across the county to Stanton. It was a long way to go, but that was the safest bet, right? Put Mr. Nadler in the river not far from his nursing home. Everyone would assume he'd wandered away on foot and died. But the truck? The truck couldn't be anywhere nearby. You didn't want anyone to connect Nadler to the F-150. So after that, you went over to Shelby Lake and wiped down the truck and left it behind. Then you took your motorcycle and you drove home."

Adam didn't look at me. His gaze wandered across the field, following his hat as it blew away toward the trees. When he finally said something, he was the old Adam. The arrogant James Dean Adam. The hero with the inferiority complex.

"That's a hell of a story, Shelby."

"It's a true story. Right?"

"I'm a cop. I know the difference between evidence and speculation. I know when somebody has proof and when somebody has nothing."

"Oh, I wouldn't count on that, Adam. We'll be able to prove you were at the resort, because we've got the voicemail to Agent Reed. And when we search along the road between here and Witch Tree, sooner or later we're going to find Jeremiah. Even after all this time, the FBI forensics team will find something to connect him to you and your bike. Count on it. But you can save us the trouble. You can admit what you did right now."

"Why would I do that?"

"Because you've been living with the guilt for ten years, and it's killing you. The only thing that will make it go away is to admit the truth. The only way to save yourself is to give up the secret. Tell me the truth, Adam. Tell *us* the truth."

"Us?"

I gestured over his shoulder. Adam turned around. They were all there in the snow behind him, their faces grim.

Ellen.

Dennis.

Adrian.

Agent Reed.

They stood there watching him like a silent jury.

"We're here so you can take us to Jeremiah," I said. "Don't you think it's about time, Adam? It's time for him to come home. Tell us where he is."

Adam tried to say something, but nothing came out of his mouth. He swallowed hard. He sucked his upper lip between his teeth and bit down. He blinked over and over, until he blinked out a single tear that ran down his red cheeks. His fingers clenched into fists.

"Please, Adam. Take us there."

He staggered away from me through the drifts. He didn't run; he knew there was nowhere to go. No one said a word. The Sloans were quiet. So was Agent Reed. No one made any attempt to stop him. I followed in his footsteps. We hiked through the clearing and back into the trees and down to the turnaround at the end of the dirt road. Adam went to his car. I saw him freeze outside the driver's door. He squeezed his head with both hands, as if he could shut out the memories flooding through his mind. Then he looked back at me, and our eyes met, and he gave me an expression that must be like a drowning man when his lungs run out of air.

Adam got in his car. I got in mine. I knew where we were going.

The two of us headed down the dirt road in tandem back toward Witch Tree. Adam drove slowly, letting me trail behind him in the ruts his car made. We went around a sharp curve. Then another. And another. And then, ahead of us, the road straightened for half a mile. At the end of the straightaway was a swooping S curve with a sign warning drivers to slow down.

I heard the roar of the engine in front of me. Adam accelerated his cruiser like a jet unleashing its engines on the runway. His tires squealed, and the car fishtailed as he built up speed. Snow shot up in clouds behind him. I thought for a moment he was trying to escape, but he wasn't. The reality of what he was doing dawned on me, and I lowered my window and shouted.

"No, no, no, don't do it!"

He was too far away to hear me. I sped up, too, but I couldn't catch him. Adam rocketed down the straightaway. His brake lights never flashed, not once. The bend of the S-curve loomed ahead of him, but he didn't slow down or turn the wheel. The cruiser burst through the snow and took flight, shooting off the road, lifting off the ground and jolting to a lethal stop an instant later as it slammed into the trees beyond the curve. I heard the tortured squeal of metal and the shatter of glass.

I brought my own car to a stop, and I got out and ran. The shoulder of the road dipped down to the frozen creek ten feet below me. I half slid, half fell into the valley. Adam's car was upside down among the trees, its tires still spinning. Steam hissed into the air. I pushed toward the wreck and squatted to look inside, but the front seat was empty. I peered through the skeletal branches and saw Adam crumpled on the ground not far away.

He'd gone through the windshield like a bullet. When I reached him, I knew that he was already dead. His face was ribboned with blood. His head was snapped sideways like a broken doll. He was warm, but he was gone.

I listened to the loud, fast, in-and-out of my own breathing. My sweat was wet and cold, and my feet inside my boots were soaked. Around me, the forest continued its winter sleep, undisturbed. There was nothing but me and the trees and the snow and the creek, but I wasn't alone. I had the strangest feeling of someone being with me, of someone who'd been waiting for me to arrive. I turned around in a slow circle. No one was there. But squeezed among the oaks and pines was a stand of birch trees, their bark flaking away like old paint, their black-and-white trunks rooted in the ground like the legs of elephants. One of the thick birches called to me, and I fought through the snow to get to it.

That was when I saw the sign.

A cross had been carved into the trunk.

Ten years ago, it must have been invisible among the summer foliage, just two slim gashes cut out of the bark. But it had grown along with the tree. As the trunk bulged and thickened, so did the cross, begging for someone to notice it and understand what it was.

My body felt enveloped by a warm glow even among the frigid cold. The earth at my feet felt sacred.

Someone was buried below me, and I knew who it was.

CHAPTER FORTY-SIX

Ten years after Jeremiah Sloan disappeared, we finally brought him home.

With the help of propane fires and insulated blankets, we melted the frost in the ground and dug carefully through the soft soil at the base of the birch tree. Three feet down, we found the skeleton of a child. Adam had buried Jeremiah with his arms folded across his chest. If it was possible for bones to look peaceful, then his body looked as if it had been at peace all this time.

His Sunday suit had long ago disintegrated, leaving behind only the leather and rusted buckle of his belt and the rubber remnants of the sneakers on his feet. He still wore his backpack. Parts of it—the zippers, the thick vinyl, the plastic-encased pockets—had survived the freezing, thawing, moisture, and bugs. His badminton racket was caked with dirt but otherwise intact. His dead cell phone was safely locked inside a zippered pocket and a boy-proof indestructible case. Agent Reed took it for analysis by the FBI team. If any photos could be retrieved from Jeremiah's phone, I wanted his parents to have them.

We were at the scene for most of three days. The time was

reverent for all of us. The Sloans were there, all three of them, when we brought their boy into the light again. We kept the media away, so that they could have a private moment with him. From where I was, I saw Adrian whisper something to his brother, and I was pretty sure he said *Welcome back*. Ellen and Dennis held hands and hugged each other fiercely. The love of that moment wouldn't last, but for a little while anyway they cried the tears of a family that had been reunited.

On the last day, as Jeremiah was brought back to Everywhere, I thought about the first day when he disappeared. Strange as it sounds, my father had been right all along. He hadn't believed in a stranger abduction. He'd had faith that the people here were basically good and that we would find an innocent explanation at the heart of the mystery. And we did.

Sadly, it came without a happy ending.

Three weeks later, Jeremiah finally had his funeral, and we all got to say goodbye. It seemed as if the whole state came. Thousands of people braved the cold for hours to pay their respects. The bend in the road where he'd waited for us to find him became a shrine, covered over with flowers freezing into brittle china. His face and smile no longer haunted us from missing-person photos the way they had for years. He had a permanent home.

Before the public service, the Sloans held a small memorial of their own at their church. They wanted to say thank you to the town and to the police for never giving up hope. The minister spoke. Ellen, Dennis, and Adrian spoke. And then they went from person to person to shake every hand. We all cried, but the tears were cathartic, letting go of ten years of pain.

When Ellen came to me, she slipped something into my hand. I looked at my palm and saw a smooth, flat stone, the kind of stone you'd place among the rocks of a cairn to honor the dead.

"I kept this stone in my pocket every day for the past ten

years," Ellen whispered to me. "It came from Jeremiah's room. I swore I would never let go of it until we found him. And now we have, thanks to you. I want you to keep it."

I tried to say something, but I had no words.

Ellen kissed my cheek, and she moved on.

It was a day of closure for all of us. Lucas was there, apologizing to the Sloans for what his grandfather had done. Dennis Sloan wrapped him up in a bear hug and told him that God hadn't wanted Paul Nadler to be alone when he died, and that was why he'd brought Jeremiah to him.

I'd like to believe that's true.

Agent Reed was there. So was Monica, carrying Moody in his urn. And Rose. And Violet. And Jeannie Samper and all of her kids. And Dad, looking handsome in his suit. I wished he could understand that the long mystery had come to an end, but he was already deep into his own mystery.

Everyone was there except the one person I wanted to see. Every time the door opened, I kept hoping, but the service began and ended without her.

Anna didn't come.

*

Later that same day, my own life took a turn I wasn't expecting.

I was back at the Nowhere Café with Monica and Dad, and Violet came through the door and made her way straight to the booth where we were sitting. She sat down next to my father, and he smiled and called her "young lady," because he didn't remember who she was. Violet nodded at Monica, who didn't look at all surprised to see her there.

"Deputy Lake," she said to me.

I tried not to roll my eyes at the formal greeting. "Hello, Violet."

"I know the congresswoman has already thanked you, but I wanted to say thank you myself for everything you did on her behalf."

"That's not necessary, but I appreciate it."

And I did. Violet and I were never going to be friends, but she was looking at me with something I'd never seen from her before.

Respect.

"Obviously, I'm not on the county board anymore," she went on, "but my former colleagues thought I'd be the best person to sound you out about something."

"Oh? What's that?"

Violet took another quick glance at Monica before focusing on me again.

"The board would like you to consider an appointment as interim sheriff. They also wanted you to know that if you'd consider running for the position in the November election, you'd have their full support."

"Me? Sheriff?"

"Well, you've pretty much been filling the role anyway since Adam's death," Violet pointed out. "So I assume you've thought about it."

In fact, I hadn't thought about it at all. I know I should have, but I really hadn't had time to think about the future. There were too many details filling up the present. The trouble was, now that the opportunity was staring me in the face, I did think about it, and I knew what my answer had to be.

"Tell the board how much I appreciate their confidence," I replied, "but no."

"No?"

"I'm sorry. No. I'd love to do it, but I can't."

Violet didn't ask me why. She seemed to know why. She got out of the booth and then bent down and put a hand on my father's shoulder. "Tom? Mr. Ginn? I wonder if you'd mind giving me just a moment alone with Shelby and Monica. Would that be okay?"

"Violet," I said in protest, but Dad simply slid his big body out of the booth.

"Why, certainly, I know how women like to chat."

I watched him make his way to the counter, where Patty brought him a slice of tollhouse pie.

Violet sat down across from me again. "I assume Tom's the reason?"

"Yes."

"You have your own life to live, Shelby."

"I know that, but my father is everything to me. I'm not going to put him in a facility. I'm going to take care of him myself."

"At some point, you won't have a choice."

"Well, for right now, I do, and my choice is to be with him. I can't do that and be sheriff at the same time. It's hard enough the way things are."

"You could get help," Violet said. "You could find someone to live with you and look after Tom when you're gone."

I had to laugh. "Live-in help? Are you kidding? Do you know how much that costs?"

As I said this, Monica reached over and took my hand. It was as if she'd been waiting for that moment. "In fact, Shelby, it will cost you nothing at all."

"What do you mean?"

She continued to hold my hand with the calmness of someone who would never let go. "I'm quitting my job, dear. It's time for me to retire. If you can find a place for me—and Moody, of course—then let me move in with you and Tom. That's where my heart is. That's where I can be most useful at this stage of my life. With me around, I think you should be able to balance your career and your devotion to your father, don't you think?"

The offer took my breath away. I shook my head and tried not to cry. "Monica, I can't believe you. I don't know what to say."

"Say yes," she replied. "And say yes to Violet."

"I don't know if this will work. It's still too much."

"Well, we won't know until we try, will we?"

"I guess that's true."

"Tom always wanted you to be the sheriff."

"I know he did."

"If you're honest with yourself, I think you'll realize that you've wanted this, too. And you'll be good at it. Truth be told, you were made to do this, Shelby. Everyone I talk to in town says the same thing. They all want you."

"She's right," Violet said.

I glanced at my father, who was sitting at the counter with his cup of coffee and his pie. Yes, this was what he'd always wanted for me. And yes, as a girl, I'd imagined the day when Dad would hand me his badge, and I would take over. I just never thought the circumstances would be like this.

I extended my arm to Violet, and we shook hands. "Okay. I can't promise to run in November. Let's see how the year goes. But for now, you can tell the board I'll take the interim post."

Violet looked pleased with herself. She had a way of getting what she wanted, and I was pretty sure she'd worked this all out with Monica in advance.

"Congratulations, Shelby. You're the new sheriff of Mittel County."

CHAPTER FORTY-SEVEN

Slowly, the town of Everywhere exhaled.

The media and the strangers went away and left us alone. February became March, and the snow began to melt. March became April, and buds appeared on the trees. Life returned to normal day by day. My own life was a constant juggling act, but Monica and I became master jugglers. Somehow, I found time to wear my many hats. I was a daughter. I was a sheriff. I was a volunteer helping Lucas and Jeannie with the owls. I was a girl with a guitar.

I had everything I needed, but I couldn't get past my biggest disappointment.

You see, I'd lost Anna. I'd failed.

Yes, I'd wrested her away from Will Gruder. She was back home with me, but the fire had gone out of her eyes. I actually missed her defiance. Ever since we'd found Jeremiah's body, she'd become an empty shell, drained of passion. Her father, Karl, reached out to her, but she pushed him out of her life the way she did everyone who tried to help her. She wouldn't go to therapy. Her drinking got worse, and the physical signs told me she was using drugs, too, as if the chemicals would deaden her.

She was a beautiful girl, only twenty years old, but she acted as if her life was over. I tried to talk to her, but she simply dug a hole for herself that got deeper each day. Now that Jeremiah was safe, it seemed as if Anna was the one buried in the woods.

Sometimes the dead are easier to find than the living.

This went on for weeks. I was losing hope that it would ever change.

Then, on May 1, I brought home a package from Agent Reed, and I thought what was inside might be what I needed to open up a little door into Anna's heart. It was like a message from her childhood.

Midnight had come and gone by the time I got home that day. I often got back late in my new job. Thank God for Monica, who put up with my hours without a single complaint and was always there for Dad. I checked on both of them. Monica was asleep in her room, with Moody on the nightstand beside her, and my father was asleep in his. But I knew that Anna hardly ever slept. She'd be awake for hours. In the middle of the night, I would hear her moving around downstairs like a fitful ghost.

I found her in her room. She lay on her back, eyes wide open, staring at the ceiling. The older she got, the more she reminded me of Trina. It wasn't just how she looked. With the benefit of time, I could see some of my old friend's flaws in her, too. Trina had always been emotionally distant, someone who was willing to cut off the highs in order to never face the lows. Karl had confided in me a while back that Trina suffered from severe depression her whole life. I never knew about it. I didn't know if that could be passed down from mother to daughter, but Anna had clearly followed Trina's path. If you don't want to feel bad, then the safe thing is to feel nothing. Unlike me, who felt everything way too much.

"Hey," I said to her.

Anna didn't look at me. The one lamp in the room was dim

and cast shadows. Her face was dark as she stared at the ceiling. "What do you want, Shelby? I'm tired."

"I have something I thought we could look at together. I think you'll want to see it."

"What is it?"

I held up a plastic bag with a thumb drive inside. "The FBI finally sent me what they recovered from Jeremiah's phone. I thought we could check it out on my computer."

"No, thanks."

"Look, I know it'll be sad, but if there are pictures, don't you want to see them? It's the last little bit of Jeremiah we have. I thought it might make you feel close to him again."

"I don't want to see any pictures."

"All right. Maybe later."

"No. Not later. I don't want to see them ever."

I shoved the thumb drive back in my pocket. I sat down next to Anna on the bed and stroked my fingers through her blond hair. She didn't react at all. All I could feel from her was numbness.

"Is it really so hard to think about him?"

"I don't think about him at all."

"I don't believe you."

"You can believe what you want. When people go, they're gone. Dwelling on it doesn't bring them back."

"No, it doesn't. But forgetting them isn't any better."

Anna closed her eyes. "I'm tired, Shelby."

"All right. Good night. Try to get some sleep."

I left her bedroom and closed the door softly behind me. I went to my own room and kept the lights off. I opened the window, letting in crisp spring air. Outside, the forest and the cemetery were lit up in a gray glow by the moon shining through misty clouds. I stood there for a while, watching the world. Spring was my favorite time of year, but my heart was heavy.

I took the thumb drive from my pocket again. I felt as if I were holding Jeremiah's soul in my hand. I didn't want to wait until morning to see what he'd left for us. I booted up my computer and pushed the device into the USB slot. According to the note from Agent Reed, the FBI had recovered nearly five hundred photos and a similar number of text messages from the boy's phone. This was like his last will and testament. His last chance to speak to us.

I checked the texts first, which took me into the past. Jeremiah was alive again, and we were all more than ten years younger. We'd lived the "after" of this case for so long that it was strange to be reminded of the "before." I smiled as I read the texts. He'd messaged back and forth with his brother during the long summer days. He'd sent Adrian silly jokes, the kind little boys tell.

What did the dog say to the tree?

Bark.

He'd exchanged texts with his mother, too. Ordinary things. What's for dinner. When do I have to be home. Yes, I took a shower. One of the messages broke my heart. It had been sent to Ellen two days after her father's funeral.

Where did Grampa go?

Ellen texted back: *Heaven. We talked about this, honey. He and Grammy are in Heaven, and they're happy, but they miss us just like we miss them.*

Jeremiah texted back: *Okay.*

But I remembered that he was still wearing his Sunday suit when he disappeared.

There were messages to his friends in the archive, but I was surprised to find only one message to Anna. The recovered texts went back for over a year prior to his disappearance. The boy hadn't deleted anything else on his phone, as far as I could tell, but at some point, he'd erased his texts with Anna. They'd been best friends the previous summer, and I was sure they'd sent hundreds of messages back and forth to each other. But the texts were all gone.

The only message that was left was a text that Jeremiah had sent to Anna in the early spring.

It said: *Are you still scared of the Ursulina?*

There was no reply.

I closed out the messages, and I loaded the photographs.

What I saw was the world through Jeremiah's ten-year-old eyes. He took photographs of everything. A rabbit in the middle of the yard. A june bug on a soccer ball. Cheerios spilled on the floor. Adrian playing a video game. His father napping in a hammock. A leaf. A doorknob. Most of the pictures were blurry because he never stood still long enough to focus

The photographs began that summer, but then they went backward in time to when Jeremiah was in school. I recognized dozens of students from different grades. Teachers I knew. Classes, desks, and blackboards inside the school building in Everywhere and the sprawling athletic fields outside. *Click click click.* I smiled at everything I saw.

What stopped me was seeing a photograph of Keith Whalen.

It was nothing unusual. It was simply a photo of Keith taking a drink of water from a hallway fountain. Jeremiah took plenty of pictures of random things, but I wondered why he'd taken that photograph.

And then, as I scrolled through more pictures, I saw Keith again, getting out of his car in the school parking lot.

And again in the cafeteria.

And again grading papers at his desk in an empty classroom. All in all, I found almost twenty different pictures of Keith Whalen taken around the school grounds.

That wasn't a coincidence. Jeremiah had been spying on him.

When I located the earliest photograph of Keith in the picture gallery, I checked the date stamp, and it looked familiar to me. Jeremiah had taken the photo on the same day he'd sent his one remaining text message to Anna.

Are you still scared of the Ursulina?

I felt an odd sense of foreboding. A sense that something was very wrong.

Around that same time in the roster of Jeremiah's photos, I began to see pictures of the cairns, too. Whenever he built a tower of rocks near Black Lake on Keith's land, he took a picture of the stones. I found eight different photographs, taken over a span of several weeks. As soon as the winter snow had melted, he'd begun sneaking off to visit the lake and assemble his memorials.

I began to scroll through the pictures more quickly.

I knew something was waiting for me.

There were only a handful of photographs taken during the winter. Mostly indoors, mostly in the boy's bedroom. His Lego creations. His boots. Crosses made with Popsicle sticks. Christmas presents. The family Christmas tree lit up with lights. Picture by picture, I went back through each month.

I found my finger hesitating with each *click*, as if I knew I would regret what I was about to see.

And then there it was.

One single photograph date-stamped November 14. Just one. There were pictures in the days before and after, but only one photograph was left on his phone from that day. I wondered if he'd deleted the others.

It was a selfie. A night-time selfie, lit up by the flash.

Jeremiah had stretched out his short arm to take the picture. I saw the familiar face of that happy, innocent boy, the face that had haunted us for a decade after he went missing. He had messy hair in need of a cut. One crooked tooth in his huge smile. But I wasn't focused on Jeremiah, because he wasn't alone in the selfie.

No, he had his face pressed against the cheek of his best friend, who wore the same big, fearless grin that he did. They were two children off on an adventure. Hunting for the Ursulina.

Jeremiah. And Anna.

She was with him.

I recognized the background in the photograph. The two of them stood in front of the apple-red door of Keith Whalen's barn. The night of November 14. The night Colleen had been killed.

They both saw it happen.

CHAPTER FORTY-EIGHT

Anna was gone. Her bedroom door was open. My first thought was: She knew. She knew I was going to find that picture.

I rushed out of the bedroom to search for her, but my sixth sense made me turn around and go back inside. I felt an unspeakable horror in that room. I went directly to her dresser and ripped open the top drawer and threw the clothes inside onto the floor. I pulled out everything until the drawer was empty.

It was gone. I knew she always kept it there, but it was gone. She'd taken her gun with her.

I flew down the stairs in the grip of a desperate fear. Few things have ever scared me in my life, but I was terrified. The door to the backyard was ajar. She'd left it that way, as if knowing I'd follow her sooner or later. I pushed through the screen door onto the wet grass and screamed her name into the gauzy moonlight.

"*Anna!*"

The frogs croaked, the insects buzzed, but I heard nothing else.

I saw the tracks of footprints leading through the grass past the gazebo, disappearing onto the cemetery path. I ran. When I reached the trees, I was blind, because the moonlight couldn't

penetrate the crown of the forest. I was crying, and I kept screaming her name.

"Anna! Where are you?"

I stumbled my way down the trail. Roots and rocks tripped
me up. Branches and wet leaves slapped my face. The thunder of
the frogs made me want to cover my ears. I broke free into one of
the cemetery groves, where the sky opened up and the graves were
bathed in silver light. It was empty except for the dead. Anna wasn't
there. I made a silent plea to the people under the headstones to
help me find her, but the ghosts had nothing to say. I was alone.

I knew I could hunt for hours through the dark woods and
never find her. She could be anywhere, and she wasn't answering
when I called. But I kept going, running through the maze of
trails, driven on by panic. Every time a branch cracked under my
feet, I flinched, because my mind was expecting a gunshot.

"Anna!"

I passed more graves silhouetted by the moon. Among the
crosses and angels topping the stones, I saw a snowy owl observ-
ing me with silent grace. Somehow, I'd expected it to be there.
Every crossroads I faced was marked by an owl. It made me finally
grasp the truth of what I'd been trying to understand my whole
life. All those years ago, the owl that had called me to rescue a
child hadn't come to me because of Jeremiah.

The child who had needed me all along was Anna.

God had rescued me for this moment.

I'd been saved for tonight. Right now.

This was why I was alive and not dead on the doorstep of my
father's house.

I kept running. I knew the path I was on. It was the path
that led up and down the shallow hill where Anna and I had
skied in the winter, past the diseased old beech tree we called Bartholomew, down into the hollow where Trina's grave was waiting

for us. But not just Trina. Suddenly, I knew why Anna was so reluctant to visit her mother, so unwilling to make her way into the small meadow with those silent spirits. It wasn't Trina she was afraid to see.

Colleen Whalen was buried there, too.

The trail took me downhill. I ran with the wind pushing me faster and the moon guiding me toward the gap in the trees. I burst into the solemn meadow, and there she was. Anna was a motionless shadow standing in front of Colleen's grave. Her back was to me. The wind swirled her hair.

I saw the pistol in her hand.

"Anna."

She didn't turn around.

"Anna, put down the gun."

I made my way carefully through the monuments, not wanting to alarm her. I passed Trina and put my hand on the angel adorning her grave, and I could feel something electric, like a voice that said: *Save her, Shelby*. I glanced at the thickness of the forest surrounding us, and I could feel the hidden eyes of the owls. They were all watching us.

"Anna."

We were only a few feet apart. I'd come around in front of her. Colleen's grave was between us, just a flat stone on the earth, with the wet grass and weeds closing around it.

Tears streamed down Anna's face along with the mist.

A flood, a deluge of tears.

"Anna, tell me what happened that night with Jeremiah."

She tried to talk, but her throat choked off the words. She shook her head back and forth, and her whole body shivered.

"Please. Tell me."

Finally, she got the words out, and her voice begged for mercy. "It was my idea."

"What was?"

"To find the Ursulina."

"And why go to Keith Whalen's place to do that?"

"Because I was sure he was hiding it. He was the one who wrote the Halloween story. He knew so much about it. I told Jeremiah that he had to be keeping the Ursulina at his place."

"So the two of you went over there that Saturday night."

"Jeremiah didn't want to go. He was scared, but I made him go. I told him to sneak out of his room and meet me in the woods. And then we took the trail past Black Lake to Mr. Whalen's place."

"What did you see there? *Who* did you see?"

"Nobody."

"It's okay, Anna. None of this was your fault. Tell me what you saw. Was Keith there? Did you see Will and Vince? Who was it?"

"Nobody was there," she moaned. "Just us."

"Anna, I don't understand. What happened?"

She tried to tell the story through the tears. "I said we should search the barn. I said maybe he kept the Ursulina in there. I thought he would have it in a cage or something."

"You went in the barn?"

"Yes."

"What happened?"

"The Ursulina wasn't there. Nobody was there. Except I found—"

"What? What did you find?"

She tried to talk. She tried to say it. But she couldn't. Her whole body heaved with sobs. Her eyes squeezed shut, and her face twisted with misery. Her head hung down against her neck.

"*A gun.* I found a gun."

I nearly felt my legs collapse under me.

I'd been wrong. So wrong.

"Oh, no. Oh, no, no. Oh, Anna."

"Jeremiah said we should leave it, but I said, what if we saw the

Ursulina? So I had it in my hand. And we left the barn, and it was so dark, and we couldn't see anything. We were near the big house—"

I waited. I waited for the truth.

"And there was this noise! Somebody was there! I couldn't see who it was, but I saw someone, and I was sure, I was sure, I was sure it was the Ursulina. I just pointed the gun at it, and I wasn't trying to fire or anything, but it went off. It went off. It was so loud. And Jeremiah was like, 'You got it! You got it, Anna!' So we went to look, and there was this woman lying on the ground, and all this blood. I just dropped the gun, and we ran. Oh, God, I'm so sorry, Shelby. I'm so sorry. I didn't mean to do it. It just happened."

"Oh, Anna."

I thought of this girl nursing her horrible secret day after day as she grew up. I thought of the weight of that one night crushing her for ten years. I took a step toward her, toward Colleen's grave, but as I did, Anna lifted the pistol in her hand and placed the barrel to her temple. She could barely keep her hand steady.

"Anna, *no*. Put down the gun. Please. Put it down, honey. Don't do this. Do not do this."

"I killed her! It's all my fault. Everything's my fault. All of it. Mrs. Whalen. Jeremiah. My mom. They sent Mr. Whalen to prison, and I didn't say anything. I'm being punished, don't you see that? I don't deserve to be alive."

"That's not true. That's not true at all."

"It is!"

All I could see was the gun pressed against her forehead.

"Anna, listen to me. If Mrs. Whalen were standing here with us, she'd tell you it was an accident. She wouldn't blame you."

"It doesn't matter. I killed her."

"You have your whole life ahead of you. Don't throw it away. That's not what Colleen Whalen would want. That's not what your mother would want."

"Her cancer came back right after. It was because of me. I did it!"

It didn't matter what I said. She was determined to believe the worst of herself, and she wouldn't hear anything else. I didn't know what to do. In my head, I called for an owl to swoop down and knock the gun away from her hand. Or for the ghosts to rise up and talk to her. I needed help. But it was just the two of us in the cemetery. This was up to me and no one else.

"Anna, look at me."

Her red, lost eyes stared into mine. I could still see the child she'd been so long ago.

"Anna, give me the gun."

"No. I can't live with this anymore."

"I understand. I do. It hurts, it hurts so much. But what made it so hard was living with it all by yourself. You never have to do that again. You told me the truth. I'm here for you, I'll always be here, I'll always love you."

Anna shook her head.

I saw her finger slip over the trigger.

"Don't you get it, Shelby? I murdered her."

"Oh, Anna, honey, listen to me. You were *ten years old*."

She quivered where she was, her knees knocking together. I watched the gun, and I saw her finger twitch. We were at the brink of a cliff from which there was no turning back. She would stop or she would fall. I rushed on, desperate to reach her.

"You said Jeremiah has been coming to your dreams for years. Why do you think he kept coming back? Why couldn't he rest in peace? It was because he wanted to save you. You need to listen to what he's been telling you all this time. You need to forgive yourself."

Anna sobbed and gasped for air. "I miss him. I really miss him."

"I know you do."

"I miss Mom. I miss her so much."

"Oh, honey, I know, I know."

I took another step forward. Colleen's grave was under my feet. I reached across the stone and gently put my hand around the gun and pointed it at the ground and separated Anna's fingers from it. I took it into my own hand, laid it in the grass, and covered it with my foot.

"I'm so sorry, Shelby."

"Don't talk. Don't be sorry. It's over. It's all over."

She wrapped her arms tightly around me and held on. Her head crushed against my cheek. Around us, the gentle mist turned into rain and became a kind of music beating on the trees and the graves. We stood there for a long time. I listened to Anna sobbing as she let go of the past, and I stroked her hair and let her cry.

CHAPTER FORTY-NINE

We all have to let go of the past. Either that, or it eats us alive.

I was there when Keith Whalen was released from prison after the judge voided his conviction for murder. So was Anna. I was proud of her for that. She'd already testified in court about the night of November 14, but she wanted to be there when Keith was set free to ask for his forgiveness. Like I expected, Keith gave it to her with no hesitation at all. He embraced her and let go of the ten years he'd lost.

He said he forgave me, too. I'm not so sure about that. We'll see what the future holds. He's moving back to Everywhere to rebuild on his old land. I guess it doesn't matter if your home treats you badly. It's still home.

Setting Keith free was the last chapter in Jeremiah's story. The ripples that had changed so many lives finally faded away into the lake. I found myself thinking about all the "if only" moments that might have changed what happened.

If only Paul Nadler hadn't escaped from the nursing home.

If only the bus to Martin's Point had arrived five minutes earlier.

If only Adam had called for help that night at the resort.

If only, if only, if only. On and on. Jeremiah would be alive.

Breezy would be alive. Adam would be alive. If only. But we all had to let it go.

Ellen and Violet went back to Washington. I heard rumors that Ellen was planning to run for the Senate and Violet was thinking of pursuing her congressional seat in the next election. I'll vote for them. Of course, I'll be pretty busy with my own campaign for sheriff. Yes, I'm going to run.

The county board voted the money to clean up the ruins at the Mittel Pines Resort once and for all and turn the land into the Jeremiah Sloan County Park. There will be a grand opening and ribbon-cutting ceremony next summer. I'm sure there will be more tears.

Dennis Sloan got another DUI. Not everyone lets go in the right way.

Will Gruder sent me his medal of St. Benedict. I was right that it was actually the medal that had belonged to Keith Whalen. Anna had slipped it around her neck that night in the barn to ward off the Ursulina, and years later, she gave it to Will. He asked me to return it to Keith. I did.

Given Anna's age at the time of the shooting, she won't face any legal consequences. And I knew she had already punished herself enough in the years since it happened. She's started therapy. She's got a long way to go, but at least she's on her way. Yesterday she slept through the night for the first time in a long time, and Jeremiah didn't come to her in her dreams.

In all these years of searching, no one has ever found the Ursulina.

And me? I needed to let go of the past, too. My father's past. I didn't know what had happened the night after his mother died, and I had to make peace with the fact that I probably never would. After all, the past had already let go of him, and he had no more answers to give me.

I confess that in a locked drawer of my office desk, I have a file where I've looked at maps and researched the distances someone might have traveled through a blizzard on a bitter night in January thirty-five years ago. It encompasses a universe of hundreds of town, county, and state police officers who might have rescued Sheriff Tom Ginn in a snowy campground. Maybe one of them was my birth mother. Or maybe I just needed to believe she was out there for me to find.

Last night, I came home late. Monica and Dad were in the great room. Monica was tired and went to bed, but my father and I went outside to the gazebo in our yard, as we often do. I brought my guitar. It was a warm spring night. The moths beat their wings against the screens, and the humid air felt thick. We sat together, and Dad listened to me play. I'd been working on a song off and on for a while now. I finally had it done. I called it "The Deep, Deep Snow," because it's about the secrets we keep and the places we hide them.

The chorus goes like this:

So we know
We know
We always know
That what we did
Is under the snow

And we know
We know
That spring will show
The thing we hid
Is down below

I sang it all from start to finish. When I was done, I put down my guitar in my lap and looked at my father with an embarrassed blush. "Well, that's what it is. I know it's nothing special, but I like it."

"It's beautiful," Dad told me.

"Oh, I know it's not, but thank you."

He shook his head and gave me that same amazing smile that I'd known my whole life. "I mean it. Play the song for me again. I could listen to you sing all night. You have such a pretty voice, young lady."

I smiled back at him.

I pretended not to hear those words. Young lady.

"Sure, Dad," I replied, picking up my guitar. "I'll play it again. You just close your eyes and listen."